Waldwick

Waldwick...Let Go

Kenneth Linde

Waldwick Books
www.WaldwickBooks.com
McHenry, Illinois

Waldwick: Let Go

Kenneth Jon Linde

Waldwick Partners, Inc. dba Waldwick Books
www.WaldwickBooks.com

January 03, 2022

Printed in Wisconsin, United States of America

ISBN: 979-8-9852613-0-1

ISBN: 979-8-9852-6130-1

9 798985 261301

WHEN EVERYTHING
MEANS NOTHING
AND NOTHING MEANS
EVERYTHING,
IT'S SIMPLY TIME TO
LET GO.

I am what I am:

My name is Amelia Harris. I earned the moniker Melia to differentiate me from my mother, who is also named Amelia, but is more commonly known as Amy and also my sister-in-law who, believe it or not, is also called Amelia. Other than Amelia Erhardt, the name isn't that common and to have three of us in the realm of one family is quite something.

Beyond my name, I'm always closely associated with my parents, George and Amelia Terrill, my brothers, Derrick and George, better known as 'V', and my maternal Grandmother and Grandfather, who were Douglas and Dr. Marie Williams, which is where this story will begin.

As a little girl, my life was filled with dreams of being a princesses. Not once, when I was small, did I realize that I was living a life that so many others only dreamed about. My grandfather was John Douglas Williams, better known as The Duke, who started life in the hardscrabble neighborhoods of Milwaukee and clawed his way to the very top of the financial food chain, where he was master of the universe and primary owner and CEO of a company called Wilco. Along with his intellect and drive, grandpa's profound understanding of people and what motivated and intimidated them allowed him to create a profound sense of loyalty to his passions, aspirations and even to him, and was the secret of his success.

Grandpa's life was not always a bed of roses. The trials and tribulations outside the bounds of business stunted what could have been a fairytale in itself. After a few years of marriage, the lady who would have been my grandmother died of ovarian cancer and grandpa was devastated. His respite from reality had him simply stop everything and become a vagabond in search of happiness.er

An abrupt change of plans that initially had him going to Puerto Rico diverted his life two hundred and thirty-one miles to the island of St. Martin. While there, he took part in what he recalled was one of his depression-induced "fermented escapades", used to simply wash away his sorrow. The combination of too much booze and too much sun resulted in a sunburn that must have been profoundly painful as grandpa had the will of steel against all but the most discerning odds. Instead, grandpa made his way to a local clinic for some sort of remedy and relief from his foolishness. While there, a young, female doctor attended his condition and grandpa was smitten. The next day, he returned to the clinic and noted that he had 'lost' the medication and needed to see the doctor again. While being administered to, grandpa had the audacity to ask this woman of African descent, if he could take her to dinner that night.

Story tells that this kind doctor called her mother to ask for advice, who indicated that she didn't want her daughter running around with a white man, simply because she thought only had one thing on his mind. Instead, the kind doctor agreed, but the dinner had to include her mother, as well. Grandpa concurred and both the doctor and what was to become his mother-in-law became enamored by the man, who simply charmed his way into their lives.

As his recovery time took place, he and Grandma Marie had dinner several more times – all above board – all proper and, according to grandma, the Duke was all she could have ever asked for in a gentleman. Grandpa said goodbye and flew back to Chicago. Upon landing, he went to the ticket counter, purchased a return ticket to St. Martin, arrived at the clinic with a dozen roses, got down on one knee and proposed.

Grandma and grandpa knew it wouldn't be easy, yet they didn't care. The social ostracization of a mixed marriage only melded them closer together as they had each other and were deeply in love. Grandpa's business acumen was so great that wealth allowed them to escape the bondage of overt racial discrimination, while grandma continued her education at Marquette University and became a world-renowned specialist in pediatric oncology.

All was not work. Grandma and grandpa had two children - Derrick and Amelia. Derrick would have been my uncle, but the pressures of life and the temptations of drugs were too great and he overdosed on some Phentenol laced heroin and died. Grandpa said it was the saddest day of his life.

Amelia became the focus of grandma and grandpa's lives and all was well until she was diagnosed with Leukemia. The prognoses didn't look good until she was admitted into an experimental program at the Carbone Cancer Clinic at the University of Wisconsin that harvested her 'T' cells and mitigated the cancer in her blood. The treatments were quite arduous and to resolve the three-day period of recovery, the decision was made to purchase a condo in Madison.

While having the treatments every month, one of the administrating nurses was a Native American woman by the name of Ann Wolf, who became Amelia's good friend. Ann sensed Amelia's loneliness and, after what might be called a terrible experience with a patient that Ann endured, made arrangements for Amelia to 'accidentally' meet the young man who had upheld her dignity by the name of George Terrill. The attraction was almost instant as Amy and George became virtually inseparable and sure enough, they became mom and dad to my brothers Derrick, George and me.

Growing up at our house was unlike that of most children. There was never a material need that couldn't be resolved. There was never an instant where money was an issue. There was never a time when we went without, in terms of items or programmed experiences. Little did we know that not all families had their own jet or homes on Pine Lake, Wisconsin; Aspen, Colorado for skiing, a farm in Northern Wisconsin with our own small lake that we used as a summer cottage and grandma and grandpa's House-On-The-Hill in St. Martin, where we could go to erase winter's chill. We always did things as a family when business allowed it, but always knew that the family business came first and controlled what we did, along with when and how we did it.

Growing up wasn't as idyllic as one might seem. Dad was always working and mom, well mom would have her 'spells' as my brothers and I would call them where, no matter what we did, they never seemed good enough for her. When you grow up rich and there aren't kids your own age around, you have to learn to adapt and become accustomed to being alone. I don't think it made me any better or worse, just a little lonelier than others. My friends were my Barbies and my joy was playing school, reading and music. I always loved to leave the hubbub of Pine Lake and Milwaukee and come to Waldwick, where I could go out to the family farm, ride horses, help with chores and go for walks in the Forest.

Grandma Marie became my hero. I looked up to her and thought the world of what she accomplished. Here was a Black woman, whose mother sold straw hats on Orient Beach in St. Martin, who became recognized throughout the world for her care and compassion for children and I wanted to be like her.

As I grew and matured, I became aware of the family's incredible wealth - the airplanes and special seats wherever we went. The fact that people were always going out of their way to serve us, was not only somewhat gratifying, but also somewhat mystifying and irritating, as it all seemed so synthetic to me.

Next:

As I was preparing to graduate from high school, mom and I went to lunch and she told me about Georgetown, where she went to college. She said that she'd asked grandpa to allow her to be herself and it was then she changed her first name from Amelia to Amy, as she wanted nothing more than to be 'normal' as she called it, with none of the baubles and beads that came from massive wealth. Grandma and grandpa agreed and helped mom ground herself in reality and be accepted for who she was, instead of the family she belonged to.

I pondered mom's advice and agreed. For college, I wanted to get out of Milwaukee and found UW Madison too big. We looked at all the schools and I chose UW Oshkosh as they had a program in Nursing, which is what I initially thought I wanted to do. I chose Oshkosh because it was big enough to have everything and small enough to feel like you're a part of it. UW Madison is beautiful and prestigious and I was accepted there, but I wanted something smaller and more personal, particularly when our family represented one of the largest donors to the UW, every year.

Mom and dad promised to keep the baubles and beads to a minimum. I enrolled and was assigned a dorm and roommate named Annie Johnson from Madison, who quickly became the best friend I never had. While I was somewhat introspective and reserved, Annie was just the opposite – liberal, outgoing and funny - just what I think we both needed.

We lived in Evans Hall for two years and decided on an apartment for the remaining two across the street from WOSH radio. Annie never knew my parents developed and built several buildings in Oshkosh, of which we leased a two-bedroom unit. Designed for transient students, the apartments were soundproofed and each bedroom had its own bathroom with a common living room and kitchen in between.

Annie and Teddy Franklin met at Madison East High School and I don't know who followed whom to Oshkosh. Like me, Teddy was the quiet, serious type and the two of them were meant for each other. I knew that money was always a problem for both of them and when Annie asked if I minded having another roommate to share the expenses, I thought, "Why not"? Annie offered to pay more, but I said no, simply because we were each paying for half the apartment. Teddy could help Annie pay her half and chip in for food. I'd known Teddy for the two years at Evans and loved him like a brother and so the three of us lived together for our junior and senior years. Not once did Annie or Teddy know about my family's wealth and that's the way I liked it.

Annie was getting her degree in Music Education. Her real dream was to perform. She loved to write lyrics and compose music and fiddled with her keyboard for hours on end to get just the right sounds for the words she wrote. Teddy's interests were sports and politics and, because he was on such a strict budget, joined Navy ROTC for the monthly stipend they provided. As for me, it was pre-med and I wanted to continue the work Grandma Marie had begun. Socially, I tagged along when we went to the bars and one somewhat inebriated, karaoke night realized I could sing, but that's part of the story I'm about to tell.

I felt I needed a break before pre-med and took a job in Madison working at the Wilco office located there. My tasks were menial to say the least, but I got to feel the power The Duke had over associates, employees and others. The family still had the condo grandpa bought when mom was going through Leukemia treatments and so it was quite convenient for me to live there, as it was only a three block walk to the Wilco offices on King Street. Annie and Teddy were also home that summer with Teddy working construction and Annie as a server at a State Street restaurant and so we'd hang out and even rent a sail boat on Lake Mendota every now and then. I met a guy named Chip whose real name was Charles and had one of those summer flings both of us knew was more of a physical convenience than anything else.

On June 21st Annie invited me out to celebrate my birthday. She asked me if I wanted to invite Chip and I told her I'd already thrown in my chips and it was going to be over between us, even though, other than the physical part, it really never started. As the night approached, I was finally able to legally do what I'd been doing in Oshkosh, which was go to the bars. However, after my Uncle Derrick died from an OD and stories of grandpa's infamous binges, I decided, other than a periodic glass of wine, alcohol and certainly not drugs, weren't for me.

Annie got some of our fellow Oshburgers together and had my birthday party at Upstairs/Downstairs, a two-story bar on State Street, where upstairs is a lot quieter than the raucous noise of inebriated college guys watching sports on TV down below. It was nice to see everyone, knowing that in one year we'd be scattered like leaves in the wind and our adult lives would mean new friends, as we tried to make our dreams come true.

Jackie Stillman was one of our former neighbors in Evans Hall and a really nice girl. As an African American in a white bread world, she and I had somewhat bonded due to the fact that, even though I'm relatively light-skinned, my frizzy brown hair identified to those in the know that I had some 'color in me' and I was always proud to report that I was one quarter black.

As the party progressed, Jackie made her way downstairs and returned, noting she'd run into some guys who were fellow Oshburgers who she thought I should meet. I shook my head 'No' and said, 'Thanks anyway'. School was just a summer away and I knew it was going to be a challenging year with my double major in Biology and Chemistry filling my schedule.

The year flew by and I graduated from UW Oshkosh and

was accepted into Johns Hopkins Medical School. While I'd been at the top on my class as an undergrad, this was a whole new ballgame and I quickly realized that life wasn't going to be as easy and school a lot more challenging. Time allocation meant eighteen-hour days with the demands growing incrementally as well.

With so much on my plate, I needed what was literally solitary confinement so mom and dad purchased a house for me in Baltimore within walking distance to the Johns Hopkins School of Medicine, hospital and children's center. The medical school was founded in 1899 and was in an older part of the city that was being regentrified, but still represented a new twist and turn to my existence, particularly after living on Pine Lake, Madison and Oshkosh.

I persevered, where the only thing that really got to me was living all alone. For four years, I simply engrossed myself in my medical education, attempting nothing more than to emulate the achievements of Grandma Marie. I graduated in the top ten of my class and was relieved and exhausted when it was finally over. Mom and dad would periodically visit, but it had been a long time since I'd seen my brothers and their significant others. Derrick was working at Wilco Law and dating Andrea who was from Germany. 'V' had finally grown up and was living in the Madison condo I'd vacated, while working at the Derrick Williams Foundation in Mineral Point and was enthralled by Amelia Whitehorse who, along with her parents, were mom and dad's best friends that my brothers and I had known our entire lives.

After the grueling four-year stint, I needed a break and mom and dad offered what would probably be our last family vacation together. It sounded great to me if we could tear Derrick and 'V' away from their girlfriends for a week. Instead of our yacht, my brothers and I asked mom and dad if we could go on a typical Caribbean cruise, where the family could all enjoy the love of each other, while still having the freedom to experience those things in life parents and kids like doing alone. As fate had it, a former Oshburger named Jack Harris and his mom, had chosen the same voyage to celebrate Jack's 25th birthday.

After we'd all settled in, Derrick, 'V' and I made our way to the ship's health club and began working out. While there, Jack walked in and I guess, was enamored by me, but was too bashful to approach, or perhaps because my brothers were there and he didn't know who they were.

Because of my sequestered love for the stage and singing, dad asked that I honor him by participating in the ship's amateur show. Reluctantly, I abided. That evening I stood before 500 people in the main theater and sang one of the songs from the play *'Jekyll and Hyde'*. Upon completion of my performance, there was a sustained period of silence before the applause began. As I attempted to leave the stage, the chant, "Encore! Encore! Encore!" resonated throughout the audience, which I'm certain started with my brothers and probably included the still strangers, Jack and his mom.

The Cruise Director, sensing something special, asked me to return to the stage where the roar of approval transcended the night as I sang *'Somewhere Over the Rainbow'*. As the silence of anticipation gripped the air, the Cruise Director, took the microphone and told the audience he was about to do something he'd never done before - offer a contestant a job as an onboard entertainer, right then and there - to which the crescendo began again.

My plans were set to do my residency and the offer put me at one of those quandaries of life - stay onboard the ship and continue singing or politely say, 'No,' and return to reality - I chose reality!

As is the case on many cruises, the amateur entertainment was recorded and re-broadcast over and over and over throughout the ships closed circuit television system for others to enjoy. To my embarrassment, I quickly became a minor celebrity within the realm of the 3,000 guests aboard!

The night after the talent show, my brothers and I made our way to one of the lounges where Karaoke was taking place. Word quickly spread that I was the girl who'd been offered the entertainer's job and I was asked to sing again. Reluctantly, I took the mike and sang another set of songs.

While I was at the microphone, Jack made his way into the bar and saw that there was an empty seat next to my brothers. When I'd completed my songs, I returned as Jack sat next to me. In the next two hours, we quickly learned we had much in common - city, university, friends and experiences and he knew Teddy, but not me.

It was then that Jack realized that it had been me who he'd been invited to meet that June night at Upstairs/Downstairs in Madison. When it got to his job, he told me, he was about to start practice teaching in a small town called Mineral Point that I'd probably never heard of. I thought Derrick and 'V' would spill the beans that our family not only owned land there, but started the Derrick Williams Foundation. Instead they just smirked to see what I would say.

I replied, "I've heard of Mineral Point. It's down by Dubuque isn't it?"

The cruise ended in a woven tapestry of memories and promises to stay in touch. We returned home and I prepared for my residency, while Jack began his year of practice teaching and coaching football.

At first, the promised correspondence took place as I went on to a life that made Johns Hopkins seem easy, while Jack went back to coaching and teaching as the spark that had briefly burned between us slowly diminished. Time and space became too great and we simply lost each other in the challenges of life. I'd already learned that time has a funny way of taking the intensity of events and circumstances situations and relationships and smoothing them out. Add in the dynamics of other people and other relationships and even the brightest hues of short-term situations can fade into the pale colors of a diminishing rainbow. Promises of staying in touch! Promises of telephone calls! Promises of getting together, slowly erode until they become nothing more than memories. Like the last embers of a dying flame, the intensity that once burned brightly went dim and Jack was gone, buried beneath the demands that filled every minute of every day of my life.

Claustrophobia:

Claustrophobia normally refers to the fear of confined spaces. From a medical perspective, it can be triggered by many different stimuli and is typically classified as an anxiety disorder, which often results in panic attacks. While normally associated only with confined physical spaces, I sincerely believe that a form of claustrophobia can also exist in one's social, professional and/or family world, where one feels trapped and afraid that everything is closing in on them. I also sincerely believe I became socially and professionally claustrophobic and I guess that's what this story is all about.

My dream had been to become a pediatric oncologist and follow in Grandma Marie's footsteps, I felt confident after four years at Johns Hopkins. Little did I realize what the next four years were going to be like. My biggest challenge as an intern, or serving in my first year of residency, was being at the bottom of the totem pole, especially after the childhood I'd had. In my new role, I was expected to do every job from moving patients, to administering medicines and writing case notes.

The nurses and doctors were inherently nice people and yet they were always giving me a hard time on the menial work that I'd either forget or failed to do. There were days when the glamour of being a doctor would evaporate and I felt I could simply disappear and people wouldn't notice, until the reports weren't picked up or case notes weren't written.

When you're on the bottom, you have no authority at all. You can't ask anyone, not even the nursing assistants or nurses, to do something. Then, I was always comparing myself to Grandma which wasn't fair to either her memory or me. I had to constantly remind myself that being a resident is virtually a form of modern- day slavery where I was forced to do work in a setting I had little or no control over. Each day blended into the next and I became overwhelmed with work, irrespective of the department I was in. It was personally an affront to take eight years of education and do 'clerical work' rather than the doctor things I dreamed of, let alone do it for so little money that wouldn't even cover most student loan payments, let alone life itself!

I guess it was the way I was raised where everyone came to us that made me a little more sensitive, but you can only hear so many, "Do this! Do that! Write this! Go there!" before you're numb, indifferent and afraid - and even after you've done this and that or gone here or there, you end up feeling screwed! I'd heard about the hours and commiserated with my fellow rookies and yet, I don't think I could have imagined what it was going to be like. Night shifts? Don't even talk about them! I knew they were coming, but not like this. Some shifts stretched for 36 hours straight and sometimes they happened twice a week. In the end there wasn't time to sleep, eat and almost all my days were spent in the hospital, while, during my free time - if I actually had any – I had little energy to do anything at all, simply because I was so alone and too tired to think of anything else but sleep.

Mom and dad tried to be supportive and when dad came to visit one day, the time with him was a rush and I felt so bad. Selfishly, I justified it simply by thinking I wasn't in this alone and every physician in America had endured what I was going through. What made it difficult was seeing the bronze plaque of Grandma in the hospital lobby, while aspiring to simply do what she had done and realizing I wasn't Grandma and wondering how she did it. How did she endure?

As I rotated through all the different departments I finally made it to where I thought I wanted to end up – Pediatrics – helping little kids get better. That first day seeing all those little ones fighting for their lives was devastating. That first night, hearing the cries for mommy and daddy, simply pierced my heart. Those first encounters with concerned parents looking for answers left me bewildered, wondering how could I possibly face them every single day for the rest of my life.

It's never a question of if, but when, how and why. It was three o'clock in the morning and I'd been on duty for two days and was almost in a stupor of exhaustion when I was called into pediatric ICU to replace the on-call physician. The room was dark, other than the night light above the little girl's head. Her favorite doll was cradled in her left arm as her right was filled with IV's and she looked like an angel lying there.

I remember her face as if she were with me now. She was only three and had spent nearly half of her life in a hospital. The cancer had begun in her pancreas, which was extremely rare for a child. Of the two types, that include ductal adenocarcinoma and acinar cell carcinoma, she had the later which represents just 1% to 2% of all pancreatic cancers and a survival rate averaging 18.7 months, with just 68% of adults living one year and even less for children.

This brave little girl's cancer had metastasized to her spine so she could no longer walk. Her pain must have been excruciating to the point of being beyond human comprehension and yet I was told she never cried nor complained. Her "little monster" as she called it, ate away her energy. Life was waning, as the 'little monster' slowly made its way to her brain and there was nothing we could do to stop it.

Reports were that she'd asked about the little girl in the white dress standing in the corner of her room. The nurse indicated it was quite common when someone's time was near. I took a deep breath and hoped it was more than her imagination and simply her Guardian Angel waiting to take her home.

I looked at the little girl and the deep creases of pain that were carved into the corners of her lips. Her once radiant smile had withered to nothing more than a thin line across her burdened face. I held her hand and she whispered, "Will my dolly go to heaven with me?" I assured her she would, as she nodded one – last – time and slowly closed her eyes, as the monitor went flat and she was gone. My heart was broken as I slowly removed

my hand from hers, tucked her dolly in next to her for comfort and wiped a tear, not sure if it was for her or me.

Her mother was asleep in the parents' room and I was instructed to awaken her. I went in and gently tapped the exhausted woman on the shoulder to which she opened her eyes. Words weren't necessary. She knew. I helped her down the hall and will always remember the silent scream as she walked in to see her daughter nestled beneath the sheets. She turned to me and buried her head on my shoulder and began to cry. Her baby was gone and all she could whisper was, "Why?"

I imagined the rest of my professional career and wondered how many times would I need to do this? How many goodbyes? How many tears flowing freely and realized I would meet the little ones in their darkest hours, along with their families and be required to hug them all goodbye time after time after time. It was then I began to feel I couldn't do it, simply because my heart couldn't take one more time when someone so little, so precious and so innocent would be gone. I'd learned to accept that we will all go some day and to hope my patients would go gently. I vowed, I would do all I could so that they didn't die alone or in pain, but not the little ones, whose only dream was about the tomorrow they would never see.

I did my best and held my emotions until reality slapped me across the face as I was filling out the Death Certificate and going to the physician's lounge to find the on-duty physician to sign the document, simply because I didn't have my license yet. Perhaps it was that moment when I made up my mind. Perhaps what happened next was simply the culmination of all that I'd seen, felt, believed and disbelieved, as I gently tapped the napping doctor on the shoulder to awaken him.

"What?" was his curt inquiry.

"I have a death certificate that needs to be signed."

"You woke me to sign a goddamn death certificate?"

I cautiously nodded yes.

"Jesus Christ, it could have waited until I got up!"

"I was told…"

"We have people die here every day and you didn't think to ask what we did when the doctor was sleeping? You put the time of death on the chart and leave it at the nurse's station. I'll sign it when I get up. **Now leave me alone!"**

I was sick to my stomach. I wanted to throw up. A child just died and her mother was in tears and I was reprimanded for simply caring, because I awakened a sleeping doctor. What had I gotten myself into?

The pressure, the exhaustion, the loss of a personal life! I think I could have handled all of these as they were transient in nature and there was a dim light at the end of the tunnel. Dealing with the loss of a patient, especially children, was already the most demanding and challenging encounter I could imagine. How did Grandma Marie do it every day? Was I one of those who wasn't capable of coping with patient death? If so, would I be inadequate in supporting dying patients and their family and be emotionally destroyed each time one of "mine" was gone, to the point that I minimized the quality of end-of-life care? My God, what had I gotten myself into?

I stood alone outside the lounge door as tears welled in my eyes. I made my way back to the room where the little girl had been. The mother was gone, as was the little girl. The room would be remade first thing in the morning as it waited for yet another sorrow. For now, it remained filled with the memories of the little girl and dolly, as it slowly erased the profound sadness that accompanies death as the final emotion.

I paused for a moment and looked at the little girl's doll. Someone had carelessly placed it on the night stand. My promise had been broken and with it my heart. I gently picked the doll up and placed it amongst the small stuffed teddy bears on the window ledge that took me back to when I was a child. For some reason, I picked up a small brown Gund teddy bear that resembled one that had been with me during my childhood and always made me feel secure and pressed it to my face. I could almost feel the little girl and then my heart reflected on the little girl still inside of me, full of hopes and dreams, love and laughter, who only wanted to be a princess someday. I began to cry, not the silent tears of professionalism, but the loud rasps of sadness that permeated every bone in my body,

I turned and looked one last time at the empty bed. The pillows were askew as if they were headstones knocked over by some malicious storm. The monitors that had measured life were silent and now reflected death where the only sound was that of my breaking heart - thump, thump, thump - pounding out a cadence in a room made silent by eternity.

Why did it have to be this way? Why couldn't I save this little girl who wanted nothing more than to be a princess in her little pink gown? I shook my head and wiped the tears from my eyes. I walked to the wall, pulled the string and turned off the night light, made it to the door and slowly opened it to reality. There were other children to see. Other children to feel. Other children trapped in the jaws of death. I quietly closed the door and heard it click, as it became the final sound in the life of a little girl who had simply reached out and touched me and made me also wonder, "Why?"

Recompense:

Life and death go on as all tomorrows become yesterdays and within a few moments, I was required to regain my composure as that was what being an intern is really all about. My night was far from over and each step took its toll upon my soul until I was but a walking shadow working on impulse, who had been drained of love and compassion that had been slowly eroded hour-by-hour, day-by-day, week-by-week, month-by- month until I could be rebuilt to fit the mold Hypocrites had planned for me that outlined medical ethics regarding confidentiality and nonmaleficence, but never speaks of care, concern or compassion.

I had a short break around four-thirty when all was still and went out into the cool Spring air simply to feel what life was like again. The streets were still empty, except for the periodic sound of a car passing by. It had rained and the streets glistened with the smell in the air of purity. As the dark clouds had passed, the first whispers of sunlight were stretching across the horizon such that I could see down the street towards Lake Michigan when my pager went off. They needed me again in ICU. Some child was reaching out and the nurses were concerned. Reality struck, as I quickly walked to the elevator and glanced at Grandma Marie's plaque, always there, always reminding me of her divine greatness.

I finished my shift and headed for the condo. It was a little after 7:00 and I knew Derrick and Andrea would be up and so I called.

"Hello"

"Hi. It's Melia. Do you have a few minutes?" "Ah, sure. Where are you?"

"Just arriving at your building. Can I come right up?" "Sure, of course!"

Derrick buzzed the outer door lock and I walked to the

elevator. I got in and realized I didn't remember his floor. Exhaustion had overtaken me physically, mentally and emotionally. I backed out and called again.

"Hello" Derrick answered, now somewhat perplexed. I began crying as I said, "I forgot which floor." "Seven."

Once again, I entered the elevator, pressed the button, buried my back in the elevator corner and watched the numbers slowly change – four, five, six, seven. As the door opened, Derrick was there and I fell into his arms, sobbing.

"Melia, what happened?"

"I'm sorry," I whispered through the rasps of remorse. "I didn't have anywhere or anyone else to go to."

"Come on. Let's go in," as Derrick guided me to the open door where Andrea stood in apprehension.

"What happened?"

"A little girl died in my arms last night," I sobbed. "Oh Melia, I'm so sorry. Here sit down and rest."

I sat upon the couch as Andrea came and sat beside me. "I'm sorry to bother you. I didn't have anyone or anywhere to go," I repeated.

Andrea asked in her Americanized German accent, "Can I make you some coffee?"

I shook my head no and replied, "I should go," feeling as if I was intruding.

"No, sit here." Derrick countered. "You two need to go to work."

"We can be late. You're more important."

I took a deep breath and let it all out. "She was three years old and holding her doll. She asked me if her dolly was going to heaven with her and I said, "yes". She closed her eyes with a slight smile on her face and it – was – over," I sobbed. "I went to have her death certificate signed and the doctor on call reprimanded me for waking him up. I went back to the little girl's room and she was gone, but her doll was still there and I completely lost it. All the education! All the training. All the exhaustion, emotion and frustration streamed from my eyes and I began to cry and cry and cry."

After a few minutes, I regained my composure and thanked Derrick and Andrea for their support. I wiped my tears and was about to rise from the couch when Derrick offered. "There are other ways to use your knowledge and education and still be happy."

"What about Grandma Marie?" I asked.

"She'll be proud, no matter what you do."

"But everyone will think I couldn't make it."

"Perhaps they will, but those who truly love you will understand that not everyone can do what those people do. Many are noble servants to mankind just like Grandma Marie who have the ability to emotionally distance themselves from what they see and feel each day. Others, like you, wear it on your sleeve and Melia, I think I've seen this coming since you got here. It doesn't mean you failed. It simply means you're one step closer to finding the true happiness you deserve."

I looked at the wall clock and realized it was now after eight. I excused myself and thanked them for their support. I walked to my building, called Wilco and asked for mom.

"Hello Melia, what's going on?"

"Mom can you, dad and I have lunch?" "OK! Where?"

"Kopp's?"

"OK, we'll meet you there." "Noon?"

"Fine."

The conversation was over and the next three hours had me running on adrenaline as I took a shower and did everything I could to scrub the pain from my body. At 11:30, I texted Uber and typed in 5373 N Port Washington Rd, Glendale, Wisconsin. Traffic was light and my silent ride allowed me to arrive early, such that I garnered an outdoor table away from the masses who would begin arriving shortly. For them, it was just another day.

For me, it was a point in life when things were about to change. "What is it?" dad asked.

I just shook my head and said "I'm sorry."

"About what?" dad looked at me with one of those paternal looks only dads can have.

"I've let you down." "What?"

"I wanted to make you proud. I wanted to replace Grandma and it's just not for me."

"Oh, honey." Mom never called me honey. "We are proud of you."

"I'm not making it." I replied. "I - really - don't - think - I can be a good doctor."

Dad looked at me with sorrowful eyes and a concerned expression and asked, "Did something happen?"

I shook my head no and then detailed how unhappy I was and how exhausted, as I shared the little girl and the doll and began crying once again, before saying "I'm sorry."

"Sorry for what?" dad inquired. "Sorry that you realize now that it's not for you? It took me fifteen years to realize I was making a mistake and put you, mom and the boys through almighty hell. It's better to know now than after years of misery."

"Are you sure?" mom asked.

I nodded in the affirmative as my head tilted back and the next thing I knew I was in the back of an ambulance with an IV in my arm. I 'd fainted.

As we reached the emergency room, I tried to sit up, but the world was spinning and I knew better than to try. They rolled me in on a gurney and I saw the concerned look on mom and dad's faces as I mumbled, "I'll be all right" and passed out again.

When I awoke, I was in a hospital room and it was evening. Mom and dad were sitting in the chairs. I had an IV in my right arm and a cannula for oxygen under my nose and so I knew it was more than just fainting.

Mom called for a nurse, who then called Doctor Rochard, a family friend. Within a few minutes, the doctor was there as he checked to see if my skin, lips, or fingernails were still looking bluish, before adding, "well, Ms. Amelia Terrill, you thought you could go on forever without eating or sleeping and it caught up with you. You can't keep pushing yourself the way you have or the next time could be much worse. Right now, you're anemic and your oxygen level is low."

"How low?" I asked. "74."

"Hypoxemia?" I inquired and Dr. Rochard nodded in the affirmative.

I looked at the IV in my arm with two bags hanging from the IV pole and inquired, "Reason?"

Dr. Rochard quickly answered, "Glucose for your anemia and tachycardia."

"How fast?" I inquired knowing that tachycardia was the diagnostic for a high heart rate.

"135 at admission," Dr. Rochard replied and continued. "Normally, it should have fallen, but yours didn't drop as it should have, which could be the result of the anemia, anxiety or stress compounded by fatigue, heavy caffeine consumption or an electrolyte imbalance. We'll run some tests in the morning to see what's going on, but my initial prognosis is a combination of stress, fatigue and poor eating habits.

I took a deep breath, realizing why I fainted.

"You've been pushing too hard and taking it too seriously," Dr. Rochard added.

I shook my head and asked, "How did you make it?" knowing that Dr. Rochard knew I was an intern.

"I don't remember," was all he said, as he handed me a small paper cup with a sleeping pill in it.

"What about work?" I inquired.

"You're not going anywhere for a few of days and then we'll see."

The pill Dr. Rochard provided, began to take effect and I fell into a deep sleep.

I awoke and the sun was up. I'd slept for twelve hours. I rang the call station and one of the nurses came in.

"I need to go to the bathroom." "Can you make it on your own?"

I nodded in the affirmative as she helped me to the bathroom door. When I was done I looked in the mirror where dark circles surrounded both eyes, my hair was a mess and my complexion was a pale yellow, as were the whites of my eyes. I checked my fingernails and fortunately they no longer had a bluish tint to the lunula, or little half-circles between the nail and the cuticle, which I knew was a good sign.

A few minutes later the nurse came in with a menu and instructed me to call down for lunch. I couldn't remember the last time I ate and was almost afraid to try. After they brought my coveted peanut butter and jelly sandwich, obligatory Jell-O and a slice of white cake, Dr. Rochard came in and shut the door, which concerned me.

"Melia, last night you asked me how I made it through being an intern and residency and I lied and told you I didn't remember. I do remember all the horrible circumstances of feeling like I was a nobody, going for what seemed to be days without sleep and implicitly knowing what was in each row of the vending machine."

"I remember my first patient to die. He was in his eighties and it was his time. He was all alone because his wife had died before him and they had no children. I sat with him and watched as he was about to take his last breaths and put his hand in mine and saw a weak smile on his face as he knew he wasn't alone."

"Some of us can handle it. Some of us cannot. Some of us build up an immunity. Some of us are too sensitive, too caring and too conscientious to have nothing but their heart and soul rubbed raw every time they lose a patient. While one would think that compassion is good, it can be a true detriment and that's where the challenge comes in. We all need to care, but we also need to remember that life is but a fleeting moment and then it's gone. It's only because I truly believe in God and an afterlife that it doesn't bother me as much as others."

"Your grandmother was one of those people like you. The

difference between the two of you is that, for every child she lost, there were dozens she saved and that's how she made it. For you, Melia. I don't think you'll ever be happy doing what you've wanted to do. First of all you're too sensitive. Second, you're trying to hold yourself up to the standard set by your grandmother and only a few in the world can or should be held to those standards. Melia, you have most of your life in front of you and the most important thing is to be happy."

Dr. Rochard stood, came over and gave me a kiss on the cheek. "You're a wonderful girl and had you been my daughter, I would tell you to choose a different road to travel."

His professional demeanor returned as he opened the door. All your numbers are up and other than total physical and mental exhaustion, you're in good health, but you desperately need an extended period of time to rest. If you go back to what you were doing or do anything too soon, you'll be right back here and I don't think your numbers will be as good. It's up to you and you did NOT fail."

I spent two days in the hospital and on the third day mom and dad came as I was wheeled out, riding in a wheelchair for the first time, other than the crazy wheelchair races we had at Johns Hopkins. Dr. Rochard called Milwaukee General and noted that I required an extended medical leave of absence due to exhaustion and emotional trauma. The head of the hospital said he understood. It was over and I was done.

Sadly, I was nearly 28 years old and alone. While others had 'settled in', my decision meant I needed to literally start all over. How? Where? What could I do that would allow me to be   happy?

Doctor Oldman:

It seemed strange to be outside in the middle of the day without the pressures of Milwaukee General superseding every thought, emotion or intuition. It had been three weeks since *IT* happened and I knew others were right, including my mom and dad. I truly needed to talk to someone else - not family, not friends, but someone 'professional' who could dig a little deeper and do so from an analytical perspective that would provide a level of confidence concerning what I was about to share that would stand between just the two of us. Like everyone else, there were feelings and emotions, loves, hates and fears that were buried inside me that needed to come out.

An appointment was made and I put the address of Dr. Sharon Oldman in my GPS. It seemed strange to be directed to a grocery store parking lot with a Mariano's on one end and T.J. Maxx on the other, with a few stores in between. It was so discordant that I almost called for clarification until I saw a nondescript entry that led to a courtyard where the ambiance transcended from retail to professional. I parked my Rover, perused the directory, saw "Dr. Sharon Oldman PHD", suite 423 and entered the elevator.

The sounds of the elevator punctuated my singularity as the doors closed, while the soft groans of the hydraulic elevator permeated my mind and opened to an arrow pointing towards suite 423. I checked my watch and had three minutes to spare. Being punctual, I paused until precisely two o'clock and turned the office door handle and entered a small foyer with cream colored wallpaper, white woodwork, a small wall mirror and a bouquet of artificial flowers on a table. Trepidation set in and I was about to turn and leave when a woman, who appeared to be about mom's age, entered and politely smiled. "Melia?" she inquired.

I nodded in a shy way simply to let her know it was me.

"Please come in," as Doctor Oldman beckoned me towards her inner office.

Matching the entry, her office was immaculate, with a large glass desk to the side and two love seats facing each other in the middle of the room, separated by a glass-top coffee table with matching end tables of which one had a box of Kleenex and small wastebasket strategically placed nearby.

Dr. Oldman motioned for me to sit adjacent to the Kleenex table and I followed directions.

"Tough few weeks?" She inquired.

I nodded in the affirmative as the first Kleenex was pulled from the box.

"Well, let's see if we can't help."

For the next forty-five minutes, the Doctor listened to all that transpired until she discretely glanced at the wall clock and I knew the session was over.

"Tomorrow?" Dr. Oldman inquired.

I nodded in the affirmative, shook hands with the doctor and departed.

The 24 hours went by quickly and I returned. Everything seemed frozen in time - same plants, wallpaper, furniture and tears.

"What was your childhood like?" The doctor inquired.

"Which part?" I countered.

The Doctor seemed surprised by my inquiry and replied. "Any way you want to share it."

"I don't remember much before age five except going to the farm where my paternal grandparents lived and riding horses. When I was seven or eight years old, it was all about being a princess."

I knew this was common as all little girls want to be young, beautiful, wear fancy clothes, have adventures, get rescued by a handsome prince and live happily ever after. In other words, the perfect life, which I shared with the doctor, made more believable simply because my Grandma Marie had shared the fact that her great grandfather had been the king of an African nation.

There was a pause in my soliloquy as the pains began to surface and I continued. "No child wants to be less than others, not intellectually, not financially and, at that point in life, physically."

The first Kleenex of the second session was pulled and dabbed as the words *'cinnamon girl'* erupted from within my heart, mind and soul as I was reminded that I was different and therefore 'not as good' as other middle school kids simply because my skin was a little darker than the white kids and too light for the sisters.

The third Kleenex was pulled when I poofed the frizzy hair upon my head that only had one style - a total mess. I probably could have lived with both the skin and hair as society began to accept my heritage, but the wounds were simply too deep about so much else, even though I still thought, "Thank you mom and Grandma Marie for being so brave!"

I continued on, "I thought middle school was a challenge until junior high. They call it puberty, I called it hell. I started seventh grade at five-feet-two inches tall. The following September, I was five-foot nine. I grew seven inches in one year. By high school I was not only the tallest girl, but one of the tallest students in my class. Physiology taught me that it's supposed to be growth and development, yet all my energy went into growth as my weight and other 'features' stayed the same. Names like scarecrow, lurch and lanky were accompanied with laughter, that added tears of sorrow to my cauldron of sadness."

I grabbed another Kleenex as I remembered the pain and embarrassment of being ridiculed. "Eighth grade began and I dreaded every day. Mrs. Blomquist's American Literature class began with the study of *'The Legend of Sleepy Hollow'* and when she asked one of my classmates to describe Ichabod Crane, he simply turned and pointed at me. All bones, no shape or form, living as Cinnamon Girl, with a broken heart as the name Icky Bod followed me from class-to-class, forcing me to withdraw socially and emotionally into a world of science and academics, where I did everything I could to prove to my peers I was more than a very tall, walking skeleton. Gone was any self-respect, superseded by the social cocoon I created that had only one goal – the day I would be able to finally escape from high school."

"You're taller than that now and have certainly filled out proportionately." Doctor Oldman offered.

"I tell everyone I'm five-eleven, but I'm actually almost six-feet-two and taller than my brothers. I find it interesting that the number one thing guys lie about is their height, simply wanting to be taller, while the number one thing I lie about is trying to be shorter. Only female basketball and volleyball players want to be tall and being an athlete is one thing I'm certainly not."

"Did you have many friends in school?" The doctor inquired. "Not really, and while other girls thought about guys, my world became focused on showing everyone I was more than the

loser they made me out to be."

I paused and took a drink of water and continued. "I knew Grandma Marie was respected and treated with awe wherever she went and began using her as my role model - someone I could aspire to be. I thought if I could reach her level of achievement, perhaps the pain and humiliation would go away by emulating all that she'd accomplished as a black woman in a white man's world."

I paused for a moment realizing I was gradually evaporating one layer of my emotional shield and continued with Dr. Oldman. "One day, I asked Grandma why I was so tall and she said it was my African genes as her great, great grandfather had been from the Tutsi tribe in Rwanda, who are some of the tallest people on earth."

My emotional door had opened, if just a crack, and I wanted to continue on only to notice that Doctor Oldman had glanced at the clock and my time was up.

"Tomorrow?" she asked.

I nodded in the affirmative.

The next day came quickly and the burdens that had been on my shoulders for so long were beginning to dissipate as day three became an extension of my thoughts as I went deeper and deeper into my emulation of Grandma Marie. While the first two sessions had been somewhat free form, Dr. Oldman took command with questions concerning the consequences of wealth and power as did my relationship with my parents and brothers.

"What was the saddest day of your life?"

"There are two. The first is the day Grandma Marie passed away." I exclaimed with no hesitation.

"Why?"

I took a deep breath and pondered my answer before responding, "Death is not a question of if, but when and how. Closure can only happen when you understand and accept 'why'. In Grandma's case the entire concept of woulda, coulda and shoulda transpired simply because of big business. Even with our family's wealth and political power, we couldn't save her and yet, we all believed we could have."

The next Kleenex dabbed my eyes as I continued. "When your guiding light's beacon goes out and you sincerely believe it could have – make that should have - continued shining, you quickly become lost. Not only was she a wonderful person, the tempering effects of her tranquility gave me hope and reality. We would talk and talk and Grandma was someone I could confide in – someone who allowed me to share my hopes and dreams, who mentored me and take the fears, frustrations and foibles and softened the blows when I didn't meet my own levels of expectation."

I paused for a moment and continued. "With Grandma's passing, my mentor was gone and with it any realistic reference to her achievements that allowed me to understand she was a woman, doctor and person, with strengths and weaknesses, just like everyone else and not some form of medical goddess, whose reputation reached mythic proportions."

"In other words, unreasonable expectations?"

I nodded "yes" and continued. "I'd spent nine years focusing on one set of objectives and was beginning to realize I'd made a huge mistake. Unfortunately, when you come from a family where failure and even trepidation aren't words included in your daily vernacular, to spend nine years preparing and then - then realizing I'd made a mistake, was devastating."

"What kicked things off?"

"That was the second saddest day – the combination of things all culminating in the little girl who died in my arms, compounded by the indifference and ambivalence that was beyond my emotional comprehension. Perhaps I was still that little girl who wanted nothing more than to be a princess. All I desired was to feel wanted, needed and loved. All I needed was to find out where I fit in."

The doctor looked at me and simply inquired. "How?"

"First, I do need a break to put some time and space between what was and what will be the rest of my life. Then I need to examine what makes me happy and proceed from there. My family understands and there is no financial pressure. For my own self-edification, I would like to find something, somewhere that would allow me take my knowledge, experience and love of children and apply it, simply to provide an accurate internal belief that the time spent was not wasted."

"And if not?"

"Then you and I will be having a lot more conversations."

The proverbial clock struck and it was time to go. With

each day, the sun seemed to be shining a little brighter.

"Tomorrow?" Dr. Oldman inquired as she politely stood. I shrugged my shoulders, nodded and departed.

It was Friday and the week had flown by and I felt as if Dr. Oldman and I were beginning to bond. I arrived and everything was the same except that she intentionally sat in the Kleenex chair, which caught me off guard.

"Melia, the most important thing in life is to be happy and that starts by accepting yourself for who you are. What happened when you were an adolescent has passed and you need to let go of the pain and embarrassment you felt. It's an awkward time for everyone and those who were mean did so, not to hurt you, but to try and elevate their own self-concept."

"Today you're a highly educated, intelligent, articulate, attractive woman and your time is coming. You reacted to the pain you incurred in the only way you knew how, yet today you understand the source and that's the critical first step."

"My suggestion is to take that time off and then move on, where your only goal should be doing something for yourself and not trying to always please others. You're not nearly as mixed up as you think and when you find the right person, all of this will quickly become a distant memory. We really don't need to keep meeting unless you want to and so, let's reconvene in six months if you think you need to."

The doctor looked at me and provided the salve I needed, "Melia, only twenty-seven percent of college graduates end up working in the field they got their major in, so don't feel like you failed. You're lucky because you realized in the beginning and can make a change instead of feeling miserable the rest of your life, because you feel trapped. Over the years I've developed what I call the tree of life which is a set of priorities that allow the person to keep everything in perspective. Other than those who've had a traumatic experience, it seems appropriate to probably 80% of the patients I meet with, who simply have their priorities out of order."

"In the center of your existence is you and the number one thing any person needs to do is maintain and enhance their health. This is from physical, mental and spiritual perspectives. You spent five years learning about the physical aspects that all boil down to the combination of genetics, rest, exercise and nutrition. There's nothing you can do about your genetics. You demeaned yourself over your height, the color of your skin and type of hair, but there's nothing you can do about them. I tell my patients to only worry about the things they can change and height, skin color and hair type don't fit that realm."

"The second aspect is mental health. Today we live in a stressed-filled society where we're constantly being told we're not good enough if we don't buy this product or that and are besieged with phony messages about how socially integrated everyone else is, when in fact, America is the loneliest and most acerbic society on earth. Our culture is overworked and under constant pressure to try and find happiness based on material possessions and programmed experiences that are supposed to make us feel like we're part of the Happy Tribe as I call it. Happiness only happens when one naturally feels wanted, needed and loved."

"Your mom and I have had numerous conversations over the years and the two of us have developed a series of relaxation and self-acceptance exercises that I hope she shares with you. While I'm supposed to be the 'expert', it was your mother who taught me about her program and is one reason why I sincerely believe she is the incredible person she is today. Stress can kill you and being able to quantify and prioritize different stress points is not only mentally good, but helps substantiate your physical well-being as well, which you learned the hard way."

"The next aspect is our spiritual health. This isn't about organized religion, where some group of men somewhere, decided right from wrong and good from bad. It's the inherent feelings we have when we act or react to any situation and the subliminal feelings we get when doing so."

Doctor Oldman paused for a moment to collect her thoughts, took a small sip of water and continued. "Once we've focused on our health, the next aspect is our spousal relationship. Marriage, or long-term relationships, are not easy and require work every single day. I have seven components here that include, attraction, association, communication, understanding, trust, compromise and forgiveness."

"When I meet with couples who are having marital problems, I can normally determine in five minutes where the relationship is weak and what needs to be worked on. With an ever-declining sense of satisfaction in so many different segments, I also see a profound increase in the level of marital boredom that results in increased levels of physical, mental and social ambivalence towards their spouse."

We initially chose a person to marry because we thought they were special and yet, nearly half of all marriages end in divorce. Why? Because it's the easy way out which has become the real American way of life."

"The next component concerns a parent's relationship with their kids. At first, the combination of oxytocin, prolactin, adrenaline and dopamine elicited by the brain are enough to naturally bond the parent to the child. It's when the child reaches age four or five and those inherent chemicals dissipate that the real challenges of being a parent begin."

"Initially, a parent must be a teacher. Sadly, in our society today, many of those who have procreated, either don't have the time, knowledge or skills regarding what it takes to teach their children well and end up failing to share the basic social mores that will allow an individual to create their own level of spirituality."

"What's profoundly sad is the reality that the psychological profile of today's child is the same as that of children in the 1940's except, we're talking about kids being raised by parents today, versus those raised in orphanages in the 1940's. Because of these inherent inabilities, we find a totally dysfunctional subset of children and then adults who crave the love and attention they never got at home, who are ill-equipped to properly act within the basic social standards deemed necessary, where the one thing missing is respect – for authority and each other."

"It's not all their fault. Our world has changed and today, we live in a society where the pressure to succeed socially, emotionally and academically is measured in dollars in a world that is instantly connected to and crippled by loneliness. Today, people are globally conscious, yet bitterly divided where the outlook on life has been shaped by decades of divisiveness and fear and information has been splintered down into political subsets aimed at a certain segment of the populous, supported by social media that promulgate falsehoods that people actually believe simply because it provides an avenue to a sense of belonging. Tragically, the underlying goal of social media was to bond. Today's it's to generate more money for the stockholders, with no consideration of the social, political and emotional calamity it is creating and affecting us all."

I sat amazed and aghast at the succinct elocution as Dr. Oldman continued. "Sadly, we look at others in an ethnocentric way and, because they are discordant from us do things from a perspective of disdain and fear, simply because we've become a confrontational society, afraid to express our offense for public profanity, vulgarity and self-centered narcissism. We quietly accept socially inept members and purposely fail to react to their public outbursts that go beyond what we consider appropriate. Today, instead of saying something or doing anything that might give these people an indication that their behavior is wrong, we sit silently shaking our heads, wondering what happened and why - too afraid to speak out where, because of our silence, we're the ones who are simply allowing it to continue to happen."

Dr. Oldman paused took a sip of tea and then continued. "I'm a strong believer that today, we are a tribal nation based on race, religion, ethnicity, country of origin, language, level of education, economic wellbeing and/or sexual orientation, that has splintered our society into segments with differing concepts of right and wrong, good and bad who distrust, demean and denigrate other tribes, simply for not having the same set of social mores we do." I took a deep breath and realized how spot-on Doctor Oldman was as she continued. "Who's at fault? It all starts at home where a parent must first garner a level of trust and respect from their children. We cannot rely on teachers to do the work of parents, particularly when we've eliminated the ability to reprimand and teach right from wrong as decreed by politicians and enforced by the onslaught of litigious threats that permeate all social and educational environs."

"Parents need to teach and earn the trust and respect of their children. Then, they need to realize that their role needs to change around the time their children reach puberty, simply because the parent needs to transcend from teacher to counselor. The human species evolved by trying new and different things and attempts to restrain a child will always lead to consequences that could be alleviated, if only the parents and children are open and honest. If parents have earned the respect of their children through more than authoritarian decree, trust and respect can be established and if the trust is there, counseling, instead of mandating, can be much more effective where open discussions can prevail."

"It appears to me that we find so many parents either too busy or too inept to have meaningful conversations with their kids, who feel isolated in their own homes. Today, over 30% of America's families with children under 18 years old are single- parent families. Incredibly, that number has tripled since 1965 in a society where material expectations of what we 'need' has seen a profound expansion, to the point where, unless you're wealthy, you need two incomes simply to get by and one working, single parent doesn't have the time, nor the resources to live the American dream, which is why today it is **truly** the American tragedy, socially, psychologically and economically."

There was a pause as I digested the treatise Dr. Oldman had provided, as she continued. "Next on the list of priorities is one's job. It cannot come before family! It cannot come before one's spouse and, as you learned, it cannot come before one's health. When job comes first, there will be problems. The components of career achievement are four-fold - opportunity, ability, desire and dedication. As an individual moves up the social pecking order, they quickly find that their ability level is no greater than the next people to the point where the mantra should be 'never try to be the best, but always try to do your best'."

"We celebrate achievement in so many different arenas - sports, entertainment, business - you name it, but most people really don't understand or realize the sacrifices made to accomplish what has been done by those on top, where the entire question of dedication comes into play and every moment doing one thing means one less you have to do something else. You just spent five years dedicated to one goal and, in so doing, other important aspects of your life were eliminated. As dirty little secrets come out about celebrities, sports and entertainment stars and even business tycoons, any correlation to feeling wanted needed or loved seems usurped by infidelity, anger and greed. Is it ego? Is it because they're wired different than others? Who knows? The question then becomes at what cost does success and happiness intersect?"

I was in awe of the depth of knowledge Dr. Oldman had as she continued. "Next is your non-nuclear family and friends. You don't choose your family and some you truly wish you didn't have to be associated with. As for friends, if you're lucky, you'll have two or three that will last a lifetime and need to be cherished, simply because so many things can change the dynamics that can risk that they'll be gone."

I thought of Annie and how much she meant to me as Doctor Oldman added. "There are three criteria to family and friends - mutual trust, mutual respect and mutual reward, in terms of some form of emotional gratification. Take away any one of them and the relationship will wither. To sustain it, you need to use the same criteria as marriage that will allow for the creation of deeper and more meaningful associations".

Doctor Oldman took another small drink of water and continued. "There are two more critical components. First is having hobbies and interests as they allow you to move beyond here and now and should create pleasure. The most tragic things are those people who hobbies and turn into careers and then have nothing else. For the lucky ones, the hobby is such that they say they never have to work another day in their life. Hobbies should give you an outlet for your passions. When they become your career and you lose that outlet, that sense of release and what was once fun, it can become a task."

"The final aspect is our relationship with the universe. Whether it's Mother Nature or other members of humanity, we must all respect and judge each other on **who** we are and never what we are and celebrate our differences as it is the difference that gives our world depth and beauty. If we could all learn to do this, our world, our existence and our lives would certainly be a whole lot better."

There was a pause as I sat in reflective awe, realizing that, in the matter of minutes, I'd been given the blueprint I needed for a happier existence and the parameters needed to move forward. That last bit of remorse was eroding as I saw I wasn't alone and thanked God for the little girl who was giving me a second chance at life.

My time was up and I stood and hugged Doctor Oldman. As I left the office, the sun seemed to be shining a little brighter, as the glow in my heart whispered, "It's not your fault! It's not your fault. It's not your fault."

Day One – A Date With Spike:

As things were finally falling into place, I was beginning to understand what dad had gone through when he first retired. It was like sitting next to the Apple River in Somerset on a warm summer's day, fully clothed and watching those in innertubes floating by. Life was becoming a spectator sport instead of being profoundly buried in my work.

My release from the hospital had me go home to Pine Lake for recovery instead of wallowing in my despair alone in my condo. As each day had taken a small toll, the net sum was much greater than I'd anticipated and while my numbers were going up, I was still in need of rest and recuperation and, for the first time in my life, I readily admitted that it was the case and not something I could poo-poo, with the belief that it would go away. For the next week, all I did was sleep. Twelve-hour nights became the norm and during the day, I simply laid on the couch with no energy whatsoever.

It seemed strange to be home. After four years away at college, four years of medical school and nine months as an Intern, it had been nearly ten years since I lived at home and been a part of the daily routine called life. As the days progressed, I became much more comfortable and secure in my decision that being a pediatric oncologist wasn't for me.

After a month, I knew it was over and wrote a letter to Dr. Worthington, head of the hospital, and formally resigned. I don't know if it was his compassion, Grandma Marie's plaque in the lobby or the fact there was the Dr. Marie Williams children's section in the hospital that the family had donated in her name, but Dr. Worthington's confirmation was heartfelt. He called and said he understood, noting that my efforts had been exemplary and perhaps, just perhaps, my total and profound commitment was the root cause of my demise.

As more days passed, I started becoming 'whole' again while doing things around the house where one of my joys was making dinner for mom and dad. The adage that dad could burn water was certainly true and mom's respite from his efforts appeared to be appreciated. One night as the three of us were having dinner, mom offered to go to the House-On-The-Hill with me for what she called a 'girl's week out' even though it was for fourteen days. We hadn't done anything together for a long time and it sounded fine. Mom made the arrangements and planned time for just the two of us. While a lot of young women would have been reticent to spend two weeks alone with their mother, simply getting away sounded quite enticing and so I said, "Yes".

With our own 'air force' as dad called the Wilco's charter plane division, there was always one plane designated just for the family and was denoted as Amelia^X. I never knew where the 'X' came from and deduced it was because the initial version was the tenth plane in our thirty-plane fleet. However, like Air Force One for the President, it was the family plane.

Mom and dad always had a passion for the Cessna Citation Plus as it was the family mainstay from Grandma and Grandpa's time until Wilco invested in a Boston Company that developed the Spike S-512 SSBJ personal aircraft designed to cruise at Mach 1.6 or 1227 miles per hour. As Spike's primary stockholder with 'V' sitting on their board of directors, Wilco received the first plane off the assembly line, that was designed just for our family with the burgundy and cream color scheme that Grandma had chosen for the Citation·

Normally, the S-512 had seating for eighteen, but our new Amelia^X was configured for eight with an additional sleeping or "casual" quarters in the rear. The engineers and interior designers had literally created a bed that could be 'flipped' so that it faced the belly of the fuselage and was the floor when not in use. It was cool, to say the least.

The S-512 incorporated what was called Quiet Supersonic Flight Technology that removed the sonic boom so that Amelia[X] could travel at Mach 1.6 over land, which was really neat, especially when you took off and felt the plane literally jump forward at ever increasing speeds going to altitudes as high as 60,000 feet. However, at greater altitudes, fuel economy greatly diminished simply because the oxygen levels are too low and so the S-512 normally flew at 45,000 feet and above commercial traffic.

Like the Citation, Spike as I called it, had a private liquor compartment that was electronically controlled by a combination of a family member's fingerprint and eye scan. One other really unique thing was that, instead of windows, the fuselage was solid and used exterior cameras and large LED screens to show the outside world and even the curvature of the earth in front of us. When you got tired of the view you could watch regular TV or even Netflix when you wanted to. Dad not only loved the speed, but the avionics which were so sophisticated Amelia[X] could actually take off, fly and land herself. Her computers examined both radar and digital weather reports and so she flew at different altitudes and around thunderstorms without any intervention by a pilot or co-pilot, although we always had them on board, just in case.

The distance in air miles from Milwaukee to Phillipsburg is 2,250 miles and we could now make it gate-to-gate in two- and- one-half hours. With a 7,100-mile range, Paris and Hawaii were both just a little over four hours non-stop, which to me, was almost incomprehensible.

The day came and mom 'closed up shop' as she called it and the following morning dad drove us to the Wilco terminal at Mitchell Field. The plane stood ready and waiting and it wasn't long until both of us hugged dad goodbye and were off.

Mom asked if I wanted anything to eat and I said no. She asked if I minded if she had a glass of wine to which I gave the same response as she poured herself a glass and offered me one. It had been four years since I'd consumed any alcohol and thought 'what the heck' as we slipped off our shoes and leaned back in our seats. I drank my wine, closed my eyes, zonked out and before I knew it, the captain came on and announced we'd be landing in fifteen minutes.

There was no need to radio ahead or even call dad and tell him we landed as Amelia[X] had air-to-ground software that was tied to an app Uncle Frank, Wilco Flight and dad all had on their phones so that they knew exactly where we were, what our altitude and air speed was and what time we were scheduled to land. The other neat thing had Spike 'talking' to the Princess Juliana control tower computer to automatically adjust the flight plan to ensure an uninterrupted landing.

As we were approaching Princess Julianna airport, I zoomed in the front camera and could actually see Uncle Frank with the Range Rover on one of the video screens talking to the customs agent. Because this was the first time Spike was in St. Martin, I also knew the 'inspection' would be more thorough, simply because everyone wanted to see our new toy. Sure enough, the cursory, 'Hello, thanks for coming,' took fifteen minutes as the inspector examined our newest addition and smiled in affirmation as he stamped our passports and waved goodbye.

Hello Again, Hello:

It was always good to see Uncle Frank and accept his bear hug hello. It didn't seem possible that in a little more than three hours, dad had literally done the same thing simply saying goodbye in Milwaukee.

Because it was June, the Caribbean heat and humidity had already settled in and it was 'quiet time' on St. Martin as the tourists were gone and most of the cruise ships were on their summer itineraries. That was fine with us, as it meant less human and vehicular traffic and virtually no crowds anywhere. We chit- chatted with Uncle Frank as he drove to the house. Mom had picked out food she thought we'd need and it was already delivered and put away and the liquor vault was filled.

We made our way to the top of Hope Hill where House-On- The-Hill is located. At an elevation of 290 feet above sea level, Hope Hill is the tenth highest point on St. Martin and one of the reasons why grandpa built the house there. The house was designed to emulate Le Prieuré Saint-Martin-des-Champs with a modified and more contemporary French Romanesque architectural style that retained thick walls of the original design but large sliding glass doors instead of small windows and twelve-foot ceilings on both first and second floor. Inside, grandpa was somewhat traditional with large wooden beams, matching bookcases and a huge fireplace. The chef's kitchen was totally new and literally unused while including Sub Zero and Wolf appliances that dad imported from Madison.

The grounds are surrounded by white stucco walls with orange tiles on top that matched the roof except the wall tiles have broken glass imbedded in the tops to keep the "critters away" grandpa used to say. While the wall is twelve feet tall on the outside, it's only five feet tall in the courtyard, thereby allowing for fantastic views of Orient Bay to the east and Grand Case to the northwest with Anguilla just beyond.

Looking inland to the southwest is Mont Careta and a little beyond Careta sits Pic Paradis which, at 1391 feet, is the highest point on the island. What's really neat is that both peaks are surrounded by lush nature preserves where grandma and grandpa used to go hiking. To really set the house off, Grandpa had large wrought iron gates designed and installed by Cacciola Iron Works that were manually forged by a blacksmith on site. What's really funny is that grandpa was notorious for his love of 'spirits' and had the gates created to emulate those of the Toronto Distillery that were used in several films including the movie 'Chicago'.

While the house and walls are impressive, the gates are what people always remember simply because they project a feeling of exclusivity and privilege, while connoting the sense of profound privacy that grandpa coveted more than anything else, except perhaps his wine collection. God only knows what the gates cost, but I do know they need to be re-finished every few years and it costs thousands of Euros to have it done.

As we drove up to the front gate, Uncle Frank simply put his index finger on the remote as it had been upgraded from the old- fashioned code type to recognizing fingerprints and the gates swung open and I felt like it had been forever since I'd been there. Yet, as we opened the front door, it was like everything was frozen in time with all the same furniture and fresh flowers on the dining room table, which was Uncle Frank's trademark way of saying 'welcome'.

Plans were made for dinner with Aunt Julia for the following night as Uncle Frank gave us both warm hugs and said goodbye. Mom went to what had been grandma and grandpa's suite and I took the other second floor suite, leaving the downstairs, where mom had stayed during her recovery from Leukemia, empty. It didn't seem possible that, in less than five hours we'd left Pine Lake, driven to Mitchell Field, flew to St. Martin, driven to the house and unpacked and it was still only four in the afternoon, St. Martin time and just two at home.

We went to our respective rooms and unpacked what little we'd brought as we already had our St. Martin clothes in the personal closets that only needed to be opened and moved into the appropriate vestibules. It took me all of five minutes to slip into clothes I hadn't worn in six years and headed downstairs in my standard St. Martin attire of shorts and a tank top.

A few minutes later, mom appeared wearing her infamous thirty-year-old short shorts. She was 54, but had the body of a twenty-something as the entire aging process seemed to have been slowed by a combination of mom's dedication to her health, exercise regimen, and genetics. After hearing about dad's Uncle Hank, who did 100 push-ups and sit-ups every day until the day before he died at age 93, mom put it into her daily regimen and it showed.

As for the genetics, as a medical student, I remembered reading about telomeres and their correlation to the aging process and how telomeres protect chromosomes from damage and fusing together. It seems that every time a normal, non-stem cell divides, somewhere between 50 and 100 of the telomere cells cease to exist and the telomeres get shorter and shorter, which is simply the aging process, until they reach a minimum length, at which time the cell division stops altogether. The cell then goes through what is called apoptosis or cell death. Discovered by a man named Leonard Hayflick, the entire process is called the 'Hayflick Limit'.

There appears to be a genetic link to both the initial length and number of telomeres each person has that correlates to why some people age faster than others and are more prone to disease and even a shorter lifespan. Scientists not only have measured the length of telomeres but determined that stress can shorten them at a much faster rate in those people who lead stress-filled lives. *"My God, mine were probably already used up"*, I thought.

The speed of change seems to be attributed to elevated levels of the hormone cortisol and may be one reason why stress can cause cancer. I accepted that it's impossible to eliminate all stress. However, identifying and reducing stress, had been proven to slow the aging process and improve the overall quality of life and perhaps even prevent cancer.

I knew there was another component to aging that deals with the thymus gland, which plays an important function in the immune system. Physiology taught me that the thymus was classified as a lymphoid organ located behind the heart similar to the tonsils, adenoids and spleen. While also considered an endocrine gland like the thyroid and adrenal glands, the thymus is a chemical messenger that emits hormones into the circulatory system to regulate other organs that convert white blood cells into what are called T-lymphocytes or T-Cells, where the 'T' stands for thymus-derived cells, that are used to protect the body from bacteria, fungi, viruses and other pathogens.

I recalled there are actually three different types of T-Cells. The first are called Cytotoxic T-cells, where the word cytotoxic means "to kill" and these cells are accountable for directly killing infected or mutated cells, including cancer and viruses that enter the body. The second type are called Helper T-cells which are responsible for creating antibodies and activating other types of T-cells to address foreign invaders. The third type are called Regulatory T-cells which function as 'police' to suppress both Helper and other T-cells to make certain the body doesn't overkill and do damage to healthy cells, as well.

Once the T-cells have learned to identify specific pathogens, they travel to the medulla, which is the lower half of the brainstem that regulates several basic functions including respiration, cardiac function and vasodilation - which is the dilation of the blood vessels that controls blood pressure – while also controlling reflexes like vomiting, coughing, sneezing, and swallowing, where the cells undergo what is called 'negative selection'. In the medulla, mature T-cells are introduced to the body's own antigens and/or other foreign substances, which then induce an immune response which stimulates the T-cells.

In most instances, only about 2% of the T-cells are released into the blood stream. Their job is to circulate and, when they encounter the molecular signature of a pathogen, attack the invader, while also activating other immune cells and producing proteins known as cytokines that play a role in regulating the level of the immune response.

In the normal person, the thymus reaches maturity 'in utero,' or before a child is born, and is at its largest and most active state in children. Starting in puberty, the thymus gradually becomes less active and the glandular tissue begins to shrink. By the time someone reaches their mid-60s, the thymus is largely inactive. By their mid-70's, the gland is no longer functioning.

What made mom different was her treatment protocol for Leukemia. When she was in her twenties, they harvested her T- cells, preserved them and were reinstating a small dose every year. In so doing, while other people had declining T-cell activity, mom retained the same level as a young woman and was therefore more impervious to the challenges facing a post- menopausal woman.

While mom appeared to have the genetic disposition to extend the aging process, she maintained her youthful look through a combination of diet, exercise and, as I was soon to learn, forms of holistic practices, intended to lower stress levels. The combination results in the subsequent elicitation of cortisol and does so to a point that it's only elicited to fight inherent challenges and not social or mental derived stress-fueled activities.

To say mom was physically fit would be an understatement. The combination of yoga, isometric weight training, push-ups, sit-ups and running, kept her bodyfat at around 20% or on the edge of the range of professional athletes, but well below the average woman in their twenties, let alone their fifties. While her musculoskeletal structure was optimum, mom also focused on her 'inner health' as she called it, through a nutritional regimen that included daily intakes of organic vegetables supplemented by periodic, but limited consumption of flour and wheat products, where the mantra *'if it's white it ain't right'* referred to the composition of food and not a racial evaluation, along with limiting red meat and white wines. That's not to say mom didn't like dad's favorites of steak and cake, with Chocolate Shoppe ice cream, all topped off by a glass of red wine, it's just that when she splurged, mom would compensate somewhere else, either through other dietary limitations or increased cardiovascular activity.

This had been the way mom lived for over 30 years and it was automatic and without thought, planning and certainly limitation. Not once, did I ever see or hear her pontificating about what others should be doing, nor mention the protein supplements she was taking to enhance her dietary intake. While many people become cloistered in their own limitations, mom has the innate ability to adroitly modify her intake through compensatory adjustments to the point she never lets on she's watching anything and everything she consumes, while privately participating in the exercise regimen developed to not only look good, but feel good as well. Needless to say, I was both impressed and envious of her willpower and dedication. More than often, when we were together, people thought we were sisters.

Uncle Frank had made reservations for our first night's dinner at L'Auberge Gourmande, which was mom's favorite St. Martin dining place. We drove over to Grand Case and parked the Rover in the public lot and walked the short distance to the restaurant. Phillipe, the owner, had been the head waiter on a luxury cruise ship and brought all the details of fine dining with him to this small seven table destination. As we arrived, mom was welcomed with open arms as Grandma Marie and Grandpa not only had been loyal patrons, but assisted with a long term, no interest loan after Hurricane Irma. Beyond that, everyone on the island knew our family was the second largest land holder on the island, only behind the government.

As always, the exquisite food was only superseded by the incredible service, where everyone on staff, from Phillipe, to the wine steward, to our server and the head chef made certain our entire meal was above and beyond what you would ever expect, even at a five-star restaurant. When the meal was completed and the complimentary shot of rum poured, mom and I toasted each other and a great vacation, as I thanked her for thinking of me.

"I never stop thinking of you," Mom replied, which pulled the strings of my heart.

On the ride back to House-On-The-Hill, mom asked what I wanted to do the next day and I shrugged. We had so many options and yet we'd done them all so many times before. "Why don't we wait until tomorrow and see what that brings?" I asked.

"How about a massage?" mom inquired.

I thought about how long it had been and it sounded wonderful.

"I'll call Felix, and see what he and Claude's schedules are like for tomorrow. Would ten o'clock be OK with you?"

I nodded in the affirmative as mom picked up her St. Martin phone and pressed the speed dial. "Felix its Mrs. Terrill. Oh yes, we're fine. Thank you for asking. I know it's a surprise to have someone here in June. No, it's not too hot. Are you and Claude available tomorrow at ten? No, my daughter has accompanied me and so there will be two of us. See you then."

Mom looked at me and smiled. "Felix and his husband Claude normally spend the summers in France, but aren't leaving for a while and so they can see us in the morning."

"Are their facilities far from the house?" I inquired, trying to plan my morning.

"They make house calls and we can get massages out by the pool."

It all sounded so inviting and with that, we both yawned and knew it was time to call home and go to bed, so I punched facetime and dad came on.

"How are you two doing?" he inquired. "We're fine." I replied.

"The trip report indicated everything went well. Do you like the new plane?"

"Dad, I love it. It's SO fast!"

"Let me see, first night, I'll bet you had dinner at L'Auberge Gourmande."

"You got it!"

"Phillipe still working his magic?" "As always" was mom's reply.

"What's happening tomorrow?" dad inquired. "A morning massage," I offered.

"Felix?" dad asked.

"And John Claude." I added.

"Have a great day and we'll talk to you tomorrow night." It was time to go to bed and that's exactly what we did.

The Massage:

I awoke a little after eight, slipped into another pair of what were now considered antique shorts and tank top in the world of fashion and headed for the stairs. As I passed mom's bedroom door, I noticed it was open and she was already up. To my surprise, the house was empty and the only insurrection of total tranquility was the low staccato hum of the Sub-Zero refrigerator. I glanced out to where we'd parked the Rover and noticed it was gone. On the table rested a small piece of paper with the note "5:00 - I'm walking the beach and will be back shortly after eight. Don't eat breakfast. I'll stop at 'Good Morning' for croissants. Love Mom".

My head turned as I heard the crunch of the driveway stones beneath the Rover's wheels announcing mom's return. As she saw me peering out the window, she smiled and waved. Entering through the sliders by the pool, I felt the first vestiges of the insipient June heat and humidity invade our air conditioned environ and it reminded me of Wisconsin on its very worst summer day.

"Good morning!" she announced in a very chipper way. "Did you sleep well?"

"Great" was my response, which was total truth.

"I didn't know if you would like plain or chocolate croissants and so I bought two of each. They're still warm and so let's eat," as we injected dabs of butter and raspberry jam within the folds and let it melt while the Keurig finished making our coffee.

"How was the beach?" I inquired.

"Wonderful! The sunrise was gorgeous and there was just enough breeze to keep the mosquitos at bay. I walked from the green steps where Pedro's had been, all the way down to Mont Vernon and then jogged back, jumped in the water and let the ocean breeze dry me off. What a wonderful way to start the day!"

Mom was wearing a pale blue, mid-thigh smock and was barefoot, as we sat at the kitchen table and devoured the delights she'd acquired. Mom took a deep breath and closed her eyes. "I love it here!" she exclaimed, as I witnessed some of the last vestiges of corporate tension evaporating from her demeanor. In front on me, instead of the somewhat uptight, quite direct person who could dominate any interaction, I saw gentle smiles and a softening of her expressions that were brushing away the last level of mother-daughter friction that always seemed so natural. "So, we have massages at ten and hopefully we can go for lunch at Le' Anse Marcel and then whatever you want to do this afternoon. Tonight, we've got reservations at Astrolab for their steak and lobster special with Aunt Julia and Uncle Frank. I do hope you still like lobster."

I did and smiled, thinking of one of the restaurants grandma and grandpa also helped save after Hurricane Irma.

"Do you know what type of massage you want?" mom inquired.

I hadn't given it any thought.

Why don't you think about it and I'll call Felix so that he doesn't need to bring anything you're not interested in. Mom arose from the breakfast table, opened a kitchen drawer and pulled out one of Felix's brochures. I really had no idea – Swedish, Aromatherapy, Hot Stone, Deep Tissue, Shiatsu, Thai, Prenatal, Reflexology, Sports or Tantric – with explanations pertaining to each. This was more complicated than eating in a five-star restaurant!

I scanned the list and ended up at deep tissue as the brochure said it was 'a focused, therapeutic massage that targets adhesions and specific problems areas in the deeper layers of muscle and connective tissue.' It continued, saying that the masseur would use deliberate, slow strokes or friction across the grain of the muscle to address chronic tight or painful muscles, repetitive strain, postural problems, or injuries."

At 9:45, Felix and John Claude appeared on the pool deck and began setting up their tables. Both were dressed in white polo shirts with their logo on them, white shorts and white tennis shoes, all designed to accentuate their gorgeous tans.

At exactly 10:00, they wrapped on window and it was time for our massage.

"What type of massage do you wish today, deep tissue or tantric like last time?" Felix inquired to mom. Mom got a somewhat embarrassed look on her face and replied deep tissue as a tantric massage is more uh 'personal' in nature.

John Claude was about 6'3" and had an incredible body, with blond, stylishly long hair. If I hadn't known better, I could have easily seen me with him. Mom's table was set up on the west end, while mine was on the east, as if fifty feet of pool water was some sort of magical privacy curtain between us.

I'd wrapped a towel around my torso and replicated mom's face down position as John Claude sensed my modesty and carefully placed the towel across my butt.

The massage tables had small speakers built into them and Felix pressed his I-phone as soft piano music began to play. For the next hour, John Claude worked his magic on my shoulders, back and legs removing the last vestiges of Milwaukee General tension from my body. As I neared a deep sleep mode, John Claude touched me on the shoulder indicating I needed to flip over. Without reservation, I followed directions, looking west to see that mom had done the same.

John Claude began and gave me a facial that was wonderful! Moving 'south' he then massaged my shoulders and continued to my arms as he added oil and continued on. At first I was uncomfortable and then transcended as he worked his magic while I became narcotized by the sensations created. I began breathing deeply. Not from arousal, but relaxation. My God, this was wonderful! John Claude began giving me a foot massage and then the front of my calves and my thighs, only stopping when he reached the lower edge of the modesty towel that had been strategically placed, to which I was not only oblivious, but no longer seemed to care.

As I lay there in a state of semi-bliss, totally relaxed and profoundly refreshed, the world came back into view as the session was over. My eyes opened and I blinked at the blue, cloudless sky and really didn't know if I could move or not. I probably would have spent the rest of the day simply encased in my own pleasure if it weren't for the fact that Felix and John Claude needed to pack up and move on.

I stood and wrapped the towel around me and peered across the pool where I saw mom speaking with Felix and laughing about something. It seemed strange to see my naked mother laughing and joking around with any man other than dad and realized I was in St. Martin and things were 'different'. I concluded, I wasn't quite ready to totally morph into mom's St. Martin world, even after my week with Doctor Oldman.

It's weird seeing your mother naked anytime and especially with two men, even though they are gay. I stood by and realized just how good of shape mom was in. I mean for in her fifties and tight as a drum with square shoulders, abs and tight legs, all her efforts at exercise certainly were on display.

Claude and Felix seemed oblivious and thanked us for our business and left without any money changing hands. I knew we had open accounts with virtually everyone on the island and a billing structure where they remitted the bill to Aunt Julia and were paid by our St. Martin Corporation that included a substantial remuneration that made their efforts worthwhile and our need for money or even credit cards miniscule.

After their departure, mom and I slipped into the pool. The cool water on the hot, humid June day was refreshing.

"Should I book them for next week?" Mom nquired. I nodded in the affirmative and smiled.

"Next Monday, you can have Felix and I'll take Claude. Claude is good, but Felix is simply wonderful!"

Charlie:

We got out of the pool and regaled ourselves in shorts, tops and sandals and headed for Anse' Marcel - mom's favorite restaurant for lunch. The design of the restaurant was done to respect the environment, with individual gazebos connected by a series of small paths. We walked up the path from the parking lot and on the side of the building was a bronze plaque of Grandma Marie denoting the family's support after Hurricane Irma.

As always, we were warmly welcomed and appeared to be one of the few guests eating, supported by some of the locals who hadn't left for France yet. The theme of the restaurant is "One leitmotiv: happiness, smile and good humor". We'd been coming here forever. Besides having what was considered one of the top chefs on the island, the setting is simply incredible, as you look out at the ocean between two bluffs and see Anguilla a few miles away. Regardless of the breeze and subsequent waves upon the ocean, we were encased in a sheltered cove where one could relax and enjoy the view, as well as the finest lunch you could imagine.

Sitting at the edge of the rocks, it was always interesting to see the imaginary dividing line between the restaurant and the beach that not only delineated proper attire, but was closely guarded by two very large Iguanas who, I was told, were almost like pets, in that all they were looking for was some extra lunch some generous diner threw their way.

To our left was a steep hill covered with all forms of growth that I peered at until I caught mom's attention. "We own the hill," mom offered. "Someday, dad wants to build a house there." I just shook my head wondering how you could drive up there.

Jacques, the day manager came over and thanked us for coming, while our server simply stood at attention until the pleasantries had been shared. As I peered out towards

the beach, I noticed a mother sitting on a chaise lounge watching her two small boys playing in the shallow water that brought back memories of my childhood when we would come here and play. As I sat watching their aquatic fun, one of the boys crumpled into the water in an almost fetal position as his worried mother jumped and ran to him. Frantically, she picked him up and took him to her chaise lounge looking around for anyone who could be of assistance. I looked at mom, pointed and took off through
the shrubs to the mother's side.

In broken English she spoke, "He has cut his foot" as I looked down at his bloody big toe. Mom had followed and I beckoned her to get a first aid kit. Within a couple of minutes, she and Jacques came running. Seeing the blood on the blue and white striped towel with me examining the wound, Jacques deduced that we needed more than a Band-Aid and quickly retreated back to the restaurant, returning with a bucket of ice and bottle of vodka. We'd been taught in medical school that unflavored vodka is nothing more than ethanol and water and can be used as a makeshift antiseptic. I remembered seeing doctors in Haiti after the 2010 earthquake, using vodka as an antiseptic due to the shortage of medical supplies and realized that Jacques had done this before.

The little boy was crying and I knew he was scared.

"Do you speak English?" I inquired, knowing my French wasn't good enough to properly communicate to the little boy who nodded in the affirmative.

"How old are you?" I asked attempting to change his point of focus from his foot.

"Four," was his reply.

"Have you ever had a cut before?" To which he shook his head no.

"Well, what happens is that you actually have three layers of skin and each one needs to be fed with food that is provided by your blood. What has happened is you cut the skin and the blood doesn't know where to go. We can fix it and you'll be as good as new in a short time.

I asked for some ice and looked at the little boy and asked, "What's your name?"

"My name is Charlemagne but everyone calls me Charlie"

"Charlemagne was one of my ancestors," I offered as I

attempted to divert the little boy's attention and fear away from the cut.

Charlie nodded as I added, "one of the things that will tell the blood to stop coming to your toe is making the area cold and so, if it's all right, I'm going to put some ice of the bottom of your foot. Can I do that?"

Charlie nodded as his crying became gentle sniffles, while I took an ice cube and wrapped it in a cloth dinner napkin and held it to the bottom of his toe.

"Do you feel the cold?"

Again, Charlie nodded in the affirmative.

"We won't leave it on too long and you're being very brave."

I continued with the cold compress and held it in place for about three minutes as I inquired. "Are you here on holiday?"

Charlie shook his head no and added, "We live here, my daddy is the chef."

"So, he makes all the wonderful food people love to eat?"

Charlie nodded and proudly smiled.

"Now, Charlie, what I need to do is check to see if there is any dirt or anything in the cut. If there is, you could get an infection and you don't want that, do you?

Charlie again nodded.

As the bleeding subsided, I inquired, "Is it OK if I check? It might hurt a little bit, but I know you're brave and I'll be careful." I had Charlie lean back in the chair as I examined the wound and determined it was simply an incision through both the epidermis and dermis, but did not penetrate the hypodermis or deeper subcutaneous tissue, which was good news.

I looked at Charlie's concerned mother and reported, the cut had penetrated the outermost layer of skin and the layer beneath, but did not penetrate the third layer, nor any of the connective tissue. Because of the shape of the cut, I didn't believe stitches were necessary and saw the relief in Charlie's mother's face as I added. "I do recommend that you go to the pharmacy up on the hill and purchase some medical grade honey."

Charlie's mother looked at me like I was crazy and so I explained that honey's antimicrobial properties would speed the healing, simply because the honey deprives the microorganisms of the water they require to survive. "Make sure it's medical grade honey and don't use honey from the grocery store!"

Turning back to Charlie I said. "Charlie, you're really a brave boy and so I know that what I'm about to do, you can handle."

"What?" Charlie inquired with a concerned look on his face. "I want you to think of the smallest thing you possible can.
What would that be?"

"A bug!" Charlie proudly replied.

"Very good. Now think of that bug being so tiny you can't see it. Can you imagine that?

Charlie nodded in the affirmative.

"Well sometime when we have cuts, those tiny, tiny bugs called bacteria, get inside and try living in your toe. You wouldn't want that would you?"

"No!"

"We need to make sure there aren't any bugs in there. This means I need to sterilize the cut with some alcohol. Now what I'm about to do will sting, but only for a minute and then it will go away. Do you think you can let me do that?"

Charlie nodded in the affirmative.

"I want you to close your eyes and make really, really

tight fists."

Charlie nodded and did as I directed.

"OK, here we go!" I dipped another napkin in a glass of vodka that had been brought from the bar and indicated one more time that it was about to sting. It did and Charlie let out a tiny whelp.

"Now that wasn't too bad, was it?"

"No, I'm brave like you said."

"Now we need to make sure those bugs don't get back in," and so I added some ointment, wrapped the toe in gauze and told the now relieved mother she would need to re-bandage the wound twice a day.

"Charlie, I think you're one of the bravest boys I've ever met and you deserve some ice cream, if it's OK with your mom and dad."

Charlie nodded excitedly as I inquired. "Is it Ok if your brother has some, too?"

Charlie reluctantly nodded yes and so ice cream was ordered. Charlie's mom thanked me profusely as mom and I went back to our table, only to learn that the head chef wanted to repay us for our trouble, which I immediately refused. The entire restaurant calmed down and what was supposed to be a light lunch became an infusion of gourmet delights as Jacques, the lunch chef wanted to make sure we were aware of his gratitude.

As always, the food was superb and the only bad thing was the summer heat and humidity. As we got to the Rover and slid inside, it was like an oven and the ride home required maximum air conditioning, before I slipped into the pool. As was always the case for mom, the heat and humidity didn't bother her, just as the Wisconsin winter cold was never anything more than a mild intrusion.

The rest of the day flew by and it was time for happy hour. Mom opened a bottle of her favorite Leroy Domaine d'Auvenay Mazis-Chambertin Grand Cru Pinot Noir and we toasted our first full day and the wonderful massages we both had. We then changed into what we called dressy casual, consisting of more formal shorts, top, jewelry and sandals and went to Astrolabe in the heart of Orient Bay, where Uncle Frank had reserved grandma and grandpa's favorite corner table by the pool.

From previous trips, I knew that Uncle Frank would go into great detail once again that an Astrolabe was an instrument used to make astronomical measurements which were typically the altitudes of celestial bodies for calculating latitude that was used before the development of the sextant. In its basic form, the Astrolabe consisted of a disk with the edge marked in degrees and a pivoted pointer which was now simply the name of a wonderful restaurant on St. Martin. With my anticipation came a soft smile, as I truly love Uncle Frank.

We arrived fifteen minutes early with Aunt Julia and Uncle Frank already there and awaiting our arrival. It seems this happens a lot when you get old and don't have anything else to do. We hugged as if we hadn't seen Uncle Frank in a month and it had only been a little over twenty-four hours. Aunt Julia was aging and it was beginning to show, but her spirit and wit was still about her as she began teasing the server about virtually anything and everything, including the fact that it was surf and turf night and included live jazz.

Chit chat mainly dealt with the family as both Aunt Julia and Uncle Frank knew we never talked business in St. Martin. Mom went through everyone but me as the attention finally turned to what I was doing. It had only been a few weeks since my departure from Milwaukee General and I felt uncomfortable talking about it.

Aunt Julia spoke first, "You know, your grandmother was an exceptional woman. I never knew anyone as intelligent as she was and also so compassionate, particularly with children. I remember when she came home from Medical School in Antigua and told your great grandmother she didn't know if she was going to make it. Our mother told her that some people could and some couldn't and it all depended upon their ability to cherish the good and forget the bad."

"Your grandma said she knew and realized that your great grandmother had sacrificed everything and I mean everything, to afford to send her to college and medical school. I think that's why Marie kept going, first because of what our mother had sacrificed and then in her honor. It's never easy and for some people. Being a doctor is so, so - emotionally challenging they become miserable themselves. Life's too short for that. What people need is to be happy and not force things. It will all work out in the end. You don't want to end up an old lady regretting the decisions you made. I mean, other than the wild womanizer I married, life would have been perfect for me." Aunt Julia deftly applied a smirk to her face.

Dinner was served consisting of a delicious filet accompanied by a Caribbean lobster tail as the entertainment began, which consisted of Frankie, who'd been at the restaurant for over twenty years, playing background instrumentals while singing the lyrics. Every now and then a patron would walk up and place a request for a song and a few dollars on the piano and Frankie would sing their song. As the music played, Uncle Frank got up, walked up to Charlie and as Frankie finished his previous song, whispered something and slid twenty dollars into his hand.

Frankie announced, "This song goes out to a very special young lady from the Broadway musical *Jekyll and Hyde* entitled *Take Me As I Am*' at which point Frankie sang the lyrics that left me with tears in my eyes. Through the lyrics, Aunt Julia and Uncle Frank were telling me I wasn't a failure and they accepted me simply for being me and would always love me. It was a wonderful gesture and one more step to recovery for which I was profoundly grateful.

Walking The Beach:

The third morning arrived and I was up before dawn. Perhaps it was all the rest I was getting. Perhaps it was total relaxation. Perhaps, it was me simply wanting to walk with mom on the beach at sunrise. I came downstairs and mom was already taking the last sips of her coffee. She had her push-ups and sit- ups already in the bag and was dressed in her favorite Saint Martin clothes...a boy's white ribbed, undershirt dad called the 'wife beater' and her grungy denim shorts that had the bottom of her butt hanging out.

"Do you mind if I walk with you?" I inquired.

"Of course not," Mom replied, almost incredulous that I would ask.

I was already in my two-piece, totally conservative bathing suit that was left over from high school when we came as a family, while curious to see what mom would be wearing. We drove down to the beach and parked the Rover. Mom went to the back bumper and put the keys in the little vault and took off her cover to show her attire that made my suit look like something straight out of the fifties, as we began walking.

"I love it here, especially this time of the day. I can come down here and feel the ocean breeze and no one bothers me. I'm not judged, cajoled or in any way hassled," Mom professed.

As we walked the shore, the sounds of the waves began to relax me as I was becoming attuned to the natural rhythm of the earth. As we made the bend between Kon-Tiki and Bikini Beach restaurants, the sun was just below the horizon and its radiance was such that the clouds above us had turned bright pink.

Mom stopped and, as we looked east, announced "Watch this," as the very tip of the sun toppled the edges of the waves and broke into our souls. "This is the instant I seek when I come here. This is like being reborn each and every day. It will only last a minute and then the majesty will disappear, but during these next few heartbeats, we will be in touch with God and he with us, as life begins again. This is why I come and why I hoped you would walk with me – to be reborn and to know there's absolutely nothing wrong with the decision you made. God put us on this earth to not only appreciate its beauty, but to accept the fact there will be times when it isn't quite as beautiful. Whether its people, events or circumstances, there will be instances when you will question why. When this happens you simply need to remember the majesty of these moments and the rebirth that surrounds them."

I was humbled by what mom shared. Our relationship hadn't always been so pristine and to have her express her beliefs was something I knew was coming from the heart and emboldened me to seek more as I inquired. "When did you become so, uh, introspective?"

Mom looked deeply into my eyes and replied, "When I was recovering from Leukemia and weighed less than 100 pounds. I was skin and bones and most people looked the other way when they saw me, as they never wanted to make eye contact. It was then I realized my body was simply the support mechanism for the real me – my mind, my heart and my soul and when I began to see the value in *who* we are instead of *what* we are."

We stopped for a moment as mom regained her composure. "One day, as I was walking, I was in a deep depression and almost turned and walked out into the sea."

"Suicide?"

Mom nodded "yes" as she continued, "Then I thought about all the pain my brother had caused and realized it would be bad all over again and I was already putting mom and dad through too much as it was. Instead, I went back to the house and began studying relaxation therapies that would allow me to accept myself for who I am. You've asked me how it is that I can run a company and yet never seem on edge. It's because I've trained myself to relax and take each day as it comes. I hope that while we're here, I can help you begin to accept yourself for who you are and not what you think other people want you to be. The self- acceptance program I've developed might not be for everyone, but it works for me and I hope it will work for you, as well."

We made it to Mont Vernon and began our return. The sun was now above the horizon and soon it would be eight o'clock, which meant those who were without clothes would need to either be dressed or on the 'other side of the green stairs' as mom called them. This was because after 8:00 AM, the consequence on the west side could be an anti-nudity ticket the Gendarmes periodically issued in the name of tourism. Even though properly attired, at 7:55 we were back at the Rover as the first patrol slowly made its way along the path behind the beach. Today wouldn't have mattered, but mom still had the timing down perfect.

We climbed into the Rover and, as we were driving through the retail complex, mom pulled into the parking stalls in front of Good Morning Bakery and we went inside as they were just filling the freshly made eclairs with homemade egg crème. We each smiled, ordered cups of coffee and sat at one of the picnic tables outside and had breakfast. It truly was the beginning of wonderful day.

"This is how it should be," mom declared. "A walk on the beach and a chocolate eclair with no deadlines or pressure and nothing more than a beautiful morning to look forward to."

It took us almost an hour to eat our breakfast and head back to the house. While walking the beach is wonderful, the combination of salt breeze and sand makes one sticky and so I slipped into the pool and felt the cool water cleanse my body as the sun had cleansed my soul. As I got out and was drying myself off, I realized that each hour mom and I were moving closer together and it was simply wonderful. I thought, "My God. I was lucky to have the mother I did."

We spent the rest of the morning by our pool as I pulled one of John Grisham's books from the library and mom got caught up on the email on her I-pad. When it was lunch time, we decided to return to Orient Beach.

"Let's start at the east end and eat our way west," mom offered, referring to a different restaurant every day as we headed back down Hope Hill.

I concurred as mom pulled the Rover behind the small retail complex that had been replaced when Hurricane Irma showed her wrath. There was a water sports shop, three apparel shops and Le' String on the west end that was known for its chicken kabobs, which was where mom hung out when she was recovering 30 years before. The lunch crowd was small and, as was the case at all the restaurants, we were treated like royalty. We sat down and ordered a bottle of water as we waited for our food, simply watching the world walk by in all forms of attire or lack of, that no one seemed to mind.

"This is where your dad and I met up with Uncle Rodney and Ann when they were on their honeymoon," mom lamented. "It all seems so long ago."

The food arrived and I quickly remembered that Le String's reputation was not an exaggeration. We slowly ate our food and when we were finished waited for the bill. Once again, it was 'on the house' as grandma and grandpa had helped out here, too. Wilco rebuilt and owned the complex, while keeping the rent at rock bottom levels in memory of my great grandmother and the sacrifices she made.

I looked at mom with a pensive stare and asked, "When we were walking the beach you said my goal should be self-acceptance. What you mean by that?"

Mom stood and asked for a moment so that she could retrieve another bottle of 'flat' or non-carbonated water from the bar. I knew this meant it was probably going to be a lengthy discourse as the venture to the bar was giving mom time to organize her thoughts.

As she returned, mom began. "Melia, there have been times when I really disliked myself in many ways. There was a period when I really didn't want to be here and it was only through counseling that I came to see that I'm all right and there's nothing wrong with me. We're all different based on our physical and mental composition and socialization and so it becomes difficult to really explain self-acceptance as some of it might be applicable to you and some of what I'm about to share, not applicable at all."

I could tell this was going to get serious as mom added, "While I'm identified as mixed race and face the challenges that come with a mixed identity, you're considered Caucasian and that means some of the racial self-doubt I endure, you're able to avoid. However, there are some basic tenants that still apply."

"First, you need to love yourself for who and what you are. This means accepting your habits, skills and how you look. You need to accept your situation and circumstances and stop hating them or getting angry when everything isn't perfect, then you need to stop having goals intended only for approval from others."

"Next, you need to have compassion for yourself and be less judgmental, simply because self-acceptance means knowing that no one is perfect, including you, thereby accepting any failings you might have. You just went through a difficult period and you need to stop dwelling on past choices and embrace who you are. This means looking forward and not back. You had a goal that was beyond achievement. You thought you could work your way through the challenges and yet, in the end, they were insurmountable. You need to accept that and move on. However, accepting your behavior and weaknesses and then doing nothing to improve, is not the right kind of self-acceptance because it doesn't contribute to real progress and improvement."

"Accepting yourself for who you are, is only the first step

that helps you realize your good and not-so-good qualities which will alleviate feelings of guilt, lack of self-esteem and the unhappiness you have. Self-acceptance doesn't mean simply accepting what you are and doing nothing to change and improve yourself, nor does it mean accepting your fate and life as it is. What self-acceptance does mean is becoming aware and acknowledging your behavior, habits and personality and not being afraid to honestly examine yourself as you are."

"When you begin to accept yourself, you'll be in a better position to begin moving closer to the one goal we all should have – to be happy. To do so, you need to move your own personal boundaries away from what you think other people expect of you, to what you want them to be. When you do this, your world becomes larger and your perspective broader. My mother told me that the greatest thing a person can ever learn is their own limitations, and she was right!"

"Knowing yourself affords the possibility to see what you can do to improve your life by seeing your failings, accepting and acknowledging your present position and looking for ways to improve, without comparing yourself and your achievements to others like Grandma Marie, as you acknowledge your skills or the lack of them. This will bring some sort of inner peace, lightness and happiness and help rid those burdens you have within you right now."

I looked at mom and realized she'd been where I was and, for the first time in my life, I saw a woman who was so much more introspective than I'd ever thought, as I inquired. "But how do I do that?"

Mom unscrewed the cap, filled her glass, took a sip of water and continued. "When I met your dad, I had a lot of issues. Because of our love for each other and his profound levels of patience, commitment and decency, the challenges I brought with me became circumstances we overcame. In so doing, many of the hang-ups I had were somewhat resolved and I can honestly say I'm truly happy. I have a husband who shows me every day he loves me and three children who not only love me, but fill me with pride, who have never made me question my existence again. It hasn't been easy, but it has happened and I thank God every day for your father and you kids."

I looked at mom and nodded as the feeling of love went both ways as she continued. "Here are few steps. First, try to pay attention to your thoughts and what you're thinking. This can help you learn one or two things about yourself and your 'inner- attitude'. Next, become more attuned to your behavior and actions in the various situations of everyday life so that what you do becomes commonplace and not exceptional."

"Next, begin to accept yourself and your life and find those things, events or people that make you angry and unsatisfied with yourself and change them by practicing positive thinking where the insipient woulda's, shoulda's and coulda's go away. Finally, become comfortable with yourself physically, mentally, emotionally and socially and set your own bounds and not those prescribed by other people, society or culture. Freedom deals with the ability to be yourself and once you know who you are, you can be what you are and then be free."

"One of the reasons I love coming to St. Martin is because I can be free without the social limitations and pressures we have at home. Beyond the physical thing, it's the social thing where my inner tranquility can come to the forefront and I can be more introspective as I recharge my self-concept and therefore my levels of self-acceptance. I know that coming here and adjusting to a different lifestyle can be a challenge, but you need to realize and accept that because it's different, doesn't mean it's wrong. The beauty here is that the spectrum of acceptance is much broader and people have the ability to seek out who they are without judgement, recrimination or permanence and that's what life should always be about."

The summer shadows were slowly inching their way

across the bay and had reached the ends of our chaise lounges. It was time to head back to House-On-The-Hill. The day had begun with a walk on the beach that initiated the dialogue we'd just concluded. During the hours of daylight, I was enlightened and came to the realization that my mother was much more than just my mom, she was an incredible, insightful, splendid woman who was dedicating her time to our time, not only for the experience, but the goal of helping her daughter heal and begin again, for which I knew I would be eternally grateful.

That night, we had dinner reservations at Le Piment which meant driving back to where we entered Orient Beach. As always, the restaurant was busy and, as always, we were warmly welcomed. Richard came to our table to say, "Hello" and personally welcome us, while offering an entire bottle of his famous banana rum of which mom and I each had one 'polite" glass'. It had been a long day and we wanted to call home, so the 'night owls' were back at the house by nine o'clock.

Mindfulness:

It was barely five when I awakened and headed downstairs. Mom was in the midst of her morning push-ups and sit-ups and so I didn't interrupt. The dark sky was in the first throes of morning light and, once again, it looked to be a glorious day.

As I ran the grinder and made fresh coffee, mom appeared. "Good morning!" mom announced.

"Good morning" I said with a short smile on my face. "Coffee?" I inquired.

"Better make it to go, if we're going to see the sunrise."

I poured the coffee into two thermal mugs as we set off for another day's adventure. With few others on the beach, we parked the car exactly where we had the day before.

Mom slipped out of her cover and put it on the back seat of the Rover as I noticed she was in a somewhat conservative one-piece bathing suit and was about to lock the keys in the back bumper. I turned to mom and said, "You can wear whatever you'd like, including nothing. I don't think it's fair that you have to follow my lead."

Mom smiled and looked at the ground and then at me. "I'm fine. Perhaps tomorrow".

We began our walk and had just about reached the bend when we stopped to watch the sun hit the waves. Nary a word was spoken as it had all been expressed the day before.

After the pause, we began again as mom added. "There's a movement today called Mindfulness which is the basic human ability to be fully present and aware of where we are and what we're doing, while not being overly reactive or overwhelmed by what's going on around us. Football teams have begun implementing the program into their training regimen as it allows players to balance their emotions and focus on the next play instead of being too jacked up and overwhelmed by the entire situation."

We were progressing towards the rocks at the north end of the bay, watching the sun's rays began their journey down the walls of the Mont Vernon condos as mom added. "While Mindfulness is something we all naturally possess, it's more readily available when we practice it on a daily basis. Whenever you bring awareness to what you're directly experiencing via your senses, or to your state of mind, via your thoughts and emotions, you're being mindful. When you train your brain to be mindful, you're actually remodeling the physical structure of the brain itself."

I was trying to process each word and thought, as mom continued. "Mindfulness is available to us in every moment, whether through meditation or practices, like taking time to pause and simply breathe. Right now Melia, you're probably thinking, "suuuure," simply because you don't realize there's a difference between regular breathing and relaxation breathing or Mindfulness."

Walking still further, mom added. "The power of active breathing—voluntarily inhaling and exhaling to control our breathing rhythm - can calm the nervous system by reducing our heart rate and activating our parasympathetic nervous system. In this way, our bodies become calm, and our minds also quiet. There are actually three phases to Mindfulness breathing – 'the in-breath' which is simply inhaling only through your nose. The 'hold-breath', which is obviously simply stopping the process and then the 'out-breath' or slow exhaling, again, only through your nose. The secret is in the timing, which is called the four-five-six method. Inhale to the count of four. Hold for the count of five. Exhale for the count of six and repeat the process seven times."

Mom stopped for a moment to look at the pink clouds. "Why does this work? Findings show that our "in-breath" is like a remote control for our brains. By breathing in through our nose we are directly affecting the electrical signals in the olfactory or 'smell' regions of our brain, which indirectly control the electrical signals of our memory and emotional brain centers. In this way, we can control and optimize brain function to have faster, more accurate emotional discrimination and recognition, as well as gain better memory, while the hold- breath allows not only the brain to begin to calm, but provide time to remove some of the stress that has built up."

"But what about the out-breath?" I asked.

Mom continued, "Slow, steady, breathing activates the calming part of our nervous system, and slows our heart rate, thereby reducing feelings of anxiety and stress. So while the in-breath specifically alters our cognition, the act of slow, deep breathing, whether the inhalation or exhalation, is beneficial for our nervous system that calms the body."

Once again, we were walking as mom added "Mindful breathing emphasizes not only the breathing component, but the mental component of paying attention as well. When you become aware of your mind, body and breath together, you are able to literally watch your mind and feel your body more clearly and that will allow you to focus on here and now."

I looked at mom and must have had a questioning expression as she continued. "I'm certain you're still skeptical and so, why don't we stop and give it a try? In-breath to the count of four - hold for the count of five - out-breath for the count of six." Mom had me repeat the process seven times and I could actually feel myself begin to not only relax, but have a better focus of what was around me.

Mom smiled and added. "This program will not only help reduce stress, but make you more attuned to your world as your ability to listen becomes that much greater. Remember, one of the really important elements of self-acceptance is the ability to listen and understand your own self, as well as the thoughts of others and not just words."

I remembered back to my physiology classes and realized that breathing was regulated by the autonomic nervous system such that inhaling oxygen is an unconscious process. I also remembered that the amount of oxygen we inhale influences the amount of energy released into our body cells that progresses on a molecular level, via various chemical and physiological processes. I shook my head thinking I should have remembered that from my neurochemistry classes, but didn't and what mom expressed was not only logical, but effective.

As we began our journey back to the Rover, I continued the breathing exercise and could actually feel my body let go as mom continued. "Melia, one thing that will help you relax is to listen to music. As you know, the human body is an electrochemical device. This means you have electric current running through your nervous system. If you can find music that is a harmonic to your natural rhythm, it will soothe your nerves and reduce stress."

It was then I realized why they were beginning to use music in hospitals with noise cancelling headphones to reduce the time needed in intensive care by as much as 20%, while improving the patient's overall recovery time as well. Give the brain something that's soothing and it can focus more on restoration of its homeostatic existence which is, was and will always remain the ultimate objective of medicine.

We continued walking as Mom added. "Another component is a practice called Grounding or Earthing, which is a therapeutic technique that involves doing activities that 'ground' or electrically reconnect you to the earth. You've been to The Forest and felt its ability to affect people simply because three positive ley lines intersect there. To a much lesser degree, there is electrical radiation everywhere and, therefore, electrical conductivity exists within the matrix of the bottom of your feet and the earth. This connection serves as an immune system defense similar to antioxidants where, through grounding, the natural defenses of the body can be restored, thereby reducing pain, stress, depression, and fatigue."

I reflected on the course I took in holistic medicine that

the medical school was not happy about. Medicine is a very big business that's based on cause and effect and, while pontificating certain aspects , such as weight loss and avoidable cancer, is not based on the prohibition of causes.

Mom continued. "While we can't always run around barefoot, we can do so at home and particularly outdoors and both will lead to greater levels of relaxation. When you're relaxed, you can better focus. When you can focus, you can listen and understand more. When you can listen and understand more, you'll have a much greater probability of enhancing your self-acceptance. While not for everyone, to simply be unencumbered allows your entire body to have its senses completely bathed in nature. For some it's a turn on, for others, it's simply a way to interact with nature and the complete consequence of Earthing."

We were past the bend as mom continued. "The final aspect of self-acceptance is the spiritual segment which has nothing to do with religion, but knowing right from wrong, good from bad and only doing what is right and good, even when there are no consequences for doing wrong or bad. People at peace with themselves know this, accept it and understand the critical importance of the word 'no' to any recommendation that calls them to act in a way they don't believe in."

Stopping in our tracks, I took a deep breath and became somewhat introspective as I looked at the water, while mom continued. "I think one of the saddest things that has happened to our society in the past thirty years is that we've become a no- fault world. There's always a rush to blame someone when in fact, people shouldn't participate in acute finger pointing or the blame game. Those at peace with themselves don't always think that someone has to be right or wrong simply because there are times when this isn't the case."

We'd reached the rocks that delineated the clothing mandatory from the clothing optional segment of the beach as mom concluded. "When you finally reach a point of self-acceptance and make a mistake, you admit it, learn from it and try not to do it again. Making the same mistake over and over and over is reserved for the insane and the government and not for those who seek internal happiness."

We turned right and went to the Rover. Mom unlocked the car and we got in.

"Good Morning?" mom inquired referring to breakfast, as I nodded in the affirmative.

We drove to the bakery and walked into the sweet smell of delicious. In my delirious need for some sort of gastronomic delicacy, I realized, I'd never put my shirt on and was standing there in my bathing suit, to which nary a glance or evocation took place. Surprise Melia!

The lady at the counter remembered us from the day before and inquired about coffee. Mom looked at me and declined the inquiry. We were heading back to the house, to grind our own coffee beans and eat our croissants by the pool.

We made it back to the house and had breakfast. Mom indicated she had to make some calls and so I took my Grisham book and headed to the pool, slipping in the water to cool down and reflect on all that mom had shared. It was going to be another hot one! I read for almost two hours, cooling off as needed when mom came out and inquired. "How about some shopping?"

There wasn't really anything I needed, but it looked like mom was in the mood and so I nodded in the affirmative as mom justified the suggestion. "Tomorrow is cruise day and so Phillipsburg and Orient Beach will be crawling with cruisers and I thought I could call Penny and Paul and have them take us over to St. Barths. We can rent a Jeep and make a day out of it. They've got better shopping over there and either go to Anse de Grande Saline or Anse de Governeur beach for a change."

While tourism is the lifeblood of St. Martin, you also knew

that when the ships were in that disgorged several thousand cruisers, you needed to stay away from the popular cruiser places and so I agreed.

While most of the people were simply looking to expand their horizons and be able to say "we did that" we realized that up to 10,000 cruisers all trying to do the same things at the same time would mean a lot of congestion, which we really didn't want. It was almost noon and so I slipped back into my shorts and top as we headed for Wai, which was the newest restaurant on Orient beach. The food was very good and mom and I took our time simply 'people watching', before heading back to the house. It was in the low 90's and I only wanted one thing, to jump in the pool. Mom joined me and we spent the next hour simply floating, relaxing and doing nothing. I thought of what had transpired and how I hadn't been able to simply do nothing for over five years –
five years of pressure and stress, now simply floating away.

At five, it was cocktail hour and we switched to drinking the all new Terrill Reserve Pinot Noir as we sat by the pool and finished the bottle. Little did I know at the time, that each bottle of Terrill Reserve cost $1,000 and there was a case in the wine vault.

The hot spot for dinner was La Villa in Grande Case, just down the street from L'Auberge Gourmande. La Villa was supposed to have great drinks, great food and great service and it did. Mom and I shared the Lobster Bisque, then both had mahi mahi and dory dishes, all topped off with special strawberry soufflé for desert.

The best part was, because it was new, no one knew mom and that made it special, as we weren't being fawned over the whole night. It's certainly amazing how you can grow tired of people trying to make you feel special.

St. Barths:

I'd been to St. Barths numerous times, but never on a shopping trip with mom. She was known as a serious shopper who could drop thousands and think nothing of it. Penny and Paul arrived at the ferry dock to Pinel Island at precisely 8:00 AM and we climbed aboard. Both of us had a 'day bag' as mom called them, that contained beach towels, suits, lotion and a change of clothes.

Penny and Paul were originally from Paris and had met nearly twenty years before on Orient Beach, where they fell in love with the island and each other. Uncle Frank hired them to operate one tour boat and Wilco hired them to run the entire charter boat business. They were good friends of the family and were discrete about what they saw and heard and always made us feel very welcome.

At a distance of sixteen miles, we would be in Gustavia in a little less than an hour while the car rental company would have the jeep waiting at Hotel Christopher where we could change and leave our belongings. Paul radioed ahead and the hotel courtesy car was waiting for us at the dock. We said goodbye to Penny while mom told her she'd call when we were ready for them to pick us up.

"Let's go to the beach first," mom offered. "Then we can come back, have lunch and shop."

It all sounded good to me as we changed into our suits, grabbed our towels and made our way in the Jeep out to Governor's Beach on the south side of the Island. While winter's day, could result in the surf being quite rough, summer waves only gently lapped upon the shore as we parked the Jeep and headed for the beach.

Governor's Beach is a crescent shaped inlet that has outcroppings on both ends. The west end was furthest from the parking area and for some reason, mom thought it would be 'our spot' as we trudged there and set up our base camp.

I pulled off my cover-up, stood and watched as mom

followed suit, if you want to call it that. There's old saying...'when you got it, flaunt it, when you don't hide it.' Mom sure still has it! Yikes! She never was one to be modest even with me around.

There wasn't a soul around and it seemed as if we were the only people on earth. After the popularity of Orient Beach, it was really cool simply to be all alone. Mom looked at me and offered a treatise on Shinrin-Yoku which, she noted, translated into English means 'forest bathing' while referring to taking in the forest atmosphere during a leisurely walk.

Developed in Japan during the 1980s, Shinrin-Yoku had become a cornerstone of preventive health care and healing in Japanese medicine and something I learned about in my holistic health class. Researchers in Japan conducted studies on the health benefits of spending time amongst the trees, demonstrating that forest bathing positively creates calming neuro-psychological effects through changes in the nervous system, reducing the stress hormone cortisol and boosting the immune system.

Every study conducted demonstrated reductions in stress, anger, anxiety, depression and sleeplessness amongst the participants. Simply following the regimen could result in a change after just fifteen minutes as blood pressure drops, stress levels are reduced and concentration and mental clarity improve which is why, along with a better diet the Japanese have the longest life expectancy on earth.

Mom had adapted the program to the ocean, beach and the sound of the waves and wanted me to try it as there is something profoundly peaceful about being all alone at the edge of the sea, with the waves gently rolling in and the real reason why we were there.

"I've been practicing this, along with Yoga since I was sick," mom offered, "and have found that, as long as there is solitude and singularity, it can work virtually anywhere."

We definitely had both the solitude and the singularity as the crescent shaped beach was deserted with only our footprints in the sand commemorating our arrival as mom continued. "First there are some basic rules which is why we didn't bring our phones or camera with us. I don't believe there can be any other distractions so that we can be fully present in the experience. Now comes the hard part for you, Melia. I want you to leave behind your goals and expectations about today and wander the beach aimlessly thereby allowing your body to take you wherever it wants to go."

This was getting interesting as mom added. "As you're walking, you need to pause from time to time, and look more closely at anything that catches your attention or notice the sensation of the path beneath your feet. Next, you need to find a spot to take a seat and listen to the sounds around you and see how the behavior of the birds and other insect or animals change when they become used to your presence."

"As you're sitting, close your eyes and simply listen and do so for an extended period of time. We have the five basic senses - the tongue for taste, the nose for smell, the ears to hear, the skin to touch and the eyes to see. However, our vision provides up to 80% of all sensory information and simply dominates the other receptors, thereby reducing our dependence on them. By closing your eyes, the other four senses can begin to compensate, and soon you will hear things you didn't hear, smell things you didn't smell, taste the salt in the air and finally feel things that were there, but you didn't notice."

"If you're lucky, you'll be able to begin focusing on any part of your body you want to, like your toes or fingertips, and simply feel what they are feeling. Normally, when I'm alone and walking on Orient Beach early in the morning, I love to have my entire body exposed to the world around me without being sequestered, but that's up to you."

I put my hands to my mouth as if in contemplation and didn't know if I could go that far. Mom sensed my reticence and made me feel more at ease as she continued. "You don't need to. Some people don't have the inner self-confidence to simply let go of their reservations and there's nothing wrong with that. Right now, it's just the two of us and so what you do is what you want to, with no pressure from me or anyone else."

"When you're ready to start, I think you need to walk alone. I'll sit here and let you explore your senses. You need to resist talking until the end of the walk or even thinking about anything but the instant you are in – not me, not dad, not Milwaukee – not anything. When you return, we can share your experiences if you want to. Now, let's sit for a while with our eyes closed to allow your body to adapt so that you can begin your journey."

For what seemed like an eternity, I simply sat and watched the waves roll in before closing my eyes and opening my ears to the sounds around me. Periodically, I'd hear the call of a gull or listen to the waves slap against the rocks as I felt the warm breeze tousle my hair. As my mind slowed to a crawl, I began to feel the grains of sand between my toes and then the warmth of the sun on my face and it felt good.

"Ready to walk?" mom inquired.

I nodded in the affirmative as I opened my eyes.

I began and didn't look back as I didn't want to break the spell. Slowly I walked towards the adjacent hills perched on the other end of crescent. Below me, the spume was washing away our previous footprints, filling the indentations of our insipience with matter that softened and finally deleted our previous incursion. Like life itself, there was symmetry and persistence, until there were only memories of what had been.

I did as I was instructed and quietly allowed my body to take me where it wanted to go and not where my mind would have decreed. At first, my body wandered further along the shoreline and then had me gradually angle up to where there were small dunes of captured sand that been splattered helter skelter by some former wrath of the sea until they became covered with vegetation marking the zone between botanic life and the thin strand of crumbled sea shells in which I was becoming immersed physically, mentally and now emotionally.

I stopped for a moment and peered at the vibrant green leaves and orange flowers and followed a small butterfly as it nestled beneath the shade of a sea grape leaf before continuing on. My body found a spot within the shade of an angular palm whose leaves stretched out over the sand and it became my eternity.

I thought of mom's exposition on totality and for the first time, sincerely felt free, allowing my body to be bathed in the majesty of nature as the warm breeze caressed my face. This is what mom meant by freedom. This was the narcotizing sensation that called her back time after time and allowed her to calm the storms of life into gentle waves upon her sea.

Quietly, I sat down and closed my eyes and all that mom had portended began to evolve. First was the sound of the waves whose repetition beat out a cadence that never ceased to exist. Next, I began to smell the succulence of the ocean as it filled my nostrils with a purity not known, felt, nor enjoyed before. Then, I began to taste the tangy residue of the salt in the air as my tongue slathered the sputum within the confines of my mouth. Finally, my bodily senses came into play and I began feeling with my finger tips and then my toes, the warmth of the sand as it permeated my loins as I sat in solitary bliss and could literally feel my tensions erode as I began to see what was so narcotizing.

I don't know how long I remained, nor what changes took place around me as it could have been but a few minutes or longer. When I finally opened my eyes, I stood, brushed the sand from the back of my legs and began walking again towards the eastern bluff. As I reached their demarcation, I turned and saw mom's distant form sitting in a lotus position, palms up, outlining the hills where my journey commenced.

My trance was over as my mind again took command and I began walking back towards where I came. Gone was the intimacy. Gone was the ambivalence. Instead, was the awareness of one objective, to regain the company of my mother.

I stopped and began my trek back to mom who was in the process of folding our towels, denoting it was time to go. We'd been at the beach for over two hours and her actions inferred we needed to head back to Gustavia. I silently agreed as we began walking back to the parking lot. So much for my trials and tribulations, fears and apprehensions. In one episode, another one of my foibles had been eradicated, replaced by the sincere belief there was a profound beauty in solitude and I needed to continue to explore a place simply called peace.

As we got to the Jeep mom looked at me and smiled.

"Well?" "Wonderful." Was my only response.

"Any regrets?" "Not really!"

"Want to do it again?" "Most certainly."

We headed to the hotel, got cleaned up and called the Concierge to make reservations at Orega on the pier. We left the Jeep at the hotel and rode in the hotel courtesy limo as Gustavia parking was always a notorious nightmare, even in June. Orega's food was spectacular and expensive to the point that, when I glanced at the bill, I almost tried to give it back. I knew St. Barths was expensive, but the cost of our meal could have fed a family of four in Milwaukee for a week.

Mom and I were casually dressed and started at one end of Quai de la République with a goal of hitting all the stores on Rue du Général de Gaulle and then Rue de Roi Oscar, as well. At first, things were going quite well until we entered a small, very high-end clothing store where the clerk looked profoundly bored, never taking her eyes off her cellphone, nor us.

As mom examined a €1,000 silk blouse, the clerk came over and noted the price, inferring her doubt it was something mom could actually afford. Perhaps it was our casual attire. Perhaps it was because we're mixed race. Perhaps, just perhaps, by the tone of her voice, the clerk decided we were intruding on her texting and she needed to insult someone and we were the chosen ones.

Just then the front door opened and two Gendarmes appeared, stared at mom and me and that was all it took. Mom looked at the clerk and began speaking French, "tu m'as insulté ainsi que ma fille » articulating each and every word to make a point, as I watched the clerk's eyes widen.

Mom looked at me and then the police as we headed for the door and exclaimed, "Perhaps, next time I come shopping on St. Barths they'll have something with a little more class for me to examine," as she turned to the trio and said "maintenant vous pouvez tous aller en enfer."

Mom was angry! Mom was hurt! Mom was embarrassed and for the first time, I saw my mother in a different light and realized she had a lot of grandpa in her, where she would ask for little, but only take so much and then watch out!

It took a while for mom's whitecaps of anger to flatten and with it, the joy of the day was simply destroyed. Mom called Penny and told her we'd take the ferry back to St. Martin that was leaving in fifteen minutes. By the tone of mom's voice, I'm certain Penny realized something had happened.

"What about our stuff in the hotel and Jeep?" I inquired.

"I'd rather get off the island than worry about the clothes and the rental car company will come and pick up the Jeep," mom said in a tone emitting profound authority that I knew I'd better not question.

The turmoil of the day became exemplified as the ferry blew its horn and we boarded. The forty-five-minute trip seemed like a long ride back to Phillipsburg and an even longer silent, taxi ride back to the house. I understood there was pain that needed to be extricated that only time could take away. As we entered the house mom looked at me as said "I should have just bought the fucking store." I knew right then that the clerk had cut mom to the bone.

Wim Hof:

Once again, I awakened before five and headed downstairs as I listened to the sounds of mom doing her syncopated push- ups and sit-ups to simply take away her anger and frustration. When you're wealthy, the memories of racial prejudice are normally forgotten. Sadly, to have them slammed into your face had simply been too much.

A few minutes later mom appeared in the kitchen and looked at me while lamenting, "I'm sorry about yesterday. I probably over-reacted."

I looked at mom and shook my head no. "Mom, if we don't stand up for what's right, then people will continue to do what the clerk did and never realize it's wrong."

Mom had a slight smile on her face as she inquired. "Ready for our walk?"

I nodded in the affirmative, noting that my only bathing suit was on St. Barth's as we climbed into the Rover and headed for Orient Beach. I had a sincere belief mom needed some sort of tacit statement that all of her efforts, all of her elocutions and all that she was sharing with me was having an effect.

"Let's walk east this morning," Mom suggested and we walked to the very edge of Orient Bay where the protective rocks separated the turmoil of the sea from the tranquility we enjoyed. It was only when the fierce storms of life breeched the wall did the wrath of Mother Nature spew her destruction upon the otherwise placid bay that God and man had created.

We made it just in time to watch the sun snatch the last morsel of darkness as it clipped the horizon and began another day in paradise. Beyond the rocks, the waves were strong. On our side, the water was calm. I guess that's somewhat like life, where a few rocks can make the difference between rough seas and tranquility.

Being a much shorter distance travelled, we made it back to the delineating rocks as the oppressive heat of summer began its incessant attack on our being. While I was in the throes of the combination of heat and humidity, mom seemed oblivious to the rapidly accelerating discomfort level. As we stopped, I wiped my brow and asked mom why the heat never bothered her.

Mom looked at me and replied. "That's another piece of the puzzle. Through studying the principles of the Dutch athlete Wim Hof, I began to practice his methodology of using my mind to artificially induce a stress response that helps me resist the effects of extreme weather which for all intents and purposes, becomes a case of 'brain over body'. In so doing, it allows me to activate an internal painkiller through the implementation of a more extensive set of breathing exercises than the Mindfulness I do before exposing myself to the extremes."

Mom continued. "At first, I thought the procedure was a bunch of hokum until I realized our body has the ability to adapt to the environment instead of changing the environment to meet our comfort levels. Through my gradual adaptation, I'm now able to comfortably function in a full range of temperatures where others would either hide indoors to escape the heat or bundle themselves up against the cold."

Mom looked at me and continued. "Quite honestly, I'm to the point that I haven't worn a winter coat in years and only wear gloves to protect my hands from frostbite and feel quite comfortable right now. The net result is that my body's healthier and I'm less susceptible to colds and the flu to the point that, when I do get one, my recovery time is a fraction of what it had been previously."

"Can I learn it?" I inquired.

"Sure, but it will take several years to master the program. It requires that you let go of all your preconceived ideas and practices. I can help you, if you like."

Mom went through the details. "The technique first requires relaxation which means removing as many thoughts as possible from your brain, which mom noted is easiest when you lie down or are walking on a quiet beach at sunrise. Next comes an intense version of the deep breathing exercises, that takes the Mindfulness program to a deeper level that needs to be sustained for several minutes. If you are effective, it might prompt a kind of tingling in parts of your body."

"In other words, a sign of hypocapnia, or low carbon dioxide in your blood," I added as mom nodded and concurred.

Mom continued. "Research has shown that this exercise makes a person's blood more alkaline as it becomes saturated with oxygen. This can activate a part of the brain that releases opioids and cannabinoids that inhibit the signals responsible for telling your body you are feeling pain or cold while the chemicals then trigger the release of dopamine and serotonin, to create a kind of euphoric effect on the body that lasts for several minutes." "In other words, the VTA, nucleus accumbens, caudate nucleus and thalamus." I offered, as I dug back into my neurochemistry memory bank.

Looking out at the bay which would soon be filled with people frolicking on jet ski's or lifted up when tethered to a huge parachute, mom continued. "Your brain has the power to modify your pain perception and that's particularly important for human survival. Too much heat and humidity or too cold of temperature creates an imbalance where the body begins the process of homeostasis as it works to correct it through sweating or shivering as you try to restore temperature balance."

"What's interesting is the fact that the pain mechanism isn't always useful. Imagine spraining your ankle while being chased by a tiger. You probably won't actually feel the sprain in the thick of the moment since your brain senses the greater danger presented by the tiger and uses the opioids and cannabinoids to inhibit the pain signals. This allows you to run away and save yourself, despite the injured foot."

"But how did you learn how to do it?" I inquired.

Mom looked at me and replied. "It's taken years and began when I was here recovering. I spent a lot of time reading and then cultivating my mental and physical skills simply to make certain my Leukemia hadn't metastasized. What was surprising was that the scans began showing a difference in not only form, but function from those taken before I began to practice."

I had a slight smile appear as I deduced, "In other words breathing, often thought of as an autonomic function, can be willfully controlled?

Mom nodded in the affirmative as I added, "And harnessing breathing can result in increased activity in the parts of the brain that deal with thought and action which, over time, can lead to actual physical changes in the brain, as well."

Mom nodded in the affirmative again, adding a smile to denote her pleasure that I understood, while adding that the response is normally short lived, but the physiological change remains constant unless you stop your routine, as she continued. "Think of it as a form of mental weight training, where stopping your exercise program results in an atrophy of the muscles. Where Wim Hof is different is that, through repetition, and over an extended period of time, your anticipated response begins to generate a stimulus in the brain's cortex before the breathing exercise even begins and does so as a type of expectation that triggers the release of more opioids, serotonin, and dopamine in a kind of self-fulfilling cycle. In other words, Melia, the longer you continue with the program, the easier it will get as your subconscious becomes more confident of its expectations, while you take greater control of your own autonomous nervous system."

I simply shook my head as mom continued. "Walking unencumbered on the beach isn't for everyone and there are those who aren't doing it for non-prurient purposes, but for me, it periodically allows me to begin the entire process that melds my mind into my body to achieve a level of both mental and physical homeostasis that creates the internal peace I desire. This is why I can handle the pressure and altercations such as yesterday and allow my life to be filled with the beauty and joy concerning what's really important and why I sincerely hope this week is showing you it's available to you, as well."

The sun was up and mom suggested we take a swim. I had my choice, the clothes I was wearing or nothing at all. I might have gone in the clothes except one of the ladies from the little shops next to Le String was pulling up the security awning and not only recognized mom but waved and beckoned us in. It would have been a social affront if we didn't and so we reluctantly made our way into the small store, jammed to the brim with all sorts of hats, beach toys and swimwear.

The lady's name was Lucille who was the proud owner. She smiled and said something in French to mom, who got a slight grin on her face.

"What did she say?" I inquired.

Mom reluctantly offered, "Lucille said you looked like you needed something to wear."

I'd always been somewhat modest when it came to my own body. I really don't know why. I spent five years studying and applying my anatomic knowledge and working on cadavers without any trepidation. Perhaps, subconsciously I didn't like the way I looked – somewhat of a gangly half-breed, or would that be quarter-breed? Other than self-centered plastic models, I don't think any woman truly likes the way she completely looks.

I reluctantly agreed to try on some bathing suits – something that most women prefer doing alone and especially, not with their mother. After wearing what was called a two-piece bathing suit that had a conservative top with a bottom that came up to my waist, anything smaller was going to be a challenge. Mom and Lucille went to work offering this suit and that, requiring me to step behind the curtain into this tiny dressing room and try them on. While there might have been conservative swimwear somewhere in the store, I couldn't see any. Lucille validated that the suit of choice for most women in Europe and St. Martin were bikinis with bottoms that exposed some of their buttocks, which was the fashion statement for my generation.

Lucille noted. "It wasn't that many years ago when a Brazilian bikini, thong, or skimpy cut bottom was only worn by only the most daring."

Mom added, "times have changed!"

As Lucille picked up another suit and said, "One of my most popular styles is the Brazilian cut bottom which is known for its conservative coverage, where the bottom is typically a small triangle on the rear, similar to the one in front."

I rapidly shook my head to indicate a very strong "no".

Lucille acted as if she didn't hear me and continued. "Feel the excellent quality of the material that won't sag and will hold its shape very well. Girls of all ages who've tried them, love these bottoms as they are often more flattering than moderate, full- coverage bottoms."

Lucille looked at me and added. "Women who are concerned with the appearance of their backside often think they'll hide more with more coverage. In fact, more coverage adds to the visual perception of a larger bottom, which is just the opposite result you're looking for."

"Melia, please try this one on for me. If you've never tried one, consider buying one for your next vacation and mix it in with your other suits. I have many excellent brands to choose from but they all fit a little different."

I tried one on and found it to be brief, but OK. Lucille offered another that was a little briefer and then another and another until I began to feel uncomfortable. I preferred solid colors and came out of the dressing room wearing a relatively conservative, chocolate brown bikini with a deep "V" neck line and bottom that rode down around my hips, while looking to make sure no one else was in the store. Mom looked at me, smiled and announced, "It looks great on you," instructing Lucille to put it on the counter. So much for my opinion.

With each iteration, I'd step out and model the suit and look in the mirror and try to convince myself, "Melia, you're not in Wisconsin anymore!" Lucille had a long way to go before being done and handed me another and then another and yet another. I actually think Lucille could have sold ice cubes to Eskimos as she continued to bring out smaller and smaller versions to my dismay, until I thought she'd just hold up a couple of strings for me to wear.

Lucille continued. "Everyone has heard of the Thong Bikini, but another style that's growing in popularity is the Tanga, which is a modified version of the Thong."

"Tangas are a little more conservative than a classic Thong. The front of the bottom is a small triangle attached to the back piece by strings, side ties or thin piece of Spandex. The back piece is a small triangle that provides approximately three more inches of coverage than a Thong."

We were finally reaching the bottom of Lucille's pile of options when she offered a brief, but attractive bright yellow bikini that had a deep "V" top like the brown suit with a bottom that had string sides and the Tanga back that had about half of my butt hanging out. I put it on and the contrast with my tan made the suit look quite good on me. Yes, it was brief, but everything was at least partially covered and I guess that's all that mattered. I simply acquiesced to the social norms of a liberated environment, while mom and Lucille added it to the chocolate suit on the counter.

Next Lucille brought out a few thongs for me to reluctantly try. Lucille offered, "A traditional thong covers the front with a

V- shaped design in the back that's often described as a "whale tail."

The fabrics I use to make my thongs are much sturdier than fabrics used in cheaper suits and the construction of the hips is a lot thicker and more reliable."

I tried on what Lucille called the "Sailor Suit" which had blue and white horizontal stripes on the top and bottom. While other suits had fuller coverage on top, the Sailor Suit top was cut much narrower and was adjustable. I guess it looked good, but the suit remained beyond my tolerance level and I said "no thanks".

Finally, Lucille offered what was nothing more than three tiny adjustable, triangles that were connected by top and bottom strings that left nothing, and I mean nothing, to the imagination.

Lucille really knew her stuff as she continued. "A G-string, is simply a string that creates a T-shape in the back and provides no back coverage whatsoever. G-strings have been donned the affectionate nickname 'floss' and it's no surprise why, as the only coverage is in the front."

Holding up the bottom, Lucille continued, "The adjustable front attaches with this thin, really sturdy elastic string around your hips and is for those special moments as G-strings have become a symbol of empowerment thanks to the sex appeal and scandal they bring to the table, which makes them a wonderful garment for those who want to express their liberation and sexuality."

Lucille had three options in her hand. One was black mesh. The second was a white, open weave mesh pattern and left nothing, and I mean nothing to the imagination and the third was a thin floral print that I deduced would be the best one to try on simply because you couldn't see through the material.

I took the suit and went in the dressing room, put it on, looked in the mirror and simply went 'gulp' and walked out onto the store floor as Lucille said, "Wear this one now Miela while you still can. When the babies come, it's too late." I looked at how trim and fit mom was and hoped I could look like that at her age vowing fifty push-ups and sit-ups each day.

Lucille and mom concluded the brown and yellow ones were right for me as I submitted to the peer pressure, nodding and saying, "OK", to the generous smiles of both of them.

I simply shook my head in disbelief, realizing how the tables were turned. Normally it's the mother telling her daughter to cover up. In my case it was the daughter informing her mother that the brown and yellow bikinis were almost beyond what she could imagine herself wearing in public, while the three miniscule triangles represented less than what most of those bold enough would wear, even for the topless French beach in St. Martin, with total nudity less than a hundred yards away.

I slipped back into the dressing room and put on the brown suit and attempted to regain my conservative composure when I heard Mom offer to pay Lucille. Of course, there was a discussion about how it should be free with mom vehemently saying, "Non" which even I knew meant "no" in French. As I re-appeared, I immediately christened the brown suit Itsy Bitsy and the yellow Teenie Weenie, and the transaction was complete. Teenie Weenie was already in a bag small enough to hold a sandwich and still have room for the peanut butter and jelly. As we were about to walk out, mom redirected Lucille's attention toward yet another suit hanging up high in the rafters and quickly slipped two 100 Euro bills under the receipt tablet on the counter.

As such, mom's maternal spell was broken as we walked into the bay and the warm water to invigorate our souls, thereby washing away the depth of discussion and my level of contemplation. In so doing we began cavorting like two little kids with a sustained water fight until the laughter erased the anger that had festered throughout the night, along with my initial modesty, replacing it with the depth of introspection that had just taken place.

As the waves were a bit larger than normal and the undertow a bit stronger, mom and I held hands and climbed back to the beach. We stood for a moment feeling the warm breeze, as mom looked in my eyes and said, "Melia, you have made me so proud to be your mother. I don't know of a single thing you could have done to make it any better. This week has been what we both needed and yet, you've made it special for me and I thank you for that."

I think I was a little taken aback by mom's elocution and yet, I sensed its sincerity. We still had several more days until we were scheduled to go home and I wanted to make mom realize how much I appreciated all that she had done, all that she had shared and how she had made me feel that my life was worthwhile. Standing there, soaking wet, I pulled mom in and gave her a hug and simply said, "I love you, mom."

We both pulled back and wiped the tears from our eyes. No more words were spoken, nor needed to be. Emotions, enhanced with a touch or a hug, can always say so much more. We headed back to the Rover and slipped on our t-shirts as

I inquired if we were going to stop at Good Morning to which I got the affirmative nod. "Oh goody", I thought. "Another pound or two, but then, at that point in time, I really didn't care."

We stopped and selected the warm croissants and headed for the house where we indulged in the baked delights, accompanied by freshly squeezed orange juice, doing so just as the sun came over the security wall, telling me it was almost time to simply lay out and finish my first Grisham in years.

The Pageant:

After breakfast, I opened the bag. Sure enough, Lucille had included not only Teenie Weenie, but the infinitesimally small triangles as I whispered, "Oh, my God!" I glanced at mom with one of those, 'this must have been your idea' looks and she feigned innocence and proclaimed, "Don't blame me. I didn't do it," as I examined the suits and really didn't know what to do.

I was still in Itsy Bitsy when mom suggested, "Go try on the others."

I had reservations, but went into mom's old bedroom and slid into Teenie Weenie, looked in the mirror and said to myself, "Welcome to St. Martin"! I thought it was too brief and vowed it would never see the light of day.

"Try on the other one," mom urged.

I returned to the bedroom and slipped into the three tiny triangles. To say they barely covered anything would have been an understatement. Connected by thin strings, the two adjustable top triangles were literally transparent, while the bottom consisted of a tiny matching tiny front triangle and a thin string to hold it in place to which I thought "Oh my God" and duly called the suit "OMG".

There was a tag on the suit written in French that read:

« La vie, ce sont les aventures que vous vivez, les défis auxquels vous faites face et la façon dont vous gardez la tête haute. Prenez le contrôle et sentez-vous sexy dans ce bikini exclusif *Barely-There*. "

"Le tri top est vraiment un classique avec son cou et son buste réglables qui assurent un ajustement parfait à chaque fois tandis que le matériau ultra-mince se fond simplement dans votre corps comme le string assorti, avec son dos sensuel dit simplement que vous êtes fier d'être une femme. "

...soyez courageux, soyez audacieux, soyez belle dans cet ensemble *Barely-There* sexy et impertinent qui fera savoir aux hommes que vous êtes prêt à conquérir le monde."

Mom beckoned me out into the living room.

Upon reappearing, I raised my arms and did one of those ta-dah poses as mom suggested. "Turn around and let me see" mom directed and I obliged while handing her the tag as she began whispering as if she were some sort of sportscaster…

"And then, the whole world stopped. Psychics,

"What started out as a normal St. Martin day with the sun high and perfect for the beach found Melia Terrill with enough courage to grab her things and head out, wearing the newest addition to the world of sexy swimwear beneath her cover. Upon arriving at Orient Beach, Ms. Terrill claimed her chair as everyone...and I mean everyone, stopped in their tracks. Men ogled as women provided long, envious glances, wishing they were as beautiful and brave enough to join in the endeavor. For a long moment, the world stopped with all eyes locked on Melia as a whisper of 'Go girl,' cascaded from those unable to fill what Ms. Terrill had simply worn that day."

"Now mom, what does the tag really say?"

Mom smiled and read "Life is about the adventures you have, ʏe challenges you face and the way you hold your head up high. Take ɔntrol and feel sexy in this exclusive *Barely-There* bikini."

"The tri top is truly a classic with its adjustable neck and bust that nsures a perfect fit every time, while the ultra-thin material will mply melt into your body as the matching thong, with its sultry back, ays that you are proud to be a woman."

"Be brave, be bold, be beautiful in this sexy, sassy *Barely-There* nsemble that will show men you're ready to take on the world."

I shook my head for an embarrassed moment that quickly ırned to laughter and said "that had to be written by a man," as

I promised myself to simply tape the tag under *just one of those things you only do when you're young'* in my very narrow scrap book of crazy memories that had five years of blank pages.

I took another look at my reflection in the sliding glass door to the pool and shook my head as there was virtually nothing left to the imagination. I reflected back to my college days when mom had given Annie and me full spa treatments in Oshkosh as a Christmas present that included the full body laser hair removal option. At first, I was reticent and then realized the hassle of shaving my legs and pits would be gone. When it came to the bikini area, I almost said "no" but Annie was all in and I followed her lead. At first it seemed weird and then my only regret was that I hadn't done it before. With each of the seven treatments, I became more comfortable with my body and the way I looked and for some crazy reason, I felt less naked than ever.

Annie, being Annie truly enjoyed the new "look" and was willing to show anyone and everyone. As for me, well, it was mom's and my little secret as she'd been the pioneer and said she too had no regrets.

"Do you really think a person should wear something like this to the beach?" I seriously inquired.

Mom sensed my trepidation and added. "Right now, it's probably less than you're willing to wear. However, that's up to you. You need to wear what you feel comfortable in and not what you assume other people will think you should be wearing or what some fifty-year-old fat, balding, copywriter imagines. If this were Milwaukee, it would be one thing, but this is St. Martin and Orient Beach. One-fourth of the women are topless and if we walked a hundred yards east from Lucille's, you'd be over- dressed in the eyes of others. It's totally up to you and no one else."

"But I'd feel so – so exposed," I replied.

"Then don't wear it. There's a fine line between personal inhibition and public exhibition that only you can determine, which is one of the great things about being here, simply because you get to decide and not society or the government. When the day comes and you're comfortable with yourself, you'll know what you're comfortable in, until then, wear what you want.

Mom looked at me and continued. "Tell you what, whatever you wear, I'll wear. If you go conservative, I'll go conservative. If you go contemporary, I'll go contemporary. If you want to join the 25% and go topless, I will too. If you decide to wear OMG, I'll buy one as well. If you want to go down to the clothing optional section of the beach, that's fine with me. Melia, the goal is to have you learn how to accept yourself and that's one of the reasons we're here."

One year for Christmas when we were in college, mom gave Annie and me matching laser "treatments" as she had done for herself. I thought it was a strange gift until I saw the advantages of no longer needing to shave my pits or legs.

I stood for a moment, pondered my options and slipped back into Itsy Bitsy, grabbed Grisham and headed for the chaise. Mom noted she had a 10:00 o'clock Zoom meeting and would need to dress appropriately as she didn't think the group presidents wanted to see her in a bikini top with gnarly hair and no make- up. My retort was I thought she should do the meeting topless as that would certainly get the old geezers talking, which resulted in a smirk to say the least.

Following the mantra regarding Wim Hof, I began the deep breathing exercise and started to feel what mom was talking about as I let go of my inner turmoil and placed my noise cancelling ears buds in place. Closing my eyes, my mind raced in a dozen directions until I finally began to calm down and simply let go mentally. In so doing, it wasn't long until my mode changed from one of relaxation to one of restful sleep as the music serenaded my inner psyche and I became totally relaxed.

Around 10:30 mom came out and inquired, "Was the pool guy here?"

"I don't know," I replied as I shrugged my shoulders and smiled a sheepish grin.

Lunch meant KaKao where we both had seafood salads that we scrumptious. Whereas we really hadn't spent much time at the west end of the beach, we rented two chaise lounges and an umbrella and sat reading, drinking rum punch and watching the world go by. At first, I felt a bit uncomfortable about all the topless women parading by until I visually surveyed responses of those both on the beach and eating lunch, to which there was absolutely no response at all. After drink number three, or was that four, I no longer cared, thereby adding another chapter of meaning to mom's mantra, 'Let go!'

I went to the bar to order some appetizers and noticed a woman standing there in **my** OMG. While I'd been reticent and concerned about glances and stares, I quickly realized no one cared and vowed, if the time and place was right, I'd get up the courage to duplicate the adventure. I thought to myself. "My God, my values are changing."

I came back with the nachos and reported my sighting and mom said, "We can move east and you can get totally naked if you want."

"Ahh, No thank you!"

After all the rum punch, nachos, chicken and lobster, we decided we needed to get out of the sun and joined the crowd at the bar. It wasn't long until we began talking to a couple from France who thought mom and I were sisters. Needless to say, that put a big smile on mom's face.

At four, we headed up the hill and mom popped open a bottle of the soon-to-be-famous Terrill Pino Noir. While I had been a sipper early in the week, I realized I'd become quite the gulper simply because, between the two of us, we finished another bottle on top of the drinks at the beach and then in the bar.

Dinner was at seven at Le Taitu, which is a tiny little, outdoor restaurant owned by two brothers who have a passion for food and always served some of the best, freshest and most reasonably price seafood on the island. The restaurant made the word casual seem over-dressed and we went casual consisting of somewhat short shorts, tank tops and flip flops where, other than having glass topped tables that seemed out of place, the outdoor ambiance and knowledge that the two brothers loved what they did, made every morsel that much better. Another bottle of Pinot Noir hit the table and left empty. My God, I was becoming a lush!

After dinner, we headed back up the hill. Awaking before five, the walk and then time at the beach, all followed by a wonderful meal, not only made the day complete, but so, so relaxing. It didn't seem possible that it was only nine o'clock and I was ready for bed as I whispered "Good night, moon!" and smiled at the memory of the book dad read to me when I was a little girl.

Surprise:

It didn't seem possible that the first week was over and the distance between mother and daughter had appreciably narrowed, with my trepidation about leaving Milwaukee General quickly dissipating as if it were nothing more than a rain puddle in the sands of time. I began to realize mom's objective – simply help me let go of the pain and pressure that comes from profound disappointment.

Once again, I awakened before five. Once again, I heard mom's sounds as she did her sit-ups and push-ups. Once again, I wanted to walk the beach and share more. The night's darkness occluded the clouds on the horizon as a rare summer's storm was brewing.

Mom appeared and we went through our coffee ritual before I asked her, "Are you ready to go?"

Mom looked at me and then outside before turning on her I- Pad and going to the weather app. "Looks like rain this morning."

"Rain? It can't rain!" I lamented.

With that, there was a loud clap of thunder and it began to pour as I turned to mom and sheepishly said "Well I guess it can!" Mom motioned with her hand and we walked out into the downpour. I felt the huge warm droplets splash against my face and they were wonderful. People forget the simple pleasures in

life, and this certainly seemed to be one of them.

I looked at mom with her head tilted back and she was smiling. "This is glorious!" she announced. "Oh my God, this is wonderful!"

We stood for a few minutes and let mother nature run her course until the cloudburst abated. I realized that, even with this woman's immense wealth, who'd been everywhere and done so many things others only dream about, she was simply excited by the feeling of a warm rain. I smiled at the little girl who stood before me and realized why dad had fallen in love with her so many years ago.

Mom looked at me and smiled. Her head tilted down and then up at the sky and it was then I realized she was so much more than I had ever realized.

"Melia, I remember this very spot and a day like today where the rains came and cleansed my soul as they washed away so many of the traits that had been in me that left me innocent. It was then I made a vow that no matter what happened I would always put quality above quantity in terms of not only material possessions but people, experiences and relationships as well." "I've never known poverty nor want for material things and was blessed to have a mother and father who taught me one very important lesson. 'It's not what you have that's important, it's the hearts you've touched'. To covet material things can result in an endless shallowness and the monotony of empty wishes for more and more and more if we substitute possessions for people."

Mom looked out at the horizon and said. "I like coming back to St. Martin because it grounds me in my reality. Not only because I once came here to die, but because I can see and experience the struggle my grandmother had and the love my dad had for your Grandma Marie. Thanks to them, we've never had the wants and needs of other people. Yet, because of the majesty of their existence, the questions of the number of cars, number of kids or number of trips that others measure their lives by has never been there."

"It took leukemia to make me realize that baubles and beads made no difference. It took a trip into space for your father to see the same thing. It took our love for you and each other to allow us to go past all the material things and enjoy the true majesty of love, for which I will always be eternally grateful.

In you Melia, I already see someone different, someone who doesn't measure things. Someone who doesn't care about material possessions, but still has a passion for all that is good which starts in the heart and ends in your soul."

Mom stopped for a moment to collect her thoughts and then continued.

"Sadly, your brothers still emphasize quantity over quality where their idea remains   bigger/better, bigger/better, more/more/more which erodes the innocence of satisfaction in what they've got. They're not alone. We live in a "quantocracy" where everything needs to be counted and judged simply on the basis of how many of something we have. When in fact, happiness does not come from what we have, but from the lives we touch." "I hope and pray your brothers someday understand the hypocrisy our society preaches that we need to care about how much or how many things, ideas and even people we have, yet devalues the important task of understanding the qualities, experiences and meanings of what those things that are already
ours."

"Our family has been blessed! We have no material wants or needs! We are lucky that way and yet also cursed and I only hope and pray that you three kids all learn to appreciate what you've got without taking them for granted."

"Your father once asked me, 'which is worse to have nothing or everything?' I've pondered that question since it was posed to me and now pass it along to you as I did to Derrick and 'V'. There is no perfect answer, but there is a great solution and that is to appreciate what you've got and share your goodness with those you love."

I wiped a gentle tear from my eye as our trance evaporated, the clouds cleared and the sky became illuminated by another summer's day. We went inside and dried ourselves off as the chill of the air conditioning made me want to seek out the warmth of what had been, in more ways than one.

We climbed in the Rover and headed for the beach. "I'll bet we're the only ones there." Mom announced.

"I think you're right." I replied and sure enough there wasn't another car parked in the lot and the beach was devoid of the silhouettes that normally punctuated the sand.

We began what had become our standard route when mom asked, "Have you ever tried Yoga?"

I thought for a moment and simply replied, "No". For the past six years, I barely had time to breathe, let alone relax.

"You should, as it will tie all that I have shared with you this week together."

"What's the difference?" I inquired.

Mom looked at the water and then at me and said, "With Mindfulness, Earthing and Wim Hof, you're simply trying to let go and relax, while the fundamental purpose of yoga and Tai Chi is to foster harmony between the body, mind and environment to create a complete system of physical, mental, social, and spiritual development.

"What's Tai Chi?" I inquired.

Mom continued to look forward, replied and began mimicking her description. "It's actually a form of low impact, slow motion exercise you go through without pausing. As you move, you breathe deeply and naturally as with Wim Hof, while focusing your attention on your bodily sensations. What's different is that the movements are circular and never forced and not done to alter your autonomic nervous system. When you're in motion, your muscles are relaxed rather than tensed, while your joints are never fully extended or bent, and the connective tissues are never stretched."

Wow! Two forms of breathing. Connecting with Mother Earth through my feet and now linking my body and soul together as one, the trip was going way beyond bonding into a potentially life- changing experience as mom continued, "As you progress, you'll enter a state of internal harmony that can help you remove the toxins from your body and bring you conscious peace."

"Do you do all the things you're sharing with me?" I inquired.

"I mix them up and apply what needs to be done based on my forecast of the day I'm about to have. By starting in a position of personal peace, even the challenges of the most difficult day or circumstance can be overcome."

"Is this why you are the way you are?"

"I'm the way I am simply because I thank God for every single day beyond when I thought I was going to die. I do what I do simply to make certain that those I love and those I come in contact with receive both tacit and explicit messages that they are important to me in many ways."

"My life hasn't been perfect, nor am I. Yet, I believe I've been able to let go of the demons that made me a lesser person. In so doing, I hope I 've become a better wife, mother, leader and friend. It hasn't been easy. Still, I'm grateful for all the knowledge I have and for those in my life who have had the patience to allow me to transcend towards my goal, which is simply internal peace, that only comes from external goodness."

I was profoundly impressed by another of mom's soliloquies that captured the past six days and made me see beyond here and now. I began to sense the immense greatness she contained and how much of grandma and grandpa she had acquired.

When we arrived from home, I'd been this harrowed, defeated, pessimistic waif who had no concept of self, other than comparing my failures to my grandmother's achievements. In a short period of time, I'd come to accept myself physically, mentally and emotionally in manners never before perceived. Gone was the trauma of failure! Gone was the insecurity of defeat! Gone was the self-induced inhibitions that had been based on doing, feeling and believing what I thought other people expected from me, for which I would be judged. In their place was a pattern that showed me the way to what I really aspired and that was to simply let go of all that had been a burden, be happy and finally accept myself.

We continued our morning march and made the bend as more dark clouds evaporated to allow mom to experience the coveted birth of a new dawn and a new day. My mother was a woman of incredible wealth and profound experiences where nothing more than a sunrise allowed her to relish one more declaration from a point in time so long ago that had once punctuated her probable demise.

It was all making sense. All of it! The freedom! The relaxation! The communication! The acceptance of each other simply for who we were – mother and daughter – traversing a peril so great that it could have meant my demise where, in such a short time, I was healing and creating a map to a destination that many covet and few achieve – self acceptance for who I am.

We stopped for a moment and I looked at mom and smiled. "Mom, have I told you that I love you?"

A soft smile caressed mom's cheek as she offered, "You don't need to tell me. You show me each and every day."

We walked a little further as the bright beams of the early sun ricocheted off our souls just as we reached the rocks and turned back again.

"What do want to do today?" mom inquired.

I shrugged my shoulders and said "I don't know, other than being with you, there's really nothing else I'd like to do."

We made it back to the Rover and dried ourselves off and climbed aboard.

"How about skipping 'Good Morning'?" mom inquired.

I nodded in the affirmative as five straight days seemed to be enough. Instead we made it back to the house and had Frosted Flakes and orange juice after which, it was 'Grisham time' as I began calling it. Mom and I headed to the pool and our three- hour sojourn. At eleven thirty, mom arose and suggested we go to Le' Anse Marcel for lunch, which was fine with me, because I, too, love the place. "Why don't you drive?" mom suggested. I simply nodded OK.

We made our way to Etang de la Barriere and then

between Pigeon Pea Hill and Red Rock and down the curve. Mom requested I let her out and parked the Rover. It seemed strange, but I did as asked and walked around the side of the building to a chorus of "Surprise!". It was my 28th birthday and I'd forgotten all about it. The staff appeared with a white frosted birthday cake inscribed with 'Happy Birthday – Melia' on it.

I smiled a shy smile and said thank you as they sang 'Happy Birthday' to me.

Lunch was special as I simply shook my head in disbelief. As our gastronomical sojourn ended, we got back in the Rover and headed for the house. I opened the door and saw birthday balloons and streamers in the kitchen and stood profoundly surprised, simply shaking my head as I elicited, "You shouldn't have."

"You can thank Uncle Frank and Aunt Julia."

"Are they here?"

Mom shook her head no, as she turned on her laptop and hit Zoom as Derrick, 'V' and dad were all there to wish me a happy birthday.

"Thank you. Thank you very much. What a pleasant surprise!" I evoked.

The boys excused themselves as dad remained encased in the screen as he inquired "Are you enjoying yourself?

"Oh, yes," I replied emphatically. "It's just what the doctor ordered."

"Mom has a surprise for you." as mom presented a large envelope.

"Open it," dad instructed.

Inside was a birthday card signed by everyone in the family. I looked at it and smiled and simply said, "Thank you!"

"Open the other envelope!" dad urged.

I did and almost fainted. Inside was a notarized letter stating that my inheritance was officially mine, as I had reached the age of maturity outlined in Grandpa's Living Trust. As of that day, I was worth $3,313,954,616.11. I couldn't comprehend the numbers and started counting backwards until I realized my birthday present was over three billion dollars in investments. My hand went to my mouth in disbelief. I was obviously aware we were wealthy, but never realized how much.

"This is for me?" I inquired incredulously. "It's your share," Dad offered.

"Oh my God!"

We've set up a basic distribution program that deposits $10,000 each week into your checking account for your expenditures. At this disbursement level, your portfolio should actually continue to grow. If you need more, you have the right to take whatever amount you want. However, any amount that exceeds twenty million dollars will need to be authorized by the trustee."

I was dumbfounded. Three billion dollars? $10,000 per week?

As I slid the papers back into the envelope, there was the sound of crunching stones on the driveway as Mom smiled and said, "We've got one more surprise for you", to which I simply shook my head.

As the door opened a huge smile crossed my face. Standing there was my dearest friend Annie, suitcase in hand.

I stood and walked over to her and gave her a hug as she whispered "Happy Birthday".

"Oh my God?" as I turned to mom and simply shook my head.

Mom offered, "Dad and I thought it would be fun for just the two of you to have some time down here.

I was incredulous as I looked at Annie and inquired,

"What about Teddy?"

"He's somewhere on duty and can Zoom us." Annie offered.

Looking at mom I inquired, "So you're going back?"

Mom replied, saying, "the jet's waiting".

"Mom, we had such a wonderful week, can't you stay?"

Mom shook her head 'no' and detailed, "I really need to get back. If you like, we can do this again another time."

Looking at the I-Pad and then at mom, I simply stated, "Mom, dad, how can I ever thank you?"

Dad excused himself and mom's I-pad screen went to its screensaver mode with a photo of Derrick, V and me, as mom went to her bedroom and grabbed her purse. Little did I know that when she awakened, she'd already put all of her clothes away and all she needed to do was change and be on her way.

In a moment, mom reappeared and gave me a hug as she handed me the St. Martin cellphone that had all the local numbers on speed dial. "Have a good time and I'll see you next week. I'll take your papers home. Call Uncle Frank if you need anything. You do remember the opening sequence to the vault? Andrew has made some arrangements and will be calling." Andrew headed up Wilco Security and I knew what it meant – better safe than sorry.

Yin and Yang:

Human beings never travel in parallel paths and in most instances, we are either getting closer or moving further away from where we once were in time, space and each other. For four years, Annie and I were part of each other's daily existence and then we went our different ways. Annie, back to Madison to teach music, and me, to Baltimore to become enmeshed in a dream that turned into a nightmare. We never stopped thinking of each other or even texting, but the immediacy that had been paramount to our existence withered, simply by time, space and others. Yet, we were and will always be close – dear friends, who shared so much, for so long that the thought of being without her simply never existed.

Annie and I were as close to being Yin and Yang as I think you could possibly get. I'd always been the quiet, conservative and reserved one - never willing to take chances - never wanting the limelight. Annie was outgoing, who had a devil-may-care attitude and craved the spotlight. Perhaps, that's why we got along so well, as we complemented each other in so many ways and were interdependent in so many others. Annie's husband, Teddy, was a lot like me. I guess that's why he and I were such good friends, simply because we understood the dynamo and accepted the reality that her eclectic energy was enough for all three of us.

Mom hadn't been gone fifteen minutes when the phone rang and it was Andrew, "Hello Melia, Happy Birthday".

"Hi, Andrew, thank you," I replied.

"Your parents asked that while you're there, we take a few precautions. Nothing major mind you, as the island is relatively safe, but they just want to make sure."

"Andrew, I'm twenty-eight years old and went through all of your Jujitsu classes."

"Still, Melia, they've asked me and I've agreed."

I'd been down this road before and knew there was no reason arguing as I inquired, "I'm not going to have another 'companion' am I?" thinking back to my European vacation.

"No, we're beyond that. In the kitchen drawer next to the Sub- Zero, you'll find a new Apple watch. Please go and find it."

I did as directed and saw the watch that was actually pretty good looking.

"Put it on please."

Once again, I did as instructed.

"Now press the upper right-hand button twice." I did as Andrew instructed and stood there.

"What time is it?" Andrew inquired.

"3:47" I replied.

There was a pause on Andrew's end and then a knock at the front door.

"Go open the door please."

Again I did , as instructed, and to my surprise a man and woman were standing there.

"May help you?" I inquired.

"I'm Martin and this is Sofia and we're your security team for the week. Any time you press the button twice we'll be here."

I looked at the watch and realized Andrew was still on the phone and asked, "Is this really necessary?" knowing that it was, especially after learning about my inheritance. "Andrew, it's cool. Thank you."

"Please, wear the watch anytime you leave the compound. It has GPS tracking in it and we'll know where you are. It's 100% waterproof to 150 feet so you can wear it even if you're going diving. If there's a problem, simply press that button twice and Martin and Sofia will be there. Melia, promise me, you'll wear it."

"I promise."

"Great, I hope you and Annie have a great time. Your mom's flight is almost to Texas and should be back in

Milwaukee in a little over an hour. Keep in touch!"

Andrew hung up and I turned around to see that Martin and Sofia had departed too.

Annie looked at me and simply smiled. It had been a long time since we'd been together alone. As a wedding present, the family had provided a jet and residence for their honeymoon and so she was familiar with the house.

"How was the trip?" I inquired.

"Incredible. I love the new plane and it's so fast!"

"How are you?" was my second question.

"Doing fine, but having trouble being a soldier's wife. Teddy's gone a lot and when he's home, he never gets it out of his mind."

"Are you happy?"

"Oh sure, but I wish he was home more."

After some more short pleasantries, we went upstairs to the room where I'd been staying and Annie and Teddy had used. I told Annie it would only take a few minutes for me to move my clothes as I opened the dresser drawers and laid everything out on the foot of the bed. I was about to pick up the pile and move it across the hall when Annie spotted Teenie Weenie and OMG. "Melia, it looks like you're not quite as reserved as you were
in Oshkosh."

I explained the whole Lucille scenario and told her I'd never worn either one of them and didn't intend to. Annie laughed and offered to buy OMG.

"You can have it if you want." "You don't want it?"

"Not really." I replied. "Are you sure?

"I'm sure. It's just not me." "OK. Are really sure?"

"Yes, you can have it," as I thought of Lucille who slipped it in the bag that I vowed I'd never wear.

I moved into mom and dad's suite and put my clothes away and came back just as Annie was putting her suitcase in the closet. On the foot of the bed was a long tube and I asked her what It was.

"It's my new keyboard that you simply unroll and lay on a table and plug into a computer. I can adjust the piano sound to any type of piano I want from a basic upright to a concert grand and can also add percussion, brass, guitar and strings. It also has a built-in microphone so I can sing along. It's even got auto tune, which is an audio processor that measures and alters pitch in both vocal and instrumental music that compensates for any weakness in a voice to make it sound rich and pure."

"Isn't that cheating?" I inquired.

"All the studios use it on virtually every song with every artist. That's why so many less-than-great singers are in the business today. What's really neat is that I can record what I'm playing and listen back through headphones to see what it sounds like. I can then hit the score app. and what I've played automatically goes into a printed form with vertical scoring lines that connect the successive staves. If I want to, I can then either type the lyrics below or using voice recognition, have what I sing added as well." "If I don't like something or want to change a few notes or words, I can literally go into any part of the score and change it and, there's even a built-in equalizer that allows me to adjust the tone so that I don't even need to spend money in a recording studio. When I'm done creating, editing and enhancing, I can put it on the thumb drive or link to a modem, press send and it will be transferred to my I-cloud account that I can download later either in the studio or at home."

I was impressed. Annie literally had a recording studio that consisted of nothing more than a flexible pad no more than an eighth of an inch thick with 88 keys that rolled up and allowed her the creativity few people could even imagine.

"Need to freshen up?" I inquired.

"How about the pool?" Annie replied.

"Sure."

We both changed into our suits and met at the pool."

Annie looked at me with serious expression and said, "your family really made Teddy and my honeymoon special. Without you, we probably would have gone to the Dells for the weekend."

As we were drying off, I looked at my best friend and said, "Thank you for coming."

Annie replied, "Thank you for inviting me. Let's see if we can't have some serious fun this week."

Not knowing what Annie meant by serious fun, I really didn't care. I needed to simply catch up on five years of solitary existence and was literally ready for almost anything as long as it included laughter.

I called Uncle Frank and asked him to make reservations for seven at L'Auberge Gourmande and confirmed dinner with he and Aunt Julia for Monday night at Astrolab. After that, I thought we'd play it by ear.

Annie and I got ready and went to L'Auberge Gourmande that was great as usual with yet another birthday cake compliments of mighty mouth Uncle Frank spilling the beans. After the cake and all, I simply signed the check that would be remitted to Aunt Julia.

As we were driving back to the house, I remembered mom had made ten o'clock reservations for massages and asked Annie if she wanted to take mom's place, to which she readily agreed while asking, "Is it still Felix and Claude?"

"Yup."

My birthday had certainly been special. Inheritance and best friend. What more could you ask for?

There was still a half bottle of the Terrill not yet famous Reserve Pinot Noir in the Sub Zero and so Annie and I finished it off and headed for bed. It had been a long day for both of us.

Imbibing in Many Ways:

Monday morning found me sleeping in for the first time and when I came downstairs Annie was hard at work on her next musical creation. We'd missed sunrise and I was too lazy to drive down to Good Morning and so breakfast consisted of the remains of the Frosted Flakes and orange juice, which was fine with me. At 9:45, Felix and Claude arrived and set up their tables by the pool. At 10:00 they wrapped on the door and were surprised to see Annie.

"Annie, it is so nice to see you. Is your husband with you?" Felix asked.

"No, he's on assignment and Mrs. Terrill had to return home and so I came down for the week."

Annie went with Claude and I went with Felix, where I was directed to lie down on the massage table. Doing as directed, Felix offered a pair of black shades and I was instructed to put them on for the entire massage. Once again, I did as directed and lay face down as Felix removed my towel and I began hearing soft music. I waited for the towel to be placed in the modesty position, but it never happened. For the next half-hour my back was oiled and massaged. At first, I was uncomfortable and then Felix's magic began working and I no longer cared as his hands went here and there and everywhere and I slipped into a somewhat euphoric stupor that transcended to one that simply tantalized each and every muscle and nerve he explored. Perhaps it was his methodology. Perhaps, the seven days with mom had finally allowed me to relax. All I know is that it was wonderful.

As Felix finished my back, he tapped me on the shoulder indicating I should simply flip over. At first it was a facial and then my shoulders and arms, then a foot massage as Felix gradually made his way up inside my legs. What reticence there had once been gave way, as a deep sense of profound relaxation permeated my inner being, as I allowed this man to simply take me to a depth of relaxation I'd forgotten existed.

As I lay there, I yearned for more, yet the totality of the experience was such I simply lay totally spent, immersed in a profound sense of tactile satisfaction. I don't know how long I was there.

When I finally came out of my subliminal trance, I removed the blinders to see that Annie was in the house and both Felix and Claude were gone. I tried to stand, but realized I couldn't garner my balance. I sat up for a moment, got my bearings and understood it was nearly two in the afternoon. I thought, 'My God, what a wonderful way to spend the day.'

Without adieu to my now former state, I arose and simply walked in the house where Annie could tell by my expression it had been wonderful.

"And so?" Annie questioned.

"Oh my God!" was my short reply.

"I'll never forget that first time when Teddy and I were here and even today, it was incredible." Annie offered with a wry smile on her face.

Dinner with Aunt Julia and Uncle Frank was at seven and so Annie worked on her next creation as I began reading yet another Grisham. God, that guy can write! At 6:30 we got in the Rover and headed for the restaurant. I warned Annie that Uncle Frank would be detailing what an Astrolab was and she just smiled, having heard the story before.

We arrived and had the same table as mom and I had the week before. Charlie was singing and the food was grand, only outdone by the company. As Charlie was about to take a break, Uncle Frank went up and whispered something in Charlie's ear. "Ladies and gentlemen, I've just learned we have one of America's rising recording artists in the audience. Perhaps, through your applause, she could come up and sing one of her new songs."

Annie shook her head as Charlie pointed at her.

"Come on Annie, show them what you got!" Uncle Frank urged.

Annie arose and went to the piano and spoke to the audience. "Thank you, Charlie, I only hope to be one of the rising artists. Tonight, I have the honor of having one of the finest voices I've ever heard with me, Miss Melia Terrill. Melia, will you join me?"

I shook my head "no" and wasn't going to go until Aunt Julia said, "How about one for your mom and me?"

I stood and went to the piano, passing an evil stare at the smiling Annie.

"Somewhere Over The Rainbow?" Annie inquired and I nodded in the affirmative.

The song went well to polite applause. The seal had been broken and so I looked at Annie and said, "How about *Ave' Maria* for my grandma?"

Annie nodded and informed the patrons who the song was dedicated to, as I sang the lyrics to a song we played at Grandma Marie's memorial.

We sat back down and the conversation got around to our plans and I inquired about getting my hair cut. One of the dominant hereditary traits in racially mixed children is that, while hair color can change, the curly hair remains and so, it was always a challenge for me to find someone to cut it.

Aunt Julia said she knew just the woman, whose name was Florence, who'd been doing Aunt Julia's hair for 30 years.

"Where's she located?" I asked.

"Oh, I'll have her come to the house if you want," Was the reply.

"When?"

"When do want? Let me give her a call." Aunt Julia took her phone from her purse and called Florence and the conversation went to Creole, which is a mix of Dutch, French and all kinds of other languages, that always ends in a smile.

"How about Wednesday morning at 9:00?" Aunt Julia inquired as she looked at me and I nodded my affirmation.

It was getting late – like 8:00 o'clock - and that meant Aunt Julia and Uncle Frank would be heading home. We said goodbye and thanked them for a wonderful evening and all their help. Annie asked if there was a bar we could go to that had any music and I thought of Le' Telegraphe which was right on the edge of Orient Beach, yet only a few blocks from where we were.

We took the Rover and, for a Monday night, the place was busy. We went in and started drinking rum punches and it wasn't long until neither one of us was feeling any pain. Annie wanted to dance, but we would need to go into Phillipsburg for that and were in no shape. As we were sitting there, I realized neither of us was in any condition to drive. I thought about Uber and then in my somewhat inebriated manner realized that at the push of a button - make that two pushes - I could resolve the issue.

I looked at my Apple watch and it was 1:40 AM and pushed the button twice. I looked around and sure enough, here comes Martin and Sofia as they scoured the place looking for trouble.

"Is there a problem?" Martin asked in a concerned tone.

"Sorry, we're both pretty drunk and I didn't feel that I should

be driving." I replied.

Sofia looked at the two of us and nodded before adding. "You did the right thing. Give me the keys please and I'll drive you home."

We found the Rover and made our way back to the house. Martin opened the door and scanned the entire premises before we were allowed to go in. I was beginning to regain my senses and apologized to Sofia, who said we did the right thing as their responsibility meant keeping me safe at all times, including driving drunk late at night. I promised it wouldn't happen again as the couple departed.

Annie was in much worse shape than me and I offered to help her up the stairs. When we got to the top she looked at me and smiled an inebriated smile as she leaned forward to kiss me on both cheeks in a typical French style, but completely missed as she mumbled "we certainly did make a nice couple tonight, didn't we?" as she turned and stumbled into her room.

I was somewhat embarrassed and really didn't know what to think, as I fell into my bed. As I lay there watching the slowly rotating ceiling fan I began to wonder if it was the fan or me that was actually revolving.

The Threshold:

When I awakened, reality hit me, along with one great big headache. I looked at the clock at it was nearly 10:00. My God! What a difference a week was making. I got up, took a quick shower, which really made no sense as I was going in the pool, brushed my teeth, swallowed three Tylenol, put on my bathing suit covered by one of mom's antique white ribbed boy's undershirts she forgot to put away and slowly made my way downstairs.

Annie was sitting at the kitchen table with headphones on creating something. She didn't look any worse for wear as she slipped off her headphones and smiled at me while inquiring, "rough night?"

I nodded in the affirmative and retorted, "How about you?" "What I remember was fine, but we need to promise
ourselves we're not going to do that again."

I wondered which part she meant but elected not to say a word. It was too late for Good Morning and almost time for lunch, as I asked Annie if she was hungry.

"A couple pieces of wheat toast and some orange juice would be fine."

I popped four pieces in the toaster slots, got out the Irish butter and raspberry preserves and set them on the table. We proceeded to eat our gourmet breakfast in a somewhat muted fashion, as we both continued to recover, vowing never to do that again.

Annie looked at me and simply shook her head. "What?" I inquired.

"Last night!" "What?"

"Well, last night for the first time in God knows how long, you laughed."

"What?" I asked, somewhat incredulously.

"You actually laughed. I don't ever remember you doing that."

"I laugh." I responded, realizing that Annie was probably right as it never had been part of my nature.

"When you started laughing, you were like a different person and you seemed like a different person. Not so…so uptight and guarded."

I sat for a moment and really didn't know what to say. Annie had sort of stuck a dagger in my heart and yet, I realized she was right as I vowed I'd try harder.

As we finished, Annie inquired about Martin and Sofia and I realized I needed to finally let her in on the family and so I began, "Annie, our family is quite wealthy."

"I realized that Melia. I mean you're the only person I know whose family has a jet."

"Well, we actually have thirty of them." "What?"

"Our family is the primary stockholder in a company called Wilco."

Annie's mouth dropped open as she inquired, "You mean like Wilco Security and Wilserv?"

I nodded in the affirmative and added. "We own nearly 200 car dealerships and a lot of property in Wisconsin and here on St. Martin."

"Oh my God!"

"Several years ago, my dad decided to start a medical research foundation that's named after my mother's deceased brother – the Derrick Williams Foundation."

Annie was in shock as she pondered, "That's your family?
You mean your family invented Mediglove?"

Again, I nodded in the affirmative as I added, "In Milwaukee General Hospital, the pediatric wing is called the Marie Williams Center, which our family paid for, as she was my grandma."

Annie was incredulous as I continued. "Here on St. Martin, we own numerous houses and commercial buildings, along with a great deal of land and so, if we go somewhere and are treated – uh, differently – it's because they know who my parents are and grandparents were."

Annie just shook her head as I added. "My grandpa's will set up trusts for my brothers and me that we received on our 28th birthday."

"Sunday?"

I nodded in the affirmative and continued. "The amount of money is substantial. With it comes a great deal of personal risk and I'm only telling you because you're my best friend. Martin and Sofia work for Wilco Security here on St. Martin, where the company provides services to most of the hotels on the Dutch side and private businesses, as well as our properties. I received a new Apple watch for my birthday that has been modified with an extra button on it and all I need do is press it twice and someone will be here, which is what happened last night."

Annie's hands dropped to her sides in disbelief as she offered, "You've always been so, so normal."

"That's been my goal. I've always wanted to just fit in."

"How about at school and the apartment?" Annie inquired.

"My family owns the complex. In fact, hold on a minute." I got up and retrieved an envelope mom provided as she was leaving when she whispered, "When the time is right, give this to Annie."

"What's this?" Annie inquired. "Open it!"

Annie's mouth dropped open. Inside was a summary of all the rent she and Teddy paid while we were living together and a check representing the full amount. Annie was in shock. "You mean, your family is giving Teddy and me all the money we paid in rent?"

I nodded in the affirmative.

"Oh, my God! I, I don't know what to say." "There's one caveat," I offered.

"What's that?"

"You never let anyone know who I am or who my family is. Promise?"

Annie nodded in the affirmative.

"I've been taught that with wealth comes risks and I want to live my life as normal as possible. I've already seen what money can do to people and I don't want that happening to me."

"What about Teddy?"

"Why not let me explain it to him personally, if you don't mind?"

"OK."

"Our secret?"

"Our secret!" as we locked pinkie fingers as if we were still in fifth grade.

Annie sat in shock and looked at the check. As reality returned, she asked what was on the agenda for the day. With it being Tuesday, I knew that most of the restaurants were closed for dinner except Le' Taitu and, after Monday night, felt we needed a day off from anything and everything. However, I asked Annie what she wanted to do.

"I don't care," was her response.

"Well, we have snorkeling, scuba, parasailing, jet skis, hiking, taking one of the boats on our own or shopping?" I knew Annie didn't have a lot of discretionary money and so I minimized the shopping experience.

"Isn't it a little late to schedule those things for today?" Annie questioned.

"It's June. The tourist business is slow and we own the activities company. All I need to do is call Penny and tell her what we want to do."

"Your family own's that company too?" Annie inquired incredulously.

"Yes." I said somewhat surprised that she didn't already catch on.

"We can take a boat?" Annie inquired.

"If you want."

"Just the two of us?" as I saw Annie's eyes light up.

"If you want, or Penny can go with us, which I recommend." "That sounds like fun."

"Tell you what, how about we eat lunch and have Penny take us to a different beach

"Where we can snorkel?" "Neat!"

I picked up the St. Martin phone and punched Penny's speed dial and asked her what her plans were. With Wednesday being cruise day, I knew she'd be busy. With it being Tuesday in June, she said Paul was in town and the day was wide open as I laid out the options while inferring snorkeling sounded the most appealing.

"Are you two OK?" Penny inquired. "Sure, why?"

"Well, I heard you two really uh, celebrated last night at Le' Telegraphe."

My God, word spread fast, as I replied, "We're fine and by noon will be back to normal."

Penny recommended Tintamarre Island, as it was an uninhabited nature preserve that had a white sand beach where the water was calm. Because of the time of the year, there'd be few, if any people, so the stingrays, sea turtles and fish come closer to shore and perhaps even a dolphin or nurse shark too. Penny said she'd bring the necessaries, which meant food, water and an emergency kit, just in case.

"What time do you want to go?" I asked Annie. "Whenever."

"Penny, it's 10:30 now. How about 13:00?" I inquired and agreed to meet her at the ferry dock where mom and I'd met her and Paul the week before.

Annie and I simply went to the dock as I knew Penny would have lotion, towels, food and drink on the boat. I put the Rover's keys in the 'vault' as we called it, under the rubber top on the back bumper. When Uncle Frank had the vault designed, he did it with what he called a floating code, where you simply put in any four digits, turned the dial, and then moved the four digits to different numbers. This allowed you to have different people use the vault and not be required to remember a code.

Penny was waiting and both Annie and I gave her the obligatory French hugs. We pushed off and headed for Tintamarre Island. Penny has been on the island for as long as I could remember and had become accustomed to the lifestyle to the point that, about twenty yards out, she took off her top and was topless. Annie had been on the island twice, looked at Penny shrugged and followed suit. "Welcome to St. Martin" I thought as we bounced along the waves in more ways than one.

It was one of those glorious summer days and I regretted not taking my walk on the beach. We made casual chit chat until Penny slowed and gently slid the boat onto the sandy beach. Annie looked a bit perplexed until Penny noted that to drop anchor would have upset the ecosystem on the ocean floor and we were over a conservation area. She also added, it disturbed the sea life less and by sliding on shore and meant we'd probably see more.

We spent the next two hours snorkeling with Penny taking us to where the sea turtles normally were and providing a big thrill when we saw three of them. Annie was a bit perplexed about potentially seeing a nurse shark until Penny pointed out that, although they did periodically bite humans by mistake, almost all the time they were sedentary and simply looking for food on the ocean floor. While growing to up to fourteen feet in length, nurse sharks were quite amenable to human interaction and the one most often seen was named Gladys and actually appeared to like seeing humans every now and then.

It was only 3:30 when we were done and Penny needed to get back to the marina. "Do you want to go back to the dock or Orient Beach?" Penny inquired.

I looked and Annie and shrugged. Annie inquired about the Rover and whether we needed to pick it up. Penny noted she'd have one of the marina guys bring the Rover over to Orient Beach and park it behind Lucille's, which made sense to me. Penny called the marina and talked to somebody in French as I gave her the code for the key.

"What number do you want them to put on the lock when they have the car there?" Penny asked.

"Uh, 0630" I replied, as it was the date.

We shoved off as Penny jumped in the boat, started the engine for our ten-minute ride. As we approached, I saw a small, flat-bottom skiff heading out to meet us. Larger boats weren't allowed close to shore for safety reasons. Penny stopped the boat, dropped anchor and Philippe came along side in the skiff.

"You two make a wonderful couple" Penny as we climbed aboard the skiff while Penny waved goodbye and was gone. Annie then realized, she'd left her top on Penny's boat while Phillippe asked where we would like to be dropped off and I indicated by Pedro's green stairs, which everyone was familiar with and we were on our way.

As we were approaching the shore, I simply took off my tank top and gave it to Annie. The protocol on Orient Beach was topless on the beaches, in the water or sunbathing, but wearing something in the bars and beach restaurants was required.

Phillippe slid the skiff on shore and Annie and I got out as the porter who brought the Rover, pushed the skiff back into deeper water, jumped in and headed back to the marina. Needless to say, it was all very convenient for us. We got on at the ferry dock, snorkeled and got off on Orient Beach and the Rover was there waiting for us. There are some things in life that money can buy and one of them is certainly convenience.

Annie and I looked left at Club Orient and then right at Chez Leandra and then Le'String and decided to have "just one" dirty lemonade. While not nearly as famous as its predecessor, Chez had, for all intents and purposes replaced the eclectic and infamous Pedro's and their glorious grilled chicken, ribs and lobster, but was even more famous for the integration of those from both sides on the "rocks" that delineated Club Orient from the rest of Orient Beach, where no one seemed to care.

In Oshkosh, no matter where we went, people knew Annie. She just had one of those effervescent personalities that drew attention and a crowd. I assumed it would be the case in St. Martin and it wasn't long until the spotlight was on my best friend and sure enough Annie's antics led to laughter and it felt good.

Annie was in her 'conservative' bikini bottom and my tank top while I was in shorts and the Itsy Bitsy top and we both actually felt a bit over-dressed as the eclectic mix from both sides of the rocks resulted in a nonexistent dress code that allowed virtually any attire, or almost lack of, you desired.

After so much great French food, the BBQ ribs looked appealing and we decided to have an early dinner and made pigs out of ourselves right then and there. As we finished our meals, the server came with the bill and it was then I realized neither of us had any money. Needless to say, it was a bit embarrassing!

I stood and went to Z, the owner and apologized, explaining what had happened and, well let's just say, he wasn't really too happy. I thought, "My God, what do I do?" Our family owned the buildings next door, Grandma Marie's plaques were hung in several of the top restaurants on the island and yet, the last thing I wanted was to name drop, as I had been counselled about sustaining our anonymity. I simply punched the Apple button twice and explained that someone would arrive with the payment shortly. With no action on my part, other than the discreet press of the button, Z was less than confident.

About five minutes later, Sophia and Martin arrived and inquired about the problem. They knew exactly where we'd been and realized the quandary as well — two twenty-somethings, somewhat inebriated, with no money.

Martin couldn't resist. "Well Melia, I guess you'll just have to see if Z has any dishes that need washing and Annie, can you please start cleaning the tables?"

Z didn't know where this was going until Sophia opened her purse and asked for the bill which totaled a hundred and twenty- five Euros, to which I raised two fingers indicating two-hundred Euros, and told the server to keep the change, as I apologized for the inconvenience.

It was then that Martin discreetly let the secret out as Z stood completely in shock. Instead of two twenty-somethings trying to scam a free meal, he had the daughter of the owner of the buildings next door, whose family was the largest private land owner in St. Martin, whose grandmother was the matriarch of several restaurants Wilco saved after Hurricane Irma, who'd simply made a mistake and left her money at home.

Z tried to apologize and return the money, but I simply shook my head no. It was my fault. I called Aunt Julia and explained what happened and assured her that Martin and Sofia had taken care of everything, but asked if she could speak with Z to set-up the signature program we had elsewhere. I handed the phone to Z and watched his head bob up and down as he spoke to Aunt Julia before hanging up.

"Again, Miss Melia, I'm so sorry. I made arrangements with your Aunt Julia and only ask that you come back and have lunch with us again during your holiday. I, too, am honored that your family considers me to be a welcomed member of your vacation experience included with so many other fine establishments."

Annie and I were quickly recovering, which can happen when there is fear and trepidation and so I politely nodded and said to Z. "There is one thing that I must ask."

"Anything!"

"When we visit again, we're treated as regular customers and you give me your word you won't share who we are with anyone or even that we were here."

"My word!"

"Your promise?"

"My promise!"

"Then we'll come again. However, I must warn you, any indiscretion and not only will I leave, but your name will be removed from the Wilco vacation list."

Z became a bobblehead as he nodded again and again and again. I think he was somewhat relieved he was being paid for the day's food and drink and had a regular, high-tipping customer. For the first time in my life, I'd used the leverage that comes with wealth. I don't know if I liked it or not, but he needed to understand that exposure meant risk and risk meant trouble, which is just what I didn't really want or need.

The circumstance quickly ended as Annie and I headed for the Rover with Sofia and Martin close behind. As we got to the Rover, I went and unlocked the keys as our security duo made certain we were not only safely in the Rover, but sober enough to drive. I turned to the dynamic duo as I began calling them and said, "Annie and I are going back to the house and won't be going out anymore tonight."

Annie had been very quiet the entire time and when we got into the Rover and headed for the bend in the beach she asked, "Melia, your family really is **that** wealthy!"

I was looking out the front window and really didn't know what to say or how to say it. For a moment I thought and then replied. "If we caught a one-pound fish in the ocean, it would be considered quite small. If we took that fish home and put it in an aquarium, it would seem quite large. It's all in perspective." The answer seemed to suffice. I'd already offered enough about the family and really didn't want Annie to know that two days before I'd inherited three billion dollars and had $10,000 per week spending money.

When we arrived at the gate of the house, Annie's top was somewhat woven into the bars. Penny had found it and had one of the guys deliver it which was considerate.

After Monday's debaucherous escapade and then Tuesday afternoon, the night was designated as quiet time. Teddy Zoomed Annie and we filled him in on our adventures and then I let the two of them have some time alone.

Around 9:00, I asked Annie if she was hungry and she said she was. I asked if pizza would be OK and she said "Sure," and so I called Pappadan's and ordered a cheese, sausage and mushroom pizza to be delivered. Forty-five minutes later it arrived and we snarfed it down with one bottle of the Terrill Reserve chilled Pinot Noir whose label probably cost more than the pizza. Nothing like living the good life with pizza and what I would learn later, was a $1,000 bottle of wine.

The Gawkers:

Wednesday was "Gawker Day" on Orient Beach. The cruise ships disgorged thousands of tourists, some of which took a special tour to Orient Beach with cameras in hand, simply to gawk at those simply enjoying uninhibited life where Club Orient had been. It always seemed crazy to me that people would spend money to go to a beach simply to judge naked people who were minding their own business. For Penny and Paul it meant the clothing optional snorkel tour that was so popular there were both morning and afternoon trips scheduled and were always filled months in advance. Crazy!

Once again, 5:00 AM wasn't even close to when I awakened. Once again, when I got up, Annie was hard at it on her keyboard, with headphones on, oblivious to her surroundings.

"Morning!" I shouted as Annie slipped off the headphones. "Morning!" Annie replied.

"Why don't you keep working and I'll drive down to Good Morning and get some croissants."

"Sounds great," Annie said with a distracted nod.

I grabbed the keys, drove down, got the croissants and headed back to the house as we sat on the veranda and ate the still warm delicacies drenched in Irish butter and raspberry jam. Florence was right on time, politely knocking on the front door. She had to be in her late fifties and was a bit overweight and, like most of the indigenous of St. Martin, had one of those
infectious, glorious smiles.

"Do you have any preference?" Florence asked after our brief introduction.

"I've had the same hair style forever, what do you recommend?"

"A little shorter perhaps?"

"Whatever you think would look good on me," I replied.

"Florence had me sit on a kitchen chair by the pool and worked her magic. Forty minutes later she was done and I looked in the mirror and my mouth dropped open. For the first time in my life, I actually liked what I saw.

"You like?" Florence inquired.

"Sorry, Florence, I don't like it - I love it!" which got a huge smile from Florence as my reward.

"How about you, little lady? Can I make you pretty, too?" Florence asked Annie.

Annie had always worn her hair shoulder length and, to be quite honest, very boring and so I said, "Come on Annie, let Florence work her magic on you too."

Annie nodded and took my place. Forty minutes later I was looking at a totally different, incredibly beautiful woman, whose hair was very short to the point that it resembled a boy's. Through her magic, Florence had removed the dullness that permeated Annie's facial features and highlighted her high cheekbones and she looked wonderful.

Florence handed Annie the mirror and I saw the look in Annie's eyes as her mouth dropped open and she exclaimed, "It's wonderful."

As Florence was sweeping up, I went for my purse. "How much do I owe you?"

"Oh Miss Melia, you owe me nothing. Your Aunt Julia is my friend."

"No! I insist. Please take something!"

Florence raised her hands in objection, but I shook my head no and handed her two one-hundred-Euro bills as she said, "I cannot accept this. It's too much!"

"This is what we'd have paid in the States and not received half of what you did. If you don't take it, I'll call Aunt Julia and tell her we don't like what you've done."

Florence acquiesced and nodded in a humble way while saying "Thank you."

As Florence packed up her gear, Annie and I both thanked her again. She'd worked wonders and I vowed I would only have her cut my hair from then on, even if it meant a trip to St. Martin to do so.

Annie and I both smiled as I announced, "Today's Gawker's Day and so all the water activities will be packed, along with Phillipsburg and so, what do you want to do?"

As noted previously, Annie is, was and will always be a 'free spirit' on the outside. If someone said up, she'd go down. When someone said left, she'd go right. When someone said "You can't do that", sure enough Annie would do her very best to try and do the opposite. I guess that's what I always have loved about her as we truly are Yin and Yang.

"How about hanging out here this morning, going somewhere for lunch and sitting on the beach this afternoon?" Annie inquired. There are eleven restaurants on Orient Beach where, to me, the closer you got to the former Club Orient, the more 'liberal' they seem to be in terms of attire. With this in mind, my initial plan was starting on the west end at Coco Beach and moving closer and closer and closer as we tried all the restaurants we could while 'in town'. After lunch, I thought we could rent a couple of chaise lounges set up on the shoreline and simply "people
watch" as the parade of humanity passed by.

The problem is that on Gawker's Day, all the restaurants are packed with cruisers and so I suggested Le' Anse Marcel, knowing that Annie hadn't been there since her honeymoon.

"Sure!" Annie replied as her eyebrows raised in pleasant expectation.

I sent a text to Jacques asking him for a table which he quickly confirmed and grabbed my third Grisham and headed for my lounge chair. About an hour later Annie came out wearing OMG which I never thought she'd be brave enough to wear anywhere and my reaction must have caught her eye.

"If the gawkers want a show, I'll give em one!" she said with a giggle. To which I simply shook my head and smiled, realizing once again, that when it came to inhibition Annie never learned the meaning of the word and certainly met the criteria of being called an extrovert, which is why we got along so well.

At 11:30 we headed for Le' Anse Marcel and, after Charlie and the bloody toe, the attention we got was almost beyond belief, only exceeded by how our server kept staring at Annie in here shorts and OMG top. We each had a crab salad and ice water and it – the crab salad, that is - was scrumptious. I asked about Charlie and the server reported he was doing fine and how he told everyone about the nice lady who said he was so brave.

As we finished our lunch, I motioned to the server I wanted to sign the bill. I'd learned from previous trips, it's always proper in an upscale French restaurant to denote you've completed your meal and ask for the check instead of the server simply slapping it on your table as it is back home. The server returned and noted the meal was compliments of the chef. I said it wasn't necessary, but also knew that to refuse would be an insult and simply asked for a piece of paper to write 'Thank you very much,' as well as giving the server his tip.

We'd packed for the beach and I asked Annie where she wanted to go. Her immediate response was Chez Leandra. It seemed she enjoyed the eclectic integration of the previous day. We drove over and parked the car behind the stores and got out and noticed that all the beach chairs at Chez Leandra were taken and so I suggested Le' String instead. Lucille was standing behind her store and waved and I waved back as she motioned to us to join her. Out of courtesy, we walked over and saw her infectious smile.

"Miss Melia, you look so nice in your new suit." Lucille noted. "Thank you," I offered, somewhat embarrassed.

"Is this your partner?" Lucille inquired.

I guess I took a little umbrage to the inquiry and responded, "This is my roommate from college whose husband is in the military and she came down to spend some time with me."

Lucille peered at Annie and said "she looks very nice in the bathing suit. Melia, you should come in and let me choose one for you. You know, the style is quite popular right now and your mother was too generous last week and it would be compliments of me."

The last thing I wanted was something smaller than Teenie Weenie and so I politely said, "No".

We made our way to the counter at Le'String and Filipe smiled in recognition as he came over and kissed me on both cheeks.

"Lunch?" Filipe inquired.

"No, thank you, we'd like a couple of chaise lounges if possible." I replied.

We were escorted to the front row or 'ocean view' and set up shop. Annie began slathering lotion on her body. I was beyond the lotion stage and felt quite reticent about removing my cover and exposing myself to the world until a topless woman walked by and I realized that my reluctance was a social issue and not a physical one. I took a deep breath and simply took off the cover, lay down and continued my Grisham.

About thirty minutes into our sojourn, Annie called the server over and ordered our first rum punch and inquired whether I wanted to join her in the ocean. At first, I thought no and then realized it was nearly ninety degrees and the water would feel good. When I thought few, if anyone was watching, I quickly made it to the shore and joined Annie in the refreshing water.

"This is wonderful!" Annie exclaimed as a sense of joy permeated her face.

I felt the same sensation as I dipped under the water and felt its succulent cooling effect. We simply stood and felt the gentle waves undulate beneath us until we saw that our drinks were delivered, at which time we walked back to our chairs.

"Want to go topless?" Annie inquired.

I thought 'God, no!' and Annie could tell by my facial expression it wasn't on my agenda.

"Come on, let's give the gawkers a cheap thrill."

I quickly shook my head no, as I looked over at Annie in OMG and noticed a small tattoo on her lower abdomen. "When did you get that?" I inquired.

"When Teddy finished basic and was about to be shipped out, I thought what the heh, and got a small teddy bear tattoo to remind of him while he's gone."

Not being a real big fan of body art, I really didn't know what to think until I realized what it took to be noticed and its purpose and then thought it was fine – her body, her husband and her love.

"You ever think of getting one?" Annie inquired.

"Not really." I responded. "I don't have anyone in my life and quite honestly, don't like needles."

"Your day is coming Melia. Trust me, one of these days, the right guy is going to come along."

I savored the words and hoped and prayed it would be true. The five years of med school and my year of residency had certainly taken a hunk out of my social life.

We spent the rest of the afternoon under the umbrella, sipping rum punches and ogling the guys who walked by. What was more fun was evaluating the gawkers who were slowly making their way up and down Orient Beach in search of the forbidden thrill. I don't know if it was the sun, the drinks or the "show" but Annie got me giggling. I don't ever remember giggling in my life, but did so as our afternoon progressed as Annie became more flamboyant in her whispered descriptions of the passersby.

Dinner was set for 7:30 at Bistro Caraibes and we needed to get somewhat dressed up which meant longer shorts, a nice top and jewelry. Annie added her wedding ring to her ensemble. I selected a black onyx ring to match the face on my Apple watch. Dining competition in Grand Case is simply intense, either you're great or gone and great was certainly the case at Bistro Caraibes. The food was excellent as was the wine! The service was amazing, while the special appetizer of snails in cream mushroom sauce was a gem. We had to decide between lobster, red snapper or lamb shank and decided to share all three. Annie being Annie, mentioned to the server she was inclined to try the red snapper as she'd never eaten turtle before, which got a somewhat weird look from the poor guy before I told him that my friend was simply joking.

With gullets filled, we toasted our friendship with the complimentary shot of rum and headed back to the House-On- The-Hill where two elderly twenty-somethings realized it was only nine o'clock, but still time for bed. We said goodnight and I was totally zonked from too much sun, too much food and too much wine, but loving it.

As I lay in bed, I thought of the day and watched the slowly swirling ceiling fan while another smile pursed my lips in gratitude for the crazy lady who was doing everything she could to make me enjoy life. I closed my eyes in total satisfaction realizing I was partaking in more sleep in one week than I formerly got in a month and laughing more in one day than I had in five years.

Scuba Diving:

With the ships gone, the tempo returned to the idyllic pace that was so alluring. Gone were the gawkers and with them, half the marauding beach vendors who preyed on their need for St. Martin memories manufactured in China.

I knew that Annie had never gone scuba diving and so I called Penny and asked if she and Paul could take us in the afternoon to one of the basic spots. Penny noted they had one couple scheduled and wondered if we could go with them. I thought, "Why not?"

We met at the long pier in Grand Case at exactly 2:00 and met the middle age couple from New Jersey. Paul was operating the boat and Penny helped us onboard. We set out for the HMS Proselyte, which was a 32-gun frigate of the British Royal Navy.

Along the way, Paul filled us in that the Proselyte was built in Holland in 1770 and was originally called the Jason. In 1796, the crew mutinied and took the ship to Scotland where it was refitted under its British name. She was 133 feet long and 35 feet wide. In September of 1801, she hit the Man of War Shoal and sank in high seas. The crew made it to shore while she sits in 20 to 55 feet of water where the wreck is covered with coral and is the home for all types of marine life.

When we arrived at the site, Paul dropped anchor as Penny went through all the diving basics in terms of communication, safety and security. I'd been diving since I was twelve, but the couple from New Jersey and Annie never had. Because I was certified, Penny asked me to team with Annie as she teamed with the couple, which was fine with me.

We slipped out of our shorts and tops, got into our scuba gear and had the obligatory on-deck photos taken. Annie really looked funny with the mask over her eyes, snorkel in her mouth, weight belt around her hips and air tank strapped to her back all highlighted by the three tiny triangles of OMG to the point I simply began snickering at the sight, shaking my head at my uproarious friend. The New Jersey couple seemed to get a kick out of Annie's antics as Annie was in one of her giggly moods where she could find something funny in just about anything and everything.

As we jumped in the water, I detailed how to put on her fins and away we went. For the next 30 minutes, Annie was mesmerized by the sites, particularly when Peggy opened her feeding bag and watched the fish literally come and eat out of her hand. Peggy handed the bag to Annie who was like a kid at Christmas, feeding the fish who were literally within inches of her. Peggy took her underwater camera and snapped a group of photos that would be emailed to us when we got home. Needless to say, it was a wonderful experience I knew Annie would never forget.

When it was time to go, Penny opened the cooler and we drank a toast to another great day in paradise. Landing in Grand Case, Annie and I disembarked and made our way to the Beach Bar where we planned on spending the rest of the afternoon in their famous red chairs, simply watching people and boats and the periodic planes fly into L'Espérance Airport located on our side of the island.

Annie asked why Amelia[x] didn't land at L'Espérance and I informed her the runway was too short and, by the time we went through their customs, Uncle Frank would have us already at our house, as he knew people at Princess Juliana and no one on our side of the island.

It was almost five by the time we made it back to the house. We had reservations for dinner with Uncle Frank and Aunt Julia at JAX Steakhouse, which was one of Uncle Tommie's Wagyu beef customers. After French food all week, I thought the change would be good and it was.

Aunt Julia asked us what we'd been doing and so I filled her in about the snorkeling and scuba at HMS Proselyte with Penny and Paul, leaving out the French guys. Annie informed Aunt Julia and Uncle Frank that she was putting the finishing touches on her album and promised to send them a copy.

At nine, both parties looked beat. Aunt Julia and Uncle Frank from being old and Annie and I simply from a full day at sea. We said goodbye and thanked them for their hospitality. In my entire life, I never got tired of being with them and their laughter and love, which made any day better than it would have been otherwise.

Flying Hi:

I awakened at 4:45 AM and realized I could walk the walk I had with mom and watch the sun rise and so I quietly left a note and headed for the beach. I parked Rover behind the stores and made my way to the shore as the pink fingers of today slowly stretched across the darkened summer sky. I set out, not thinking of what was either before or behind me, instead simply focusing on what lie immediately ahead. Periodically, I'd see one of the beach crew aligning the day's chaise lounges, making certain they were properly set for another day in paradise or raking the seaweed that had been deposited in front of their assigned enclave.

As I made the bend, the sun's first speckle of intensity reached the horizon and I stopped to think of mom and Grandma Marie and how one instant could mean so much to them that meant so little to so many others. The thought of rebirth crossed my mind and I vowed I would find the one thing I really needed and that was love. Not maternal or paternal, but passionate love from someone who truly wanted and needed me. I realized it wasn't something that could be forced and assured myself that the only way to at least find it was to begin to look, which I promised myself right then and there I would do.

I made it to the rocks, reversed course and headed back towards the Rover. My singularity had been divided into cusps of others simply walking upon the sands of time. For many, it represented sharing a moment with another. For some, like me, the events and purpose were singular, where my only hope was that my social monoblastic condition would someday cease to exist. I felt safe and secure as I walked alone, avoiding visual contact with those who appeared to have a different purpose in their morning adventure and quickly made it back to the Rover where I simply got the key, climbed in and drove back to Good Morning for warm croissants.

While a week prior, I would have been totally embarrassed by my brevity, I'd become indifferent as the magical, mystical, wonderful liberation of what transpired on the island took place. What mom had decreed was certainly coming to fruition, I was gradually becoming comfortable with myself, while the artificial social bonds I'd placed upon my psyche for so many years were slowly eroding, leaving me mentally, socially and emotionally free and, for the first time in years, doing so to the point I no longer felt inadequate, for which I was profoundly thankful.

I arrived back at the house a little after eight and Annie was already working on her computer. She informed me that she'd already Zoomed Teddy and all was well and had also just finished the last song she wanted to put on her first album while asking, "Do you want to hear it?"

I frowned as if to reflect the innocuous reason for the inquiry and said "Of course, if you want me to" adding "Let's eat first and then listen, as the croissants are still warm."

We slathered our treats with Irish butter and raspberry jam as the dark coffee accentuated each bite until all that was left were the sounds of satisfaction. I stood and put the dishes in the dishwasher and returned to stand behind Annie, while she queued up her musical creations in the order she felt was most appropriate.

In a world of rap and hip hop, Annie was a purist where her songs were ballads that evoked thoughts that rolled along with the rhythm of syncopated chords designed to accentuate each syllable and create the desired emotion. As her first song began, the three-chord intro had me hooked and I knew what I was about to hear would be special, as it communicated the emotions felt the first time a person met someone they fell in love with.

As we listened, I began to sense the frustration and loneliness that was pervading my best friend. She was in love with a man who was away. Their relationship was an electronic one measured in minutes instead of hours and days controlled by bits and bytes instead of touches and tenderness. I felt her frustration and sensed her pain and realized that the happy go lucky persona was simply a façade that shielded a broken heart – alone, afraid, aware of her singular existence and the reality that she was and would always be second in line behind a career that enveloped Teddy in every single way.

As I focused on the lyrics upon the screen, I put my hands upon Annie's shoulders. Perhaps for comfort. Perhaps support! Perhaps simply to communicate that I understood and felt her pain. In so doing, her head leaned to the right until she nestled my hand between her head and shoulder as the soft wisps of trickling tears permeated our now common existence.

I stood entranced by the melodious sounds that emanated from the small speakers until all the creations had transcended from Annie's heart to my mine. I closed my eyes as if to shield them from the darkness of singularity that transcended both of us, but for different reasons. Perhaps we were a couple. Not physically, but emotionally, walking in our solitary worlds hoping, praying, dreaming of one thing, simply to feel wanted, needed and loved. Not as the second option, but the first choice. Not as an afterthought, but a primeval urge that transcended another until they too felt they simply could not live without us.

Reality began permeating the room as the sounds of the Sub Zero replaced those of a broken heart, reminding us that it was time for the day to begin where we spent the rest of the morning quietly by the pool, almost as an after-thought, reading for me, listening for her, with mutual glances toward each other that said it all.

For lunch we went to Le' String and had salads while wearing nothing but our bikinis. Our waiters cavorted in front of Annie, doing everything they could to try and break our solidarity and initiate what they hoped would be some sort of one-night tryst and another notch on their bedpost.

Penny made reservations for Annie to go parasailing. This was not my thing and, as she flew above the tranquil seas of Orient Bay, I sat and watched from a chaise at Wai and did my best to take photos she could show Teddy that life could be good, even without him.

Dinner that night was back in Grande Case at Le Cottage for a traditional French five course meal. The food was scrumptious and the escargot, for which Le Cottage was famous, simply out of this world. This was fine dining and our dress and demeanor matched the ambiance as we both sat quietly enjoying its gastronomic pleasure.

As we got to the Rover, I turned and Annie whispered, "Thank you for the wonderful week and memories." as she hugged me and held me tight.

I slightly pulled back and smiled, not knowing what else to do say or do. Without word, we rode back to the house and I unlocked the front door. The hot, humid summer air had permeated our clothes and the cool house seemed resplendent in comfort.

"Care for some Terrill Bourbon?" I inquired. Annie looked at me surprised. "Terrill bourbon?"

"Yes, dad and Uncle Tommie distill it. They can only sell 90 proof, but make some 150 proof for personal consumption."

"Where is it?"

"In the wine vault. Let's have some!"

I went, looked into the retinal scanner and then dialed Wilco security in Milwaukee. On the second ring, the representative answered. "May I be of service, Ms. Terrill?"

"I'd like to get into the wine vault please." "Which level?"

"Level one will be fine." "May I ask the reason?"

"Terrill Private Stock bourbon."

"Please place your right index finger on the scanner"

I did and heard the 'ping' "Your access code is 37363"

I spun the five dials until they read 37363 and the vault opened as Annie's mouth went agape as well. Inside were several hundred thousand dollars-worth of vintage wines and aged liquor, some of which had been Grandpa's.

"Oh my God" Annie exclaimed.

"This is nothing," I lamented. "If we really wanted to get to the great stuff, we'd need another code to allow us to go down to the wine cellar, which is thirty-feet down. Once you get there, there's another vault that requires another combination that takes you into a room filled with I don't know how many millions worth of rare wine and spirits, some of which is over two hundred years old, including one bottle that is from Napoleon's personal stock."

"Why so much security?" Annie inquired.

"Not only because of the value of the contents, but because the vault can also serve as a fall-out shelter or safe haven during a hurricane. Grandpa had the company design it that developed the bunkers that were used to protect the nation's communication system in case of nuclear attack. The room is about 12x18 with walls that are over a foot thick and made of steel-clad concrete with gamma-ray sensors and equipped with an air-tight door. I've only been down there a couple of times, but it has everything you'd need to live for a month including food, beds, running water and both communication and air purification systems."

Annie just shook her head in disbelief as I continued. "The reason for the second combination is that the contents are kept in a vacuum sealed environment where the second combination actually releases air into the vault so that you can open the door. If someone were to break into the vault, the door would automatically close and the air would be sucked out."

"They'd suffocate!" Annie deduced.

"Yup! You never messed with Grandpa's booze."

I took a fifth of Terrill Private Stock Bourbon and closed the vault door, listening to the remote locks click into place, went to the kitchen and took out two glasses and poured three fingers in each and brought them into the living room.

Handing one to Annie I said, "Here's to good friends."

We sipped the bourbon as Annie proceeded to her computer to see if Teddy had called. He had and she returned his overture. For an instant, I felt jealous and then my jealousy was gone as I poured three more fingers of dad's booze for myself.

Independence Day:

There's a zone between deep sleep and being totally alert when your subconscious does things your logical mind would never consider. As I awakened, I slid my left foot across the sheets as if to touch "Hello". To my surprise, the sheets were empty and I was alone. Had it been a dream? Had it been something I created? For an instant, I had no idea.

As reality permeated my mind, I realized I was alone in bed and not wrapped in another as a form of remorse rushed through my bones to remind me of my singularity. I took a deep breath of solace and arose, walking into my bathroom to discharge the results of too much Terrill bourbon and wine, once again.

I looked in the mirror at the face staring back and realized it was me. Now twenty-eight, the sun had darkened my otherwise naturally tan skin, while my light brown frizzy hair looked as if it had exploded from my scalp. Even the magic that Florence had worked had become a morning mess, while my brown eyes stared back and asked, where have you been?

I slipped into a pair of old shorts that crazy Annie had 'modernized' by taking the inseam from six inches to the point they'd became bootie shorts, that I highlighted with a red tank top. It was the Fourth of July – Independence Day in America and for me personally the culmination of my independence from what I had become, to what I was now. Normally the Fourth of July would mean a family dinner and fireworks at the Grand Geneva Resort that had become the family tradition. Here on St. Martin, it as just another hot, humid, summer Saturday.

Mom had been right about needing time off. My week with her was introspective as she shared thoughts on ways to not only survive, but thrive. I'd begun the breathing exercises and could already sense some results and promised myself I'd not only look into, but begin practicing all the other things she'd shared.

The week with Annie had been, well let's say 'interesting'. We'd let our hair down in many ways, cavorting through some sort of temporal existence that manifested itself in ways I had no regrets realizing that she had been right. Previously, I never smiled and yet, the smiles, laughter and guffaws punctuated our week and I was beginning to develop an internal peace where, for the first time in a very, very, long time, didn't think about medicine or trying to live up to Grandma Marie, and began to accept that what was right for her, wasn't right for me.

I made my way downstairs to find a quiet and empty house. Perhaps, Annie was still in bed. I walked into the kitchen and put a cup beneath the Keurig and pushed the button. Nothing happened. In our late evening stupor, I forgot to add water to the reservoir.

I took a deep breath and looked out at the pool and noticed the top of Annie's tilted head in one of the lounges. I opened the slider and made my way to Annie's side where I found her sound asleep with the towel she'd used the night before as her cover.

"Annie!" I whispered.

Annie's eyes opened and she had a perplexed look on her face.

"Are you OK?" I inquired.

Annie nodded in the affirmative and smiled, while simply saying "Nice" as she looked at me and closed her eyes again.

I was concerned and repeated "Annie!" whose eyes opened again and inquired. "What's going on?"

Annie looked at me and smiled again and began to return to reality, as she responded, "We went to bed and I couldn't sleep and so I came down and wrote a song for you. I don't know where it came from, but the lyrics and melody just came to me and it's on my computer. I was so excited, I wanted to wake you up but it was three o'clock and I called Teddy and we had a fight because he knew I was drunk."

Annie continued, "I was so wound up about – well, about everything, and knew I couldn't get to sleep without taking one of the sleeping pills Teddy uses when he's flying back and forth, but mistakenly took two. I didn't want to wake you and so I came out here."

"Are you sure you're OK?"

"I'm fine, just a little hung over." "Let me go make some coffee." "OK!"

"What time is it? "A little after nine."

"I guess you didn't make sunrise, " Annie deduced as she looked at me and chuckled. "Boy we really did drink a lot of your dad's bourbon last night, didn't we?"

Needless to say, the night had not been what was expected. During our scurrilously drunken discourse, we reflected on those who'd walked with us through school and how profoundly important it all seemed back then and how insignificant it all was now. Beyond the basics, Annie referred to the male members of our "tribe" as she called it and her "evaluation" of this guy or that, detailing who she thought was a 'hunk' and who was not, until her giddiness evolved to a level of hilarity articulated by trickles of tears, with me realizing what a lecherous friend I really had!

I went back into the house to get the coffee and set the selector for half cup and hit it twice for Annie and then the same for me. We both needed something strong to get us going, as it all came back and my only thought was, "oh my God!" with an internally elicited smirk about all that transpired.

"Are eggs OK for breakfast?" I asked.

"Sounds Great! Let me jump in the pool and wake up."

I returned to the kitchen, got out a frying pan, cracked our remaining eggs and put some butter in the pan. Annie finished her quick swim, wrapped the towel around her torso and came in the house where the air conditioning immediately began giving her the chills.

"Go put on some clothes and the eggs will be ready."

"Can we eat out on the patio?" Annie inquired. "Sure, why not?"

Annie simply put on the t-shirt that she'd washed the day before and began taking the dishes and setting the table as I cooked the eggs, put bread in the toaster and squeezed oranges for the fresh juice. I brought the food out to the table and set it down as Annie slid into one of the chairs and offered, "I think you're going to like the song I wrote."

"How about you and Teddy?" I inquired, more concerned about their marital status than a song she'd written.

"He'll calm down. This has happened before. He's too serious and I was too drunk."

"Tell me about the song." I inquired.

"I wrote it and it's just for you and I want you to sing it."

"Me?"

"Sure, you've got a great voice and it really fits you."

"What's it called?"

"Dream!" Annie replied. "Dream?" I inquired.

"After breakfast, I'll play the melody and you can practice the lyrics and can sing along."

It had been a long time since I'd done any singing other than our duets at Astrolab and I was reticent. Yet, I also knew it was time to turn over another new leaf as we finished breakfast, carried the dishes into the kitchen and put them in the dishwasher.

Annie went to the computer and turned it on as the lyrics appeared on the screen. "Here, let me play the melody," upon which Annie pressed a key and the sounds of a piano began. I listened and realized Annie had truly written the song for me, as it was about dreaming and tomorrow. To say I was touched would have been an understatement.

"Why don't you finish getting dressed and let me practice and then, when you come down, I'll sing It," I offered.

Annie went upstairs and came down a few minutes later as I perused the lyrics as she handed me the microphone and I put on her headphones and sang along with the melody.

Annie turned and gave me a big hug and said, "I'll still need to add some more instrumentation, but Melia, you nailed it."

"Where do you go for instrumentation?" I asked.

"Here!" Annie replied with a look as if I hadn't been listening all week. "Why don't you take Mr. Grisham out to the pool and I'll put down the other tracks? It shouldn't take long."

I grabbed another Grisham and headed back outside. Two hours went by and the slider opened as Annie called "All done. Come on in and listen".

I stood behind Annie and watched the lyrics float by on her lap top as we listened to her creation. Beyond the lyrics and piano, Annie adjusted the chords so that they were in the background when needed and forefront to establish the mood. Annie added her voice for harmony along with light percussion and strings to fully compliment what I'd recorded.

"Wow! It really came out nice," I offered. "Do you like it?"

"I love it."

"How much auto tune did you have to use?" I asked, remembering how electronically Annie could alter any voice to give it depth.

"None!" Annie proudly responded.

"You mean that was just me with no echo, reverb or anything?" Annie nodded in the affirmative, making me even more impressed. "Cool" I replied with a broad smile on my face.

Annie looked at me and then the computer and then back at me before saying. "I wish I could sing half as good as you."

"You've got a beautiful voice," I assured Annie, while she retorted, "But not like yours."

Not-So-Happy Bay:

We went out to the pool as I asked, "What do you want to do today?"

Annie shrugged and I offered. "I've got an idea, instead of going to Orient Beach, I'll call Penny and see if she can take us to my favorite place on all of St. Martin, called Happy Bay. What's neat is that it's a long walk from the road and there's nothing commercial, including no ladies selling hats and scarves, so few people use it. We can stake out our area and hang out for a while. Afterward, we can go back to Chez Leandra if you want."

Annie shook her head to infer her approval of the plan.

"If you could go back to one spot for dinner, where would it be?" I inquired.

Annie looked at me and then came the surprise, "Le' Taitu".

We'd been eating in fancy restaurants all week and, other than Pappadan's Pizza, she chose the most basic, as I asked "Why?"

"It reminds me of Wisconsin. You know, down to earth and great food."

It was fine with me and so I called Penny and discussed our idea. "We'd meet at the ferry dock and proceed to Happy Bay. When we wanted to come back, one of the marina staff would bring us back to the Rover and we'd drive over to Orient Beach.

"How about lunch?" Penny inquired.

"Anything will do, but what I'm really hungry for is peanut butter and jelly."

The agreed-to time was eleven and so we drove the Rover to the pier and Jon-Claude was waiting with a twin-engine run- about. I had decided to get brave and wear Teenie Weenie while Annie was in OMG. I was shuddering is self-awareness, while Annie was indifferent to the slight smile and extended looks from Jon-Claude.

On board was all we needed – towels, water, wine and sandwiches including peanut butter and jelly, [thank you Penny] along with gobs of fresh fruit. We took off and went around Eastern Point, Petites Cayes and Pointe des Froussards and saw Le' Anse Marcel nestled between the hills in Baie des Froussards where Jon-Claude said Froussards meant "fearful" or "funky" in English. We made our way between Creole Rock and Petite Plage and saw all the new condos being built on the west side of Bell Hill. I knew where the line of demarcation was as our family owned the top of the hill and dad vowed he was going to build a house there some day.

Next was Grand Case from the ocean side that Jon-Claude pointed out was built on the border of ancient salt mines from Salt Pond that divided Grand Case from N7 that circled the island.

We continued on around Pointe Molly Smith and then a little further as Jon-Claude slowed the boat and I pointed out the small inlet called Baie Marie, which is what Grandma Marie was named after, and where both grandma and grandpa were 'buried', leaving out how grandpa passed away.

As we continued, Jon-Claude outlined that there are 37 different beaches on St. Martin of which five are clothing optional that included Pinel Island and Orient Beach as Jon-Claude added. "Petites Cayes is one of the island's top hidden beaches and is accessible via the Froussards Trail, which is a narrow, steep and rocky trail that traverses St-Martin's last unspoiled forest."

Jon-Claude continued, "Cupecoy Beach is located on the island's southwest tip and the Dutch side of the island and consists of a set of three beaches surrounded by limestone cliffs. While many people go for the sun, it's the sunsets that have to be seen to be believed while the clothing-optional section is on the beach's northwest end."

With it being both summer and Saturday, Happy Bay would probably be deserted, as it was 'transfer day' for the few summer tourists, while the locals were still working, and the fact that it was a long walk from the parking area to the beach helped keep the gawkers away.

As we rounded Smith Hill a broad smile crossed Jon-Claude's face as he said, "Welcome to Happy Bay Beach" as a matching smile set in Annie's face.

Jon-Claude continued. "Small in comparison to Orient Beach at about a quarter of a mile in length versus over one-mile including Club Orient, Happy Bay Beach is isolated and quite tranquil."

Jon-Claude cut the engines as we coasted into shore. We were on the east end where two palm trees resided as Jon-Claude quickly carried our chairs, towels and cooler to what he thought would be the best spot while explaining that it was the furthest from the path to the highway.

We agreed to have Jon-Claude pick us up at 3:00PM and set up 'camp' with our belongings neatly spread to ensure we got just the right amount of sunshine as Yin and Yang came into play with Annie looking at the deserted beach and then at me and asking, "Do you mind if I work on my tan lines?"

I had to think for a minute and realized she was asking me if she could take off her bathing suit. Consisting of the three tiny triangles, the lines were hardly there and I thought 'whatever turns your crank'.

I accepted that Annie had always been satisfied with the way she looked and indifferent towards who saw her body. It had been that way in college and remained so. I, on the other hand, only saw my flaws and had lived a life of self-induced modesty, somewhat ashamed of my appearance. After four years of seeing Annie run around in her underwear or with a towel wrapped around her, I guess I appreciated the fact she even asked and replied, "That's up to you."

Annie casually removed her suit, turned on her I-Pad and we listened to a mixture of oldies-but-goodies, along with her new album and soaked up the sun. For the next hour, we simply relaxed and listened to music, totally enveloped in the tranquility around us. Whereas the temperature was nearly 90, Annie stood and announced she was going in the water to cool off and asked me to join her.

As I stood, Annie inquired, "have you ever gone swimming naked in the ocean?"

I looked at her and shook my head in a very definitive manner to express the fact the answer was "no" and then added, I've never gone swimming naked anywhere.

"You should try it! It's a totally different sensation." I shook my head as if to communicate "no", again.

"Come on! There's nobody around. Take a little risk every now and then!"

The Bumpin Uglies song "Morning After" had just played on Annie's I-Pad and the lyrics:

"... But there's a thin line between haste and action
And now I'm crossing lines in search of satisfaction Truth of the matter, it's as simple as this
Happiness can't exist unless you take a little risk..."

rattled in my head and I realized I'd missed out on a lot simply because I was too hesitant and too self-conscious.

"Come on, Mela, try it!" Annie urged again.

I took a deep breath and shook my head 'no' again and then hit a compromise as I took off my top and walked out until we were neck deep and just stood there.

Annie looked at me and announced "This is simply wonderful." I concurred as there was a sense of freedom and a different set of tactile nuances that actually felt good.

After cooling down, we made our way back to shore and Annie asked if I wanted to walk the beach. I thought, 'Why not?' and headed for my suit.

"Heh, why don't you go naked with me?

There was no way I was ready for that and simply shook my head no.

"OK, at least go topless, that way you can get your boobs brown." It was Annie's way of suggesting, inferring, cajoling, coaxing, enticing and proposing something to me as if we were still in college and reminding me of the first time she wanted me to try a little weed.

I gritted my teeth, was quite reticent and then remembered the woman wearing OMG on Orient Beach with no consequence, but remained reticent. Here we were, Annie naked and me topless in the briefest bathing suit bottom I'd ever worn, as we began our westward journey.

The beach was totally void of humanity and my discomfort quickly dissipated. This really wasn't as bad as I thought it would be. However, like the different shades of green women can see, but men can't, I sensed we weren't alone. Someone, somewhere was watching and I could feel it and all of a sudden felt very exposed and uncomfortable in more ways than one.

The distance from the Buttonwood shrubs to the water had to be twenty yards and yet, as we passed a tropical abutment, we came upon a couple who'd purportedly taken advantage of the tranquility and perceived solitary existence. All would have been fine, if they hadn't abruptly flipped over and were facing away from both us and the water.

I knew right then who it was. It certainly wasn't some random couple who'd walked a half mile to the beach and just happened to be sitting behind some shrubs and out of sight, it was Martin and Sophia spying on me and I was royally pissed.

"Damn It!" I exclaimed.

"What?" Annie said, startled by my elocution.

"It's Martin and Sophia and they're spying on us!" I was livid. I was beyond all levels of control and wanted nothing more than to do something, anything, to send a message that I'd had enough. Enough planning! Enough schedules! Enough safety! Enough security! Enough of never being myself!

We stopped walking as Annie appeared in shock. Stoic Melia had blown her top…(anyway my mind, as the top was still back with our towels by the palm trees)…and Annie had never seen the vitriolic side of her best friend before.

Right then and there, I wanted to give Martin and Sophia something to report other than mild-manner, milk toast, Miss Goodie Two Shoes, walking the beach. I really wanted to go and confront them and tell them to leave me alone, but knew better.

Annie sensed that any overt act of defiance could mean more trouble and knew I needed to mellow out as she offered, "Come on, let's walk and you can cool off".

I looked at Annie and, to her surprise, literally pulled her in. My response to Martin and Sophia's intrusion was to make it look like our hug was a romantic gesture. I believed or at least hoped, Annie understood my intent as Annie's hands slipped down to my waist until she pulled me in as our bodies pressed against each other.

Annie whispered "let's make it look real" as she leaned back and kissed me on the lips and slowly rubbed her hands up and down on my back and kissed me again.

"Oh no!" I thought. "This isn't what I wanted."

I was literally in shock and stood frozen with my mind rampant in conflict. 'My God, what am I doing'? What would mom and dad think of me enmeshed in the arms of a naked woman?

It certainly wasn't what I'd planned and yet, I was still seething at the spies' intrusion. I obliged, simply because I had enough of the planning, scheduling, structuring and controlling part of my life and wanted to be free… free of it all. No more limits! No more concerns! No more worrying if what I was doing was what everyone expected!

Being nearly eight inches shorter than me, Annie's face

was almost at the same level as my chest. As our eyes met, Annie looked down and then began kissing my breasts.

Oh my God! I was breathing deeply in anticipation.

"Feel good?" she whispered.

I was too frozen to respond as her hands continued their slow, gentle massage as my breaths became shorter.

I stood shaking. It had been so long since I felt this way. "Oh God!" I whispered. I didn't want her to stop and yet, I felt we needed to. I wanted more, but then I didn't. This was…so much…more than I'd intended.

My head tilted back as all my neural energy became focused on one spot.

Why? Why? Why? My mind repeated. Why did I want her to stop? Why did I want her to continue? Oh my God, is this wrong?

Oh my God why am I enjoying it? Oh my God! Oh my God! Oh my God! Yes! Yes! Yes!

I bent down and Annie and I kissed again. As our mouths disengaged, Annie glanced toward the bushes, and nonchalantly announced, "they're gone," at which time she nonchalantly stepped back leaving me with a somewhat clumsy, embarrassing disconnect. What had begun with me wanting to shock the interlopers, ended up with me wondering whether we'd gone too far - profoundly afraid that it would affect our friendship as I whispered, "Sorry".

"For what?" "For…for this."

"Why? Didn't you want to?" Annie asked as her brow furrowed in confusion.

"I don't know. It's just, just so difficult for me."

"Did you enjoy it?" Annie inquired.

"I think so." I reluctantly replied.

"I did too and just because we enjoyed it, doesn't mean it's wrong." Annie said as she looked into my eyes.

"Are you sure?" I asked.

"You've never been with another woman before, have you?" Annie asked.

"No!"

"Do you regret it?"

"No!" I replied in a somewhat sheepish manner.

Annie offered in a detached manner. "I thought it was nice.

Now that it's over, let's keep walking,"

I bent down to retrieve rearrange my suit bottom as Annie said, "don't you feel liberated?"

I actually felt uncomfortable.

"If you want to go back and put your top on, go ahead. However, if you give yourself a few minutes, you'll quickly see you've acclimated and will find it liberating."

I thought of mom and began to think that perhaps it was all right. I realized for me, it was everything and for Annie it was nothing…just another form of Yin and Yang. I took a deep breath and thought of the interlopers and decided to follow Annie's lead and did so as we began walking again.

I felt I needed to change the subject and, after about twenty paces asked, "Annie, what's it like to be in love?"

"You mean with Teddy?" Annie inquired.

"Yes. I've never been in love like you and that's what I miss the most… to put someone on a pedestal, so that you think and feel the world revolves around them?"

"It's a different type of feeling. At first, it's exciting and you think you're different than everyone else. Then, reality sets in and you begin to see all the cracks in the armor and realize it's just another person and you adjust and hope they do, too.

"Other than my immediate family, there are only two women in my life I've loved – Grandma Marie and you."

"Me?" Annie inquired, in an almost incredulous way.

We stopped as I turned and noted. "Yes, you. I love you. I always have. You'll always be my best friend and I'll always love you. It's not a physical thing and I apologize for our little, uh, scene, but it's a deep-down emotional feeling."

I paused for a moment to let my words sink in and then

continued in a very concerned way, "Do you think it's wrong that I love you?"

"Not at all!" Annie responded, somewhat concerned and somewhat honored.

I felt I needed to clarify what I was saying. I didn't want her to take it the wrong way and quickly added, "I'm not talking about physical love and hope you didn't take it that way."

We stopped again and Annie looked at me and recited, "if you're inferring, les amoureux, that would be fine. If you're not, that's OK, too."

"Les amoureux ?" I asked, not speaking or understanding French.

"You know...'lovers'." There was a lackadaisical tone to Annie's voice denoting a sense of ambivalence. I didn't know how to take it. In the end, I had a sense of relief pass over me. Annie would accept me either way and that's what I really needed to hear – acceptance without pressure knowing what I wanted was to keep the relationship the way it was, without all the sexual pressure that comes with intimacy.

There was another long pause as Annie continued. "Do you think I've pushed myself on you this week?" as her expression became one of concern. "I mean, I'm so much more...uh liberal, than you, and hope and pray I haven't put pressure on you to do things you didn't want to do."

"God no!" I said firmly, "It's been a relief. When we were in school, you were my guiding light. You showed me how normal people live. You have to understand, before and even now, my life was and remains incredibly sequestered with everything planned and controlled. Sure, our family has an incredible amount of material possessions and does things other people only dream about, but everything and I mean everything, is planned, calculated, scheduled and measured and, as you just saw, I'm never really alone."

I continued on, "From the first day we became roommates, I saw what it was like to be liberated and yet normal. For the first time ever, at school I didn't worry about what other people would think and security wasn't an issue and I was free. You taught me how to laugh and became the first real and honest friend I've ever had and for that I'm profoundly grateful."

"I don't understand," Annie replied.

"Our family is very wealthy, Annie. Last Sunday, I learned how much and it was a lot more than I imagined. Now wealth sounds wonderful and exciting, but with money comes control, limitations and risks. First, as you just saw, I've lost all privacy. I only need to push the button on my watch and Martin and Sophia will come out of their hiding place and be here in less than five minutes. This means they know exactly where we are right now. Monday night when we got drunk at Le' Telegraphe and I pushed the button on my watch, I was miserable. I wanted to simply be like everyone else and then I had to rely on the company."

I slowly shook my head, somewhat in remorse as I continued. "I've always been so conservative simply because I felt big brother was watching and didn't want the company to know who I was with, or more important, if I'd done something that would have been 'outside' standard values in terms of actions, dress or even inclinations."

"Until you arrived last Sunday, I was feeling cloistered in terms of what I could or couldn't do on this trip and in life. Perhaps it was because mom was with me. After I left my old bathing suit on St. Barths, and she picked out Itsy Bitsy, I began feeling a little more 'normal'. Before that, I wouldn't have worn a suit like that for fear they didn't fit the company standards."

"But, that suit is probably the most conservative suit on Orient Beach," Annie countered.

"For you and others, yes. For me, you have to realize, I'd never worn anything that brief in my life."

"How about today?" Annie inquired.

I shrugged my shoulders and replied "I don't know. I thought we'd be alone and I'd give it a try."

"And?"

"Well, at first I was quite aware, but after we began walking, I began to feel comfortable."

"How about now?"

"I was really reluctant, but that's gone too." I replied.

"In other words, you're adapting and realizing it's no big deal."

Annie offered

"I guess so." I replied and countered, "would you have gone topless if there were other people on the beach?"

"Sure, why not?" Annie inquired "What if they were naked?"

Annie looked at me as if I was asking the dumbest questions and answered, "Why not?"

"What if it was two men or two women?" "That wouldn't have made any difference." "Really?"

"How about you. Now that you've worn Teenie Weenie, do you think the world is going to stop spinning?"

"No." I grudgingly answered.

"Do you think anyone will remember – 'Oh that Melia Terrill, in Teenie Weenie?' Melia, people don't care and neither should you and if they do care, do you think a week from now, or a month, or year, they'll remember?"

"I don't know, it's just so…so different for me."

Annie vigorously responded, "Then don't do it! However, perhaps, and just perhaps, if you'd let go, you'd realize there's a sense of freedom you're keeping locked up inside of you, that when released will let you be happy. What I'm saying is, you need to learn how to be comfortable with your body, accept it and then get comfortable with yourself. You said your mom talked about all kinds of relaxation exercises to bring down your level of stress and yet, what I've seen here is that you're biggest hang up of all is your own self-concept regarding the way you look, when in fact, you're gorgeous."

"You really think so?"

"I see the way men look at you." "But I don't feel that way."

"Maybe, you need to forgive yourself for how you looked fifteen years ago and begin to accept yourself as you are today. When you do that, you'll see you're an attractive woman that men covet and many women are intimidated by."

"Intimidated?"

"Yes, intimidated! You've got the body of an athlete and the build of a professional model. Your complexion is something most women would give their eyeteeth for and those big brown eyes and incredible smile are enough to capture any man and a lot of women's hearts. What's missing and has always been missing, is an aura of self-confidence that attracts people instead of making them feel they're not important to you.

Annie looked at me with a very serious expression on her face and said, "you know I love you like a sister and will do anything for you, so please don't take what I'm about to say the wrong way."

I cringed not knowing where the conversation was going as Annie continued. "Melia, at times the words you use are…well so much more…ahh…complex than the normal person. For some people, it shows your intelligence and they appreciate it. For others, it seems like you're trying to impress them."

I looked at Annie and apologized. "I'm sorry, I don't mean to. It's just how I think and express myself. Do me a favor, if the words get too big or it seems like I'm 'showing off' please let me know, OK?"

Annie nodded in the affirmative and I think one of the things that had always bothered her was finally coming out. As for me, there was a lot to think about and, for the first time, I was beginning to feel as though my lack of self-confidence were some of the elements restraining me from achieving my ultimate goal, which was happiness. I realized, you can't be happy with others if you're not happy with yourself and perhaps, just perhaps, that's why I was so lonely. I wasn't letting anyone 'in'.

Annie continued, "when you laugh, it's infectious and yet, you hardly ever do. When you smile, you can brighten a room and yet again, it's rarely there. Because you don't laugh and rarely smile. Sadly, IF people do think of you, they have the wrong impression - that you're a dour person, while underneath is this funny, witty, incredibly intelligent, profoundly wonderful friend of mine."

"I don't know how," I confessed.

"Well, I know I'm the extreme and probably too gregarious and too…uh, liberal, but feel there's got to be somewhere in between that's right for both of us."

"But don't you feel the least bit self-conscious wearing so little?" I asked.

We stopped walking and Annie looked at me and continued. "You said you weren't uncomfortable when you had the massage and yet those guys know who you are. So what if someone sees your body. Who cares?"

Annie looked down as if to measure her words and added, "You explained the whole concept of acclimation and the same thing happens with what you're wearing. At first it might be titillating or uncomfortable and you'll be nervous, but once you acclimate, you'll think nothing of it. It's not putting on a show…well not too much of a show…as long as it fits the culture you're in."

Annie questioned. "Would I walk the beach topless in Wisconsin? No! But here, why not? Would I walk naked on Orient Beach? If the time and place are right, why not? I understand the social limits! However, this is a clothing optional beach and there's no one here, so I'm naked and think nothing of it."

Annie shook her head as if in dismay and continued. "The Europeans have it right, most of them have a complete disconnect between nudity and sex that's a lot healthier than the uptight, hyper-sexed American society that has turned the human body into one more way to sell everything from cars and cigars to shampoo, beer and SUV's."

Annie looked at me and almost pleaded. "Come on Melia, just let go. You're always so hard on yourself."

Our walk reached the outcropping beyond which civilization began again and we turned back. It was almost profound to see our own footprints becoming nothing more than memories, soon to be erased by the incoming tide as the intensity and emotions that had prevailed slowly began to fade towards obscurity.

I glanced ahead towards the foliage and confirmed our interlopers had departed…hopefully for good…but probably to simply meld themselves into another position where they weren't so obvious and intrusive, as I wondered what they thought of my 'statement'.

There was a long pause and then I began again. "When my medical world fell apart and I was hospitalized, it was because I was in the throes of having a nervous breakdown to the point they had me begin to see a psychologist, who correlated my childhood to both my insecurity and drive for perfection."

I shook my head and introspectively added. "The biggest mistake I made was going back to Grandma Marie's hospital and falling beneath her shadow. You have no idea what it's like to walk into a building and see a plaque of your grandmother by the elevator that takes you up to the floor your family paid for and then try to live up to their expectations and her achievements."

I continued on. "I know my world will always be different and that's why I cherish your friendship, simply because you're my beacon of reality. You're married! You have to worry about things I don't even consider and you have goals. I don't have a single male person in my life. I don't have to work if I don't want to and the only goal I have right now is to live my life as a normal human being."

I looked at Annie and continued. "On top of that, you're free! Free to express yourself any way you want. Free to wear what you want, be what you want, do what you want and I covet that, simply because I know I never can. I was angry and frustrated and you saw a side of me you'd never seen before and, yet, you were willing to calm me down, which makes me love you all the more, simply because it shows that you're a real, compassionate person who has more sides than I could have imagined."

"But I have problems too!" Annie retorted. "I'm married to a type 'A' personality, I rarely see. When I do see him, his mind is elsewhere. I'm as lonely as you are, but tied to one man, while you've got the entire world out there to look for the right person."

I looked Annie in the eyes and asked, "Do you regret being here now?"

Annie incredulously replied. "Not for an instant. I needed this more than you can imagine. I teach music part time at three different parochial schools and try to book gigs for my band. I live on what little money I have and after six years, feel like a failure. I'd love to have kids, but how can I, when I can hardly afford living as one and periodically two?"

I offered. "I hope your life with Teddy becomes more satisfying. For me, I just want to finally find some guy who wants to make me feel special and marry me so that I can lead a normal life. The last thing I would ever want is for us to share the friendship we have and do so as nothing more than a reaction to our own dissatisfaction. Life is tough enough without having an easy way out and that's the last thing I want to have."

"Me too!" Annie whispered as she tried changing the subject. "I haven't felt this relaxed in so long and I want to thank you for inviting me."

We stopped for a moment as I looked out at the ocean again and then at Annie and added, "We're best friends and this week you've helped me heal the wounds of disappointment and exonerate my sense of profound dismay that's been building up inside of me for years. You have to realize my life has consisted of virtual social isolation since

Oshkosh and I thank you for helping me escape and have some fun."

After a few silent steps Annie's right hand clutched my left and we continued walking, not in a contrived or sexual way, but one of acceptance. Even after our talk, I sincerely felt this wasn't about anything more than accepting each other for who we were – two lost souls in search of happiness. Whew! I'd been so reluctant about so many things. Maybe, I truly was letting go.

When we reached the spot where we'd 'put on the show'…or at least, I hoped it was…Annie looked at me, pulled me in and we hugged again. No kissing! No clutching! Simply a juncture of two souls who finally did what I think both of us needed to do for so long - share feelings with someone we trusted.

I'd admitted I loved Annie, but not in *that* way, and hoped she felt the same way, or anyway I didn't think so. We were simply two friends who trusted each other, respected each other and cared for each other and that was the beauty of Yin and Yang, where I felt, the very last thing either of us needed was another set of dynamics challenging our sense of self.

I wondered, "had we shared too much? I think we both were concerned that we'd crossed a bridge neither of us wanted.

After a long pause the word "Sorry" escaped from Annie.

"For what?" I replied.

"For – for what I did and what I said."

"What? We finally talked about what's probably been below the surface for a long time." I replied, not wanting to revisit our staged kiss or embrace.

We began walking and I saw John-Claude and the boat arriving, checked my watch and realized it was three o'clock. Annie was naked and I was topless and Jon-Claude was arriving while we were two-hundred yards from our clothes. Yikes!

Annie looked at me and I looked at Annie and she simply

shrugged and smiled. By the time we got back, Jon-Claude had everything, and I mean everything, loaded and never flinched as he helped us into the boat. Annie unfolded the towels and said she couldn't find her top. Claude said he thought he had everything and offered to go back and look. Annie said not to worry about it. (Later Annie realized she'd put it in the empty cooler under her I-pad before we started our walk).

As we neared Anse Marcel, I inquired, "Home or Chez?" that we were beginning to call Chez Leandra. Annie simply looked at me like I was some sort of dolt for even asking.

Jon-Claude radioed ahead and said one of the marina guys would take the Rover and park it behind Lucille's and would use 0704 as the code for the key. We reached the limits of where the boat could drop anchor at Orient Beach and Jon-Claude announced we'd need to wait for a skiff to take us in.

We were less than 250 feet from shore, the waves were calm and both Annie and I were strong swimmers so we had our choice…wait for the skiff and take our belongings or simply swim to shore the way we were. We decided to swim with Claude assuring us that he'd have the rest of our stuff in the back of the Rover when we headed back to the house.

As we reached the beach, Annie inquired, "Are you ready to try fitting in?"

"What?"

"Everyone else is going to be in their bathing suits. How about you?"

I flinched a slight expression of reservation, thought back to our dialogue and took a deep breath. My courage was finally there and so Annie and I simply swam in, walked up to the Chez porch and met our French vacation friends, with me wearing Teenie Weenie and Annie regaling in her OMG bottom.

It seemed strange to be wearing so little and still feeling overdressed, as tho fabulous, friendly, somewhat inebriated,

French men wished us a happy American Independence Day, while the topless French women in their Barely-There, thong bottoms watched with some detachment as the men ogled the newly liberated Americans.

I finally began to realize that Annie was right about why I appeared to be stand-offish, when I really wasn't. At first, I forced a smile at the conversations placed before me. Then, as the afternoon progressed and a few rum punches traversed my lips, it became much easier for me to laugh at Annie's antics until Chez became filled with enough of my own mirth for me to see that, for the very first time in a long, long time, I was a participant and not some reluctant spectator in this thing called life.

As the sun began to set, the thought of Martin and Sophia spying on me crossed my mind and I was tempted to simply press the watch button twice, have them come running and tell them to "Fuck off." Instead, we said Au revoir, checked the back of the Rover to confirm that everything was there, including Annie's top, and made our way up Happy Hill .

It truly had been Independence Day filled with anger, frustration, elocution and trepidation. As I entered the house, I paused for a moment to simply absorb the softening silence of solitude that was a welcoming respite from all that had transpired, as I shook my head and vowed to never look back.

Annie opened her computer, sent a text to Teddy and became immersed in the other things of life. I went out, took a quick shower by the pool and hung up Teenie Weenie to dry.

Annie came out and joined me in the pool and we simply cooled off.

A few minutes later the phone rang. It was mom.

"How's your vacation going?" she inquired.

"Fine"

"Sounds like you've been having a lot of fun."

"How do you know that?"

"Well…"

It was then I realized that everywhere we went and everything we did was being reported and she was getting copies of our restaurant and bar bills and I was totally pissed

"Mother! This is pure bullshit! You've been spying on me!"

"Melia! You have to realize, with wealth comes risks and we need to make certain you're protected."

"Who knows?" Who knows I've got money?" I shouted.

There was a significant pause and then mom spilled the beans. "Melia, you're on an island where we own more property than anyone except the government. We've donated millions of dollars to its redevelopment and helped families simply survive hurricanes and pandemics and they know who you are and therefore there's always a chance something can happen."

"Mom, I'm twenty-eight years old and just had a nervous breakdown. I've never done anything dangerous or been a risk to the family or the company. To sit and mother me like I'm a child is really not fair. I would like some privacy, please!"

"But what about today at Happy Bay?" Mom retorted before realizing she'd crossed the line. All of our mother/daughter bonding of the week before was in jeopardy and she knew it. Being as intelligent as she was, she quickly recognized she'd better back off and promised me she would. She finally hung up as a chill ran down my spine. I finally, emphatically realized I'd gained my financial freedom only to become a captive at the same time.

Metamorphous:

Sunday morning arrived and it was time for one last Good Morning treat.

As we were eating, Annie offered, "I wish we didn't have to leave".

"We don't," I nonchalantly replied. "What?"

"I don't have anywhere to go or anything to do. What do you have planned for the week?"

"I need to water my plants."

I laughed "One less week on St. Martin because your plants need watering?"

"I think my landlady could do it. Can we really stay?"

"I need to call and tell Wilco not to send Amelia^X. They weren't scheduled to leave until around one Milwaukee time and so, it should be OK."

"You mean we really can stay?" "Sure, why not?"

Annie was like a little kid who just got her first bike, as I called and told operations I'd decided to spend more time. At first, they seemed reticent and then they realized I wasn't a kid anymore and now a primary stockholder.

"All set!" I reported to Annie. "However, in about fifteen minutes my mother will be calling."

Sure enough, twenty minutes later mom called and I assured her that everything was fine and that, because it was summer vacation, Annie didn't need to come home. She kept pressuring me to make certain we were being careful and asking me if I was wearing the watch. I assured her I was, whenever we left the house.

I hung up and knew who'd be calling next – Andrew! I answered the phone "Hello Andrew. Here are your options, either Martin and Sofia stop reporting all my activities to my mother or your watch gets dropped in the ocean! They're security and not spies for my mother! Andrew, do you understand?"

I was royally pissed and pushed the button on the watch

twice. In three minutes, there was a wrap on the front door as Martin and Sophia arrived. "I'm staying another week. Your job is security and not invading my privacy. **IF** you report my activities this week, you **WILL** be terminated. Do you understand?"

There was a shocked affirmative on the other end as I added, "Now get out of my house and remember, your job is security when I need it, not reporting on my life and what goes on."

Annie sat with mouth agape, mealy mouse Melia had a temper she'd never seen before.

"Now Mrs. Franklin, we need to drive into Phillipsburg and go to Carrefour for some groceries."

We got dressed and headed into town as I silently vowed no more central billing. I'd put everything on my Visa card and that way mom and security wouldn't know where we'd been or what we were doing. Carrefour was jammed, as always. As we made our way up and down the aisles as the grocery pile grew until we got what we felt we needed for the week…and probably for the entire Russian army.

We checked out and put the groceries in the back of the Rover. "We've got a couple more stops to make," I announced as Annie looked perplexed.

A few blocks down Union Street at the intersection with Well Road, we pulled into the parking stalls in front of a nondescript building across from the Ace Hardware store as Annie looked at the sign above the door. "You're not really going to do that, are you?"

"Why not?" I countered. "Really?"

"Uh huh, it's about time I did something for Melia instead of always trying to please my parents."

"We walked inside and I looked at all the designs on the wall as an elderly man appeared.

"May I help you?" he inquired.

"I'm interested in a small butterfly tattoo," I replied, remembering biology and the complete metamorphosis or holo- metabolism that took place in transforming a caterpillar into a butterfly.

The elderly man showed me a few options and I chose the one I liked that was highlighted with multi-colors.

"Where would you like to place it?" he asked.

I pointed to my mons pubis or lower abdomen and off to the right side as he nodded in the affirmative. We went in the back room and I removed my shorts. Twenty minutes later, it was done. I had my butterfly tattoo as a memento of my perceived new freedom.

Annie shook her head and grinned at my enthusiastic liberation as we proceeded to the final part of the Phillipsburg run which was going down to Front Street where the cruisers usually shop. When Annie and Teddy were on their honeymoon, they never made it to this side of the island and so I thought it would provide Annie with a respite from everything French.

We parked the car by the Green House restaurant and walked down to 'Retro on Front Street' as I pointed out that it had been Aunt Julia's jewelry store before she and Uncle Frank retired. Instead of diamonds and jewels it was now filled with all sorts of clothing styles from the 60's and 70's.

We looked in the window and elected to enter. The men's side of the store was much smaller than the women's and contained bell bottoms, swimwear, big collar paisley shirts, shorts and platform shoes. I realized that back then, men were a lot more 'open' about their bodies than today.

The women's section included hip hugger jeans, bell bottoms, leotards, platform shoes; tube, halter and Dickie tops, hot pants, miniskirts, rompers, jumpsuits, oversized sunglasses and head bands, all beneath photos from Woodstock, along with psychedelic photos of the bands who were popular at the time, as their music blared on.

We went through each of the women's clothing sections and shook our heads. I smiled and thought of my grandmothers, realizing they were part of a huge social, political and sexual revolution and not just two dowdy ladies who conformed to what was 'right' when I knew them.

I spied a rack of old-fashioned halter tops and then some of what they called Hankies made of rayon chiffon, which were not only lightweight, but very soft and fell in love with the feel of a paisley rayon batiste design that literally floated off the hangar. While halter top material was thicker and more conservative, the hankies consisted of a single triangular piece of thin fabric with strings that tied behind your neck and back, thereby providing a different meaning to the term bareback.

The clerk noted that the entire hankie movement began during the woman's lib demonstrations of the 1960's and I quickly realized they left little to the imagination, wondering if I'd ever be brave or drunk enough to wear one, but at that moment really didn't care. I decided there could be safety in numbers such that Annie and I could 'share the wear' as we called it in college and so I took both the paisley and white batiste hankie intended for Annie, as she was certainly more liberated than I was.

The store had a tiny dressing room which had been Charlie's jewelry workshop when Aunt Julia's store resided there. I went in and tried on the paisley and returned. Annie just nodded in the affirmative. God it was comfortable! I then tried on the white one and looked in the mirror and thought it would take more than a few rum punches to get even Annie to wear it in public and I wouldn't be caught dead in it, but this was to be our wild and crazy week.

The clerk had been somewhat oblivious to our activities until she saw my choices and said, "You need to wear that with some 60's hip huggers or hot pants."

"What are hot pants?" I inquired total incredulous to the term.

The clerk took me to a rack of what we call bootie or short shorts, except they had wide multi-colored, rainbow belts with big peace sign buckles that rode very low in the front, while the bell bottoms weren't too appealing as I couldn't imagine wearing long pants is 90-degree heat.

"How about a Dickie?" the clerk inquired, to which I had no idea what she was referring to other than a purloined anatomical reference which sounded good to me. We went to a circular display consisting of a myriad of different styles where the idea was simply taking a hankie top and designing it so you showed some cleavage. The clerk looked at me and said, "I think I've got something you'll like," which was probably something she said to every customer who was polite enough to listen.

Slowly she perused the options until she found a white top that reminded me of an old-fashioned horse collar that you simply slipped over your head and tied in the back, down around your waist. For something so simple, it certainly looked dressy and the thought of showing off my tan was appealing, simply because I could wear it with dress shorts and be somewhat in style, which was something that had been furthest from my thoughts for so long I'd forgotten what it meant to try and be visually appealing.

I went in the dressing room, put on the horse collar and never even had to model it. I knew I liked it. While there, the clerk handed me another option that consisted of two adjustable brown triangles with gold rings on the top and one string that tied behind my neck and the other just below my boobs so that my back was exposed as well as my abdomen. Not quite as dressy as the first one, the brown one still looked great and I liked the idea of being given the option of creating my own degree of exposure, simply because the two triangles had bottom channels instead of a hem such that you could widen or narrow the material as you saw fit.

The clerk noted, "We're also offering a matching skirt," and told me to hold on as she would get it. "Size four?" to which I concurred.

As I was standing in the dressing room, her hand reached around the edge of the curtain and handed me what I initially thought was a scarf, only to realize it was a brown miniskirt that I quickly deemed 'hooker wear'. I slid into the skirt with a great deal of trepidation as it was only eight inches wide. Annie verbally beckoned me and I walked out onto the sales floor to get her opinion only to find a husband and wife who had entered the store as the man's mouth dropped open as he exclaimed, « *Magnifique. Elle doit être mannequin* » as his wife grabbed his arm and demanded that he stop staring at me.

I asked the clerk what he'd said and she simply said "he thought you were very beautiful and probably a model." It had been a very long time since anyone called me beautiful and, needless to say, I added three more items to the pile, as the clerk noted she had the same outfit in black and, through mix-and- match, I could actually have four different outfits.

The clerk really knew her stuff as she outlined. "Micro-minis were introduced in Britain in the summer of 1962 where those girls with legs as good as yours were called 'Ya-Ya girls', a term derived from 'yeah, yeah' which was a popular catcall at the time. Extremely short skirts, including the style you have on, were designed to be worn eight inches above the knee. Because of your height, you have even more leg exposure, but you'll still have four inches of coverage below your buttocks, which makes it a great fit for you."

Without missing a beat, the clerk continued. "Designer Mary Quant is credited with starting the trend and was quoted as saying that "short-short skirts" indicated youthfulness, which was seen as highly desirable, fashion-wise amongst the post-war baby boomers. However, there was actually another reason for the brevity and that's because in England, they had a special tax on women's apparel, but not on children's and by making the skirts as short as they were, micros were considered a child's design and therefore avoided taxation, making them less expensive and more appealing."

I was impressed by the clerk's knowledge and thought we

were done until she took us over to a section of what she called jumpsuits, which were one-piece outfits that had twelve buttons all the way, and I mean all the way, down the front. The clerk offered information that jumpsuits had been the fashion rage in the 1970's and came in all types of material including corduroy and denim along with some constructed of lightweight, parachute nylon.

The re-invented style included a small amount of Lycra to make them more form fitting. While the design was still loose, the current iterations included a small elastic waistband sewn in the back to create more form that fit the body. After looking at the corduroy and denim and not really being attracted, I found a yellow nylon suit that was not only attractive but extremely lightweight, not weighing more than a pound or two.

Once again, it was back to the dressing room, as I slid into the yellow romper as the clerk had called it with a wide collar and buttons down the front, from my neck to far below my waist. It certainly felt comfortable and I was somewhat ambivalent towards wearing it when Annie called out and asked me to come out and show her. I slid back the curtain and stepped out onto the sales floor and Annie smiled as she beckoned me over to her.

Annie looked me over and said, "Wait a minute," as she opened the six top buttons and folded the collar up directing me to, "Now go look in the mirror". With two pockets strategically placed to create a double layer of material across my chest, I realized I actually felt somewhat attractive with the clerk nodding her approval.

"What size shoe are you?" the clerk inquired.

"Twelve" I replied as the clerk motioned me to the shoe display and pointed to a pair of lace up sandals that had three- inch soles on them. Being nearly – ok – six-feet-two inches tall, adding three inches, had me at a grand total nearing six-foot-five and I felt as though I was on top of the world. With my short hair accentuating my long neck and high cheek bones, the clerk told me to hold the moment as she retrieved a pair a large, gold-loop earrings and directed me to put them on.

Looking in the mirror, I found my lobe piercings and did as directed, turned to Annie and the clerk to see them both smiling in complete approval as Annie offered, "You look mahvelous dearie, simply mahvelous!"

What was supposed to be a simple excursion into Aunt Julia's old store turned into one of those buying sprees mom was famous for. Two horse collar dickies, two halter tops, two hankies, two mini and I mean mini-skirts, one jumpsuit, one pair of elevator sandals and one pair of gold big hoop earrings.

I looked at Annie and inquired, "Anything you like?"

The clerk got the gist and noted they had what was called the Mary Ann collection from Gilligan's Island. I don't know who had the bigger frown Annie or me.

"You're familiar with the show aren't you?" the clerk inquired. We both nodded yes as we watched it in the afternoons in Oshkosh.

The clerk added. Viewers found Mary Ann incredibly attractive, often preferring her over because of her wholesome, natural beauty and girl-next-door charm made her relatable and appealing and the kind of woman you could take home to meet your parents. In other words sexy but approachable. With that in mind, the Mary Ann collection was created."

The clerk took us to the round display and pulled out a red corduroy jumper and noted it was a 'show stopper' for Mary Ann that would show off Annie's great legs.

Next the clerk picked out a mini dress that I thought was a top simply because it was so short and noted it would work perfectly for those semi-casual nights. Third was a form-fitting gingham crop top that could be worn off the shoulder or a tied- up button down. Finally were reproductions of Mary Ann's famous Daisy Dukes which consisted of high waisted cheeky version shorts that literally had no inseam, which the clerk noted would provide a sexier vibe.

I looked at Annie smiled and noted, "well Mary Ann, it's not Gilligan's Island but you can play the part," as I told the clerk to add one of each to the growing pile of clothes.

While Annie was eight inches shorter than me, she and I wore the same size and so, other than the shoes and jumpsuit, we could do like we did in college and trade off. Annie had been eyeing the denim miniskirts and so I went over to the rack and found three versions in black, faded blue and white and tossed them on the counter. I then went to the hip hugger display and found a pair of size four, low rise, button fly, hip hugger jeans with a peace symbol belt and added them to the pile as well, telling Annie she could wear them in Madison while doing her gigs and fitting right in.

The clerk politely asked, "Will there be anything else?" to which I simply shook my head no. Using the bar code scanner, which I was certain didn't come from the 1960's, I watched the numbers soar as I realized that, while the styles were from the sixties, the prices were from outer space, with a total exceeding two thousand Euros. I simply offered my Visa card, realizing that Carrefour, tattoo and all those clothes were still less than 20% of my weekly allowance and there would be another $10,000 deposit the next day.

As we were leaving the store, Annie inquired, "Where are you going to wear those?"

"Where are WE going to wear these? When we go bar hopping." I replied with a chuckle with Annie realizing that week two was going to be completely different than our first one.

We returned to the House-On-The-Hill and realized the housekeeper had been there and everything was spic and span. We put away the food and I went upstairs and divided the clothes, putting Annie's new assortment on her bed as I rebelliously slipped into Teenie Weenie, intent on spending the rest of the afternoon at the pool.

Annie came out with a towel wrapped around her and simply took it off with nothing underneath. It was then I realized that Happy Bay was the beginning. Annie wasn't going to wear OMG or anything at our pool again. At first I felt a little uncomfortable and then reticent and finally thought "whatever."

When it was time for dinner, we decided to do down to Le Piment and I actually decided to put some makeup on with Annie urging me to not only wear lipstick, but light blue eye shadow as well, which I hadn't done since we were roommates.

For attire, we both wore the new halter tops and added the denim skirts. We didn't have dinner reservations, but Richard recognized us, nodded to the Maître D' and we were sealed right away, out under the stars, where it was a lot more tranquil, but also a lot warmer without the ceiling fans.

As the appetizer was completed, Richard sauntered to our table with a huge smile on his face. "Ms. Melia, you look fantastic. You could be a model and Annie, if I remember correctly, you could be on the cover of Vogue. You two look exquisite."

I smiled and said "thank you", not knowing if it was a true compliment or pure B.S. Hello world! Goodbye Milwaukee! Tee Hee!

After dinner, we went back to the house and I realized how comfortable the halter tops really were, simply because there wasn't much to them – a piece of thin cloth that covered our boobs. We kicked back and had a couple more glasses of mom's Terrell Reserve wine.

By the third glass, on top of several shots of rum at the restaurant neither of us were feeling any pain as we both simply went to bed.

Buttons, Buttons How Many Buttons:

Monday morning the phone rang and it was Uncle Frank. He'd heard we decided to stay and asked if we needed anything. I told him we'd gone into town and bought groceries. He asked if we'd like to go with he and Aunt Julia back to Astrolab for dinner and I thought 'sure, why not?'

We went to the beach and had lunch at Wai. For dinner, Annie and I decided to get "dressed up" for which I selected the jumpsuit, large hoop earrings, a gold necklace and the lace up sandals. Annie wanted me to "unbutton" to number six as she had done in the clothing store, but I felt it would be improper with Aunt Julia. Annie looked great in the black miniskirt and the white horse collar. I added some makeup, looked in the mirror and realized I actually looked like a different person. No longer plain Jane, nor a wall flower. Perhaps this had been the missing ingredient and I hadn't realized it as I was too enveloped in my studies and work to care.

We drove down to Astrolab and when we entered, virtually every eye in the place was on us, with most men's mouths open. I guess that meant they found us attractive. Towering above virtually everyone in the restaurant certainly caused a stir as we were escorted to our table. Aunt Julia and Uncle Frank both stood and I really didn't know the reason why.

Aunt Julia's smile said it all – she approved – she said she loved both of our hairstyles and I knew mom would hear about them. I guess I really didn't care. Uncle Frank couldn't say enough about how beautiful we looked as he said in a cavalier way, "You look ravishing!"

Uncle Frank excused himself to go talk to the manager as Aunt Julia shook her head and added, "Melia, between the short hair, long neck and those gold hoops, you look like some sort of Egyptian goddess. What's her name? I know Aphrodite, or something like that."

My emotional core smiled as I was being associated with not only an Egyptian, but ancient Greek goddess of love and beauty. The bonus of throwing in Venus, who was known primarily as a goddess of love and fertility, really made me feel good.

Aunt Julia looked at me with a concerned expression as she offered, "you should unbutton some of those top buttons." I started - one, then two, then three as I paused and instructed Aunt Julia to tell me when to stop, which she did at button number five, just below the pocket line.

Uncle Frank returned, took one look and smiled. He knew who was involved as I thought to myself, 'now if I could only find some guy who'd go from button six to twelve, I'd be all set.'

As we were being served Aunt Julia added, "Annie, I think St. Martin is just right for you too. You look simply marvelous. I love your hair and hope you're having a wonderful time."

"I am, Aunt Julia," Annie responded with a bashful smile on her face.

Dinner was splendid and, as had been the case the previous week, the end came early. It seems old people go to bed when we normally go out. The initial "wow factor" when we arrived had somewhat worn off. Yet, I could still feel every set of male coveted eyes on Annie and me as we walked out and that made me feel good.

The Routine:

Because we'd done so much during the first week, our planned routine for the bonus week was quite simple. We'd get up and walk the beach if it was before sunrise - stop at Good Morning for whatever was coming out of the oven, come home, eat our treats out by the pool and then head to the beach. It wasn't very exciting but it was what we both needed.

Every morning Annie would work on her album, while I progressed to Grisham number seven, then we'd head for our "restaurant of the day" as we slowly gobbled our way down the gastronomic Orient Beach highway and people watched until around two or there where quitting time was totally determined by the quantity and quality of the walk-by traffic. The neat thing was, I really don't know if it was total relaxation or some sort of reaction to all that I'd been constricted by, but my uptight attitude was certainly melding with Annie's free spirit and I was loving it, as laughter re-entered my life for the first time in a very, very long time.

We'd already eaten at almost all the restaurants and always ended up at Chez Leandra in the afternoon. After careful consideration, we elected to find a permanent people viewing location and chose the area, just east of the rocks where Club Orient began, so that we would get maximum people exposure in more ways than one, I guess.

The routine was set! When we got thirsty, Annie and I would ask one of the servers from Chez to bring us some dirty lemonade and when it got hot, we'd simply walk in the water to cool off. After a couple hours, we'd go inside Chez for Happy Hour and between the tans and the fact we were both young, to say we were getting hit on, was an understatement as we became the target of every "loving" Frenchman who came along. We'd play along and finally let them down gently and head for home to get ready for another of the gastronomic delights that serve as one of the driving forces of St. Martin.

By the third day, we were calling the Club Orient section of the beach simply 'the club' where we quickly learned there was both a pecking order and an assortment of 'neighborhoods' consisting of small groups who sat together every day. I suggested we continue to sit where we were and establish our own neighborhood, if we could find people we enjoyed being with. After the first day, I went to Paula and asked her to send one of the marina guys with six chairs and reserve our spot for the entire week, which he did. Spoiled? You bet!

As the days progressed our 'neighborhood' developed where, to our west and closest to the rocks, was a couple from Paris who were very nice. To our east, was a couple from Lyon, in their mid-to-late forties who were also really nice and much more talkative. We learned he was an engineer and his wife a magistrate. When they asked what we did, Annie said she was a teacher and I said I was a financial analyst, simply because I had no idea what else to say besides thinking of the money I could spend.

The neighborhood was set and each afternoon I would simply ask both couples if they would like to have the chairs reserved for the next day. They did and we looked forward to having them by our sides simply by having them there where we arrived.

I kept my suit on but Annie was naked as a j-bird from day one. By the third day, we began judging the guys who walked by, or at least one part of them – too small, too big, too discolored. We were looking for the perfect appendage.

On the third day "he" walked by. Black wavy hair! A beautiful tan! Sparkling white teeth! I looked at him and my loins ached. I think I would have done him right then and there. Annie caught my glances and simply nodded as her way of saying "come and get it."

As he was walking by, a slight smile pursed his lips and I thought "I'm going to make love tonight". Instead, he veered to his right and away from the water and met with another guy who set up shop behind us.

Gay! Damn!

I hoped the porch swung both ways but realized it didn't as his partner slithered suntan oil onto his entire, and I mean entire glistening body.

Being so close to Lucille's meant she was always on the prowl when we were heading back to the Rover. One day, Annie succumbed and we went inside. Big mistake! Not only for Annie, but for me! I'd started my vacation in a fifteen-year-old, two-piece bathing suit I'd worn when my parents were here that was left on St. Barths. The lost suit forced me to reluctantly begin wearing Itsy Bitsy that my mother of all people, picked out while Annie stated it was the most conservative suit on Orient Beach.

I began wearing Teenie Weenie all the time, which was still conservative compared to some of the apparel on the beach. This should have been enough. However, Lucille convinced me to purchase the blue-and-white sailor-striped OMG thong. I thought to myself, 'Melia - you're changing girl! You're certainly letting go! Perhaps, after trying so hard your entire life to always do things right, you're finally letting go'.

Let's Go Bold:

Wednesday Annie and I decided to "go bold" on Orient Beach with Annie wearing OMG and me in my new Sailor Suit, that rode so low, my new butterfly tattoo was playing peek-a-boo with the roving eyes of passers-by. Surprise! We seemed to fit right in. So much for fear and trepidation.

That afternoon, I received a text from Wilco Ops, asking me to give them a call. I thought they were still upset about my last- minute cancellation. I called and the dispatcher noted they had a VIP who wanted to take Spike to Puerto Rico on Wednesday, July 14th and was willing to pay a premium, simply to say he rode in the plane. Wilco asked if Annie and I could stay a few more days, as it would save the company $15,000. I turned to Annie and asked what she'd planned for the following week and she noted, "Watering my plants".

"Want to stay a few more days?"

"Really?" she said excitedly, as I explained the situation and she enthusiastically said "Sure" as I told Wilco Ops it was all right to allow someone besides the family use Amelia^{X,} if it was OK with my parents.

Twenty minutes later, mom called and was about as nice as could be, only asking if we were enjoying ourselves and thanking Annie and me for 'sacrificing' for the good of the company. It seems, even when you're wealthy, you still need to watch your pennies to stay that way.

I informed mom, we were sitting on the beach and enjoying the weather. I also let her know that Annie was wrapping up her album and she seemed fine with that. Our little tiff of the previous week had blown over and I believe Wilco Security was giving me the latitude I needed. Little did she imagine that her straight as an arrow daughter had a new tattoo and was wearing a thong bathing suit. I know – shame on you, Melia! Tsk! Tsk! Tsk! Tee Hee!

As the week progressed, it was actually starting to get mundane and also very hot, as I thanked myself for getting pissed off and cutting my hair as short as I did. The one thing about hair, even if you screw up, it will grow back. However, the smiles and nods led me to believe I'd hit a homer in the social league. Our tans were just about maxed out and so we stopped slathering suntan oil all over each other while, other than my kinky hair, Annie was beginning to have my complexion when I hadn't been in the sun and I began to show my African heritage. Friday, I got brave as Annie went naked with me in the sailor suit to The Perch in the clothing optional area and ogled the elders, as we began calling them, who were trying to take one last gasp at virility.

The Perch sign said *"no shirt, no shoes, no clothes…no problem"*. At first, I was a bit reticent but then simply "joined the crowd" while retaining my now somewhat liberal modesty.

Our first visit seemed to break the ice in more ways than one and, from then on, we'd join the Perch crowd for a couple of cocktails, then Annie would put her bottom and head to Chez. Finally, we'd head for home, jump in the pool, have our own happy hour, get gussied up and going back to one of our haunts for dinner.

One afternoon, as we were making our way from the Perch to Chez, we were putting on our bottoms Annie inquired "why do they call it skinny dipping, when none and I mean none of the people at the Perch are skinny?"

I took out my phone and Googled to learn that the idiom "skinny dipping" was first used in 1947 simply because, up until then, swimming without attire was considered the norm that was practiced virtually everywhere. With new material that would dry fast, the act of swimming naked was no longer deemed necessary and to distinguish the new way from the old, the phrase "skinny dipping" was adopted, simply because it referred to the act of dipping nothing but skin in the water. So much for thinking our generation was more liberal, when even Grandma Marie was probably skinny dipping in her time.

I'd always loved Le Piment and that night, I asked Annie if we could wear our disco clothes and go there for dinner. I decided to wear the brown, adjustable horse collar with the gold rings and matching skirt with enough thigh showing to make it interesting. Annie was in light blue denim shorts and the white horse collar. While being somewhat biased, I must admit, I felt we both looked quite fetching with our bright pink lipstick, deep tans and eye- catching apparel as we made our way to the hostess stand with every set of male eyes upon us.

We were seated "inside" where there were ceiling fans to keep us cool. Low and behold, who was sitting next to us, but the couple from Lyon who we sat next to that afternoon at the beach. It seemed funny to see them with clothes on and I guess they felt the same way. How incredibly discordant to feel uncomfortable around dressed people, even after the four of us began gulping down Henri's famous banana rum as our after-dinner aperitif.

As the conversation continued, I found it particularly interesting to watch the eyes of the husband as he mentally invaded our privacy in a somewhat lecherous way, when a few hours before, everything covered was in plain sight. I guess the old adage about creating mystery does hold true.

Perhaps it was the rum! Perhaps it was the wandering set of eyes! Perhaps it was just me wanting to be a little naughty, but I excused myself, went to the ladies' room and slid the top triangles of my horse collar in on both the inside and out so that the man from Lyon had a better view of what he had been lecherously staring at.

As I sauntered back to the table, Annie looked at me with a devilish grin as our French friend almost tipped over his glass of rum. So much for a little skin the guy had been ogling for three days. In the end, we had a wonderful meal and incredible conversation that ended with us promising to see all of each other the next day.

Twinkle Twinkle:

The weekend slipped by as our Parisian "neighbors" said Au revoir and the group of six was reduced to four. Monday was the same as the previous week and becoming somewhat redundant. I think both Annie and I knew it was time to head home. Tuesday arrived and it was our last full day on the island. We kept our promise and met the couple from Lyon and spent one more day sharing stories and promising to stay in touch.

We went to Chez Leandra for happy hour that should have been called happy afternoon because on Tuesdays it lasted from two until six. We'd noticed two French guys about our age earlier in the week who approached us this time. After the obligatory "where are you from" and "do you know so-and-so", we let them know it was our last day.

We had drinks and, as the conversation progressed, they invited us back to their condo. I looked at Annie as she nodded yes. I was a bit shocked. Annie seemed more open and willing than I'd anticipated. Perhaps, her pain and loneliness was more than I perceived.

The condo was located in the development just behind Good Morning. It was small, yet clean. More wine was consumed until I needed to use the restroom. When I returned to the living room, the three of them announced they wanted to "party".

I took Annie by the side and asked if she was sure and she said "yes".

I didn't want to. Annie did. By the look on my face Annie knew my feelings and asked if it was OK if she stayed and played.

Looking at her I thought 'she's an adult. She knows what's going on. I didn't want to go there and would go back to the house. Looking at her, I slipped off my special Apple watch and instructed. "No matter what, don't take this off and if there's any...uhh...problems, simply push the side button twice. OK?"

"Promise?"

"Promise!"

"When should I come back?" "Six?"

"OK. I'll be outside in the Rover at six." "You're sure?"

"Yes!"

I went back and got into the Rover and headed for H-O-H. I pushed the button and the gate opened and walked into the cool air. An empty house has a way of having a different mood to it. The silence! The emptiness! The profound sense of oneness, brought back memories of my five years of solitude. For the first time in six weeks, I truly felt sad as the hum of the refrigerator was my only companion, previewing my impending singularity.

I tried reading but to no avail. I got cleaned up, looked at the clock a dozen times until nearly six, got in the Rover and went back to the condo. Annie was standing outside. She got in with no words spoken about what had transpired and simply handed me the watch. To this day, she's never shared the details and I've never asked.

I must admit, I was curious. Why was Annie so willing to stay? I began wondering if it had happened before and what would have transpired if I'd agreed to stay. We all have our little peccadillos and this one was, is, and shall always be Annie's.

I drove back to the house and parked the Rover. Annie went out to the pool, used the outdoor shower and came back into the living room. She had a somewhat laconic attitude that pervaded our interaction as she quietly went and turned on her laptop to see if there were any messages. There were none as she slowly closed the lid, took a deep breath and sadly shook her head.

I felt I needed to adjust the mood and relieve the mounting pressure and so I changed the subject to dining. After the first week, we'd been alternating restaurant selection and it was her turn to choose. Annie surprised me with Le' Taitu and its very casual atmosphere.

Having already worked our way through most of the "disco clothes" we were down to hankie tops and micro-minis. We got gussied up with Annie selecting the white 'hello' hankie, as there was no other way to describe the impression it made, topped by the faded blue denim micromini. For me, it was the paisley hankie that Annie called the 'sperm shirt' simply because the paisley design reminded her of, "a bunch of little guys racing towards ecstasy," that I matched with the black scarf - make that micromini - that was mid-thigh, even when I was standing up. (It seems that an eight-inch-long skirt on 38" hip-to-toe legs will do that.)

Once again, I thought of the grandmas and wondered if they really ever wore so little and snickered at the thought, hoping that if they did, it was only when they were young.

We arrived at Le' Taitu where there were three other couples and a pair of guys dining that had 'American tourists' plastered all over them. When you've stayed on St. Martin for a while, you get to know that French men NEVER wear tee-shirts to dinner!

We were escorted to our table on the mid-level of the three- tiered dining area. Instead of sitting "married style" or across from each other, Annie sat next to me simply because no one likes to have their backs to the rest of those dining.

We ordered a bottle of wine and were minding our own business when the two Americans approached. Gee I wonder what was on their mind? We both knew what was in store and politely deflected their initial overtures. It was nice to have some guys pay attention to us, but the afternoon had availed in more ways than one and the last thing I wanted was a second chance at a one-night stand.

To accentuate our lack of desire, Annie put her hand in mine and told the Americans we were on our honeymoon. When they continued, Annie got out her dagger and said "Isn't it great that gay people like the four of us can go anywhere without being chastised?"

Now there are good ways and great ways to end a conversation and Annie knew just how to do it. These two were macho men who coveted their own masculine traits of dominance, toughness and assertiveness as one replied, "We're not gay and can prove it."

"Switch hitters? Annie inquired. "No way!" One of the two retorted.

Annie responded and then really dug in deep as she added. "There's nothing wrong with being gay and you two might want to give it a try. I mean, all the outward signs are there."

Standing there in shock, the two watched as Annie turned and kissed me on the lips. Not a little peck but a deep dive as her hand slid way up the inside of my left thigh. For an instant I could taste my best friend as her fingers aroused my inner anguish. The kiss ended while her soft, gentle touch lingered in my mind long after her fingers were gone.

The Americans mouths dropped open and they departed to which there was a pause. All of a sudden Annie seemed insecure, as she verbally pondered, "Have I gone too far?" Annie had always been concerned about her 'outgoing' personality and 'liberated' lifestyle and was afraid she'd crossed some bounds. After living together for four years, I knew better, as she was a kind, sweet, incredibly sensitive person whose extroverted façade was her means of defense about getting hurt by someone or someway. Naturally, there had been issues along the way, but our friendship and care for each other always allowed us to discuss problems and not have them explode into some sort of rant and raging diatribe that would have jeopardized the deep friendship we had for each other.

I could sense she was beginning to believe her 'independence' was putting pressure on me and so I added. "You've shown me friendship, love and compassion that eliminated many of the bounds that have been restraining me. Along with mom, who helped provide a new perspective on my existence, you've put fun back in my life. It's just been the two of us for the first time since we lived in the dorm."

Annie paused, took a small sip of wine, looked in my eyes and put her hand in mine. I knew that what she was about to say was on the edge. Taking a deep breath Annie admitted. "If it wasn't for Teddy and things were...uh...different, being here on our honeymoon would have been all right with me."

All right? All right? what did that mean. Did it mean that because of Teddy, things weren't different? Did it mean things were not all right? Was its Annie's way of saying we would have been a couple even though it was the farthest thing from my mind?

Was it a confession or a compliment? Was it something so deep within the two of us that had finally come out? I was honored and yet, at the same time concerned. Where was this leading physically? Emotionally?

Perhaps it was my solitary existence that lowered my guard and yet I realized feelings for Annie were there as I tingled at the thought of the physical aspect, yet the emotional challenge was a barrier holding me back. I looked at Annie and wondered if it was her disappointment, sadness and subsequent loneliness that had simply lowered her own barriers and made her willing to explore so much more and I was simply a convenient escape.

After so many years together in both school and life I believe we were both feeling safe, and confident in each other's loyalty and reliability. I also knew, with all my heart, that the dedication, compromise, and willingness to grow together was there. The only barrier I could see was allowing both of us to maintain our personal identities while supporting each other's growth.

I was lonely. I was scared and disappointed with how my dreams had turned into nightmares. My wish was for liberation. My fear was that my loneliness and nightmares were making me vulnerable to things I really didn't want to happen.

It was then I made a silent vow not to let the physical aspect affect my emotional aspect and vice versa. I had my standards. I had my limits. I had what I thought were my breaking points and yet I looked at my mother and realized her standards, limits and breaking points were much wider than mine and she seemed in control.

I quickly changed the subject and asked, "Can you believe it'll be ten years next month that we began rooming together? Ten years! Because of you, I've been able to create another wonderful chapter in the dossier of memories of my best friend, whom I truly love like a sister. Without you, I'd be singular and, after tolerating five years of nightmares, there's no way I could ever do that again."

Annie seemed appeased and relieved as she proclaimed, "This vacation has been wonderful and I really don't know how to thank you."

I smiled and replied. "I'm the one who should be thanking you. If you weren't here, I'd have been here alone, feeling sorry for myself existing in a world of sequestered propriety, limited not by what I truly wanted, but what I sincerely believed I had to do simply to sustain the expectations of my family and the company. Instead, I've had a wonderful time with incredible memories that simply reinforce why I love it here and don't want to leave. There were things we did, I'd never have done and I thank you for that."

"Why don't you stay?" Annie inquired.

"I need to move on with my life." I replied. "I can't be 'free' forever." I thought of the story dad told me about when mom was here recovering and had a friend by the name of Sydney from Paris. Dad said he'd met Sydney when he and mom came to meet Uncle Rodney and Aunt Ann and she was young and vivacious. Mom and dad saw her again a few years later where too much sun, too much booze and too much of everything else had withered her body, mind and soul and made her sad. This place is somewhere to visit and not escape to, as it would be too easy to simply forget reality and end up like so many of the locals who have bad cases of Island Fever.

"Do you know what you want to do?" Annie asked.

"I need to figure that out, especially how to use all the years of education and not consider them a waste. I've dreamt a million dreams that have all been erased. We all change and with those changes, yesterday's dreams can certainly turn to nightmares. The last five years have taught me a lot. Most of all, I now know that my spirit can live on even if my physical form is gone, if I can find a way to not only make myself, but other's happy. This is where I truly envy you. You know what you want and already have someone to help you get there and I would simply love to have that."

"But, it's not that easy!" Annie retorted. "I have goals, but there are days when they seem so far out of reach. I don't know if my dreams will ever come true."

I paused for a moment and continued on. "Annie, you'll make it. I know you will. As for me, not many people have the luxury I've been given to make a major mistake and do so with little consequence. Instead, for others, the path they've chosen becomes a virtual tunnel that sequesters their dreams and confines them forever. Now that I've seen that not all dreams come true, I hope and pray I can find out who I am, where I belong and how to simply be happy. I know in the bottom of my heart, your dreams are all going to come true, you're too good, too kind, too generous and too talented, not to have it happen."

Annie almost blushed and countered. "You love kids and have an incredible medical mind. Perhaps you could go to work for your family's foundation or become a teacher."

"I don't know what I'd do at the foundation and I really don't want to be kowtowed simply because of who I am."

"Why not give it a try and see if it's for you? If not, find something else."

It made sense, but the last thing I wanted was another false start, as I inquired, "How about you?"

"What do you mean?" "Teaching? Performing? Teddy?"

Annie looked at me and replied, "I need the income from teaching and I'm trying to save enough money to have my album produced. Teddy is Teddy. We love each other and yet he's always gone."

"How much would it cost to produce your album?" I inquired. "Basically, around $10,000 for finishing and all the stuff you need to do on social media to launch it."

I simply shrugged and shook my head. Until my birthday, $10,000 seemed like a lot of money. Now it was simply pocket change. "Tell you what, I'll loan you the money and you can pay it back from the royalties you earn."

"I can't do that." "Why not?"

"That's a lot of money!"

"Annie, I'm on an allowance for the rest of my life and within reason, can literally have as much as I want whenever I want it."

"Really?" Annie responded incredulously.

"My endowment is substantial and if that's all it's going to take to get you started, there's no problem."

"What happens if the album fails?" "Then it fails."

"How would I ever pay you back?"

I could sense her concerns and replied, "OK, let's do it this way. I become your partner and invest the $10,000 in the album and let's say I get 10% of the net profits."

"Are you sure?"

"As sure as I am that you're my best friend", I replied.

I paused and wanted to justify my offer. "This whole vacation has been incredible. You've shown me a side I never knew I had and made me laugh more in few days than I have in years." I took a deep breath and reiterated what I had proclaimed on Happy Beach, "I love you and always will."

Annie's hand slid across the table and touched mine again as a gesture of gratitude. Instead of words, the loquacious Annie chose a simple touch and looked in my eyes to mutually express the same thing - we were together and would be forever, simply soul mates who knew, understood and appreciated each other – Yin and Yang, Extrovert and Introvert, Expressive and Reserved, who let her best friend tag along, doing things that otherwise would have never happened.

In retrospect, this was an expression of love and friendship, of acceptance and understanding, that I truly felt as my hand willingly, almost urgently, met Annie's as her total existence flowed through my soul.

Syzygy:

I closed my eyes for an instant to relish the glory of friendship only to awaken to the reality of the server bringing our check. It was late and we'd kept the restaurant open long after the other guests had departed. I felt sorry for the staff. We'd overstayed our welcome and so I called the server back and slipped a hundred Euro note in his hand. On our way out, I repeated the overture to both the owner and the dishwasher as my way of saying 'We're sorry'.

"Will you be going to watch the lunar eclipse?" the server inquired.

I had no idea there was going to be a lunar eclipse as the server added. "Tonight's going to be very special in that the sky has little moisture and the syzygy is in place. It's been over twenty years since we've had all the pieces align."

"What time will it begin?"

"A little after midnight. I can put a cork in your wine bottle so you can have a little wine if you'd like to go and watch the eclipse."

I glanced at Annie as she nodded and then at my watch and it was nearly eleven. Long past the time when those of us 'just visiting' would have called it a night on the sleepy side of the island. I looked up at the sky and realized that, for a summer's night, the sky was almost as clear as it is during the winter months. Dad once told me the reason for the winter clarity was that the upper atmosphere's cold air can't hold as much moisture and so having crystal clear nights in the summer were quite rare.

You really couldn't enjoy the stars or the eclipse from The House-On-the-Hill because of all the lights below and light pollution everywhere else on the island. While few people would have even noticed the difference, I knew that if we wanted to really experience the eclipse, we either needed to go out in a boat or find some really dark place.

I looked at Amy and said, "I have an idea." "What?"

"Instead of going back to the house, if we go to the beach, we can look up at the stars that are normally washed out by all the lights. The sparkles will only last a couple of hours before the moon rises and they'll be gone. Then we can watch the eclipse, if you want to."

"Is it nearby?" Annie inquired. "It's really close."

Annie added, "We can look at the stars. watch the eclipse and hear the waves as well – neat!"

"Annie, you get so much out of so little. So much joy! So much pleasure! So much fun! That's what I love about you. I mean, look at tonight, we're here and going to simply look at the stars. How many people ever do that anymore?"

We got in the Rover and drove the few blocks towards the condos at Mont Vernon and pulled into their grass residential parking lot by the tennis courts.

Slipping out of our sandals, we walked around Etang Chevrise, the small estuary that filled with sea water from high tide and some grass-covered sand dunes I thought would block the light and let us enjoy God's majesty and reached the beach. I looked left at the rocks where the turn-around was for the morning walkers as we began the slow trek south towards the bend. As we were walking, I pointed out Polaris or the North Star, then Sirius and added that it was also known as the Dog Star, because it's the brightest star in Canis Major or the 'Big Dog'. Then I pointed to Betelgeuse and Annie laughed when I told her it was pronounced 'Beetle-juice' just like the movie and is also known as Alpha Orionis, as one of the most luminous stars in the night sky.

Annie was having trouble following all my verbal directions and so I stood behind her and took her right hand and pointed to Alpha Centauri and informed her that it's the brightest star in the southern constellation of Centaurus and the third brightest star in the night sky, while noting that it was also the closest system to Earth at just a shade over four light-years away. I then added, "Much like Sirius and Polaris, it's actually a multi-star system, consisting of Alpha Centauri A, B, and Proxima Centauri."

Even with the ocean breeze, I could smell Annie's perfume as my left hand went around her waist and my head slid in next to her right cheek until my body was pressed against her back.

"How do you know so much about the stars?" Annie inquired.

"From my dad. He and mom went into space and he fell in love with its majesty."

"Your mom and dad went into space?" Annie inquired incredulously.

"Yup, dad gave the trip to mom as a special Christmas present and it changed his life. That's when he stopped working for Grandpa and started the Foundation."

"Wow!" Annie exclaimed.

Still behind her, I put my chin on her shoulder, took her hand and pointed to a bright white spec just above the horizon indicating it was probably Venus. Annie looked down at the gently lapping waves and then laconically quoted an interposed version of the title of John Gray's book *"Women are from Venus and Men are from Mars"* which my clinical psychology classes taught me was a definite misnomer.

I closed my eyes for an instant as if what I was about to say was imprinted on the inside of my lids and responded. "As for Venus and Mars, it's really a misnomer. Men and women are actually a lot alike. My clinical psychology tests indicated that the vast majority of psychological traits, including the fear of success, mate selection and empathy all validated that men and women are definitely from the same planet."

The spell broke and we started walking again as I added, "Clinical tests have shown that, instead of response scores clustering at either end of the spectrum that would mean men and women are opposites, as is the case with things such as average height or physical strength, psychological indicators actually fall along a linear path for both genders instead of the absolutes the title infers. The scores do so to the point that both sexes are pretty much the same. It's not so much gender, but human character that causes difficulties in couples where character represents your personality, especially how reliable and honest you are."

I was done with both the celestial and sociological dissertations and realized I'd taken an emotional allegory on Annie's part and reconstructed it into an analytical perspective and not the treatise she'd intended.

Once again it was Yin and Yang reflecting how we were obviously opposite yet complementary, interconnected and interdependent of one another, that provided strength, freedom and joy for me and a sense of reservation and limitation for Annie.

We were almost to KaKao where the light pollution from the restaurants quickly was dissipating our starlight theater and I suggested we turn around.

Annie inquired. "This is where you can walk naked in the morning, right?"

I affirmed her deduction, as she asked, "What time does it begin?"

"What?"

"What time can you walk naked?"

The thought never crossed my mind as I replied, "I don't know," simply shaking my head, realizing only Annie would come up with a question like that and do so to the point that it made me ponder what time it really was?

We stopped for a minute as Annie walked to where the placid waves were lapping over her bare feet, raised her arms to the ocean and let the breeze caress her body.

"Come on Melia, this is GREAT!" She announced.

I paused as Annie came back. I had no inclination to follow her, was full of trepidation and simply couldn't see myself participating. However, my inner-self asked why? Why not join Annie and see what it's like?

I smiled and was about to take that first step when Annie took off her clothes as I simply looked at her in total disbelief. Club Orient was one thing simply because there's safety in numbers. Alone? No way! Not for me anyway as I waded in. Sure enough, Annie was right! It felt really good as she suggested, "Melia, let's go out a little deeper."

I stood for a moment, reconciled my reluctance and joined Annie as I became somewhat liberated physically, mentally and emotionally and was finally able to experience what mom had talked about, which I boiled down to one word - freedom! Freedom from limitation! Freedom from condemnation! Freedom to simply enjoy the beauty of being myself without the fear of judgement from others. In other words, I finally let go.

Annie and I silently stood for what seemed like an eternity with the gentle waves lapping at our thighs and the breeze caressing our bodies as the upper edge of a supermoon broke the water's horizon and gradually dominated our attention. Gone were the stars, washed out by the prevalence of the moon as it cast its glow upon the waves.

I knew about "moon illusion", where the moon appears larger than it really is simply by what it's being compared to and realized that it can also happen to so many other things in life that seem bigger than they really are because we compare them to something so much smaller. I closed my eyes for a moment and introspectively accepted that many of my problems and challenges had been the same. I'd simply taken them out of context and therefore altered their perspective and made them paramount, when in fact, they shouldn't have been.

As we stood watching the glistening waves, the moon began to darken as the syzygy when the sun, earth and full moon align in a near-perfect line of which tonight, the Caribbean was the glorious epicenter.

With mouths agape, Annie and I stood in total silence watching the moon slowly slide into Earth's shadow until the lunar dusk upon the bay progressed from a silver-gray shimmer to an eerie shade of orange, before beginning its trek back to normalcy.

For over an hour we stood spellbound engrossed in this almost religious spectacle until the light of the moon began to intensify again and the fascination was broken.

I looked at Annie and she at me and then it happened. Annie's and I turned such that we were facing each other at which point a gentle kiss evolved into making out and I knew I wouldn't – make that couldn't stop. It had been so long and it felt so good. My God, what was I doing?

Our hands journeyed up and down each other's bodies. Our lips pressed against each other and then my tongue slid within Annie's mouth. My lips found the side of her neck as I kissed below her ear and then slipped her earlobe into my mouth.

Any reservation was gone. I no longer cared as my primal urges usurped any and all social constraints while the tactile pleasures simply over-rode any reticence. I looked down as Annie looked up and we kissed a long, deep kiss.

I stood engrossed in pleasure as Annie's tongue entered my mouth as she was slowly, ever so slowly, taking me up, up, up the ladder of pleasure.

With each caress my breaths became shorter and shorter until they were staccato rasps. No longer was I standing in the ocean with waves lapping at my knees. My mind had transcended to the land of bliss where all that mattered was the next touch, the next stroke, the next quiver until all I could do was moan and whisper, "yes, yes, yes."

"Ohhh!" I expressed as Annie stood smiling while never ceasing to look directly into my eyes. This was her way of expressing contentment that lasted for at least one-hundred heartbeats until we both closed our eyes as our lips met again and the flavor of joy permeated my soul.

As tranquility made its way back into my body, a sense of serenity entered our domain and a different expression covered Annie's face. Was it one of conquest? One of pleasure? Perhaps one of satisfaction as we stood with the gentle waves in cadence with our heartbeats until the eventual postpartum pervaded our bodies.

As my breathing began to slow, I looked at my dear friend and simply whispered..."thank you."

"Any time. Anywhere. Any way." Annie whispered making me wonder what she meant, while reticent to ask.

The eclipse was over and, after what seemed like an eternity, all the primal intensity waned until we knew it was time to go back from whence we came as we began walking hand-in-hand. Two girls! Two friends, who trusted each other, respected each other and valued each other – Yin and Yang - who solemnly knew their bond would now be forever intersected by an instance of intimacy, amplified by emotion and sealed in a moment that would last endlessly.

We reached the rocky outcrop that represented the turning point in so many junctures, stopped, stood and listened to the waves. Looking out at the again-glistening moonlit water as it ricocheted off Little Key, ilet Pinel and both of us, I looked at Annie and she at me and once again we hugged - not as a corporeal interaction, but an evocation of our trust, belief and respect for each other.

Perhaps it was the evocation that changed the mood as the sensuous moment passed and we both realized we'd ventured far enough on our journey. Instead, we quietly made our way back to the Rover and stopped. What had been a somewhat intense adventure had reached its conclusion as the old Annie reappeared and looked at me with a devilish grin on her face.

"What?" I inquired.

"I dare you to drive back to the house naked!" "What?" I asked incredulously.

"Bet you've never done that before, have you?" "No!"

"Chicken?"

"And you have?" I inquired somewhat incredulous.

"Teddy and I used to drive from Oshkosh to Beaver Dam that way."

"What?" I exclaimed in total disbelief.

"Sure, we'd be going to his parent's farm and we'd do it and then, when we got there, well, I'd give him a...well you know." Annie replied somewhat reluctant to continue the expose.

"You mean...?"

"Uh huh! Right there in the truck."

"In his parent driveway?"

"Yup!"

I didn't know what to think. It was three o'clock in the morning and my best friend wanted me to drive the Rover back to the house unclothed. I knew she was crazy, but NOT this nuts.

"Well?" Annie pondered.

"I don't know." I reluctantly responded quite concerned about legality.

Annie looked at me and noted. "If we're riding in the Rover, which has legally tinted windows, don't expose us ourselves to the public and follow all traffic laws we really aren't do anything wrong, are we?"

Annie simply opened the passenger door, tossed her clothes on the back seat and slid in.

With the door open and the Rover's melodious "bong" tone ringing Annie challenged, "Well?"

Reticence slapped me across the face as I simply couldn't do it and then realized I no longer cared. Following suit, I simply got undressed and tossed my clothes in back as well and began driving.

I was completely awake and somewhat anxious to not only be naked, but having a naked woman sitting next to me. Annie softly giggled and closed her eyes before we made it to Cul de Sac as the pale green lights of the Rover's dash illuminated her now-still body providing a celestial appearance as if perhaps, she really was from Venus or was that Mars?

My glimpse ventured across at my slumbering friend and glanced at her body. As I drove, I took it upon myself to memorize her peaks and valleys. I gazed at her legs and then her thighs. I glanced at her torso stopping to visually etch the sight in my mind. I browsed her now sanguine face for any sign of emotion and wondered if there would ever be another chance where we would or could, possibly evoke the same passion that had just taken place justifying it by thinking, other than touchy-feely and deep kisses, what had we really done?

Had this been my liberation or was it initiation? I'd crossed the line so many other women had already serendipitously done and justified it by the reality it could be temporal...simply an experience in the game of life. Yet, I was no longer taciturn by what had happened, nor was there any guilt. All the turpitude that permeated my psyche had dissipated and I felt free of the bonds that restrained me.

Annie shifted in her seat, still asleep and unaware of my glances. As I drove my eyes returned to what lie beside me as my heart convinced my mind that it's all right...it's all right...it's all right.

We made it to the Arrêt sign and I obligingly stopped as my eyes quickly drifted below the seat belt while I deliberated if I should reciprocate. Instead of any form of reluctance for my stares, my mind ambled as I pondered what it was like to give instead of get. Would it happen? Could it happen? Did I want it to happen? Would the time ever be right again? Would I really know what to do?

Even in our current 'condition', I took a deep breath and realized, there's something peaceful about the solitude of night when life stands still and empty streets evoke a sense of innocence that blend together to create the intersection of tranquility and serenity. When given the chance, in our otherwise hectic world, serenity can evoke a set of emotions that have long since departed for most Americans simply because we're always in such a hurry to simply get to tomorrow.

I carefully made it past Pappadan's, climbed Hope Hill, placed my finger on the remote so that the gates would open, thought of grandpa and the hidden message of the gates that generated a brief smile and parked the Rover.

"Annie! Annie!" We're home!" I called as my somnolent friend reacted to her brief interlude with peace. Stretching, Annie smiled and nodded as the rush of the humid air from my opened car door stirred her consciousness and she realized where we were.

Casually unhooking her seatbelt, Annie opened her door and headed for the house, gingerly walking barefoot across the crushed rocks to get there. Still somewhat asleep and in a form of detached ambivalence, she looked at me, smiled and simply whispered, "nice" before entering the darkened house, heading for the stairs and going to bed.

I picked up our clothes and followed Annie's footsteps and crawled beneath the covers. I truly believed I wanted to continue but the woman next to me was sound asleep and with sleep, the reference transformed from the present to the past and the reality that perhaps it was to be never again.

Instead, I lay staring at the slowly revolving ceiling fan, while contemplating everything that had transpired from Dr. Oldman, to mom, the butterfly and my sojourn at House-On-The-Hill to lying there, still aroused and wanting more, all the time smiling at all the antics that transpired.

I looked at the darkened walls and wondered what stories they could tell, accepting that it was best to simply leave sleeping dogs lie in the name of familial harmony, where those who came before and those who would come after could write their own sagas of life at House-On-The-Hill.

Recompense:

Sleep never came to me. I glanced at the clock and it was 5:00 AM and I was still wide awake. My thoughts were becoming redundant and I couldn't stand the repetition. Sadly, my mind was playing emotional ping pong with the previous night. Was it guilt? Was it arousal? I didn't know. All I knew is that for the first time i my life, there was a naked woman sleeping next to me. A woman I'd loved but never expected it to get physical.

I quietly got up, put on mom's smock and tiptoed past the still zonked Annie, who lay exposed to my ardent glances as I made my way out of the bedroom and to the Rover as I had decided to take a walk on Orient Beach simply to think things out.

After driving the nearly-deserted N7, I parked behind the stores, slipped out of the smock and stood naked, feeling the warm breeze caress my body. I smiled and thought of mom and her ventures here and then those of a few hours before and simply shook my head, while agreeing with Annie - it felt good, really, really good.

I looked to the east where we'd watched the promenade. I looked at the deserted Perch and thought of all those who probably shouldn't have been there. I looked at Chez and thought of the rum punches and dirty lemonades, laughter and frivolity and simply shook my head and smiled. Finally, I glanced at Lucille's and how she'd provided my independence in an allegorical way, wondering what she would think of me now, 'unencumbered' as mom would say.

I began walking west at water's edge, mentally isolating myself from those who intercepted me when their path and mine crossed while having the same objective - contemplation. A couple here! A woman there! A man passing by, probably making his way towards the distant rocks where Annie and I had been a few hours before.

Deep in thought, I became oblivious to the disjointed

stares as I reflected on our crazy vacation and my transformation while my soul justified that I'd been reticent about so many things for too long and perhaps, I could finally stop judging myself, demeaning myself and questioning myself for words spoken, taunts given, tears shed so long, long ago.

I walked towards the bend, following mom's and my former footsteps, now completely eroded by the sands of time. With each step, my hesitancy diminished and I became more determined to sincerely see and feel what it was like to be free… free of the anxiety I'd endured for so long and free to simply follow what everyone suggested – "Melia, accept yourself for who you are – nothing more - nothing less and simply let go."

I made it to a point where eroded sand allowed for a small ledge between the waves and what many would consider the now-narrow beach. I quietly sat and thought about all that transpired. In six weeks I'd changed, where nothing was greater than what had occurred last night.

In my health education classes, I remembered that studies suggest that women tend to have more sexual fluidity than men, meaning our attractions and desires can change over time. Perhaps this is why I was reluctant and now more open to experimenting. I thought back to college when I was afraid to try anything, yet now realized that female same-sex experiences are often less stigmatized or even encouraged in certain social settings and I just never partook.

With Annie, I became curious. When you're alone and then alone even more and then literally stranded on a desolate social island perhaps, the availability of Annie unleashed my hunger to explore my own sexuality to either better understand myself or see if I sincerely feel attraction beyond what now seemed to be archaic norms.

I readily admit that Yin and Yang allowed me to form deep emotional bonds with Annie where our history together always had Teddy involved. For the first time ever, it was just the two of us that finally allowed me to see beyond their relationship. Perhaps that's why it evolved into the physical attraction, experimentation and culmination that might have happened years ago if it weren't for Annie's and Teddy's dynamics.

While Annie certainly put the two jerks in their place at Le' Taitu, I accept that women face far less social pressure against experimenting to the point that a lot of guys find it to be a turn-on amplified by the media who've made it more sanguine. I look at women's magazines like Harper's Bazaar and Vogue and how they pushed the envelope thereby allowing situations, circumstances and willingness to be more comfortable than in the past. With nearly one-in-five adult American women reporting they've had a same-sex experience perhaps that's a form of justification creating a sense of security and reason for the lack of any sense of remorse by me.

It's no wonder why so many have tried it when most women, including me, are looking for a sensuous experience for both, or make that all parties, simply because it's been my experience where the men I've been with have been too rough and too demanding and their only self-serving goal is penetration.

I don't want to be a receptor! I don't want sex to be a wrestling match! I hate getting pounded while my partner does everything he possibly can simply to get himself off!

When he does finally get **his** satisfaction, I'm not a sperm repository, nor some form of recreational device, and most certainly, I'm not a rag doll and I profoundly detest the word 'screw'. I'm a woman who has thoughts and emotions who wants to feel wanted, needed and gently loved.

The men I've been intimate with have usually been there simply to fuck me as a self-proclaimed symbol of conquest where spreading one's seed was their ultimate objective as was the profound concept of subjugation. My goal with them had always only been to reduce my own sexual, social and emotional tensions brought on by what our young adult society believes other young adults want and I did so simply get it over with.

From my virginity to my accumulated needs that's all sex has ever been. Last night, there was more foreplay, longer extended physical contact and attunement to each other's pleasure that certainly culminated in a more tender and connected experience which was the most appealing aspect of the entire endeavor. Ours lasted four hours and was to the point Annie satisfied me and was happy to do so. Yet, I didn't really satisfy her.

For one who'd always felt so guilty about so many things, last night was not one of them. All that happened did so with no regrets. It happened and finally, I'd truly let go...let go of so many things that held me back.... so many things that had contained me, constrained me and made me less than what I really wanted to be and that was happy...happy with life and, in order to be that, happy with myself.

I sat looking out at the first faded fingers of sunshine and realized I'd always been 'conservative and traditional'. It was then, my mind wandered as to why, all of a sudden, my instincts changed. I realized there could be several reasons of which some are psychological, some social, some cultural, and several personal.

I know the main reason is because I love Annie. Until last night it had always been a sister-type thing and then it changed. What's crazy is I don't think I'm attracted to other women and haven't found that many sexually attractive. However, like so many other women, I've reached a point where I've become 'nonlinear' which seems to mean I want to capture a more dynamic and flexible reality regarding my identity.

I guess the next few months or years will unravel the mystery regarding my attraction, and experiences and what's really weird is the fact it neither bothers or scares me. If I'm gay! So what? If I'm bi, it no longer creates any sense of fear in me. I am, what I am. What I do know is that I no longer want or need to follow the very finite and predictable path that's been in place for my life.

Instead of a straightforward, linear progression and always knowing my orientation or following a single trajectory in relationships, I now realize I'm entering a phase of fluidity, shifts, and evolving understanding my sexuality.

Last night was exciting! Last night was rewarding! The big question now is, was it a one-time fling? Did it represent a change in my inclinations? I don't know, what I do know is that I feel wonderful simply because I now identify differently and am excited to see where it ends.

With Annie, I find myself attracted in unexpected ways that no longer fit neatly into rigid categories of sexual orientation. All the fear, reluctance and trepidation that had been there is gone and to be with her physically, even after just one time, is no longer something that scares me or be uncomfortable with. To make love with her seems exciting and my only hope is that it's rewarding for her as well.

My biggest concern is how do I test the waters. Sure Annie's totally ambivalent regarding her body, she's always been that way. Perhaps last night was an anomaly.. simply one night she now thinks we went too far.

If she wants to proceed, I believe I do too. I'm just afraid to find out whether the feeling is mutual. I don't want to create a situation where something I took one way jeopardizes our love for each other. I mean she's married. I guess If I'm bold enough, I can approach the situation with subtlety, respect, and clear communication.

Having known her for ten years, I pretty much can answer most open-ended questions about her relationships, past experiences and thoughts on attraction. If I want to send the right message how do I start? Do I maintain prolonged eye contact and lean in when we're talking? Do I find reasons to touch her with a lingering hug or a light touch on the arm or hand to see how she reacts?

With the way she dresses I think I can communicate in a slightly more intimate tone by complimenting her. I mean she really does look sexy in OMG and I guess I should have told her that. If Annie seems comfortable and there's chemistry, I guess I could consider being more open. However, if she seems unsure or uninterested, I need to respect that to maintain our friendship. If she's receptive but hesitant, she might need time to process— After being so constrained for so many years, I know I need to go at a pace that feels comfortable for both of us.

My God what a transcendence. I never thought I'd be physically involved with a woman. More important, I never thought I wanted to. Yet here I am, sitting, trying to rationalize why, why is it that Annie satisfied me in a way I'd never been satisfied before?

My contemplation was over. I felt I could continue with Annie knowing that it was a physical thing as she has Teddy and I'd simply be a sexual surrogate until his return. I stood, wiped the sand from my butt and looked out at the ocean. It was then that the very tip of the sun traversed the horizon to which I turned, paused, smiled and repeated what mom recited every morning - "A new day. A new time. A new beginning".

Perhaps it was the sun. Perhaps my conclusions. All I knew was that the urge to continue walking was simply no longer there. It wasn't exhaustion, nor trepidation, but relief. I no longer needed to go any further and the restraint within my soul dissipated like the darkness of night that encircled me. Instead, I turned and headed back - back to the Rover - back to Annie - back to my life and the road ahead that would take me down a path I prayed would lead to a happy destination.

I began walking, oblivious to the stares as I pondered the next step. I concluded that Annie and I had emotional intimacy as a foundation for a physical connection. We've had ten years of communication, trust and bonding. If we continue, I realize that touching, kissing and caressing will be essential and perhaps adding some sensory experiences like massage, cuddling and skin-to-skin contact that had always been off limits on my side, suddenly became appealing.

Since both of us have a deep understanding of what feels good, I believe we could be very attentive to each other's needs. For me, oral plays a big part of both giving and getting and then we'd have our fingers and hands. I'd like to try tribadism and incorporating toys into our love-making. Knowing Annie, I'm certain she'd like to watch and perhaps get involved in a little dominance and submission, BDSM, or role-playing.

Since every person has different preferences, I accept that open communication is essential while talking about desires, boundaries, and comfort levels that will ensure both of us have a satisfying and respectful experience. I know that none of the subjects were ever discussed with the men I crawled in bed with. If Annie and I continue, my goal would be to expand upon what she and I could do to and with each other.

My mind cleared as I reached the Rover, paused and thought of my reflections, confident I was making the right decision as I slipped back into mom's smock before asking myself, "why am I thinking this way?"

Getting in, I paused to give a longing look to the beach where so much had happened, started the Rover and began making my way down the backside of the beach. At the opening, I turned and simply drove past Good Morning and where I'd picked up Annie the night before. Heading west on N7, I drove up Hope Hill and quietly parked the Rover and simply walked into the house to find Annie quietly preparing to go home to the reality of an empty apartment, an empty marriage and empty life, measured in minutes and not years that she and every other woman never dreams about.

Annie smiled and casually said 'good morning' as I went out to the pool, disrobed and simply jumped in to wash the sand, salt and thoughts off of me. Annie slipped out of her ever-present t-shirt and joined me as we spent time luxuriating in our memories as long as possible. There was no talk of, nor response to what had transpired. It had been an experience to simply store in our individual memory drawers to be pulled out some day, some way when we thought of our time on Saint Martin.

"I'll get breakfast" Annie offered as we simply both got out of the pool, Annie into the house and me to allow the sun's rays to caress my body as its early intensity began to take the last remnants of the pool to escape into the air.

It was time to send my first message by simply drying off and placing the towel on the chaise. Totally naked, I looked to the east as my head tilted back encasing my body and soul in one last sensory bliss. While waiting for Annie to reappear, I made one last pass around the edge of the patio to ensure all the anomalies of our attendance had been eradicated and things were back the way they were when I arrived.

As I neared the sliders, I saw a reflection of myself, paused and looked at the naked person staring back and examined all the things I'd previously thought were wrong. It was then I realized that, like my butterfly, there had been a metamorphous where all my self-proclaimed shames had simply dissipated and I was accepting me as me. I paused and thought of mom and all she'd pontificated and finally agreed... you can't love someone else until you love yourself.

Annie must have looked out at me and never put on her shirt as she came out on the deck with the breakfast dishes and joined me. Quietly, we both sat exposed in an almost quirky fashion, unfettered by anything and everything, consuming the last of the orange juice and Frosted Flakes. I looked at Annie and she at me with both silently realizing this was the end of a grand vacation filled with love, laughter, libation and liberation.

Annie broke the silence. "This has been wonderful. I don't

know how I can ever thank you."

I looked at my dear friend and replied. "Annie, you've done that every single day simply by being you. I've laughed more, giggled more and had more fun than I've had since God knows when."

"Any regrets on the tattoo? Annie inquired.

I looked down at my butterfly and responded "none at all" realizing it symbolized so much more than the catharsis intended.

"How about you?" I inquired as I nodded towards Annie's teddy bear.

"Not really, I just wish I had more than a little ink holding me close."

As breakfast ended, Annie and I stood and hugged once again – a grateful hug of friendship, acceptance and gratitude and then slowly separated as the insistence of time that had been missing for so long reappeared like an all-consuming fuse, measuring heartbeats until the serenity would be over and we would return to reality.

As we were about to release each other, my hand slid down lightly brushed Annie's bare butt. Message number two had been sent as I reluctantly watched Annie depart for the kitchen, realizing all that was left were memories of joy and laughter, silly things and crazy things - of smiles and shaken heads interspersed with revelations, regarding all we'd done, as the two of us had simply let go and had fun.

I took a deep breath and slightly winced, realizing the constraints of decorum that had been in place came perilously close to being frozen forever instead of eradicated in the name of freedom. I realized for the first time in my life, I was actually willing to see if there could be more than ever before.

I stared at the pristine horizon, sighed, picked up the smock, folded the towel and slipped both of them over the back of the chaise, knowing the cleaning lady would arrive soon after we left, wash them, fold them and put them away, removing any stories they might tell

My God had I transformed! In a few weeks I'd gone from one sequestered in their own sense of inadequacy, ashamed, afraid, and incredibly modest, drowning in a sea of self-doubt to one who'd finally broken loose, no longer feeling inadequate, who'd simply let go of so many demons, so many reservations and so many self- doubts to the point I was finally happy...happy with me.

My contemplation was interrupted as my watch vibrated with a text from Wilco Ops indicating that Amelia^X would arrive around two and the pilots needed to depart as soon as possible due to potential storms over Texas. I was tempted to press the security button twice to thank whomever was 'on duty' for pissing me off and making me go beyond where I'd ever been before, but thought it would simply be too much.

Annie appeared on the other side of the glass and smiled. She was dressed and her suitcase was by the door. Opening the sliders, Annie looked at me and simply shook her head before noting. "When I arrived, there was this girl I knew who was so shy, so reserved and so...uh...inhibited and I didn't know how things would be. Instead, that girl has simply let go and stands before me a proud, positive, and confident woman."

I smiled a satisfied smile, walked into the house, slid the slider closed and stopped for a moment to simply look at Annie before sincerely saying "thank you...just for being you. You are and will always be my best friend."

Uncle Frank had been copied and responded he'd be at the house at 12:30. I checked my watch and it was nearly noon and so I reluctantly got dressed while putting my new "island" clothes in my assigned dresser, wondering if I'd ever be bold enough to wear them again while hoping someone, somewhere, someday could take my dreams of being a princess and turn them into reality.

Precisely at 12:30 Uncle Frank appeared a we secured H-O-H and departed for Princess Juliana. The jet was waiting and, after both of us giving Uncle Frank big hugs, we boarded, took our seats and took off. Looking down at the island below I quietly thanked mom and dad and then God as I knew I was returning home a different person than the one who'd arrived.

All went as planned regarding Amelia[X] as Annie and I both caught twenty winks, arriving in Milwaukee and going through the obligatory customs.

We transferred to the waiting limo. Stopping in Pewaukee, Annie kissed me on both cheeks as if we were still in St. Martin and thanked me for the wonderful time.

I smiled and whispered "thank you" and then initiated an extended kiss upon her lips while inviting, "we need to do this again".

An hour later I received a text…
"Home safe and sound.
Plants were glad to see me.
Anytime, Anywhere Any way! ☺

Love and kisses!"

XOXOX

Annie

Dubai To Buy:

Before we left for St. Martin, I'd agreed I needed to clean out the Milwaukee apartment, but didn't have the gumption to go near the place. It reminded me of death, where everything was frozen in place and time stood still, unable to move on and have closure that meant doing something, anything, regarding tomorrow. Mom asked if I was up to it and I told her, "No". Instead, she had some Wilco people go there and sort things out.

The extent of my furniture was a desk in the living room and my bed. I never had time for dishes and always used plastic cups and paper plates for the few times I ate there.

Mom asked about 'personal' items and there were none, a few clothes, toothpaste, deodorant and my laptop. I told mom to give the furniture to Goodwill and send the rest to Pine Lake. You finally realize how little substance your life has when the moving team drops off two of those cardboard boxes they use for office files representing five years of existence. I was floored, flabbergasted and embarrassed by what little I had.

I was happy to be home as I unpacked from St. Martin and took a few more minutes to put my Milwaukee things away as the absolute silence of nothing roiled within my soul. I already missed St. Martin and the fun we'd had. Dad could sense my sadness and asked, "What are your plans for next week."

I just shrugged my shoulders. "Nothing! No one! Nowhere!" "I have a business trip planned to Dubai, do you want to come with me?"

"Dubai?" I asked incredulously.

"Yes. I'm trying to set up a Middle East distributor for our Terrill branded products."

"In Dubai?" I said incredulously.

"Melia, the world has changed and Dubai is now where

East meets West. We've marketed the Terrill brand as ultra-premium products and that means going where people not only have money, but are willing to spend it. American dining habits have changed. People still go out to eat. However, what they eat and the service they receive has been degraded to formula restaurants with formula food and formula service, all devoured in noisy atmospheres that make entire meals nothing more than feeding fodder where the underlying formula includes table turns – how many times you can fill a table each day. The market is packed with goods that appeal to the American masses and so we decided to only offer our products in restaurants that offer fine dining in business or political centers of major cities, where people with expense accounts are eating and drinking what we offer."

"When would we go?" I inquired.

"I'm scheduled to leave on Monday and be home Sunday."

It was Thursday and that meant four days at home with nothing to do. "Dubai?" I had visions of camels and palm trees, where we sat in tents and ate dates. "OK".

Mom came home from work and we sat down for dinner. I broached the subject about Dubai as she noted, "Fantastic place to shop." My surprised look said it all as mom continued by justifying her statement. "Those with money have found Dubai to be an oasis of culture and sophistication. "

"It's been a long time since I bought any new clothes and so I asked, "How do I begin?"

Mom looked at me and offered her opinion. "You need three types of clothes - sport, casual and dress, all accessorized with purses, shoes and jewelry and the right make-up to do it right, and for that you need a fashion consultant."

I didn't even know people like that existed as mom continued, "While the best consultants are in New York and

Paris for trendy clothes, the real epicenter for upscale traditional fashion today, truly is Dubai."

I smiled and actually had a look of excitement about me as Dad looked at mom and mom looked at dad and they both said in unison, "Cecelia". Even though she'd retired and lived in Phoenix, she was still helping dad out on things just like this.

"Should I call her?" Dad inquired, to which I nodded in the affirmative. Cecelia had been dad's administrative assistant and closest business friend since before I was born and someone I loved.

Dad went into his office and made the call and returned about fifteen minutes later with a smile on his face and simply said, "All set, depart Monday and return Sunday."

Cecilia sent a text outlining our itinerary, "Flight time is thirteen hours and twenty-five minutes and there's a nine-hour time differential so you are scheduled to depart Monday night from Chicago at 8:45 PM and arrive at 7:10 PM Tuesday Dubai time. I've scheduled Wednesday, Thursday and Friday for business and Saturday for sightseeing because it's a holy day and everything is closed"

I just shook my head as dad continued, "We could take Amelia^X, however at 7250 nautical miles, it's just beyond her range and the refuel time and crew change would result in it taking longer than flying commercial." Knowing dad, I knew it would all be first class. Also knowing dad, there was no reason to challenge safety and security. He had his rules.

Monday arrived and I packed a bag consisting of what few clothes I thought were proper for the desert as the chopper took us to the O'Hare helipad. A courtesy van was waiting to take us to the international terminal, where we were escorted to a private room, had our passports collected and Dubai immigration papers processed.

A few minutes later another couple entered and I knew we had company for the trip compliments of Wilco security. "This is Robert and Marsha Williams," dad announced.

Whenever we had a security detail with us, they always used Williams as a last name.

We remained shielded in the faux luxury of the waiting room until the airline terminal manager came in to personally welcome us. Dad introduced me as his daughter and the Williams' as his and my administrative assistants. The Williams' had been briefed about the trip objectives and their roles and responsibilities. As was always the case, Cecelia had everything segmented into day parts, contacts and objectives, printed and categorically organized in binders.

I checked my Apple watch and fifteen minutes prior to push- back the manager returned and escorted us to the plane. All the other passengers had settled in and I'm certain the one man in first class was a little dismayed to realize he wasn't going to be "the star of the show" on his flight to Dubai.

The terminal manager took the steward aside for a discrete conversation to go over the fact that the Terrill Private Stock, 150 proof bourbon and Terrill Reserve Pino Noir, were reserved for dad and me unless we offered it to other passengers as the bourbon was placed in the first-class bar and two bottles of Pinot Noir in the refrigerator. Cecelia had thought of everything.

Just before take-off, a steward came on board with four narrow leather suitcases. The first was brown with gold trim that said 'Terrill Premium' embossed on the side. The second was black with the words 'Terrill Private Stock'. The third was cranberry color with the words 'Terrill Reserve Pinot Noir'. The fourth was navy blue and stamped 'Terrill Wagyu', with all of them carefully placed in a small closet for safe keeping.

I looked at dad and my frown must have communicated my wonder as he said "Insurance in case the samples we sent from the farm didn't make it."

With an evening departure, it wasn't long until I was yawning. The flight attendant inquired if I was ready to retire to my suite that had a full-size bed long enough even for me. I noted I would like a little more wine to complete my meal that had consisted of a chilled crab salad, cooked carrots and filet of beef, along with a small piece of coconut layer cake that Cecelia had arranged for me.

It had been a long time since I'd flown commercial and this was really beyond expectation. I finished my wine and said goodnight and slept a good six hours and was then offered the opportunity to take a shower. Can you say 'spoiled'?

As we landed, we were told to remain in our seats as the other passengers were herded off. When the plane was empty, a Dubai government representative came aboard to welcome us and asked us to follow him as we went somewhere within the terminal to a waiting white Rolls Royce that was parked inside so that we wouldn't need to go out in the heat and humidity.

Even though it was Tuesday night, everywhere I looked there were construction cranes building more and more, higher and higher. The building in front of us looked like a ship's sail and I learned it was the Burj Al Arab hotel which means 'Tower of the Arabs', where we were staying. My God, the hotel looked spectacular!

I found out Burj Al Arab was built on a manmade island 500 yards off Jumeirah Beach and is reportedly the fourth tallest hotel in the world measuring 28 stories and over 1000 feet in height. The hotel opened in 1999 and remains one of the world's only 7- star hotels. We walked inside and my breath was taken away by the 600-foot-tall atrium with dancing fountains and touches of gold leaf everywhere and could quickly see why it had the reputation it had.

The hotel is 'off-limits' to anyone but guests staying in one of the 202 suites. While dad always wanted the best, the Royal Suite was already booked, so dad had to settle for 'just' two deluxe suites on the floor below.

"Do you need to freshen up?" Dad asked.

I'd slept well, had a shower and was in clean clothes. "I'm

fine," I replied. "How about you?"

"I'm fine," he replied as he too had taken a shower and was used to long trips and immediate action as dad nodded to the security team and our luggage was taken to our suites.

Dad offered, "We've got two suites. One for buying and one for selling."

Dad asked me if I wanted dinner and whether I preferred, Al Muntaha, which is Arabic for 'Ultimate' or 'Highest' that offered views of Dubai at 650 feet above the Persian Gulf accessed by a panoramic elevator or Al Mahara, which means 'Oyster' that features a large saltwater aquarium and an entry via a unique simulated submarine ride.

I chose Al Muntaha for the view and found the food to be incredible to the point it almost made St. Martin seem somewhat pedestrian. I'd learned a long time ago that the difference between eating and dining was the time it took. When you dine, you know it's going to be a full evening affair and it certainly was. By the time dad and I finished, it was after midnight Dubai time. When we went to our suites and I was surprised to find what looked like an oversized telephone booth in the middle of my living room, with a note indicating the tailors would arrive at 9:00 AM.

I didn't sleep well, as it hadn't been that long and going east always created jet lag. As I lay there, the time in St. Martin floated through my mind and I wondered what it all meant. Had I really changed or was it simply a reaction to Annie's free-spirited attitude?

I was up early and Dad and I had breakfast in his suite. Precisely at nine, the entourage arrived with me expecting tape measures and straight pins, until I quickly realized what the booth was for.

"Ms. Terrill, we need to have you change into this gown, please."

Consisting of a material that appeared to be paper, I went into my dressing area and changed into the gown. I was then instructed to put on a pair of protective goggles, did so and was then led to the booth and told to place my feet on the outlined forms on the floor as the door was closed.

"This will only take a few moments, Ms. Terrill."

Similar to an MRI, I heard the hum as the scan took place. Later, I learned the booth was measuring my entire body in millimeters. No more tapes! No more guessing! All the data downloaded into the tailor's computer. Amazing!

Through the audio system, I was instructed to remove the gown and stand in the same place, making certain the goggles were secure. I did as instructed and sensed a bright flash of light that I learned was a spectroscope, measuring my skin tones. In a matter of minutes, the tailors had all the data they needed. Amazing! Simply amazing!

"That's it?" I inquired.

"We'll need a few minutes to program the computer and then we can begin. Would you like some tea or fresh fruit?" I thanked them and said "no", changed into "civvies" and walked across the hall to dad's suite where he was setting up his display of Terrill bourdon, wine and beef.

A few minutes later, the tailor was ready and one of his assistants came for me. Dad and I returned to my room and the 'telephone booth' was already gone. I was asked to sit on a couch with a huge TV screen in front of me as a white androgynous form appeared. With the press of a button the skin tone changed to match my Cinnamon color, including the somewhat-faded tan lines from St. Martin. There I was, a 3D model, from which the designers could create their clothing.

Waseem, the head designer detailed. "Based on your torso- to-leg aspect ratio and décolletage, we feel your wardrobe should center around jackets that are matched to longer skirts, dresses, knee-length shorts and pants. This will accentuate your overall form without drawing too much attention to your legs."

I nodded yes, as my computer model was garbed in a white blouse, cream-colored jacket and matching trousers. I simply smiled and nodded as dad had one of his big shit-eating grins on his face.

Waseem continued, "From this core, we can develop a full complement of ensembles that not only provide a multitude of options, but address the seasonality where you live".

Needless to say, they were spot on, as Waseem continued. "Based on your skin tone, we will bring different fabrics for you to choose tomorrow. Do you prefer your tanned or basic flesh tone?"

I thought for a moment and responded my basic tone, as the only time I really got tan was in St. Martin.

Waseem continued, "From that we will work on different blouses and tops that will provide even more flexibility, depending on the time of year or event you're attending along with your basic make-up. As for accessories and shoes, your father has indicated that representatives from G.J. Cleverley of Cork Street, Mayfair will be arriving tomorrow from London as a personal favor to him."

Dad loved his custom shoes and actually got mom hooked, as well. While Cleverley's normal focus was on custom shoes for men, dad had convinced them to create the 'Amelia series' consisting of more traditional women's shoes with matching purses and clutches and trust me, they were gorgeous AND obscenely expensive.

Normally, Cleverly representatives came to America and would set up in Chicago for two days for private fittings, by appointment only. Because dad was such an important customer who'd talked so many of his Wisconsin buddies into wearing 'Cleverly's' as he called them, the Monday after Chicago, the representatives would have a one-day private event at the Pfister in Milwaukee on a reservation only basis.

Back in Dubai, Waseem continued. "They'll be arriving tomorrow. We've worked together on numerous occasions and will coordinate just the right combination of style and color to match your ensemble." I thought this was getting crazy. All I wanted was some new jeans, which I learned they were going to provide as well.

By the time they were done, it was almost time for dinner and so we went to some fancy place dad heard about and spent the rest of the evening sightseeing. My God, what an incredible city, built where nothing had been before - clean, safe, well controlled, without being overbearing, where everything wreaked of money. The highlight had to be going to Etihad Towers, which was named after one of the country's airlines and means 'union' in Arabic. At one time, it was the world's tallest building. What was absurd was looking out at the steel skeletons around it that were going to be even taller and the Sky Tower on Al Reem Island and finally *Burj Mohammed bin Rashid* residence which stretches over 1250 feet in the air. I could hardly imagine that the three tallest buildings in the world were literally within walking distance
of each other!

As my visual escapade came to an end, we sat down and the server came and asked if we wanted a drink. Dad inquired "Do you have Terrill Bourbon?"

The server replied, "Yes sir, both the Terrill Reserve and Terrill Private Stock."

"I'll take the Private Stock," dad requested. "One, two or three fingers?" the server inquired.

"Three please." This meant the server would bring the bottle to the table, have dad hold three fingers to the side of the glass and pour to that level.

"For the young lady?"

"Do you have the Terrill Reserve Pinot Noir?" dad inquired. "Yes sir! Would you like that poured at the bar or here at the
table?"

"Here, please."

The server came back with dad's bourbon and my wine in some sort of stainless-steel cannister, flipped a switch on the bottom of the cylinder as I heard the whoosh of air entering the receptacle. Dad noted that the Terrill Reserve Pinot Noir was what he called 'fragile' and more susceptible to 'turning' and losing its vibrant flavor, if left open.

Dad added, "Red wine turns bad because the moment you pull the cork, air begins to mix with the wine regardless of how you re-insert the cork and is actually a form of oxidation where. Too much exposure to oxygen essentially turns wine into vinegar. While drinking old wine won't make you sick, it will likely start to taste 'off' or flat after a few days and ruin all the labor of love that went into creating the wine."

Holding up my glass of wine dad reported "the finer the Pinot Noir, the clearer the wine. When it has turned, you won't be able to see through it and you certainly won't want to taste it. We don't add any preservative and so the MadCity boys developed a special vacuum reservoir that sustains the delicate combination of sweet cranberry, cherry, raspberry, tobacco and clove flavors." Dad has me sniff the wine as he added. "The Terrill winery's Somalia worked hard to retain the fine tannin frame while developing an alluring, silky feel and its loamy, earthy scent."
After the eight bottles Annie and I drank in St. Martin, I was starting to feel guilty and glad they weren't the vacuum style.

The server asked dad, "180 or 270?" referring to the amount of wine in milliliters. Dad said 180 or just over six ounces, American style.

The server poured my wine to the lower line etched on the goblet and closed the reservoir as I listened to the air being evacuated. As he departed, dad added, "Part of the mystique of our products lies in the presentation and the server was spot on," as he raised his glass to mine and said, "Welcome to Dubai!"

We clinked what was fine crystal goblets and took small sips.   "What about the meat?" I inquired.

Dad smiled, "Terrill Wagyu beef is becoming the reference standard for the type of meat it is. Not quite there yet, but nearing that of Kobe beef. While we initially purchased our breeding stock in Montana, we went to Japan and contracted for Kuroge Washu Wagyu stock simply because it's genetically predisposed to the fine-grained intramuscular marbling that gives the meat both its flavor and tenderness. What we do, lies not only in how we raise the cattle, which has to meet certain Kuroge Washu standards, but how we wet-age the meat and then incorporate a vacuum seal method the MadCity boys also developed, that allows the individual cuts to be stored at room temperature for up to one year."

I had no idea the level of thought and technology Uncle Tommie, dad and the Madcity boys had developed as dad continued, "We take each steak and cut it to portion with 16 ounces for T-bones, 22 ounces for Porterhouse and 26 ounces for prime rib. The rest of the meat is made into hamburger and sold in 12-ounce packages. Because the meat is never cold, it never has any degradation of the interaction of the juice to the walls of the cellular structure and therefore, retains even more delicate taste and texture. To really highlight the product, we package each cut or patties in the individual 'beauty boxes' you saw, that are preformed to hold the meat with the date, cut and weight on the outside of the carton. By doing this, the restaurant has a complete overview of their inventory and which pieces need to be used first."

"This all sounds so complex."

"It is, but like everything else in the world, half the value comes in the sizzle and not just the steak and people are willing to pay a premium for what we have to offer. As an example, we take the Terrill Private Stock bourbon, which can't be sold in the US because it's 150 proof, and notify our distributors as to the amount we have for the season and their allocation. They're given 30 days to sell their share place their orders. On the 31st day, we would open up any excess to other distributors. So far, we've never made it to day thirty-one."

"Because the Private Stock Bourbon is so popular, we decided to expand the brand and came out with the Terrill Reserve wine and then bought the winery, where not only is the wine first class, but the presentation is unlike anything in the world and everyone is loving it."

"The Wagyu is the same thing. Sales are based on herd size and allocation. At first, we thought we'd sell it on a bid basis, but quickly learned that restaurants need to know what their costs are and, because of its extended shelf-life, what their allocation will be. Most restaurants have a 'preferred' Wagyu list of customers and notify them when their allotment is coming that sells out in a few weeks. Because demand intentionally exceeds supply, the value and mystique of our products remains high."

"How much does it cost?" I inquired.

Dad leaned in and said "Private Stock bourbon, $30.00 per ounce or $1,000 per bottle wholesale. Reserve and Wagyu $10.00 per ounce."

"You mean one of our T-bone steaks costs $160.00?" I asked incredulously.

"Wholesale and then you double the entre' cost for the beef and triple the cost for the alcohol."

"So, three fingers of Private Stock costs $270 per glass?"

"Normally $300.00 as its charged by the number of fingers you put next to the glass," dad casually replied, as the server returned and asked if there would be anything else. Instead dad offered his credit card and the bill with tip, for one glass of wine and one of Private Stock was $500.00. I almost tried to spit my wine back in the glass and thought of Annie and me sucking it down with Pappadan's.

Dad continued. "We have a very loyal wholesale base that's not only trained on who to sell the product to, but how its properly presented. They work on commission and a bonus plan and so everyone is making money, including us. We held off on Dubai simply because demand exceeded supply by so much. However, with the demise of so many fine restaurants in the United States, we're now opening up what we believe will be our biggest market."

As we were sitting there, another couple had seen the presentation and was intrigued as the server went through the same procedure putting a huge smile on dad's face simply because all the pieces of the puzzle were fitting together right then and there. The server had no idea who he'd served and why we were there, sitting on top of the world!

Simply Heaven:

The following morning, we took a tour of the shopping district that made Chicago's Miracle Mile, New York's Fifth Avenue or even LA's Rodeo Drive seem like Target and I had my first camel ride out in the desert, followed by a visit to Sheikh Zayed Mosque, where I wore the hijab out of respect to the culture and their beliefs. As I was covered from head to foot, I thought of Annie and me in St. Martin and sort of gulped wondering what the folks of Dubai would think if I showed up in our beach garb that Lucille sold us.

We arrived back at the hotel midafternoon as two representatives from Cleverely's were just arriving. The plan was set for the following morning and yet, because grandpa and dad had been loyal customers for so many years, they insisted on taking us to dinner. It was an early and also very expensive meal at the world-famous Zuma, where one bottle of Terrill Reserve Pinot Noir was $2,000 and that was just the wine. I made up for it with Cleverly by ordering twelve pair of shoes and six pair of sandals with matching purses, wallets and attaché cases, where only full grain leather was selected that was guaranteed to be from the same hides to ensure consistency. I know, picky, picky, picky!

Friday morning meant hair and make-up and all the data that had been uploaded from the spectrograph allowed for the creation of a set of specialized bases, lipsticks and eye shadow to compliment my complexion. I guess it meant no more shopping at the Dollar Store for me.

After lunch, it was time for choosing fabrics and accessories. Once again, I was amazed at the detail involved, as materials were matched with my skin tone and makeup along with the type and color of leather. In the end, I chose different apparel 'sets' as they called them and different accessories, to not only allow for applicability to the day, but different levels of sophistication, ranging from casual to formal. I loved the Mongolian cashmere mock turtlenecks and ordered black, charcoal gray, navy, tan and purple and splurged by getting both two and three-ply thicknesses so that I could extend my sweater season to include winter, spring and fall.

The designers wanted to do gowns, but I said no, we didn't wear what they offered and I knew the bill was already sky high. The last thing was jewelry to match the outfits and the shoes. For this, a jeweler came. I immediately said 'no rings,' as I really didn't like wearing them. I was only I interested in earrings, bracelets and necklaces to compliment my wardrobe.

Whew! We were done and I only wondered how and when we'd get my new wardrobe home. The 3-D model and clothes options were put on a thumb drive and I could simply choose which combinations I wanted, thereby making my wardrobe changes that much easier to select.

With Saturday being the holy day, the city was quiet and so dad and I hung out at the hotel, went out on dad's new distributors yacht and had a quiet dinner. I never realized spending money could be so exhausting. I had no idea what my total bill was and offered to pay, but dad said it was on he and mom. I think I would have put it all back had I known the cost.

Sunday meant coming home. There was a knock on my door and a young lady who'd accompanied Waseem came in carrying a garment bag offering, "We thought you might like to wear one of your new outfits home."

I smiled and nodded in the affirmative as she opened the garment bag and retrieved a pair of camel tan slacks and a black silk blouse. I'd already done my makeup and so it was quick change and an incredible transformation. My God what the right clothes can do! Gone was the gangly nothing and for the first time I actually felt proud of my looks. I packed the jeans I was going to wear and called for a bellman. In four days, I'd learned what you did and didn't do in Dubai and one of them was ever carry your own luggage.

The wrap on the door came quickly and, after checking through the security peephole, I opened as the bellman's mouth dropped open. I guess he liked what he saw. We went to the elevator and he pressed the lobby button. The private top floor elevators were swift and when the door opened, those in the lobby simply stopped and stared at me with several men smiling and nodding.

Dad and the 'Williams' were already there and had checked us out. I assumed the goods would be shipped and was surprised to see matching luggage with my new clothes in them. The American consulate had sent a representative who inspected everything. Dad signed the documents and the luggage was taken to a vestibule off the lobby and placed in a small aluminum air freight container where the container door was closed and an international seal put in place. On the outside was a large gold and black sticker with the letters ORD, LIFO meaning 'last in, first out' for the baggage handlers in Chicago. More paperwork was signed, and dad provided a stipend of appreciation and the documents given to the 'Williams'. This meant we'd already cleared US customs. The shoes and purses were coming from England and would take about two weeks. Dad had knuckled under to pressure and ordered three pair of tassel loafers for himself including one pair of alligator and one of some type of lizard and I thought I was becoming a clothes horse!

We made it to the airport and received the same personalized service we had in Chicago with the only difference being the stares of admiration wherever I walked. The Emirates airport manager escorted us to the plane. Once again, there was a bottle of Terrill Private Stock bourbon and two chilled bottles of Terrill Reserve Pinot Noir in the frig. Once again, the purser was instructed about security and protocol. I was realizing what money could do.

It being Sunday, travel was light and we had first class and the bar to ourselves. I asked dad if it was OK to offer the 'Williams' some of the Terrill spirits. Dad said sure, simply because we couldn't take open alcohol off the plane and so two of us drank the wine, while the dad and 'Mr. Williams' sipped on the Terrill bourbon.

We toasted a great trip as I pondered the watch on my wrist with the second button and wondered whether it was a sign of freedom or a shackle that would inhibit and control me the rest of my life. When we'd all settled in, I asked dad if we could have a private conversation. His eyes opened wide in concern and trepidation and I quickly noted I simply needed some advice.

We went back to the empty bar and I began. "Dad, you and mom have done an incredible job balancing work and life and making Derrick, 'V' and I feel special. I look at my brothers in awe. Derrick will run Wilco, you can see it everywhere and 'V' will become a great political leader where your goodness will prevail. The Terrill bourbon, wine and meat will continue to grow and you'll continue to succeed, while both you and the Foundation will always be recognized for earning a Nobel Peace Prize."

Dad nodded in agreement, not knowing where this was going as I continued. "As for me, I simply don't want any of it. I learned my lesson. My dream is to find the right person, settle down and have kids and simply be a mom. While I know in today's world, it isn't thought to be much of a profession, for me it's all I think I really want."

"Melia, being a mother, is a noble profession," Dad countered.

I looked at dad and was a bit reluctant with what I wanted to say and yet, the time was right and so I continued. "Dad, I just want to be average. I don't want all the attention I get every time someone hears my last name. Yes, I love the fine things and wonderful trips and having our own planes, but I also crave anonymity where I don't have to worry about Wilco Security or this or that, simply because of my name."

Dad had a frown on his face and a look of concern as he offered, "But it comes with the territory."

"I know, but I would like to get out of the territory, if possible." "What do you mean?"

"I'd like to change my last name." "What?" dad inquired incredulously.

"I'd like to change my last name so that I wasn't part of such a famous family."

"If you get married, you can do it then," Dad said defensively. "I'd like to do it before then, and, if the day comes I get married, which I hope it does, I'll change it again. I'd also like to have Wilco Security see what they can do to expunge me from all data that people might search that would tie me back to our
name."

I could see that dad was getting upset and so I needed to calm him down. "I totally respect you, mom, Derrick and 'V'. I know the Terrill name brings power and prestige and you've spent your entire life making certain you're not thought of as Mister Amelia Williams. I always want to be a part of the family, but I also want to feel less cloistered than I do right now so that I can go and do and be what I want to be, without worrying about security or tarnishing all that you have created."

I looked at the Apple watch and held up for dad to see. "Is this a timepiece or a shackle where someone, somewhere knows exactly where I'm at and what I'm doing at all time?"

Dad just shrugged as he saw my consternation as I continued. "While, what I'm thinking about probably seems extreme, I'm also thinking of the future and hopefully your grandchildren. If I'm lucky, the name change is going to happen when I get married and the only difference will be that my husband and my kids won't have the challenge of living up to all that is expected with the Terrill heritage every single day. I'm not demeaning the name or its integrity, just concerned about the limitations it puts on living a traditional life, filled with hopes, dreams and aspirations."

Dad was in shock as I continued. "I've looked on line into

the name change process and it's actually quite simple. All I need do is contact Social Security and fill out the appropriate form. After I receive confirmation that the name associated with my Social Security Number has been changed, I would need to complete a court petition to prove residency in Wisconsin and provide my current Social Security card, birth certificate, driver's license and photo identification. Then I'd need to file a signed and notarized Petition for Change of Name with the Waukesha County Court Clerk with my current and proposed names, Social Security number and a signed statement that I'm not a convicted felon or have any outstanding warrants."

"After filing the form, I'd need to attend a hearing where the judge or magistrate might ask questions about my reasons for the name change. If the judge signs off, which they normally do, I'd receive a certified copy of the Order, which I'd present to anyone who needs verification of my new name."

Dad looked at me and simply shook his head and asked. "What happens if you meet some guy, fall in love and get married?"

"The process is a lot easier, but my new husband and hoped for children wouldn't need to worry about all the security and challenges that come from being famous."

There was a long pause as dad was thinking things through and then I continued. "Dad, I love you and am incredibly proud of all that you and mom have accomplished. However, the burden of Grandma Marie at Milwaukee General is what really made me crack and I don't want that to ever happen to my kids. If it means losing my inheritance, that's OK. However, I won't do it if it means losing you, mom or our family. I just want to be free – to let go of all the limitations associated with wealth, power and fame."

Dad shook his head and I knew he wasn't convinced. I was afraid I'd taken a glorious trip and turned it into a downer and so I added. "If you or mom think I'm wrong, then I simply won't do it. If you think it will demean all that you have accomplished, then it stops right now. The reason I'm asking you now is because I love you and don't want to do anything that will hurt you in any way. The most important thing in my life is my family. It's just that I would like to be free of the limitations. I might be naïve. It might be extreme, but it's one option I hope and pray will allow me to the find the true happiness I desire."

Dad looked at me and reiterated, "So you'd like to change your name now so that your future husband and children will have a degree of separation and do so to create a semblance of anonymity?"

"Yes."

"But the name change would actually be transitional? If you get married, you'd only be doing it to protect your future husband and children by breaking the link?"

"Yes."

"Melia, when you first proposed it, I was hurt and dismayed and yet I can see the logic behind it and it actually makes a lot of sense, if your goal is normalcy. I guess, I never realized the cost of fame until I got it. We can't do anything, go anywhere or act in any way that won't be scrutinized by someone in some way, whether it's publicly or even by our own security team. We're going to need to talk this over with your mother, but I see the rationale and don't worry about your inheritance. Grandpa didn't give it to a woman whose last name was Terrill, he gave it to you."

I looked at dad and gave him a hug and whispered. "Dad, I only hope I find a guy as wonderful, generous and special as you!"

The 'aw shucks' tears were in both of our eyes as we simply stood and looked at each other and nodded. We were asked to return to our seats, landed in Chicago and said goodbye to the 'Williams' as dad and I were escorted down the gangway stairs and into a limo that took us to the helipad. Amazingly, less than an hour later we walked in the house to the smiles of mom who was glad to see us.

"Good trip?"

"Amazing! You and I need to go there some day. " The comment put a smile on mom's face.

"Love the outfit," mom offered.

"Thanks. Now I want to get into a pair of shorts and tank top." I didn't use the shower on the plane and so I took a quick one. When I came back into the family room, a Wilco truck was just pulling in the driveway and two guys brought the luggage into
the house.

"Doesn't look like you'll need to go back for a while," Mom commented with a grin.

I took the suitcases into my bedroom, opened them, remembered each ensemble and its applicable season and why I selected it. It's always a good feeling to get something new and this was very satisfying. Mom came in and I detailed what I'd bought and the whole procedure and logic. With so many clothes, my closet quickly filled and mom said I should put anything extra in Derrick's closet as she was certain he wouldn't be living there anymore. I suggested putting the winter clothes in the cedar closet and mom thought that made sense.

We had a small dinner and moved the empty luggage into the storage loft above the garage. I was fading fast when mom reminded me I had a ten o'clock meeting Tuesday at the foundation with Peter and then with Hsu.

"Chopper?" Dad inquired.

"Yes!"

As dad was about to go to his office, I stood and gave him a hug. "Thank you", I whispered.

Dad nodded a bashful affirmation. "I love you, dad."

I think that was all I needed until I said I had a small gift for both he and mom and gave them gold bracelets with both of their initials on one side and Derek, 'V' and my initials on the other.

"You didn't need to," Mom replied, but I knew she appreciated the gesture.

Between the jet lag and quite honestly forgetting about the meeting with Peter and Hsu regarding medical research, I was feeling a bit flustered. It had been six weeks since my meltdown and I'd recovered in many ways, but not all. Guilt still pervaded my own belief that I'd failed and the image of the little girl and dolly had become part of every night's retinue called sleep.

E-I-E-I-O:

Perhaps going to the farm would help. While it normally meant jeans and whatever, I wanted my first trip in years to be like a job interview and not some 28-year-old looking for a way to give meaning to her life. With so many apparel options and my belief that I should make a business presence, I was in a tizzy. I knew the Mad City boys would be in their normal funky farmer and Hsu in her white lab coat and I really didn't know what to wear.

It was August in Wisconsin and so I chose a light blue pants suit with cream colored blouse and some navy-blue pumps and matching purse that I formerly only wore to weddings with gold studs and thin gold necklace.

I entered the kitchen and mom put her coffee cup down and dad the paper. "Melia, you look spectacular," Mom offered

"Too much?"

"Not at all." Mom offered as dad smiled knowing the boys down on the farm would be shocked to say the least.

I drove to the helipad and the chopper was waiting. I parked the car and climbed aboard. My pilot looked at me and smiled. "Welcome aboard Ms. Terrill, it will be smooth sailing today".

Forty minutes later I saw the foundation helipad with the Suburban waiting for me. We landed and I got out to see Peter's mouth drop open. "Melia, you look - simply spectacular."

"Thank you Peter, for taking time out of your busy schedule. " I'd known Peter since I was a little girl. The years had softened the edges, but not the brilliance while the salt and pepper hair and horned rimmed glasses gave Peter the stature he deserved. We went to the 'farm', as the Mad City boys called it, and everything was set for a formal tour as if I'd never been there before. I met all the resident wizards, including some new faces and was brought up to date on

Mediglove, the kaleidoscope and how they'd taken the chip created for grandpa and created hundreds, if not thousands, of applications they'd licensed to companies around the world. To say the foundation was successful would be an understatement and the knowledge that the generated revenue was being reinvested to make the world a better place for all living things made it all worthwhile.

While Luke's original facility continued as the main core, personnel additions meant a new structure had been built halfway between Mineral Point and Darlington where over 200 more team members worked on everything from the next new gizmo to making certain the patents weren't being knocked off somewhere. Luke had selected the second site simply because it had a flat surface amongst the rolling hills where he created an airstrip. The idea was to be able to skip the helipad transfer for those flying in and have some of our smaller jets land on the 6,000-foot runway.

Luke being Luke, took it one step further. Using geothermal energy that brought 55-degree subsurface water to chemically inert conduits under the runway. The water then returned to the level from whence it came. Luke also incorporated solar power to charge the batteries for the pumps and lights which not only meant the runway would be clear, regardless of snow, at any temperature above zero, it wouldn't require any maintenance.

The Madcity boys created software that took all the weather conditions and even the runway temperature into consideration that was broadcast on a closed channel so that pilots knew what the landing conditions were. The FAA loved the design and designated the Williams runway as an emergency airstrip for other small planes, if they needed to set down. Luke also designed and built a small garage that could hold two vehicles, such that there could always be one vehicle waiting if someone flew in and needed to get to the office.

As we were returning from the 'new place' as the boys

called it, Peter asked me what I wanted to do job wise and I reported that my goal was to use the education I had somewhere and somehow. I also let him know that I wasn't looking for a handout job simply because of who my parents were. If I couldn't add anything to the equation, I didn't want to be there.

"Melia, you're more than welcome to join the team in any capacity you like. Knowing you, I know you don't want a menial task. Why don't I provide a prospectus on where we're going in the next five to ten years to see if there isn't an area you're interested in?"

I noticed that Peter had glanced at his watch several times and deduced he needed to be elsewhere and so I offered. "Why don't we do this, I'll take you back to the farm and go into town and have lunch at the Red Rooster. I haven't had pasty in a long time."

"Are you sure?" Peter politely replied.

"You've got more important things to do than hold my hand until I meet with Hsu at two."

I could sense the relief as Peter pulled into the parking lot and handed me the keys.

"If you don't mind, I could use the restroom before going into town."

"Of course."

We walked back into the facility and I gave Peter a hug. "Thank you for being such a wonderful friend."

I did what needed to be done and headed out to the parking lot. It was still a little early for lunch and the forest beckoned me. It had been a long, long time since I'd been there. I walked the cinder path and made it to Great Grandfather's obelisk and sat for a moment and pondered all that had transpired. For the first time in six weeks, everything finally overwhelmed me as tears began to flow. My pain, my sadness, my frustration and my anger simply came to the surface and were escaping from my soul.

I took a hankie from my purse and dabbed my eyes and

when I looked up 'he' was there - the big buck so many had spoken of when their own lives were in turmoil. His big brown eyes met mine as we locked into each other's soul. He nodded as if to say, "Follow me," and I obliged.

The buck slowly made his way down the path to the springs with me not far behind. He stopped and I stopped. His head turned to look at me and he nodded as if to say "It's all right," as a sense of long-lost tranquility pervaded my soul and injected a level of peace.

I closed my eyes and when I opened them again, he was gone. I stood for a moment and opened the old wooden box where the little tin cups were stored, taking one and dipping it in the cool, clear water, I pressed the cup to my lips. As each droplet entered my mouth I could feel its purity simply wash away the sadness that had been there for so long. I stood for a moment enveloped in the majesty of innocence and thanked God for all that I had been given. I put the cup away and headed back along the path until I reached the parking lot, got in and drove into town. All the pain was gone and I knew I'd reached the point of a new beginning.

The Red Rooster:

The Red Rooster had been a Mineral Point restaurant for as long as I could remember. Much like the town, it was frozen in time, as it too was worn soft and smooth by the goodness, kindness and compassion that only happens in small towns filled with memories of family, friends and folks who've come and gone.

I entered and the memories came cascading in with me. Nothing had changed! The same rooster wallpaper and decor, the same tables, the same smells from the kitchen in back. I looked at the 'island' in the middle with the backless stools that kids like me used to spin around on, and the pie display and soft drink cooler that still hummed at a slower pace than the rest of the world.

On the wall, across the island and at the 'dead end' of the island and adjacent to the soda machine, hung a faded photo of my great uncle Hank. It was there simply because that was 'his' corner and the fact that Uncle Hank and his wife Kat, had done so much to re-gentrify Mineral Point from farm town into an artist colony.

The 'big' table up front had its usual confab of locals and farmers who'd come to town for business or simply break bread, tell lies and laugh at the world going by. As was the case for every entrant, the moment the door opened you were reviewed as family, friend or neighbor with warm smiles and curious glances at the strangers who came for the famous Cornish pasty. Everyone was welcome and it had been that way forever, just the way it should have been.

It had been several years since I'd turned the knob and went inside and when I did, I was immediately slotted in the stranger category. Add my skin color and more upscale attire and the quick glances extended to stares and whispers. I didn't want to sit at the island and be the center of so much attention and the three tables for two along the Chestnut Street wall were already filled and so I progressed back towards the kitchen and garnered a solo chair at a table for four just behind the outcropping for the stairs that Uncle Hank had climbed so many times when he lived above.

I meandered past those already dining and reached the table facing back toward the bathrooms and somewhat tucked beneath the stairs. I chose my seat with my back to the wall and felt sequestered from the ongoing glances of the regulars who were probably wondering who I was. With one table behind me still devoid of customers and the last table ensconced in the huge arms of some man who was diligently devouring the Wisconsin State Journal, I felt singular in my quest for nothing more than what I'd come for, Cornish Pasty.

The server's name tag said 'Sue' and the friendly smile made me feel welcome. There's something about a place your ancestors called home that can do that to you. The water glass was filled and I was politely offered the hand-typed menu with white-out erasing old prices here and there, even though I knew exactly what I'd come for.

A few minutes later Sue returned and asked for my order. I politely indicated the pasty without the rutabaga, as I never really liked them. Sue wrote my choice on her small, green order tablet and inquired about a beverage with me asking if they still offered homemade lemonade that fostered a wry smile as Sue wondered how I knew about something normally reserved only for the locals.

With my wishes written and the page pulled from the tablet of future delights, Sue excused herself and went to the order wheel where thousands of appetites had been proclaimed and then proceeded to the table down the hall with her water pitcher. The stranger put down his paper and a rush of excitement traversed my body. It had been years and yet the man sitting there had been in my dreams a hundred – make that, a thousand times. It was Jack, a little older and certainly a little rougher than the photo I had from the cruise. His Packer shirt was sweat-stained and whisks of dirt not only permeated the shirt but his brow and unshaven jaw as well.

At first Sue's intercession captured Jack's attention and, as Sue departed, Jack's eyes glanced my way and his mouth dropped open. Jack sat perplexed with a reflective glance at the past wallowing within his heart. I could sense his reticence and so I simply smiled as he inquired, "Melia?"

I nodded in the affirmative. Jack sat for a moment, locked in trepidation. Did he approach in his gritty garb? Did he venture forth or simply continue the conversation across two tables?

I perceived his conundrum and stood and walked to his table. "Hi, Jack." I whispered. "May I sit down?"

The affirmative, shocked mood reflected the state of his emotions as he inquired, "What are you doing in Mineral Point?" "I have a job interview," I quietly responded, knowing it was

somewhat true. "With whom."

"The Derrick Williams foundation."

"Wow! I thought you were going to be a doctor."

"Long story," I relied, looking deep into his eyes before inquiring. "How about you?"

"Phy. Ed and head football coach here in town, which means I'm also the landscaper, lawnmower and goal post painter," Jack replied with a slight smile as his fingers splayed the front of his shirt.

"I can't believe it's been years," I offered, as I glanced at his left ring finger and he at mine.

"Married?" Jack inquired.

I twisted my head from side to side to ensure I communicated in the negative and replied, "My education took all my time and it's only been this summer I've begun to have a life again. How about you?"

Jack had a somewhat forlorn expression cross his face. "I had a long-term situation. When she gave me an ultimatum, I simply couldn't do it. She was crushed when I told her I was in love with another woman."

"You were dating two women at once?" I incredulously

inquired.

"No, I'd met this wonderful woman and simply couldn't get her out of my mind. We kept in contact for a while, but she was away at school. Her education was very demanding and I lost touch with her."

A tear welled in my eye as feelings of remorse flooded my soul. Even after those difficult years, those sensations from the cruise came to the forefront. For the first time in my life, I felt the empty piece of my jigsaw puzzle might finally fall in place.

Sue arrived and inquired if I wanted my pasty moved to Jack's table. I looked at Jack and he said, "please," as a profound sense of joy made its way into my heart.

For the next hour we got caught up until I looked at my watch and realized I needed to go.

"When will I see you again?" I inquired, not caring if it was the right thing to say or not.

"Where are you living?" Jack inquired.

"I'm moving to Madison in September and hopefully going back to school," I replied as I anticipated using the family influence and condo to get me in and provide a place to live. "How about you?"

"I'm living in Mount Horeb," Jack quietly announced as if to keep it a secret from Mineral Point ears. "My dad passed away a few years ago and so I'm helping mom," which I found to be a sign of nobility.

Sue came with the check and I reached for it, but Jack's hands were faster. I wrote down both my cellphone and home number and he agreed to call. It was then I realized he didn't know my last name and added "Melia Wilson", as I didn't want to spill the beans, but finally knew how the communication abstinence riddle was finally solved.

I bought three half-baked pasties, went back to the farm and had my meeting with Aunt Hsu. She was polite and pleasant and we both quickly realized medical research wasn't for me. I was grateful for her time and candor while taking one option and removing it from my forever list.

As I was driving the Suburban back to the foundation offices, I called for the chopper and was told it would arrive in thirty minutes. I pulled into the parking lot and stepped inside to leave the keys on the hook and noticed that Peter was still in his office, so I stuck my head in say, "Thank you".

"How was your day?" Peter inquired.

"I learned a lot," I replied, pausing for a moment and then inquired, "How's the Mineral Point football team doing?

"Great coach, lousy facilities. Poor guy has to do everything because he doesn't have the budget. Kids don't go out for the team because the equipment's old, the field's a disaster and there's no community support."

"Peter, if you were going to fix one thing for the football team, what would it be?"

"First would be replacing the field and fixing the lights."

"Who installs football fields?"

"Natural or synthetic?"

"I don't know," I said shaking my head.

I looked at my vibrating watch and was informed the chopper was five minutes out. Peter offered to drive me to the helipad and so we headed over and arrived just as the bird came over the hill. I gave Peter a hug and thanked him for the hospitality.

"Melia, why the interest in the football team?"

"Don't know, just overhead the folks at the Rooster talking about how bad it was."

My flight home from Waldwick was just the way you want it to be - uneventful. As we landed, a smile crossed my face, a text from Jack had arrived and I was happy. "Sorry our time together was so short. Need to make it up to you when it's convenient. Jack."

Cha-cha-cha-changes:

When I arrived home, mom was there, waiting with empty plates as I'd sent her a text that I was bringing pasty from the Rooster for dinner which we snarfed down. It was then I felt brave enough to start a discussion about the name change. At first, mom was shocked and then settled down. Amazingly, dad did most of the talking and told mom he completely understood. Change the name now, find some guy to marry me and change the name again to provide anonymity to both my hoped-for future husband and her grandkids, who were going to have a different last name anyway.

Mom thought it through, asked all the same questions dad had and concluded my strategy actually made sense. After dinner, she called Derrick and asked what his schedule was like the next day, as she and I would like to meet with him to discuss a family matter.

The next morning, I rode with mom to the office and I reiterated the entire strategy and my aspiration to be a stay-at- home mom and why I wanted to change my name. As we arrived, you'd have thought we were aristocracy. Mom rarely made it to Wilco legal and to have two of us there was something the chatterboxes would be warbling about for days.

We entered Derrick's office and mom closed the door indicating this was personal and important. I proceeded to lay out my strategy and Derrick simply smiled and shook his head before finally saying, "You mean, be free of big brother?"

"Yup!"

Derrick offered, "I think it's brilliant and very generous, not only for your family, but for you. If you get married, you're probably going to change your name anyway, so why not break the chain and have the freedom?"

I think mom was shocked until she began to realize her kids had been profoundly sequestered and she hadn't even realized it. There was a brief pause and then Derrick picked up his phone and told his administrative assistant to have Charlie Woodson come to his office.

Within two minutes, Charlie was there and was shocked to see mom and me as we moved to Derrick's conference table and Derrick outlined the strategy. Charlie had been called because he specialized in all the Wilco civil matters and was wired in at the Waukesha County Courthouse. When asked if he thought the process would be a challenge, he said, "No," and thought he could get it done in ten days to two weeks. I was shocked, thinking it was going to be an arduous process.

Derrick then said there was one more person who needed to be in the loop and called Wilco Security and asked for Andrew who immediately came on line and then Zoomed in. Once again, Derrick went through the plan and asked Andrew what it would take to go through all social media and the internet and sweep it for articles that included me. Andrew said we should include Peter and so he was added to what was becoming a conference Zoom, where it was decided that Charlie would handle the legal, Andrew security and Peter would have Simon scan the internet and literally erase anything and everything that had me and my image referenced.

Derrick then called Wilco PR and asked for Charlene Thomas to come to his office. Less than two minutes later another nervous employee arrived and was offered to sit at the boss's table with the group.

"Charlene, here's what's going on. My sister has had some harrowing security issues recently and feels challenged. To protect her, she is legally changing her last name and we are literally wiping all references to her off the global internet. What we need you to do is create a reason for the wipe and develop a destination where people will think she's gone and can't be reached and will soon be forgotten. To this end, we'll need to have your department create the story."

Charlene thought for a moment and offered, "What would you think if we said she'd joined the Peace Corps and was going to some undeveloped country to work with the poor?"

I looked at Derrick and he at mom and we all smiled. Derrick turned to Charlie and asked, "You still have contacts in Washington?" to which Charlie nodded in the affirmative.

The story evolved, Melia Terrill was joining the Peace Corps and going to New Guinea. In reality, Melia Terrill was legally changing her name to protect the future innocent from the pressures of reality, almost like the Federal Witness Protection program.

The meeting was over and we all stood as Derrick asked a very profound question, "What's your new name?"

I looked at mom and then the group and offered, "Amelia Marie Wilson," which was Grandma Marie's maiden name.

Mom smiled and knew that I was honoring her mother in a way that went directly to her heart as Derrick responded "And so it is, Ms. Wilson. Welcome to your new world."

As we got back in the car, I called dad and gave him the news. I don't know if he was really happy, but was sentimental about the name and told me he thought it was special.

Ten days later, it was all done. Charlie pulled the promised strings and I took my certification to the Motor Vehicle Department and obtained my new Wisconsin Driver's License that read Amelia Marie Wilson.

Touchdown:

After going to Waldwick, I asked dad about Mineral Point football and he just shook his head. "Great coach, lousy facilities and the field is simply terrible as it hasn't been replaced since I played there."

"Who replaces football fields and how long does it take?"

"I think the biggest company around is the Bruce Company in Middleton. They do a lot of commercial work, including all of our properties."

I looked at dad and pointedly asked, "Dad, the company and foundation donate tens of millions of dollars each year and yet the town that supports the foundation doesn't even make the list. Why?"

Before dad could respond, I continued. "Our ancestral home! Our roots and yet there are things that need to be done and the town can't afford to do it. What would make the community proud not only of themselves, but The Derrick Williams Foundation, would be our involvement."

"Why all the interest in Mineral Point football?" Dad inquired. "I had lunch at the Rooster and there was this guy sitting in the back corner who looked like a migrant worker. I found out he was the high school football coach and athletic director. I learned that, on his own time, he had to landscape the football field, repair the bleachers and do all the painting. Peter told me no one came to the games because none of the kids came out for football simply because they didn't have the right equipment or facilities. I think it's sad, especially when we give millions to the UW Athletic Department each year."

Dad had a different look on his face that I didn't appreciate and so I continued. "Your own home town! The location of our foundation! And we can't even help them have a decent place to play? It's no wonder why so few of our employees live in Mineral Point. If they've got kids who want to play sports, why have them risk their health and play on lousy fields with rotten equipment? We should be doing things to help the town, not just take from it!" Dad and I ended our conversation and I was damned if he was going to stop me. I knew who I needed to call and that was Captain Luke. Not only was he responsible for the foundation

facilities, but lived in Mineral Point.

I called and told Luke the same story and asked if we could have a Zoom call. He agreed and the following morning, I googled images of those I could find on the internet showing the worn bleachers, rusty chain link fencing and standing puddles on the football field, when it rained.

Luke hadn't seen this much passion from me in a long time as he inquired "What do you want to do?"

"A new field, get the lights fixed so they can play games at night like all the other schools and repair the bleachers and fences."

"Your personal money?" "Yes."

Luke realized my sincerity and said he'd see what he could do. I then hit him with a timetable. "It all needs to be done by Labor Day."

"Melia, that's only three weeks away and we'll need Board of Education approval."

I loved hearing the word 'we' and responded, "I know and so **we** better get busy, but this needs to appear as if it's coming from the foundation and not me, please."

Breakfast was just dad and me and so it was time to drill down. His daughter had finally let go of her past and wanted to move forward and do so quickly. To his delight, he could see his former daughter reappearing with a level of determination that had been buried in loneliness and frustration.

"Any more thoughts on the football field?" Dad asked.

"I'm moving ahead with or without the foundation or Wilco and there's one other thing."

"What's that?"

"I've decided medical research isn't for me and would like to enroll in Madison to get my elementary education credentials."

"It's really late in the registration period."

"I know, but my grades were good and with all the money we donate to the UW, you'd think asking for one small favor wouldn't be too much."

"You're getting it all figured out, aren't you?"

I nodded in the affirmative and looked at dad, while providing my rationale. "I love working with kids. I think I can be a good teacher and love Madison. The only thing is, do you think I could use the family condo or should I try and find an apartment?"

"Who's using the condo now?" Dad asked. "'V' when he's in town, which isn't that often."

"Call him and see what he thinks. If there's a problem and if he's only in Madison a couple nights a month, he can stay at the Hilton."

"He can also stay with me if he doesn't mind staying with his little sister."

I called 'V' and told him my plans and he was all in favor of it, telling me he thought I'd be a great teacher. I drove to Madison and went to the condo. While the view remained spectacular, the entire motif was really dated, as nothing had changed since mom and dad lived there when they first got married.

I called Annie and asked her if she knew any interior designers and she gave me the names of two. The first call was like oil and water. I don't like effete snobs. The second lady was named Constance and seemed wonderful. She agreed to meet with me at one o'clock. We both were on time and looked at everything from the windows and floors to carpeting, furniture and appliances and discussed an entire rework of the bathroom while adding a roof-top deck.

It was fun looking at all the options that took almost two

hours to make my choices. After selecting everything, I asked how long it would take. Constance looked at all that I wanted done and said, 'Six-weeks'. I thought, 'My God, I've got school starting and couldn't commute from Pine Lake every day.'

Dad agreed to let me fund the football field and said a Quick Claim Deed could be processed giving me ownership of the condo, as I wanted to handle it alone. Dad agreed, but offered to have someone at Wilco make the appointment for the football field. I said thanks, I'd rather do it myself.

After my meeting with Constance, I drove out to Middleton and the Bruce Company. I entered the facility and politely announced, "My name is Melia Wilson and I have a 4:30 meeting with Mr. Marksman."

"Let me see if he's available," the receptionist said as she stood up, went to a closed door and returned denoting, "Follow me please."

I entered Mr. Marksman's office to literally see piles of landscape drawings in rolls, all neatly stacked. He seemed like a pleasant man and was quite cordial, offering me to sit at the planning table while offering water, coffee or tea.

"I'm sorry Mr. Marksman to make such a late appointment as I'm here on my own behalf, but I don't have a lot of time and don't like wasting what time I have. My father suggested I meet with you and said you were the decision maker.

"Thank you."

"It's come to my attention that, due to budget constraints, the Mineral Point football field has become, let's say, less than an ideal sport's environment, not due to effort, but limited resources."

"We're aware Ms. Wilson."

"I personally have the resources necessary to assist in developing a more positive athletic environment which would reward both the students and residents of Mineral Point and would like to do so."

"That's a generous proposal."

"Thank you. The reason I'm here today is to get your commitment on the football field replacement with a deadline of Labor Day, using the same methodology of the large turf slabs incorporated in Lambeau Field. My research indicates that to scrape, level and lay the field should take no more than three days and I'm willing to pay a premium to have this done. My question is, do you have the capacity to accomplish what I need or names of firms capable of doing it in the timeline I've summarized?"

I could see the trepidation in Marksman's eyes and so I went for the close. "I've drawn up an agreement that outlines what I've detailed and have a personal check for $250,000 in earnest money with me."

"Can I have a moment please?"

Mr. Marksman excused himself as a I sat looking out the window. About five minutes later, he was back with a frown in his face. "We believe we can do it, but would like the opportunity to check with our field team to see if they have enough sod and they've already left for the day. The last thing we want to do is promise something we can't deliver. You're taking care of School Board approval, correct?"

"I believe it will be approved tomorrow," I confidently replied as I inquired. "When will you know if you have the capacity?"

"First thing tomorrow morning." "Define first thing."

"Six AM"

"Quotes by when?"

"Same time, I'll draw them up tonight so that the only question will be inventory."

I nodded in the affirmative, offering my email address and adding, "Assuming you can, please draw up the agreements and I'll have them signed and back to you no later than nine tomorrow so that you can schedule the project."

I opened my purse and took out an envelope and slid check number 1001 in the name of Amelia Wilson, along with a non- disclosure agreement across the table for Mr.

Marksman to sign. "Upon completion, the balance will also be paid by me."

Mr. Marksman reviewed the agreement, signed the document and smiled, while saying thank you, thereby taking the first steps to have my very special friend get the assistance he needed.

"Agreed," Marksman concurred as we stood and shook hands. I'd just committed to spending $400,000 and almost pee'd my pants.

Everything was falling into place and I was optimistic in a world normally filled with delays and excuses and there was a smile on my face all the way back to Pine Lake. All I needed was some place to stay in Madison until the condo was done to which I hit speed dial and called Annie. After the normal chitchat, I explained the condo remodeling project, timetable and how dad was pulling strings to get me enrolled at the UW for the fall semester so that I could get my teaching certificate. I politely wondered if she'd like a roommate for a few weeks until the condo was done while Teddy was off playing solider somewhere. Annie thought it would be great and told me she'd just moved into a lovely apartment away from the ridiculous rents near downtown. I guess I should have known it was going to be small
when she gave me the address of 1814$^{1/2}$ Spaight Street.

I made it home to Pine Lake and, as I drove in our driveway, spotted a bright red corvette in the driveway and wondered who was at the house. When I walked in, dad had a big grin on his face as he handed me the keys and said the car was a combination early housewarming and back-to-school present as he said, "If you're going to be a Badger, it needs to be in Badger red."

"So, I was accepted?"

"It took a couple of calls, but it's done" dad said with a smile.

Mom, dad and I went to The Five O'Clock to celebrate and then it was home to bed. I was up early and there was an email from Mr. Marksman with the job order. The $250,000 down payment had been accepted with another $150,000 due upon completion. I confirmed and went to the kitchen to make breakfast. For the first time, I was missing Good Morning, but knew that if it was going to remain special, it had to be sequestered in my memory bank and not something I could have every day.

With life falling into place, I needed to schedule a couple of days in Madison to check on the condo, get my books and do a dry run of my class schedule. I called Annie and asked if it was OK, I spend the night with her and she said 'sure', as she described the house and detailed that the apartment entrance was in back.

I programmed the address and made it to Madison in nothing flat, loving the ride of my new toy. The house was located on a quiet residential street and I parked out front and made my way to the back to find a set of steep gray stairs. I climbed the stairs and rapped on the back door but there was no answer. I was a bit perplexed until I saw a note from Annie "Had to go. Key under mat. Should be home around 5:00."

I found the key and unlocked the door that opened into a small kitchen. It was tidy in many ways consisting of a sink, stove, microwave and refrigerator with a small table for two. I entered what would be considered the living room that was just big enough for a couch and small TV and then the small bedroom that had a double bed and a single night stand with a small closet and bathroom that had the standard fixtures with a tub and plastic shower curtain. I went back into the living room and checked to see if the couch opened up into a pull-out and realized it didn't.

The place was tiny, but clean and neat, with Annie's plants and music gear everywhere. I put my overnight bag on the living room floor and was reading when Annie returned, as we gave each other hugs.

"Heh, cute apartment." I offered.

"Awfully small," Annie offered and continued. "But reasonable, especially compared to downtown". There was a pause and then Annie asked, "Do you want to put your clothes in the closet? I've cleaned out one dresser drawer for you."

The look on my face must have said it all as Annie added, "I packed up Teddy's stuff and took it to my parent's. He's on a six- month tour, with no chance for any leave.

I was a bit reluctant, but knew it was important for Annie and so I smiled and did as offered. We ordered from Pizza Pit and got caught up with me telling her all about my new name and why it was done and reiterating on how I'd run into Jack, even though she already knew, with Annie telling me about the gigs she was doing.

It was nearing eleven and time for bed. I asked about bedding for the couch and Annie just looked at me and added, "I thought you'd be sleeping with me. The couch is too short and really uncomfortable."

"That's OK, I really appreciate you letting me stay here but the couch will be fine." I offered.

"It's nice having company," Annie replied. "I get so lonely with Teddy gone."

I hadn't slept on a couch in years, but appreciated not having to drive back to Pine Lake when I needed to finish preparing for classes early the next morning. We put the linens on the couch and Annie was right, my six-foot-two body simply didn't fit.

Annie laughed and offered the bed. I reluctantly agreed.

I slipped beneath the covers as Annie crawled in next to me.

We both lay in bed staring at the ceiling.

"I really loved our vacation." Annie whispered.

"Me too." I agreed.

"I loved the walk on the beach that night." Annie offered.

"Me too." I responded.

"I loved the moon and the stars and…"

"Me too." I whispered.

With that, Annie rolled over and propped herself up and looked into my eyes whispering. "Do you?"

"I think so." I replied.

"Are you sure?"

"Yes" I quietly responded.

As morning came, Annie got up and used the bathroom. Coming back asking, "How was the couch?" with a smirk on her face as she slid in besides me as I noted. "This is nice!"

We lay, saying nothing for the longest period of time simply looking at the ceiling fan slowly turning reminding me of the House On The Hill.

Finally, I propped myself up on one elbow and looked at my dearest friend and asked, "have I told you that I love you?"

Annie smiled a shy smile as I knew it was something she needed to hear as she inquired, "can we stay in bed all day?

"Well not today. I've got to go finish getting ready for school. By the way, how's Teddy doing?" I asked trying to change the subject.

Breaking the spell, I got up and took a shower while Annie made breakfast. Sitting at the tiny kitchen table wearing her traditional t-shirt, Annie paused and stared at her half-empty coffee cup and I could tell she'd slipped into a funk, but decided not to dig any deeper as the weak smile on her ace was saying it all as she asked. "Will you be here tonight?"

"No, I need to go home. I've got some papers to sign and don't have any classes until next week."

"Do you want to stay then?"

I could feel Annie's loneliness digging in and wondered what to do. "Let me see what's going on." I offered, without telling Annie about my hoped-for plans with Jack.

To make Annie feel "wanted", I asked if I could stay the following Friday night, justifying that it was Labor Day weekend and traffic to and from Madison would be tough, especially with road construction and the first Badger football game of the season. Annie smiled and said, "of course." She had a gig and would be coming home late, but I was more than welcome to stay.

I vowed that my time "on the *ouch*" would be a one-night thing and went to Steinhafel's furniture in Waukesha and found a nice, comfortable sleeper couch. I figured it was the least I could do for Annie while sending a message that I thought we'd done enough. I called Annie and asked if she would be home Wednesday afternoon as I had a surprise for her. She said "yes".

I never realized the apartment was furnished and when the delivery guys arrived, Annie had to call the landlady who lived downstairs, to make certain it was OK to replace the worn-out couch with a new hide-a-bed. Needless to say, the lady said "yes" making certain Annie understood it came with the apartment and would stay when Annie left. I guess the delivery guys had quite a time getting the new couch up the back stairs and into the tiny apartment and literally dropped the old couch as they were hauling it away.

After the dust settled in more ways than one, Annie texted me and said "You didn't need to do that, but thank you."

"It's the least I can do for letting me stay." I replied.

"You're my best friend, I would have been hurt if you hadn't." Annie replied.

I guess we both knew that what transpired was only a transitory thing and not a forever situation. While some people would look back with regrets, I had none at all. I expanded my horizon and did so without physical, emotional and social consequence. Perhaps, milk-toast Melia had more of her mother in her than she thought she did.

Coaches Seats:

As I was leaving Annie's, I sent Jack a quick note inquiring what he was doing Labor Day Weekend to see if he wanted to go to the Badger game. Two minutes later, he responded that he would love to and had high school coaches' tickets. At first I thought we could sit in our skybox, but thought I'd better slowly expose Jack to the Terrill world for fear he'd be overwhelmed by what was about to transpire.

I texted Captain Luke and inquired whether the school board had approved the field and if he could get a crew to either repair or replace the rusty fence and see what needed to be done about the bleachers and lights. Fifteen minutes later, Luke called back saying the board had approved the gift and, after the new field was in, a crew would be there with a new chain link fence and support struts for the bleachers and electricians had already been contacted about repairing or replacing the lights.

I asked Luke if he knew a painter, as Jack said he needed to paint the goal posts. Luke laughed and said, he'd do it while the fence people were there, simply to stay out of their way.

I received a text from the Bruce company and received the work order stating the field would be installed the following Wednesday through Friday, weather permitting. All Jack would need to do is add water and then more water and then even more water.

I called Luke back with the news who indicated he'd contacted an irrigation company in Platteville and ordered a better pump and enough hose and sprinklers to do the entire field at one time, instead of multiple trips to simply move the sprinklers.

Everything was in place and I was as excited as a kid at Christmas.

Game On:

It's really amazing what you can learn about people on the internet if you dig deep enough. What's also incredible was what Wilco Security can do to find out even more. Before I got too far down the emotional rabbit hole, I needed to learn a little more about John W. Harris. I realized it wasn't very romantic and probably not the neatest thing to do. However, I felt I'd better see for myself rather than wait to have him vetted later on. A few minutes later, a smile crossed my face when I learned just how good a person Jack really was as it showed he was filled with good old Wisconsin values.

Instead of the traditional dating scene that allows two people to learn about each other, we both knew we had commitments that needed to be met. First, I needed to settle into the School of Education at the UW, while realizing Jack not only had to teach, but prepare for football, as well. One of the things I really respected in the man was his sincere search for excellence, which also meant less time we could be together. The net result was actually what we both needed - a gradual ramp-up of the relationship instead of with both feet right away as this wasn't a seven-day cruise.

I learned that Jack's birthday was September third, which was the Friday before Labor Day. The Badger football team was kicking off the season against Eastern, Western Southern Somebody on the fourth and thought it would be neat if we could put the two together. So I texted him and asked if we could go out to dinner Friday night and the game on Saturday.

I wanted the first date to be special and remembered back to mom and dad, whose first date started when they met in the Capitol rotunda. Dad told mom that, until she walked through the door, the inside of the Capitol was the most beautiful thing he'd ever seen.

Being the ultimate romantic, I offered to meet Jack at the spot where it all began for my parents. While it was romantic, there was another reason. Jack still had no idea about who our family was and I wanted to ease him into the entire scenario.

Jack thought it was strange, but agreed. I told him I was taking him out for his birthday. He asked what he should wear and I told him not to wear what I saw him in at the Rooster, even if he had it washed, while a sports coat and jeans would be fine and so September third was set.

With the Mineral Point school board approving the new field, I knew we couldn't keep all the changes a secret and so I called Luke and agreed that he should meet with Jack and tell him the Foundation was donating the field, fencing, repairing the bleachers and fixing the lights. I also wanted Luke's valued opinion of my potential suitor.

Luke met with Jack and said he was 'first class' which was quite a compliment from the former Navy captain and religious leader. Luke filled Jack in on all the improvements and the timetable. It was fun seeing the dynamics simply because I got reports from both sides of the proverbial fence with Jack all excited by the fact that someone was finally supporting his efforts.

The days slowly passed with me spending time in both Pine Lake and Madison checking things out and getting my books. My God, were they expensive! I also checked my class schedule and realized I was going to have a lot of downtime, as a lot of the advanced classes had prerequisites. I asked dad if I could work part time at Wilco or with the Foundation Selection Committee, concerning annual donation applications and subsequent awards, which he thought was a great idea.

Not knowing what Jack liked to eat, I chose one of dad's favorite Madison restaurants called the Graze on Pinckney Street. It was literally across the street from the Capitol and served Terrill Wagyu beef, Terrill Premier bourbon and Pinot Noir.

Dad had somebody call whomever at the restaurant and

make reservations for a small table in the corner with candlelight and the whole shebang. If you're going to make the right impression on a first date, I didn't want to leave anything to chance.

Finally, Friday arrived. I picked out a cream-colored pants suit with a white blouse, black purse and matching pumps, gold stud earrings and thin gold necklace. I parked the Vette at the condo and made it to the rotunda fifteen minutes early and stood in the middle as I imagined dad had done so many years before. At precisely seven, this tall, muscular, handsome man entered from the West Washington Avenue entrance and simply took my heart away. Gone was the dirt under his nails, sweat stained t- shirt and looks like he'd just mucked out the horse barn. I smiled and Jack smiled. A tear slid down my cheek. All I'd dreamed he would be was coming true.

Jack approached and I opened my arms and hugged him. "Happy Birthday".

"Thank you." he whispered as we separated.

"Hope you like steak." I commented.

"Love it. Do we have far to go?"

I pointed to the Pinckney Street exit and said, "Across the street."

"The Graze?" Jack inquired, almost incredulously. I nodded as he asked, "Are you sure?"

"You only turn 30 once."

We walked across the meticulous Capitol grounds and down the few stairs as Jack commented, "Did I tell you, you look marvelous?"

"Thank you." Hoping he didn't realize my new outfit cost more than $5,000.

We entered the restaurant and were immediately taken to our table. The restaurant was a little louder than I'd hoped with the pregame crowd in town, but our secluded candle lit setting was all I'd dreamed.

The server was prompt, polite and professional and read

off the litany of options without quoting prices. Little did my new suitor realize our meal consisting of Jack's porterhouse with garlic mashed potatoes, asparagus and one glass of Terrill Reserve and my small T-bone cost nearly $500.00.

As we finished, the sever brought out a stainless-steel bowl and poured cream in it as Jack had a perplexed look in his face. Next came a cylinder of liquid nitrogen and, just like Uncle Tommie, the server made ice cream in front of us and asked Jack what toppings he preferred as they were all homemade - chocolate, caramel or strawberry? Jack asked for all three. To say the kid from Mount Horeb was impressed, would have been an understatement as they stuck a sparkler in the concoction and quietly wished him a happy birthday, already understanding that he didn't like being in the spotlight.

By the time we were done, it was nearly ten. Jack had a forlorn look in his face. "I need to go home," he announced. "My car is in the shop and mom needs her car to go to work at the hospital."

At first I was afraid our first date had been a failure and only later learned that Jack was driving a nine-year-old Toyota Versa with nearly 300,000 miles on it. I felt really guilty with the fact that I had a new Corvette and my beloved Range Rover that dad called my 'winter car'.

We walked back to the rotunda and politely kissed goodnight. It was the first time our lips had met in six years and I wished it could have lasted forever. Jack walked towards the West Washington exit as I stood and watched him go, he turned, gave me one of those unforgettable half smiles, where the left side of his lip curled, as he threw me a nod of gratitude that put a smile on my face.

Hide-A-Bed:

I walked to the condo garage, got into the Corvette and headed for Spaight Street. I knew the house would be empty as Annie was playing a gig and wouldn't be home until God knows when.

It was seven the next morning when I woke up on the new and not-so-comfy hide-a-bed with Annie totally zonked in the bedroom. I tried to be as quiet as possible and don't know if it was the toilet flushing that awakened Annie.

As I came out of the bathroom Annie was propped up in bed. "Good morning!" I offered.

"Hi. I thought you'd sleep here with me," Annie expressed in a somewhat disappointed manner.

"Sorry. I thought I'd try the hide-a-bed." "And?"

"I'm stiff and sore." "Where?

"My lower back and shoulders." "Come here and let me massage it."

I didn't want to start again, but needed some relief as I made my way to the bed while placing the towel on the bedroom chair.

After Saint Martin, the moonlit beach and then when I stayed with Annie the last time, I was feeling guilty and studied what happened and why and found an interesting statement concerning couple dynamics that said. "There's absolutely nothing wrong with two women being intimate with each other. Love and attraction are natural, and as long as both individuals are consenting adults, their relationship is valid and meaningful. Society's views on relationships have evolved, and many cultures recognize and celebrate diverse expressions of love. What truly matters is mutual respect, emotional connection, and personal happiness.

Over time, in a sexually oriented relationship one partner takes on the feminine expression and one takes on the more masculine expression and the radical differences in orientation create a strong arc of sexual polarity, also known as the dynamic flow of attraction and tension between two individuals with contrasting masculine and feminine energies.'

'In relationships and intimate encounters, sexual polarity is the magnetic pull that arises from these differences where the arc represents how this polarity shifts and evolves through different phases of interaction–building, peaking, and sometimes dissipating or reversing between the energies in relationships based on the idea that strong differences with one partner embodying more masculine traits such as direction, stability, and presence and the other embodying more feminine traits such as flow, emotion, and receptivity can create a natural and magnetic attraction.'

The article noted that the further the 'poles' are apart, the stronger the sexual attraction. In long-term relationships, partners often become very much the same—they start to like the same things, do the same things—over time, the couple resonates rather than polarizes and hence has less sexual chemistry."

It also detailed that gender had very little to do with polarity practices. The only important thing was that one partner animates one end of the spectrum, while the other partner goes as far to the other end as possible for the sake of the strong polarity arc. In other words, it didn't matter who skewed which way, or how often, it was the subtle energetic differences between two people that creates the animal attraction."

Crawling under the covers I snuggled next to Annie as she whispered. "this is nice."

After so many disappointing times with the few guys I'd been with, it was wonderful to have someone who knew want I wanted, provide what I needed and gave me the satisfaction I always fantasized about as we kissed, not a passionate one, but one of acceptance and gratitude as we lay entwined in each other's minds

Annie and I simply lay there staring at each other and periodically glancing up at the slowly moving ceiling fan. In an apartment with no air conditioning, it was already getting 'toasty'.

Looking in my eyes, Annie inquired. "Any regrets?"

I thought for a minute and then said 'yes' which I think caught Annie off-guard as I added. "My only regret is that we didn't do this when we were roommates.."

"Really?" Annie responded somewhat surprised as I continued, "until Saint Martin, I'd been so modest... so restricted... so prudish, I really never let go. Remember when we lived together and I always changed clothes in the bathroom? I did that because I was ashamed of my body and now... well now, I realize how insecure I really was."

Annie giggled and noted. "I knew some nuns in grade school who were more liberal than you were."

I continued. "Until Saint Martin, I never felt that way and then, thanks to you and Lucille, I began to see what you saw and realized, freedom is a liberating thing as well."

I paused as Annie added, "in other words Melia, you simply let go."

I nodded and smiled..."Yes, I let go in so many ways."

Annie replied. "That's what I liked about Saint Martin. For the first time in my life people didn't seem so hung up on...on I don't know, I guess the differences between each other...not race, not gender, not nationality and certainly not money. I'm certain it's there, but it seems to be a lot less than here. And even with all that we did, you were still so modest."

"In my case, it hasn't been modesty, as much as embarrassment. I've never found myself attractive," I countered

Annie got serious as she asked." Melia, you know all that and yet you've been so...so I don't know, uptight about how you look. I mean you're incredibly gorgeous!"

I closed my eyes and let my mind absorb the compliment

and then responded. "A lot of American women, including me, feel dissatisfied with their appearance due to a combination of cultural, societal, and psychological factors. The media constantly portrays unrealistic, often digitally altered images of women with "ideal" bodies— thin, toned, youthful, and flawless that set unattainable expectations, making us, feel we don't measure up."

Looking at Annie, I admitted. "I've have always had a weight problem. Never too much! Always the other way around and I feel sorry for women in both arenas. American commerce includes a $70+ billion diet industry that profits from making women feel like their bodies are never good enough where, from childhood on, we were taught that thinness equals beauty, health, and success, leading to body dissatisfaction and disordered eating."

"As was my case, growing up there was a situation based on sexualization and objectification simply because my and other women's bodies are frequently objectified in advertising, entertainment, and even daily interactions to the point our self- worth became tied to appearance, where, in my case, this self- concept created deep insecurities about not looking "desirable" enough."

I paused for a moment and then continued. "You have to realize, in our society beauty and success are linked and I always felt like Hans Christian Andersen's ugly duckling simply because studies show that women who fit conventional beauty standards are perceived as more competent, successful, and likable, leading to more pressure on the rest of us to look a certain way which can affect everything from job opportunities to social interactions."

"From all this are the psychological factors which have hounded me. You have to realize I grew up in a family that had only one objective... wealth... from which there came power...from which there came perks... all based on what other people thought of us and never what I thought of myself."

"While everyone thinks we've lived the glorious life. We haven't. Like the Wizard of Oz, we never let anyone look behind the curtain where I experienced childhood teasing, bullying, and negative comments about my race and body that created incredible insecurities that has carried over in my into adulthood."

I'd put it all out on the table. For the first time in my life I was telling the truth, the whole truth and nothing but the truth. Perhaps it was because I was sharing my body that I was finally willing to share my soul.

I rolled on my side, propped myself up on one arm and added, "I always kept it to myself and then I went on vacation and my dearest friend opened a very special door for me for which I know I'll never be the same."

Annie rolled on her side such that we were facing each other and inquired, "but what about Teddy? I mean he was living with us. Wasn't he the real barrier between you and me and the reason nothing happened?"

I shook my head and responded quite directly. "No! I was the reason nothing happened. At that point in time I didn't love myself and if you don't love yourself you can never fully love someone else."

"And why now?" Annie asked while staring deep into my eyes.

"Because this is **our** time together and no one else. This is **you** and **me** sharing each other to the point it's been wonderful and something I'll always cherish."

"Do you think *'this'* will ever happen again? Annie inquired, now somewhat concerned.

"Perhaps someday, but not right now. I need to focus on one person at a time.

"In other words, Jack?"

"Perhaps. I'll just need to see if he's all that I hope he is."

"And if he is?"

"Annie, I'm a one-person person. I can love more than one person, but can't make love to more than one."

There was an extended period of silence as I knew Annie was digesting what I'd just said...If Jack and I were to become a couple, it meant Annie and I'd reached the end of our physical relationship.

I caught my breath as Annie leaned in and gave me a kiss on the cheek and whispered. "Today has been my way of saying thank you for loving me, thank you for caring and thank you for being my friend."

For the next half hour, we simply lay there waiting for the white caps of unspoken secrets to calm until the spell was broken by the realization it was time to get ready for some football.

I went in to take a shower giving me time to think if I'd gone too far. At times, I realize I'm too honest and it would have been better if things were left unsaid.

I came out of the bathroom to see Annie in the kitchen in one of her usual white tee-shirts. As she was buttering the toast, I came up behind her, put my arms around her waist and my chin on her right shoulder, pulled her in and whispered, "If things were different, you and I would have gone on that honeymoon. Today and always, I'll love you."

Annie turned and we kissed a gentle kiss of acclimation and acceptance allowing the passions that had been there to simply fade into history. We'd experienced bliss and culminated what could have, make that, probably should have probably happened so many years before. The longing glances, the shared secrets, the laughter that had been with us would always be there. This was simply the last act, this wonderful, wonderful event that bonded our friendship and preserved it forever, understanding and accepting that, to give of oneself is the greatest gift one can offer to someone they truly love.

I patted Annie on the butt and then we sat at the tiny table, drank our coffee and ate our toast and thought nothing of what transpired. What was so strange for me is that I'd always thought what occurred between us was aberrant.

Without sounding like a hypocrite, I now profess it's certainly not abnormal for two people who care for each other to be intimate. Human relationships, including emotional and physical intimacy, are deeply personal and vary widely among individuals.

Peering into Annie's eyes I realized that love, affection, and attraction are natural aspects of human connection, that can exist between people of any gender and are a normal part of human experience. What matters most is mutual respect, consent, and genuine care for one another and it's the expression that matters... the expression of love...the expression of joy... the expression of good times, bad times, happy times, sad times all rolled into one. It isn't always physical, in fact sex is probably the secondary or even tertiary part of it... nothing more than the exclamation point at the end of a profound sentence.

Friendship is the day-to-day set of shared experiences woven into an embroidery of memories to create a close and mutual bond based on honesty, understanding, and a deep connection. When it's right and in our case it is, the friendship results in trust, respect and support from which the willingness to be there for each other exists.

True friendships are those that grow stronger over time and allow for value and meaning from yesterday to today and then tomorrow, I'm honored to profess that I **love** Annie and know that she loves me.

Game Day:

The weather forecast was for a high near ninety with humidity about the same. Welcome to Wisconsin! Don't worry if you don't like the weather today, it will be totally different tomorrow.

Annie and I finished breakfast and then it was time to get into my Badger gear of a white tank top and red shorty's as I called them which, with two-inch inseams, were short enough to expose my thighs but long enough that my butt wasn't hanging out the back leaving that for the freshman girls.

I pulled on my shorts and was about to add the tank top when Annie noted, "you're not going to wear a bra are you? You're going to be stuffed into a hot, humid stadium filled with eighty thousand other profusely sweating fans."

"You don't think it's too... uh... liberal do you?" I asked.

Annie looked at me and shook her head. "Melia, first, you're going to be sweating like a pig. Second there's isn't a guy on earth who isn't turned on by a little 'pokie' music every now and then.

"You mean polka?" I asked, somewhat confused.

"No Melia, pokies...you know when you're cold or excited." "Oh my God. Do you really think so?"

"Are you kidding me? This new guy's going to love it and your tank top is conservative enough as it is."

Taking Annie's advice, I simply slipped into the tank top and put the holsters back in my overnight bag and glanced in the mirror. Annie was right!

Jack was coming from Mount Horeb with friends, as his car was still in the shop and I was coming all the way from Spaight Street, an incredible three miles from Camp Randall. We were big kids and it made no sense for Jack to pick me up and so we agreed to meet at the parking lot in the 1200 block of Spring Street, where his dad always parked and Jack and his buddies still tailgated, which was only three blocks from Camp Randall.

Kick off was at eleven and I said I'd be there around 9:00 as someone was cooking breakfast and I'm certain there would be several forms of libation.

At 8:30, I Ubered to the corner of Regent and Charter Street and walked the last block. Since Jack and I had reconnected, he'd only seen me in my dress casual attire. I hoped my red short shorts, Badger tank top and red and white Wisconsin visor met with his approval. The huge smile on his face told me, it did.

As I walking towards him, it hit me. Less than three hours ago, I was in bed Annie and profoundly enjoying it and now, perhaps, this new man was entering my life.

As I turned th corner at Spring Street, Jack saw me approaching smiled and waved. I smiled and waved back. From his glances, Jack could tell I was excited to see him.

All Jack's friends were his age and still growing up. Even with human brains not reaching full maturity until age twenty-five, it seems it's taking longer than ever for guys to mature and all I needed to do was look at my own two brothers to see that was the case.

We had egg sandwich breakfasts with Bloody Mary's, as Jack introduced me to the entire Mount Horrible gang as they called themselves who'd 'adopted' a couple of the guys who actually went to Oshkosh with Jack.

As the clock hit 10:15, the tent was down, the grill away and it was departure time and we headed for the stadium. Jack flashed his phone with the electronic tickets on it to the gate keeper and we went inside. His seats were in the high school coach's section, which was on the goal line in section 'W', row 60 or near the top on the south goal line and next to Kellner Hall.

Most of the fans around us were older, but there were a few our age, with Jack being the youngest athletic director by at least fifteen years. Jack took his share of ribbing from some of the other coaches in the conference about the new field, but was able to shoot it right back at them. For a bunch of guys bound and determined to beat each other on Friday night, it sure was interesting to see how much they respected and supported each other when they were off the field.

The game began and half way through the second quarter, Mother Nature decided to play games with us. It seems that the 20% forecasted showers actually became a torrential thunder and lightning downpour that delayed the game as everyone was instructed to head inside. We were told the storm front would pass in twenty minutes, but sitting inside a sweltering stadium with 80,000 hot, sweaty, wet and somewhat inebriated fans wasn't my idea of fun especially in wet clothes that included a now semi-transparent white tank top. So much for Jack using his imagination.

I had to make a quick decision, keep our little family secret and endure, or head for our skybox where there would be food, beverages and wonderful air conditioning. I justified the later by realizing the downpour was dumping a lot of water on the seats and it wasn't going to be much fun sloshing around in row sixty with a bunch of now, even more inebriated, football coaches, especially wearing a wet, white tank top.

I felt like one of Uncle Tommy's beef cattle and finally looked at Jack and said. "Follow me." We made our way through the sweating masses until we were at the VIP elevator below section 'U'.

"Where are we going?" Jack inquired.

"You'll see," as I pulled out my skybox ID and the Customer Care representative called for the elevator.

The door opened as a student's brow raised while he politely smiled, trying not to stare as he offered, "It's nice to have you join us Ms. Terrill, my name is Arthur and I'll be your concierge for the day," which got a total frown on Jack's face pertaining to the name, as I realized I'd forgotten to change the ID when I did everything else.

Noticing that both Jack and I were wet from the rain or sweat, Arthur inquired, "Can I provide a towel or perhaps a change of clothes from your closet, Ms. Terrill?"

Jack just stood there in shock. Concierge? Towel? Terrill? Change of clothes?

The elevator door opened and we were in a different world. A little older. A lot more formal, subdued and a lot less fun, but no wet clothes or dripping sweat.

Arthur led us to the skybox with the Wilco logo above the door and unlocked it for us. Inside sat Derrick, Andrea, 'V' and Amelia who looked at the dripping fools standing before them and could do nothing but laugh. Jack and the boys remembered each other from the cruise and so Derrick and 'V' took it upon themselves to introduce their fiancées.

I opened my closet and took out some dry clothes which for me consisted of the obligatory red and white, but in reverse. Jack looked like he was about the same size as 'V' and so I asked 'V' if Jack could borrow some of his clothes to which 'V' simply nodded "yes".

I went first, dried off and changed in our private bathroom and came out refreshed. Jack went second and came out wearing 'V's' striped red bib overalls over a white tee-shirt. The overalls fit fine but the shirt was tight which accentuated Jack's prominent muscles that simply turned me on. One would think that, after the morning I'd had with Annie, nothing could arouse me, but a set of square shoulders and bulging biceps on a guy with jet black hair, an incredible tan and million-dollar-smile was all it took.

I buzzed Arthur who came and collected our clothes indicating he'd have them dried and back to us before the final gun. Jack just simply shook his head in disbelief.

Our box was next door to the Athletic Director's and a few minutes after our introductions, there was a knock on the door and the Director came in. "Sorry for the delay. We should be restarting in about a half hour," he announced.

As one of the departments largest annual donors, the Director was well aware of who Derrick and 'V' were and smiled as he saw me and noted "Melia, it's been a long time and you look wonderful. Who's your friend"

"This is Jack Harris," I replied.

"Jack, are you the Athletic Director in Mineral Point?" The director inquired with both a smile and a frown.

Jack sheepishly nodded 'yes'.

"I've heard you've got a great football mind and with your new field, you'll be turning things around."

I don't know if Jack was impressed, scared or overwhelmed as he thanked the Director for the kind words.

"A question for you, Jack," the Director posed. We're in the process of developing an intern program for former Badger football players who want to become coaches. I know it's pretty late in the year, but do you have any need for assistant coaches for this fall?"

I think Jack was about to poop his britches as his budget was so thin it was just he and one other teacher trying to do everything.

"I could use the help," Jack responded.

"Tell you what, call me Tuesday and I'll get you in contact with the right people as we really want to kick this off and you're just the type of guy we need and the intern program certainly makes sense."

The Director paused for a moment and added. "Also, if there's anything else you can think of, let's talk about it when you call." With that the Director handed Jack one of his business cards and excused himself.

Derrick offered Jack a drink. Jack looked at me and I nodded as I thought he needed a stiff one about then.

"Has Melia given you any of our family bourbon?"

Jack shook his head no and so Derrick poured three fingers into a glass for each of us and raised his glass in a toast. "To old and new friends and go Badgers."

Just then, the sun came out and Jack simply shook his head as I inquired, "Do you want to watch the game here or go back to the seats?"

After the heat, humidity and humanity, we decided to stay

in the box as the game resumed. Needless to say, I knew there were going to be several questions that needed to be answered after the final gun.

Derrick and Andrea offered us their seats in the first row of the skybox. Andrea was generous enough to tell Derrick to stay and I told Jack to sit with the boys and enjoyed watching them get involved in the game, with high fives and groans in response to the plays, which I think they still call male bonding.

As half-time approached, Arthur returned with menus that seemed endless. Sandwiches, prime rib, salads, a dozen different desserts and ice cream from Babcock Dairy. We all filled out what we wanted to eat and just as the clock hit zero on the second quarter, Arthur appeared with lunch.

The Badgers won the game and so, even with the rain and all, it was a great day.

Arthur returned our dried clothes and we both slipped back into our pre-game attire as I told Jack to text the Horribles and tell them he had a ride home.

We waited for the fifth quarter to end and the masses to leave when Derrick asked where we'd parked and I said Spaight Street.

"We can drop you off on our way back to Milwaukee, if you want".

I nodded yes as tacit plans were made for me to give Jack a ride home.

We walked out and Jack was shocked to see that Derrick had a parking spot adjacent to the stadium. We climbed into Derrick's Rover and headed east. Small talk about Mineral Point football and Jack's opinion of the Badgers transpired. Derrick pulled in behind my car and inquired if I liked it. I retorted that I didn't think there was any way I couldn't. We climbed out and said thanks as Jack and I waved goodbye to my brother and Andrea.

"Well Lucy, you got a lot of splaining to do." Jack evoked in a meager attempt to impersonate 'I Love Lucy's', Ricky Ricardo.

I just stood and shook my head. "Tell you what Mr. Harris, let's go and I'll explain everything. How about me showing you my new apartment and then you might have a better understanding?"

"Want to drive?" as I tossed the keys to Jack. He just grinned from ear to ear as I don't think there's a guy in America who hasn't had an erotic dream about driving a new Corvette. Jack climbed behind the wheel, put the seat all the way back and followed my directions all two miles to the condo and parked in stall 205, next to my beloved Rover.

I took him on the two-minute condo tour, roof patio and view. He really thought the new floor-to-ceiling photovoltaic glass windows were neat where all I needed to do was turn a dial and the windows went from totally clear to different levels of translucency, depending on the mood. I pointed out that the roof patio was completely private and blocked from all the other buildings, but don't think Jack got the hint.

With no furniture, carpeting and bathroom, we sat on the floor and I detailed who I was, who the family was, why my last name was different and who both Wilco and the foundation were.

I explained the benefits provided, but was quite explicit in stating that my goal in life was to simply be part of a normal family with traditional goals and values that didn't need the trappings wealth offered to be happy - other than nice clothes and the skybox on a hot, sweaty day and apologized for not being more forthright, as I wanted Jack to accept me as me, and not the member of a wealthy family.

"Why the perks at Camp Randall?" Jack inquired.

My grandpa was and dad is, a major Badger football and basketball fan and, along with the company, we are major contributors both personally and corporately in many ways."

Jack just sat shaking his head in disbelief. "And you want to date a high school P.E. teacher?"

"No, I want to date an open, honest, sincere, lovable, laughable man who is caring, compassionate and humble, who will accept me as me, who realizes and accepts the fact that I am a human being with hopes and fears, strengths and weaknesses, just like everyone else."

We stood and I looked in Jack's eyes as I offered, "It's not easy being wealthy. Sure, there are benefits, like not getting soaked at a football game."

"Or having a valet take your clothes and get the dried during the game," Jack interceded.

I then continued. "But there are also challenges in terms of security and integrity. It's very easy to get spoiled and so you need to constantly keep reminding yourself, 'One leg at a time'." Jack had a frown on his face and so I added. "You're no better than the next person and put your pants on one leg at a
time, just like they do."

I finally asked, "Where do you want to take me for dinner Mr.
Harris?"

"I don't know," Jack replied, wondering if I wanted a fancy, schmancy joint that would put a big dent in his checkbook.

"How about Paisan's next door and some Sprechers root beer? Then we can have a belching contest to see who's the longest and the loudest."

The offer broke the ice. Jack was beginning to see that Melia Wilson was just another girl from Wisconsin who simply wanted to feel wanted, needed and loved.

We walked next door to find it packed with Badger fans where we could hardly hear ourselves think, but decided to stay anyway. Jack gave them his name and we made it to the bar. We both had a couple of drinks and went to our table out on the veranda where we ordered pizza and decided to hold off on the belching contest. Darn!

We finished our meal and I had an idea. "How about you taking my Rover home and using it until your car is fixed?"

"I can't do that," was the expected response, to which I

countered. "Think of it as a rental car, where our family just sort of leases them from our company and they're insured for any driver. That way you can get home without the rush and I can head back to Milwaukee."

"Are you sure?"

"Why not? The Rover is just going to be sitting here."

"How much is the rental?"

My fingers went to my chin as I responded. "Hmmmm, I'll need to figure that out, but I don't think you'll be too upset with the fee," as I reached across and touched Jack's nose.

It was getting late and we walked back next door and into the garage. I gave a Jack the keys and told him he looked good in it. We hugged and politely kissed and I whispered, "thanks for a wonderful day, Mr. Harris" to which I got a bashful smile.

"I hope it wasn't too much!" We kissed again and said goodbye and headed our opposite ways. By the time I got to Pine Lake, there were two texts from Jack and both of them made me smile.

Tuesday, Jack followed up and called the Director. Instead of the run-around he thought he was going to get, Jack was put right through. Jack called me later and said he had a conference call with the Director and the Badger head football coach who asked about his staff. In the end, it was decided that, at a minimum, a full high school coaching staff should have at least six and preferably eight assistants.

The call ended and Jack was assured that one of the Badger assistant coaches would be back to him. A few hours later, Jack was contacted by the assistant coach regarding former players who'd graduated, were majoring in education and wanted to be coaches, with a list of eight players the assistant recommended along with phone numbers and the fact that they'd all been notified of the opportunity.

Dad got involved and had Wilco contact the Athletic Department about structuring some sort of compensation program through Wilco, thereby offering the interns part-time coaching jobs. All eight knew each other. All eight jumped at the chance to begin coaching. All eight loved the idea of earning some money. Jack was ecstatic, especially when given the coaching roster. For the first time, he had a full complement of coaches that included not only offensive and defensive players, but even a Special Teams coach, as well. Needless to say, I was VERY happy and proud of my father.

Jack now had the facilities and the staff. All he needed were kids who wanted to play football and more who wanted to watch their team.

I called Irene Jackson who headed up the Wilco PR group and outlined the entire situation. We quickly summarized that it wasn't cool to play football for Mineral Point, but everyone in town loved the Badgers.

Jack initially had 36 kids signed up for football. He said he needed fifty minimum and 60 would be ideal. I had an idea, with eight former Badger players as coaches, whose names everyone knew, perhaps we could have a "Meat-and-greet" with the kids at school where we could serve burgers and fries during the lunch hour. In addition, the new assistants could show up at Jack's P.E. classes and try and recruit from there. Time was short, but we needed to do something.

Next, came money. I called Luke and asked if the foundation could designate funds for scholarships. He asked what my idea was. I thought of offering each player a free semester's tuition to any in-state school for every year they played. The original 36 would be given a full first year. The cost for the whole program wasn't that much. Luke called Wilco legal and found out it was OK. This meant that any kid associated with the football team, as a player or manager, had the opportunity to have their college costs reduced.

Next, was making it cool to be part of the team. I asked Jack how the team traveled to away games and he said by school bus. Wilco bought a used tour bus, quickly had it repainted in Mineral Point school colors with Pointer the dog emblazoned on the sides. In addition, we contacted Land's End in Dodgeville and talked with the corporate wearables program department and ordered 300 blue, hooded sweatshirts with 'Mineral Point' and an image of 'Pointer' the mascot on them. I then asked if we could also have navy blue blazers created for each member of the team to wear to school on game day.

Wilco PR examined the schedule and decided that we would have yard signs made for every house and business in Mineral Point. We then went to WDMP radio and bought all the times when the games were scheduled and hired play by play announcers. The Pointer games were going to be on the radio. Finally, we contacted the Democrat Tribune, where we spent a lot of money for our car dealerships and offered to have a column written each week that summarized all the high school games in the area. They were reluctant until we offered to consider it paid advertising and have high school kids interested in Journalism write the reports.

With the first preseason game away, it gave us enough breathing room and so I called Derrick and told him I needed his help. We knew we needed more than the original team to draw fans and so we called in favors and scheduled the UW band to perform the night before the Pointer's first home game when we were going to have the ribbon cutting on the new field. We thought it would be cool to have Bucky Badger there, as well, and have him arrive by helicopter. Strings were pulled and all was scheduled.

The school was going to be decorated by the pep club. There was going to be an old-fashioned pep rally where every student would receive the Land's End sweatshirts and honorary membership into the "Pointer Dawg Pound" with special seating at the games. It was announced that at each home game there would be a lottery of those sitting in the Dawg Pound where the winner received $100.

For the ribbon cutting, there would be free food and a DJ before the UW Marching band and cheerleaders arrived.

Bucky would fly in and a few short speeches would be given along with introductions of the players, followed by a full-scale fireworks display and photographs for the little kids with Bucky that they could pick up at the first game.

We developed a quick brochure outlining all that was going to take place that was mailed to every address in the Mineral Point school district and had banners made for each store on High Street reminding people when everything was going to take place. We watched the weather forecasts and it all looked good as all the pieces fell into place.

Touchdown:

After the assistant coaches appeared at school, the scholarship offers, travel bus and blazers, the number of kids on the squad increased from 36 to 62 with no kid rejected. Jack was able to get every talented kid he wanted to join the team and a few surprises that gave him the depth he'd been lacking in the past.

With all that done, we hoped we'd fill the bleachers. Not only were they filled, but people were standing all the way around the new fence. Jack had his hands full, but glances my way were such that words weren't needed. I knew he was grateful by the smile on his face, the occasional nod and the tear that rolled down his cheek. I don't think I could have given him a better birthday present than a full house.

As the night ended, we wanted to make certain all the adults came back and so they were given a lottery ticket for game night that not only included free admission, but use of a new Chevy Silverado for one year, compliments of Terrill Chevrolet that required attendance at the next game to win. The idea was to create the necessary interest and then establish the "habit" of looking forward to the home games.

For the first time since who knows when, the Mineral Point football team played to a full house. Unfortunately, they lost, but you could see improvement and excitement and Jack felt they were only a week or two away from being a decent football team. I began to see what it was like to be a football coach's widow and loved it.

To say that Jack and my relationship was developing quickly would be an understatement. We'd gone past the ooh/aah stage and reached a comfort level. Fall was going to mean football and I was OK with that as long as Saturday was 'our' day. After the game on Friday night, it was time to simply decompress and Sunday night, it was time to get ready for the following week.

After nearly two months, the condo was finally nearing completion after a certain Ms. Wilson put her foot down and gave everyone an edict that was supported by a bevy of Wilco lawyers who certain gave my threats more meaning with all their 'whereas' and 'here-to-for' gobbledy gook.

I took Annie to see the place and she fell in love with it. Perhaps it was the view of Lake Monona out the living room window through the floor-to-ceiling windows, or the private roof- top sundeck, or how we converted the smaller bedroom into an office with a motorized Murphy bed that folded into the bookcase. Whatever it was, Annie thought what we'd done was "cool", to use her expression. Finally, I took her in the master bathroom/bedroom, which seemed larger than her apartment and she was amazed at the size of the shower.

"You can fit four people in there!" I offered.

"Or have a lot fun with just two." Annie snickered.

The occupancy permits finally arrived and I was allowed to move in. I had a quiet house warming for Jack and I and well – let's leave it at that! My biggest surprise was how all my former experiences seemed to dissipate as our 'house warming' was soft, gentle and totally...and I mean totally complete.

It was midseason and the Pointers were starting to win games. With all the college assistants living in Madison, the condo became mission control on Sunday nights where we'd grill whatever we had and let the boys go over the next opponent's tape as they prepared the game plan.

Everyone loved the circular stairway to a rooftop patio and when the weather was nice it was where we hung out. There would be an inordinate consumption of Terrill Reserve bourbon and laughter, with moans and groans and good-natured ribbing thrown in. As everything wrapped up, the 'old couple' would thank the boys for coming, pick up and head for bed.

October flew by and the first two weeks of November meant the Pointers just made the regionals for the first time in a long, long time. The tension mounted as we were chosen to play Deforest, who'd been a well-coached team forever and play on their field. To say it wasn't pretty would be an understatement. The real issue was they had more depth and more experience and went on to State. Jack tucked his tail between his legs and it took a couple of days for the sting to wear off.

We were still going to the Badger games and sitting in the coach's section. Jack offered to sit in the skybox, but I said "No", I wanted to fit in. Perhaps someday, but not then. At the Badger game after the Deforest trouncing, I expected a lot of comments from the coaches around us. Instead, they congratulated Jack for a great season considering where he'd come from. I think this really helped salve the wounds as I realized how decent and honorable these coaches were, where the love of the game was only superseded by the respect they had for each other and the fact that they'd all been there before.

Thanksgetting:

It was the week before Thanksgiving and Jack asked if I
had plans. It was just he and his mom and I said "no". He
asked if I'd like to meet his mother and have Thanksgiving
with them. I was honored and told mom who realized, it was
getting really serious, really fast.

Jack was still driving the Rover even though he'd offered
to buy a new car. I had a better idea but didn't want to make
such a splash and so I asked dad if I could lease something
a little less, uh sporty for Jack and he suggested a Chevy
Silverado. I thought it would be great and picked out a candy
apple red, High Country, Crew Cab with a hard, quad fold bed
cover and a vanity license plate that said 'Pointer 1'.

I made it to Mount Horeb and reunited with Jack's mom
whom I slightly remembered from the cruise. She was about
the same age as my mom and dad and so I felt comfortable.
The house was small, but immaculate. On the mantel were
photos of Jack with his dad and then Jack in his football
uniforms from high school and Oshkosh. I never realized until
then that my boyfriend played college ball as a tight end, as
he never talked about it.

Thanksgiving dinner was quite traditional and I helped
clear the table. As the day was waning, I took Jack by the side
and told him that I needed to turn in my Rover, but had a
surprise for him as I handed him the keys. No more borrowing!
The dollar a month lease was in his name!

"You don't have to do that!" he responded.

"I never do what I have to do. I only do what I want to and
I want to lease you a vehicle for a dollar a month."

Jack just shook his head and looked at me. "I have so
much to be thankful for this year. Look at what all you and
your family have done for me. I can never express my total
gratitude."

"You do every time I'm with you. Perhaps not in words but
in the way you look at me and make me feel." I almost said "I

love you" but caught myself.

I looked at Jack and he at me and I spoke from the bottom of my heart. "What started off as the worst year in my life, you Jack Harris, made the best. You've shown me respect, dignity and above all else humility that I will always be grateful for."

I think we both knew this was becoming a forever thing and the warmth in my heart as I left Mount Horeb could have carried me to Timbuctoo instead of the condo if I needed to. The following morning the doorbell rang. It was Felly's flowers with a dozen red roses and a card that simply said "Touchdown!"

Take A Knee:

Saturday, we watched the Badgers beat Minnesota on TV and the media had them going to the Outback Bowl in Tampa for New Year's Day. I asked Jack if he'd like to go. He wasn't aware of our plane and thought we'd have to fly commercial or drive as he inquired "How many days will we be gone?" as he was mentally rearranging his schedule.

"Let me check with Derrick," I replied, knowing that my brother had it all figured out. I already knew the answer, but needed to ease Jack into one more of our family secrets.

The next day, I decided to spill the beans as I said "Jack, we have our own family plane which means we'll leave in the morning, fly down, watch the game and come home New Year's night," to which Jack just shook his head.

Jack and I were becoming like Forrest Gump's two peas in a pod. With Christmas quickly approaching I wondered what to get him as a present. Two weekends before Christmas we went out and bought a live tree and decorated the condo. Jack had asked if we could go back to The Graze for dinner that night. I don't think Jack had any idea how much it cost, but I couldn't say no and so he said he'd made reservations.

The weather was cool, but not cold for early December and so we decided to walk the few blocks and cut through the Capitol as both a respite from the cold and the shortest distance. We made our way into the virtually empty building by entering through the Hamilton Street entrance. As we reached the central portico, Jack stopped and said he needed to tie his shoe. With that, he knelt down and looked up and said "Will you marry me?" My hand went to my mouth. I'd already assumed we'd do the gradual thing and live together first, but simply knew it wouldn't have made any difference, the answer then or later would be the same. "Yes!"

Jack stood and we hugged and kissed and the few

people traversing within the dome probably put two and two together and realized what was going on that put a smile on the faces and a little warmth in their hearts.

"I'll need to ask your dad," Jack offered.

"If he doesn't say yes, he'll lose a daughter," I replied as the smile on my face almost began to hurt.

We kissed again as tears trickled from my eyes. From doom and gloom to incredible joy in less than a year. I thanked God and thought of the big buck and how he'd nodded. I thought of the anguish and pain and how mom and Annie helped make it go away. I thought of football and Mineral Point and all that had been a part of my dreams of being a princess as my heart filled with a profound sense of jubilation as, for the very first time in my life, I began to see my fairy tale come true.

"I can't afford much of an engagement ring right now," Jack offered.

"That's Ok. I really don't like rings anyway. Just a band of gold will be fine with me."

"Are you sure?" "Positive."

"You can have one if you want."

"Seriously, I really don't like wearing rings and a simple band of gold is all I want."

We embraced and whispered, "I love you" and agreed to cancel our reservations and go back to the condo, even though I later found out, there never was one. It didn't seem possible and yet, I knew that there was a God and my prayers were being answered.

It was just seven o'clock and I felt it was all this wonderful, wonderful dream that had been in my heart since I was a little girl was coming true. I asked Jack if I could call my parents and see if they were going to be home. Mom answered the phone.

"Hi mom, what are you and dad doing?"

Nothing really, we just got back from The Five O'Clock Club."

"Heh, Jack and I are in Milwaukee, can we stop by?" I lied. "Sure, I guess that's all right," Mom replied somewhat
hesitantly.

"We'll see you in a little bit."

We went down to stall 205, got into my new Rover and headed for Pine Lake, arriving a little before nine. I think mom knew what was going on as my poker face made it look like I had a royal flush. Dad had been watching TV in his new theater and was glad to see us, but had to show us the new ten-foot LED TV with surround sound and eight chairs in what had been the garage that was insulated and sound-proofed at mom's insistence.

We finally pulled dad out of his new playpen and I thought Mr. Tough Guy football player wouldn't know what to do or say as he simply announced, "Six years ago, I met a girl on a cruise who took my heart away. For the longest time, she was gone and with her absence so was the sunshine in my life as I could never forget her and thought of her each and every day."

"Four months ago, she walked back into my life and every minute since then have been the happiest days of my being. While the time has been short, the feelings have been there since the first time we met. While many will think we are rushing things, I know and have known for all these years there's only one woman I'll ever truly love and that's Melia."

"I'm just a school teacher and don't have the trappings that will ever match what Melia has been afforded. However, I promise you that, while I don't have in physical possessions, they will be more than compensated for by my dedication, love and commitment to your daughter."

"Tonight I repeated what you did so many years ago. We walked into the Capitol rotunda where I got down on one knee and asked your daughter to marry me. Melia said 'yes' and I've come to ask for your blessing."

"If you approve, it will be the happiest day of my life. I'm certain there will be times when you wonder why and yet, I vow I'll give my heart and soul to Melia including my love, respect, loyalty, dedication and my total commitment to her happiness."

Mom was crying. Dad had tears in his eyes and I was crying too. For an old football coach, I don't know who or how anyone could have been more eloquent as mom and dad simply said, "Yes".

We all hugged and it was time to go. As we got in the Rover and pulled out onto Highway 83 I looked across at Jack and simply said, "That was one of the most beautiful things I've ever heard."

Jack replied, "I've had six years to think about what I wanted to say. Can we call my mom?"

"Of course!" I replied as Jack hit speed dial and his mom's voice came on the speaker phone.

"Mom, I've got some news for you." "What?"

"Mom, you're going to have a daughter-in-law. Melia and I are going to get married."

"Oh, Johnnie. My prayers have been answered. I'm so happy. Melia, I've loved you since the minute we first met and I can't say how happy I am for all of us."

Jack continued. "We just left Melia's parents and so, it's still just between you, us and them, can you please keep it that way until we get some details worked out?"

"Of course, son. I'm so very, very happy. Thank you for calling and congratulations again."

With it so close until Christmas, I offered. "Why don't we wait and tell everyone then?"

A slight smile crossed Jack's face as he nodded in the affirmative, although it wasn't quite fair as Jack's family consisted of just he and his mother while I had my brothers and Annie.

"Do you think you can keep it a secret that long?" Jack asked. "Yup!" I replied.

"OK"

"I'd better call mom though and let her know," I offered.

Jack hit speed dial and the phone rang at the house. I frantically said, "Mom, Jack and I just had an argument and the engagement's off!"

"What?"

"Just kidding! We just called his mom and would like to keep it a secret until Christmas if you don't mind."

"Melia, don't scare me like that!" mom retorted. "Can you keep it our secret?"

"Of course, I can. It's your father I'm worried about. He's already making all sorts of big plans."

I shuddered. The last thing I wanted was a big wedding with all the hoopla and hoity toities. "We can talk about that AFTER it becomes public knowledge."

I think mom realized I didn't want what dad already envisioned and so I knew there was going to be some sort of negotiations involved.

During the next week, mom and I talked and she wanted to have Aunt Julia get my engagement ring. I told her, Jack and I already agreed that I really didn't want one. All I wanted was a thin gold band as I never liked wearing rings."

"Are you sure, dear?" mom inquired.

"Yes mom, I'm totally sure. That's really all I want."

Ho-Ho-Huh:

Christmas was on a Tuesday and so the Terrill Christmas with the boys, Andrea and Amelia was on Sunday; Jack's and my Christmas was Christmas Eve with Christmas day reserved for Jack's mom.

Sunday came and we headed back to Pine Lake. As always, the house was resplendent with all sorts of fancy decorations and a huge live Christmas tree sitting next to the fireplace. D (Derrick), V, and Me as we called each other, had pleaded with mom and dad not to go overboard on presents for all of us. Suuuure!

We had roast turkey with all the trimmings and then retired to the family room. Mom took me by the side and we had a short confab. "I think I've got a way to let you make your big announcement if you want to," Mom offered.

"How's that?"

"Well, there's a small box under the tree with your name on it. When you open it, I think it will all make sense."

We opened presents that consisted of all kinds of things no one needed and then mom pulled the small package from beneath the tree and handed it to me. I looked at the tag and it said, "To: Melia and Jack, From: Grandma Marie."

I already had tears in my eyes as I pulled the ribbon and opened the box. Inside was Grandma Marie's plain gold wedding band. I looked at my family and at Jack and then at the ring and then at mom as tears were sliding down my face.

D&V sat there as I looked at the ensemble and said "Jack and I have an announcement, we're getting married. As you all know, I don't like wearing rings and Jack wanted to get an engagement ring and I said, 'No'. Instead, I have the most beautiful wedding ring I could have ever imagined – Grandma Marie's."

There wasn't a dry eye in the house. I think even Charlie, dad's dog, had tears in his eyes.

The next big question was, "When?"

Jack and I had talked it over and we knew we wanted it to be soon but, didn't want to erode any of Derrick and Andrea's or 'V" and Amelia's plans and so I said, "We'd like to talk about it and see what makes sense for all of us.

I began wearing the gold band on a chain around my neck and whenever the question came up about an engagement ring, I simply showed the ring and explained my choices.

Tampaah:

New Year's Day arrived and time for the Outback Bowl as Jack and I made the quick trip from Madison to the Wilco Terminal at Mitchell Field. Jack simply shook his head as we pulled inside the hangar and the porter came out to open my door. Jack looked at Amelia[X] and was agog.

"There aren't any windows," Jack exclaimed.

"All closed circuit inside," I replied. "It allows the plane to go faster."

We entered the terminal as Derrick, Andrea, 'V' and Amelia were pulling up. Derrick had pulled out all the stops for Jack, as he was given a tour of the facility, and met with our pilot, who indicated we had a flight plan for just under 90 minutes wheels up to wheels down. I could see Jack's mental calculator spinning as he was attempting to determine our air speed, while the pilot noted we'd hit Mach 1.2 before beginning our landing.

We all climbed on board and Jack was simply taken aback by the luxury. None of us needed to imbibe and so we settled in. We left the boys to the front cabin and you got it – football – as us girls went in back. I'd wondered why mom and dad hadn't come and Derrick said dad wanted to watch it in his new theater. I thought that sounded like dad and yet knew the real reason was to allow the six of us to bond.

I had known V's Amelia my entire life. As Uncle Rodney and Aunt Ann's daughter, we'd done so much together. I was getting to know Andrea and liked what I saw. All the rubbish about stubborn Germans just didn't seem to be true. As we were sitting in back, the subject of weddings came up as I wanted to assure both of them I didn't want to take anything away from their big day, but really had no idea when they were planning on getting married. Needless to say, I wasn't surprised when both of them said they didn't have a date set simply because the Terrill boys were too busy or too involved or too something or other to think about the formality, which was normally one of the biggest days in a girl's life.

I looked at the two and said I had an idea. "What would you think if we all got married on the same day?"

"What?" Amelia questioned, almost shocked with the suggestion.

"Sure, we could have one wedding ceremony with one 'formal' reception at a neutral site and then have individual receptions closer to home."

"You mean like Black River Falls and Germany?" Amelia inquired.

"Yup, and Mount Horeb or Mineral Point for Jack and I."

A frown crossed Andrea's face as she inquired. "But what about my family coming to the wedding?"

I looked at her and replied. "I wouldn't worry about that. Mom and dad will take care of everything."

"Are you sure?" Andrea inquired.

"Which do you think would cost less and be less stress on everyone, three individual weddings or one big wedding?"

The girls just shook their heads and smiled while inquiring, "When?"

"I'm thinking late June." "Of this year?"

"Yes, haven't you waited long enough?"

They looked at each other and then at me as Amelia inquired "and how do we get the boys to agree?"

"Leave that up to me. Is it agreed?" Both nodded in the affirmative.

For everyone but Jack, the routine was pretty normal when we landed in Tampa. The courtesy car was waiting on the tarmac. We had some sort of clearance that took the vehicle literally next to Raymond James Stadium and we were escorted to our skybox that already had food and libations in place.

The boys sat in the front row and went crazy while the three of us, while somewhat football fans, didn't quite have the enthusiasm the boys did. Midway through the first quarter, the Athletic Director entered to make certain everything was OK, congratulated Jack on 'Operation Turn Around' for the Pointers and inquired whether he wanted to incorporate the intern program for fall. Jack enthusiastically said "Yes."

"Where's your dad?" the Director inquired.

"He and mom decided to ride this one out as dad's playing with his new TV," Derrick replied.

The look on the Directors face was somewhat perplexed.

"Dad got the bug and wanted a home theater, so had a new

garage built and took the old one, attached to the house and converted it, where one whole wall is a modular Samsung Micro LED unit that's 292 inches wide and added Dolby surround sound and eight theater seats."

"You mean he has a twenty-four-foot television?" the Director inquired.

"That's dad!" 'V' interjected as the Director just smiled and shook his head.

The Director looked at Jack and noted, "Reports back from this year's interns is that you really know your stuff. All of the kids indicated they not only were educated in football, but time management and sports integrity and I want to thank you for that."

"Thank you!" Jack replied in a somewhat embarrassed manner.

With that, the Director was out the door and Jack was back outlining different offensive tendencies and defensive strategies to Derrick and 'V'. We could tell that the boys were eating it up as much as they did the carved roast beef, potatoes and green beans they served during halftime.

Midway through the third quarter, Jack pointed to the Miami defensive line and told the boys, "Watch their hands during huddles, if they're on their hips, it means their gassed and it's time to spread to O-line from an 18" gap to 24" because the defensive line is tired. In college ball, there's an average of 72 snaps on both sides of the ball and both lines need be in contact that many times. With the Badger O-line as deep as it is, they've been consistently rotating players to keep them fresh. What used to be three to five-yard gains, should become five to seven and you might even see some breaks by the tailbacks who've been rotated and are fresh."

Sure enough, midway through the third quarter, the Miami defensive linemen had their hands on their hips and the Badger blocking scheme changed as they literally ran away with the game. 'D'&'V' were impressed as they simply shook their head at the depth of knowledge Jack had of something so obvious to him and overlooked by so many.

We knew that traffic would be tough after the game and so we sat in the skybox to let the crowds dissipate. With nothing to grab their attention, it was time to spring the question about a triple wedding. I felt that it would be improper for me to broach the subject and so Amelia said she'd do it.

"Guys, we've been talking," Amelia started, to which there were glances of consternation amongst the boys. "Is there anyone here who doesn't think we're going to all get married?"

All of us shook our heads no.

"In there anyone here who thinks we've waited long enough?" to which Andrea and Amelia both nodded in the affirmative.

"Don't you think having three separate weddings is going to create havoc for mom and especially dad Terrill?

Positive responses from Derrick and 'V'.

"What would you think of a triple wedding and then individual receptions?"

The guys looked at each other and at first, frowned and then smiled as Amelia continued, "We could have one big formal wedding, where dad Terrill could do what he wants to do for all of us and then have our own individual receptions."

The concept was quickly sinking in as I watched the expression on our alpha male, namely Derrick, evaluate the options as he inquired, "Where would we have the wedding?"

I piped up and asked, "where is one of dad's favorite spots?" "Camp Randall?" 'V' offered.

"I don't think so," I curtly replied. "Where did dad propose to mom?"

"The Capitol!" Derrick offered. "In the middle of the Rotunda." I nodded in the affirmative.

"What would you think if we had the weddings there? We'd all come in together and then either have separate vows or all together."

Amelia spoke up. "I think it would be neat to have individual vows," to which Andrea nodded, as I realized Amelia would like to have some form of Native American service, Andrea was Lutheran, Jack Methodist and the three of us whatever.

"When would you like to do this?" Derrick asked.

Andrea replied, "We were thinking about the third Saturday in June."

"This June?" 'V' inquired, somewhat surprised.

'V' looked at Derrick and Derrick looked at Jack and all three realized they were outnumbered at three to three.

"Do you really think you can pull this off?" Derrick asked, as all three of us replied in unison, "Yes!"

"Well guys, it looks like they're going to make honest men out of us." Derrick said with a smile as each of us hugged our respective beau and then did one of the old-fashioned hand stacking to show we were all in it together.

Surprise to the Third Power:

The plane ride home was insignificant as the boys watched even more football and we kibitzed in the back, agreeing we needed to go as a group to Pine Lake and propose our plan to mom and dad. With wheels down, we all headed to the house and sort of surprised mom and dad who was enamored in the Rose Bowl on the biggest TV I'd ever seen.

Derrick took the lead. "As you know, all of us want to get married. In so doing, we think it would be unfair to have you go through three weddings in such a short period of time and so, we'd all like to get married on the same day and have a triple wedding."

Mom was in shock as she repeated, "Three weddings at once?"

'V' replied. "Yes, and then one formal general reception followed by individual receptions at later dates."

"Where?" dad asked.

"We were thinking about the Capitol Rotunda in Madison." I offered.

Dad's wheels were spinning as he inquired, "Do they allow that?"

On the plane, I'd Googled and learned that it was possible. There were rules, but it could be done.

"Third week in June?" dad asked, almost to himself as he continued. "Block the entire Hilton and Madison Club which would mean around 500 people?"

We all nodded in the affirmative.

"We'd need to hire someone to quickly set up and take down the chairs and have Felly's do the flowers." Dad lamented. "One common entrance, separate seating areas and then individual vows?"

I again nodded to dad's introspections. "How big would each wedding party be?"

"We were thinking of one bridesmaid each and no groomsmen. We also thought about it and no one wants to wear tuxedos."

Dad was nodding in the affirmative as we knew he hated 'monkey suits', as he called them.

Derrick continued, "What would you think of navy-blue suits, white shirts and then three different color neckties to have us somewhat aligned with our brides?" which really made sense.

"Third Saturday in June? The Rotunda of the State Capitol? Three weddings? The Hilton and the Madison Club?" dad reflected as he looked at mom. "Makes sense to me, how about you?"

"It would be a little more complex, but also a lot easier. Then the kids could have their individual receptions. Amelia, I assume yours will be in Black River Falls? Andrea, in Germany? Jack?"

Jack replied, "I'd like to have it in Mineral Point or out on the farm if it would be OK."

"We'd be honored."

The excitement was building and yet everyone knew there would be a lot of planning and work that needed to be done as we all said goodbye and went our separate ways. Derrick and Andrea to downtown Milwaukee, 'V' and Amelia to Pewaukee and the helicopter to take them to Wausau, where they'd begun building the political network for 'V's' planned entry into national politics, and Jack and I back to Madison.

The following morning the phone rang and it was a lady by the name of Marie Gunderson who introduced herself and reported that Cecelia had contacted her regarding the wedding project. She noted that Ceclia had used her services several times and asked for her assistance for the three of us. Mrs. Gunderson said she'd email a corporate profile and references to which I gave her my email address and reviewed her information that noted she lived in Madison.

We agreed to meet the following day and I asked Jack to join us as he was the master organizer. The following morning, Mrs. Gunderson arrived at the condo at precisely nine. We sat at the kitchen table and went through all aspects of the wedding from location, to timing, to transportation, to the service itself and even the musical accompaniment. Jack, being Jack, began developing a Gannt chart on each aspect that included twenty- two different components. I think Mrs. Gunderson was in awe of Jack's ability to take a complex situation and break it down into components.

As the meeting ended, we called Cecelia and agreed to have Mrs. Gunderson represent us. Cecelia noted that she'd already booked the entire Hilton and the Madison Club next door and dad had a call into the Governor's office about the rotunda. She also noted that she'd asked Luke to be involved as well as Wilco security. Luke for operational logistics and Wilco Security to work with the Capitol Police to integrate our team with theirs, concerning what could and couldn't be done in a public place and how to ensure that those walking through the public building were neither offended, nor intrusive to our event.

I was amazed. In less than 48 hours, the plan was implemented and already being locked down. Two hours later, Cecelia sent a text saying dad had been in contact with the Governor's office and the space was reserved. It's amazing what a few million dollars in campaign contributions can do to open doors and get quick responses. Jack was dumbfounded at the speed at which everything was being set up as I sent a text to the fearsome foursome letting them know all that had transpired and they, too, were shocked. Quite honestly, so was I! Whew!

Spring Break:

Incredibly, Mineral Point Schools and the UW actually had spring break scheduled at the same time. Amazing! Jack and I were at the point where we needed a pause from school, wedding plans and daily life and I inquired whether he'd like a week away at House-On-The-Hill, especially after it seemed like spring would never come and the weather was less than wonderful in Madison. Welcome to Wisconsin!

Arrangements were made with Mom and Dad, Wilco Ops, Uncle Frank and Wilco Security and all systems were go. I told Andrew that my fiancé was a six-foot five-inch, ex-football player who weighed two hundred and sixty pounds and I didn't think Melia Wilson would need to wear the Apple watch, but agreed to do so anyway.

Amelia^X's speed attraction had become quite the money maker for the company to the point Wilco added three more to the fleet that weren't quite as "exclusive" on the inside as ours. In addition, Dad, in his never-ending quest for speed, ordered a plane from a company called Boom that we immediately began calling ' Boomer' that was 30% faster than Amelia^X. In the commercial version, Boomer could hold eighty passengers, but dad had it customized to "only" hold fifty. Flying at Mach 1.75 or over 600 meters per second, dad noted it would fly at 1,375 miles per hour, while flying above any turbulence, at 60,000 feet.

Boom Corp. created an app that allowed you to simply added the departure and arrival cities and it would show how long it would take to fly from Milwaukee to St. Martin, which was a little over ninety minutes, or Honolulu and Berlin in a little over three hours. Wilco Marketing had the app customized with the Wilco logo and sent a brochure and thumb drive to every potential client, even though we needed to wait a few years until the plane arrived.

There is an old saying, "the only difference between men and boys, is just the price they pay for toys." While we all thought dad was nuts buying Amelia[X], his business acumen was such that two years out, there were already deposits and a year-long waiting list for trips on Boomer.

Dad wasn't done. Not by a long shot! He went to Atlanta and invested in a company called Hermeus that was developing a 20- passenger plane that could fly at Mach. 5 or 3836 miles per hour. This meant we could fly from Milwaukee to St. Martin in a little over 30 minutes or around an hour from take-off to landing. Dad then had software developed that indicated travel times of a little over an hour from Milwaukee to Honolulu or Paris, which are both just a little over 4,000 miles away and Sydney, Australia in two- and-one-half hours. Crazy!

For Jack's and my vacation, all four Zoomers were going elsewhere and so we had to take Amelia III. Imagine, being *forced* to fly in the 'slower' private, four passenger jet. My goodness what was the world coming to, but we made the *'sacrifice'* – tee hee.

Uncle Frank met us at the airport and as always, was his effervescent self, who'd greased all the right wheels to make certain our week on the island would be wonderful. The ride to the house was as tumultuous as always considering that, other than Christmas, March was high season. During the one hour, fifteen-mile ride, Jack and Uncle Frank got to know each other as I sat in the back seat and wondered why we didn't have a chopper on St. Martin. I know, 'You're spoiled Melia.'

On the plane, I'd outlined what the French side of the island was like. Very European! Very tolerant and **very** laid back. I think Jack understood, but I was still concerned he'd be a little surprised how *'liberal'* everything was, particularly on the beach.

We arrived at the house and Jack was immediately impressed by House-On-The-Hill and the fact that the refrigerator was stocked, there were fresh flowers on the table and oranges in a bowl for breakfast juice. I'd already made our itinerary in terms of dinners, including Aunt Julia and Uncle Frank at Astrolab, which was one of the primary reasons for the trip, other than rest, relaxation and sporting activities.

Jack packed light, as I told him the island was casual. As for me, I brought nothing, which I'm certain Jack must have thought was odd, until I told him all my St. Martin clothes were there and I just needed to open my closet and put them in the dresser.

Uncle Frank said adieu and I took Jack on a house tour and went to unpack. Jack put his clothes in a couple of dresser drawers while I dug out my attire. After wearing long pants and warm sweaters all winter, the thought of shorts and tops sounded wonderful. As I put each item in the dresser, memories came back of Annie and me and our raucous time. I had some degree of trepidation about some of the items, but also knew I wanted the week to be filled with a degree of intimacy that couldn't happen in Madison, even as liberal as it was and so many time constraints as well.

I'd learned a long time ago that men loved women who were part mothers, part nurses and part, where the polite term is amorous lovers. While we'd been quite 'active', I wanted to make certain the week was filled with all sorts of adventures that would make Jack aware of how much I loved him.

I suggested a dip in the pool and Jack thought it would be great as he slid into his bathing suit. I needed to make my first attire decision - Itsy Bity, Teenie Weenie or the Sailor Suit. I looked at my farm boy fiancé and thought, 'Hmmm, what do I wear?' Remembering the theory of acclimation, where what starts out special becomes commonplace and with repetition even mundane, I decided to start with Itsy Bitsy and when Jack got 'acclimated', switch to Teenie Weenie and then, depending on his reaction the Sailor Suit.

We fiddled around in the pool until it was time for the cocktail hour and I took Jack on a tour of the vault that almost knocked his socks off, particularly the security involved. We settled on some of the Terrill Reserve Pinot Noir and toasted our first night on St. Martin. I got dressed in what I now considered conservative attire consisting of the white horse collar and dress shorts with Jack in khaki shorts and a black golf shirt.

As was our family tradition, our first St. Martin dinner was at L'Auberge Gourmande where we were greeted royally. Nothing had changed, but then, I'd hoped it hadn't. While small in size, L'Auberge was huge in ambiance and that's what I loved - small, quiet, intimate, where you have a dining experience and simply don't go to eat.

"Ms. Terrill, it's so nice to see you," Pascal offered as he kissed me on both cheeks and offered as his hand for Jack's.

"This is my fiancé, Jack Harris," I offered.

"It's so nice to meet you, Monsieur Harris. Welcome to L'Auberge Gourmande. If there is anything I can personally do for you, please feel free to ask. Mademoiselle Terrill and her family are always our honored guests."

Jack was aware of the name Terrill-to-Wilson name game and yet I think he was still experiencing a level of discordance with the entire situation. There was nothing I could do about it except hope he got used to Wilson or Terrill for the remaining 90 days until my name would finally change to Harris.

The food was scrumptious and the service spectacular. As we enjoyed our after-dinner rum, Jack kept waiting for the check. I finally realized and told him not to worry, we had an account and it would be central billed, outlining that all I needed to do was sign my name.

Being the gentleman Jack was, he wanted to pay and I simply told him, "No". He could make it up to me in other ways.

Dinner reservations were set for the entire week and neatly printed on a card on the kitchen table. Late comers, even with Uncle Frank's connections, would never have a chance to get in.

- Sunday, Bistro Caraibes
- Monday, Astrolab
- Tuesday, JAX Steakhouse
- Wednesday, Le Piment
- Thursday, Le Cottage
- Friday, La Villa
- Saturday, Le Taitu

When it came to sports activities, Penny set up snorkeling at Pinel Island, scuba diving at the HMS Proselyte, jet skiing and parasailing on Orient Beach, with all times scheduled in the morning so that we could then eat lunch there as well.

Even after Irma and the new arrivals, I knew the restaurant line-up that started at Coco Beach, KaKao, Bikini Beach, Playa Bar, Orient Bay Beach, Wai Plage, Kontiki, Orange Fever, Le String, Sun Beach Clubber, Chez Leandra and finally, The Perch Lite, where the plan was to try as many as we could for lunch and then sit by the shore and people watch as 'the strollers' passed by.

It seemed funny to me the existing impact of the former Club Orient had and how the closer you got to its former edge, the more liberal the clothing requirements became. I didn't want to make Jack feel uncomfortable and so we began on the conservative west end and ate our way east.

While mom had me motivated to do push-ups and sit-ups, Jack was incredible. Besides running up and down Happy Hill, Jack did push-ups from a deck of cards where you pick a card and match the number. Face cards called for 10 pushups. Aces 25, and the Joker 50. I thought it was crazy until we finished 25 cards in the deck and Jack said, "again" shuffling the deck and going through the same twenty-five card routine, only with sit- ups.

After the first couple of days, I realized that my fiancé was more liberal than I anticipated and so we began planning afternoon sessions at Chez Leandra to give Jack a sense of what - other than the epicurean delights - the island was really all about. I explained the sunrise walks and offered to escort him if we were ever up that early with special treats from Good Morning, if we made it in time. Jack thought it would be neat. I wanted him to dip his toes in the European way of living, but not jump in with both feet.

As for amorous adventures, perhaps, just perhaps, eight years of literal celibacy finally caught up with me as my proclivities that had been dormant for so long, were erupting in full force. The location and ambiance? The weather? The totality of feeling wanted, needed and loved? I'm not certain. Caution was thrown to the wind and the week evolved into a stretch of activities beyond what I'd planned that were, quite honestly, all initiated by me. Regrets? Absolutely none. I only hoped Jack didn't think the level of activity was the norm and would either be concerned, turned off or assuming they represented tomorrow's tomorrow, instead of just the week at hand.

Sunday, we slept in and I made breakfast of bacon and eggs with the freshly squeezed orange juice. I slid into the Mary Ann Daisy Dukes accompanied by the paisley hankie top, which received multiple stares from the man I was sleeping with.

We met Penny for the snorkel trip early enough to beat the tourists and made sure Penny kept the revenue stream flowing that afternoon. Jack loved it, even though we didn't see any turtles or Gladys, the nurse shark.

As the snorkeling ended, we made our way up and down Bell Hill to Le' Anse Marcel, parked the Rover and I took Jack to the side of the restaurant to show him one of several plaques throughout St. Martin of Grandma Marie. I thought I'd better explain why we were about to be treated the way we were at so many different places.

Next to Grandma Marie was the esteemed Gault & Millau "Les Soirees de Toques" or Chef's Hat Award plaque denoting that head chef Florian Mercadier had been named Chef of the Year.

The plaque noted that the award was based on the Gault & Millau Antilles-French Guiana Restaurant Guide that featured 259 restaurants in Guadeloupe, Martinique, St. Barths, St. Martin and St. Lucia of which 28 were located in St. Martin.

Once again, we were treated like royalty with the corner VIP table as Jacques, little Charlie's dad, personally came out to welcome us and ask Jack what type of food he enjoyed. Once again, Jacques wanted to make a special meal that Jack would never forget. Once again, Jack was flabbergasted at the offer and the meal provided.

"This is lunch?" Jack inquired as he rubbed his belly.

"Well, Jacques probably went a little out of his way, but yes."

"Oh, my God. We're going to need a cargo plane for me to fit in, to go home."

Sunday night meant Bistro Caraibes, one of the top-rated restaurants in the Caribbean. I pulled out the yellow jumpsuit and slid into it, trying to decide how many buttons to undo. Three? Nope! Four? Nope! Five? Maybe! Six? Hmm!" Seven? No way, as things began falling out. I decided I'd start at four and then 'progress' as the night wore on, with hope that buttons eight through twelve would be undone by a certain Mr. Harris.

I put on some make-up and came down stairs to a radiant smile and a "you look great!" comment from the man I wanted to entice. I gave Jack a "thank you" hug as we got in the Rover and headed for Grand Case.

As Jack was driving, I discreetly unbuttoned number five. As we were finishing our entre and Jack wasn't looking, I unbuttoned number six, with a wry smile on my face. At first, Jack didn't notice and then realized I was virtually doing a strip tease in the restaurant, just for him.

As we left the restaurant and began walking back to the Rover, I unbuttoned number seven, which opened the jumpsuit to just below my waist and sure enough there was a little, make that, a lot of peek-a-boob taking place. When we arrived at the Rover, I hugged Jack and whispered, "buttons eight-through- twelve have been reserved for Mr. Harris," as I slipped my tongue inside his mouth.

Monday meant Orient Beach with Jack 'adjusting'. Monday night we met Aunt Julia and Uncle Frank, while Jack had to hear the story about what an Astrolab was. Dinner was a smashing success and when Jack excused himself to use the restroom, Aunt Julia whispered as if he could hear us from fifty feet away. "Melia, he's everything your mother said, except even more handsome. If you don't want him, I'll take him," which was Aunt Julia's way of saying she approved.

From the swimwear perspective, Sunday and Monday had meant Itsy Bitsy. Tuesday morning, I lollygagged until Jack was downstairs and slipped into Teenie Weenie and made a grand entrance.

Jack's eyes widened as he smiled and observed, "Nice suit!"

I didn't know if he was being sincere or factious and so I asked, "Really?"

"You look fantastic," Jack responded and I knew his libido was on the rise…again.

Jack went parasailing and we had lunch at Wai and rented two chaise lounges to watch the human parade pass by. I was tempted to take him east of the rocks, but thought otherwise. However, at three, we made our way to Chez Leandra, as I thought it was time to indoctrinate Jack into Annie's and my world, from the previous summer.

As we arrived Z saw us and spread his arms almost as wide as his smile as he planted the obligatory la bise on both cheeks and announced, "Melia, my love, you have returned."

I looked at 'Z' and announced. "This is my fiancé and his name is Jack Harris."

"You mean, you're going to get married?"
"Uh huh!"
"Oh, that's wonderful news. Come, we've got to tell Maria."

"Maria! Maria! Look who's here, it's Melia and her fiancé Mr. Jack Harris. Let's have some Champagne to celebrate."

While I really didn't want the attention, it made no difference as Z offered a toast in honor of Jack and me. As Z went back to serving drinks to others, Jack offered, "Another restaurant your grandma saved?"

"No, it's where Annie and I hung out last summer and spent enough in two weeks to cover his expenses for the year."

I think Jack was a bit discombobulated by the brevity of attire of the other patrons with half the women topless and in thongs while I hoped he didn't think less of me. I also hoped he'd eventually be able to acclimate as I had done, to the point it no longer made a difference.

As we finished our celebratory toast, we excused ourselves and walked west and got caught in Lucille's web as she came from her storefront to greet us. "Melia, it's so wonderful to see you. You're suit looks so nice on you. Who's this handsome man?"

"This is my fiancé, Jack Harris."

"Oh Mr. Harris, it's my pleasure and you'll have such a lovely bride. Come into my shop, I would like to show you something I think you will like."

Jack looked at me and didn't know what to do. I decided it would be fun to watch Lucille try and finagle Jack into something he didn't really want and so I just smiled and nodded as we trudged into the den of inequity, where the ultimate salesperson resided.

"So, you're American. That means you probably don't want to wear this," Lucille reported as she held up a tiny men's bikini."

"Ahh, NO!" Jack replied.

Lucille responded, "I didn't think so and yet we need to take that 'made in America' label off you. You're such a handsome man with a great body and yet, your suit comes down below your knees."

Lucille simply shook her head in disdain as she lamented, "that basketball player who made his entire team wear really long shorts simply because he wanted to wear his college shorts underneath! What a shame for so many gorgeous men! Let me see if we can't find something that says you really belong on Orient Beach."

Lucille began offering Jack more and more of less and less and less as I simply stood and watched, silently giggling, until Lucille saw a positive response in Jack's eyes to trunks that were shorter than those he was wearing, but not one of those Lucille originally had in her hands.

"Go try it on. For you, half price – no for Melia and her mother, it's my gift to you."

Jack looked at me and I simply nodded and so he went behind the curtain and changed.

As he appeared Lucille said, "Come, look in the mirror. You'll see how you look so much more debonair. You know, like you belong with Melia, instead of someone who just got off one of the cruise ships."

In this case, I happened to agree with Lucille. Jack did look more European without going crazy, although he had the body for any suit, as I politely nodded in the affirmative.

"What do you think?" Jack inquired.

"Well, I really liked the very first suit, but then that's my opinion," I lied as Jack simply cringed.

Lucille realized she'd reached her limit, looked at the two of us, put Jack's old suit in a bag and offered "You two go now and be young. It won't be long until your youth is gone. I looked at Jack and he at me and we simply surrendered to Lucille's urging and realized if we didn't leave the store, she'd try and sell us more.

Dinner Tuesday night was at Jax as I thought my Jack needed a break from French cuisine. I wore a conservative pair of dress shorts and the white horse collar and watched as my Jack snarfed down a twenty-two-ounce porterhouse as if it were an appetizer. My, that man can eat!

Wednesday was cruiser day in St. Martin when the gawkers inundated Orient Beach via tour buses with cameras in hand. Penny was busy with her and Paul's double tours. The marina was packed with people wanting to go snorkeling, sailing, jet skiing and parasailing and so I asked Jack what he wanted to do as he politely said 'Hang out at our pool' which quickly took on a new meaning.

Dinner was at Le Piment, which was slammed. The food was great, eating alfresco was grand and we were able to go 'casual' with me in shorts and a tank top and Jack in shorts, sandals and a tight black tee-shirt that showed how buff he was.

Richard waved at us, but was really too busy to visit. We made it an early evening, although we could easily have walked across the courtyard and had drinks at Le Telegraph. We didn't, simply because I was afraid I'd be recognized after the night Annie and I had there.

Thursday, I called Penny and asked if we could go to Happy Bay for a break, got brave and slipped into the Sailor Suit Lucille sold me when Annie was there that I hid it under the red Mary Ann romper. Penny made all the arrangements for a wonderful picnic and we had a superb afternoon. Jack seemed to acclimate to the fact the beach was clothing optional, which had been my biggest concern. Some people can handle it, others can't. I was quickly learning that the man I loved was much more sensitive and liberal than the rough, tough, macho football coach let on and that put a smile on my face.

When it was time to go, I called and Claude came with the skiff, taking us directly to Chez Leandra for happy hour. Jack inquired about the Rover and Claude indicated that it had already been relocated and the bumper key vault's code was simply the date.

We arrived at Chez Leandra and indulged in glasses of dirty lemonade and talked with some people who said they were from Paris, but had American accents, until they told us it was Paris, Texas.

Thursday night's dinner was at Le Cottage and once again, it was a five course, knock-your-socks off meal to which my husband-to-be simply said, "This is ridiculous". To spice up the might, I wore the tan micro mini and the rayon paisley top. I thought Jack was going to stab himself with his fork when I simply arched my shoulders back to create a full profile.

"What?" I inquired.

"Food this good and only here. We've got to come back real soon," which put an ear-to-ear grin on yours truly.

Friday was back to Orient Beach and the same routine with me now comfortable in the Sailor Suit. That night, we went to dinner at La Villa where I wore the tan horse collar and a black miniskirt. Jack just smiled.

For Saturday, we planned on literally duplicating Friday, except it was laundry day as I started getting ready to return to reality. As I was sorting the clothes and putting them away for our next vacation, I dug down in what I hadn't worn and sure enough, Annie had tucked OMG in with my stuff from when we'd been here before.

I slipped into the suit and simply shook my head. Jack was out at the pool and so I sauntered out to where he was sitting. His head jerked back and he smiled and exclaimed "wow, where'd you get that?"

I told him the entire story of Lucille and Independence Day. "You actually wore that at Chez?"

"Uh huh!"

A sly smile crossed his face as he inquired "Are you going to wear it there today?" "If you want me to." I guess the very last drop of inhibition in my body was gone. The man I loved was excited by the way I looked and it was a wonderful feeling.

We made it to the beach and then to Chez to say goodbye. The week had been magnificent and just what we needed. We had reservations at eight at Le Taitu, or 'Annie's night', as I called it. I'd learned that Le' Taitu means "The Silent" in French and to that end, we abided with a very quiet dinner where our eyes never left each other's.

I wore the white hankie top and denim mini skirt, which I think Jack really liked. I provided Jack with a highly redacted version of Annie's and my walk on the beach, and about the stars and lunar eclipse and how Annie looked with the Rover's green dash lights glowing on her body – "like she was from Venus or perhaps even Mars", to which Mr. Smarty Pants had to add, "at least it wasn't Uranus". Tee hee, hee!

Fuseday:

I informed Jack that Sunday would be 'Fuseday'. When he asked what I meant, I told him that we'd had a week without any timetable and, on Sunday morning, we'd subconsciously light the imaginary fuse and keep looking at our watches regarding what time we were going home.

"Fuseday? I like that," Jack replied.

I received a text saying we were riding home in Amelia^X, that would be arriving from Puerto Rico, where she'd dropped off some high rollers. I was instructed to check the app for an estimated departure time from St. Martin, but plan on 1700 hours. I decided not to tell Jack about Amelia^X and make it a surprise.

Uncle Frank said he and Aunt Julia wanted to take us out to lunch at Le' Anse Marcel. I thought it was odd, but concluded they'd only had dinner with Jack and probably wanted more time with their future Grand Nephew and agreed to meet at 1300 hours.

Jack was going to pack, but I told him we could leave his clothes and store them with mine. It made no sense bringing clothes home simply to bring them back again. Fifteen minutes before our reservation, we made our way over to the restaurant. As always, Aunt Julia and Uncle Frank were waiting. We sat and shared our week's adventures.

"What do you think of our little island, Jack?" Aunt Julia inquired.

"I love it! But I wish Melia could have found some better restaurants."

Aunt Julia's mouth dropped open as Jack continued. "I only gained ten pounds eating some of the best meals of my life and I'd planned on twenty, so I guess we'll need to come back soon."

It was then that Aunt Julia got the left-handed compliment which, being left handed, I never really knew why they called them that.

As lunch was completed Aunt Julia got a serious look on her face and began. "Frank and I couldn't be happier for the two of you. You make such a wonderful couple."

"Thank you, Aunt Julia," Jack offered and I affirmed.

"Melia, your grandmother was the only person I ever had in the world. Your mother was the only niece I've ever had. And you're the only grandniece, I'll ever have. Jack, as I'm certain Melia has shared with you, Frank and I owned a jewelry store in Phillipsburg and it was always my dream to give my only grandniece one of my favorite rings that contains three stones – one for my sister, one for my niece and one for my grandniece and I would like to offer it to you to give to Melia as an engagement ring."

Jack and I were shocked as Aunt Julia handed Jack a ring box and we opened it.

"My God!" was all I could say as Jack's mouth dropped open in totally profound shock as the center stone was at least three or four carats and the two side stones were one carat each.

Jack took the ring out, got down on one knee and repeated, "Melia, will you marry me?"

I looked at the ring and then Aunt Julia, as the tears began to flow. I guess deep down I'd wanted an engagement ring. I just thought Jack would be pressured as I replied, "Of course, I'll marry you and will always think of not only my love for you, but my wonderful Aunt and Uncle every time I put it on."

"Can I pay you for this?" Jack inquired.

"Most certainly," Aunt Julia replied. "Simply by taking care of Melia and making sure she always feels wanted, needed and loved."

"You have my word on that," Jack offered. I thought there couldn't be anything else until Uncle Frank added. "Jack, for nearly forty years, we were one of the largest Rolex retailers in the Caribbean. When we announced our retirement, the Hans Wilsdorf Foundation, who owns Rolex, wanted to show their appreciation for our loyalty and gave Julia and I matching Rolex watches. While we were honored, we're too old and it's too hot to wear them here on St. Martin."

It was Uncle Frank's turn as he placed two watch boxes on the table and Jack and I were simply flabbergasted as we opened them to find his and hers 18ct gold, Rolex Sky-Dweller watches as Uncle Frank added, "Your Aunt and I would like you to have them as our wedding gifts."

Jack and I just sat there in shock. What do you say? We were given watches that cost more than some people pay for cars, from two people who only needed to continue giving us the love they always had.

I stood and gave both Aunt Julie and Uncle Frank big hugs, knowing to do anything but accept the gifts would have broken their hearts. Jack followed suit as he wiped tears of joy and gratitude from his eyes, where each tear said more than a thousand words.

It was getting late and Uncle Frank said he'd take Aunt Julia home and meet us at the house at four. We'd drive the Rover to Princess Juliana Airport and he'd come back, close up the house, set the security and go home from there.

We all stood again and hugged once more.

"See you in June! I've love you," I said to Aunt Julia.

"See you then Melia, and thank you for making my dreams come true by finding a nice boy who will make you happy," she responded

We went back to the house, climbed in the shower and finished putting the clothes away, just as Uncle Frank reappeared. I checked the Apple watch one last time to see that Amelia^X was just departing from San Juan and put the watch in the kitchen drawer until the next time we came.

Uncle Frank had it down to a science and knew fighting Sunday Marigot traffic meant an hour to travel the nine miles from House-On-the-Hill to the airport. Fortunately, the ride was filled with laughter and memories of a wonderful week and there were no delays, as we entered the private plane tarmac gate and drove out to Amelia[X].

Jack just looked and smiled at my little airplane surprise. We said goodbye with hugs to Uncle Frank as I handed him a thank you note for Aunt Julia.

We boarded and I admired the beautiful watch and ring and then looked at Jack and said. "You know what? I'm going to wear the ring on my right hand instead of my left, in honor of Grandma, mom and Aunt Julia so that my wedding ring will always be closest to my heart."

Jack looked at his new watch and simply smiled. Rolex watches are all hand-made and take over a year to assemble. Jack said he'd always wanted one, but never thought his dream would come true.

I looked at the love of my life and asked him what he thought of our vacation. He just shook his head and asked when we could come back again. I expressed a devilish grin and whispered. "The vacation's almost over. However, a little later in the flight, I think we do need to join the mile-high club!"

The Planners:

Spring was flying by. It was nice to have the weather warm again and our wedding date getting closer. With each day, I knew that my acceptance of Jack as my life partner was the right decision. For the first time in my life, I felt complete.

I transferred my winter clothes to Pine Lake and brought my spring wardrobe back to the condo. Jack thought we should rent a warehouse just for my clothes. His smart-ass remark made me warn him that **HIS** Red Corvette might be delayed as there was only room in the downstairs garage for two vehicles. Tee hee!

We had a zoom call for all six brides and grooms along with mom and dad, Captain Luke, Mrs. Gunderson and Andrew, who had forgiven me for threatening to throw the Apple watch in the ocean. Between Luke, Andrew and Mrs. Gunderson, they had everything planned including seating, logistics, entertainment, plants, flowers and security. Using Jack's Gannt chart system, each showed the progression on every aspect, along with the Hilton, transportation for Andrea's family and friends from Germany and even the menu. Mrs. Gunderson even had a contract for china with a blue and gold pattern around the edges for the Madison Club.

For the ceremony, seating in the Capitol rotunda was to be in three specific 'family sections' with a general section as well. Each bride would enter from a different lane and walk down the center aisle with their father and go to an assigned couch in front of their respective families. Music was arranged from the University of Wisconsin Chamber Music ensemble who would be located on the upper promenade so that the entire rotunda would be filled with music. Dad had contacted the Chief Justice of the Wisconsin Supreme Court who'd agreed to give the benediction. The 'altar' was designed to be a clear sheet of glass with tall plants and flowers behind to block any people walking through the

Capitol. Wilco Security was planning on 30 security guards to support the Capitol Police and there would be royal blue ropes with security staff members blocking all but the focused entrance.

Luke signed a contract with a company that specialized in rock concert set ups and tear downs, who had twenty-five experienced staff members ready to set up and take down the chairs and carpet runners. The contract with the State had a clause indicating we only had two hours before and after the ceremony to get everything back the way it was. It would be a rush, but Luke said they could do it, and they did. Go Luke!

We made a security payment of $50,000 to ensure we were on time and complete. Special parking permits were issued for the trucks to have them adjacent to the Capitol and ready to go. Permits for horse drawn carriages were obtained to bring the wedding parties from the Hilton to the Capitol, even though it was only two blocks away. Luke also had trollies ready to convey guests from the wedding to the Madison Club which is next door to the Hilton for those who needed conveyance from the Capitol or there was inclement weather.

Mrs. Gunderson outlined the reception menu that was top shelf with Terrill bourbon and Pino Noir RSVP with meal request cards that would be included, along with the 'save-the-date' and invitations along with Gannt charts indicating when they were being sent out, as well as the follow-up and RSVP counts. Finally, Mrs. Gunderson outlined the entertainment for the evening that began with chamber music during dinner and then a disc jockey after we ate. Needless to say, nothing, other than the weather, was being left to chance and, at the end of the Zoom meeting, everyone was impressed with the details in place to make it a perfect day.

Dad (actually Cecelia) made arrangements at Brooks Brothers for all the guys to be fitted for the navy-blue suits. It was the first time in Jack's life that he'd ever been custom fitted and I knew he would look dashing with black, lace-up, Alan Edmunds Park Avenue shoes, as well. Ceclia ordered striped ties from Hawes and Curtis and the guys drew straws with Derrick getting gold-and-white, 'V' blue-and-white and Jack red-and-white, to delineate who was with which bride, while otherwise sustaining a consistent look.

As for dresses, they were up to us girls. Mom wanted me in something really fancy and I politely said 'no'. I wanted it to be nice, but nothing overboard. Amelia was honoring her family and would be in the traditional buckskin with hand-sewn beads that mom told me she remembered from Rodney and Ann's wedding, as simply incredible. Andrea was planning on wearing the dirndl, which I learned was a traditional dress with a structured bodice, tightly tied and decoratively embroidered which meant that all three brides were going to have a different look to honor the heritage of our families.

With my measurements in Dubai, mom ordered a custom white wedding dress for me that was simply gorgeous with white pearls embroidered on the bodice. I vowed I'd put in in storage in case we had a daughter who could wear it on her wedding day. It was simply too beautiful to only wear once.

It didn't seem possible that the wedding day was coming so fast. I finished classes as did Jack and had a brief respite before the big day. I'd asked Jack where he wanted to go on our honeymoon and he said he didn't care. I asked him if there was one place he's always wanted to go. Again, he simply shook his head. Mr. Conservative didn't want to have our family go overboard as we knew he couldn't afford anything more than going to the Dells, which would have been fine with me.

Instead, I took out a map of the world and set it up on a board, got some darts and told him to throw a dart and wherever it landed, we were going. The ninny tossed the dart and it landed in the middle of the Atlantic Ocean. Great, just what I wanted, a glorious honeymoon floating on a raft in the middle of the Atlantic. I thought of the movie 'Titanic' and how, there was actually room for Jack on the floating door if Rose had simply moved over.

"Throw another one!" I commanded and he hit Antarctica. I vowed never to have Jack on my dart team.

"Again!" as one finally hit South Africa.

"OK, we're going on a photo safari to Africa!" I announced.

I called Wilco Ops and informed them of our desire and they said it was in Amelia^X's range, but I thought I'd better ask dad. I called and he said it was where he and mom had gone on their honeymoon and one of his favorite trips. He wanted to know if we wanted to sell some bourbon and steak while we were there, but that didn't sound like the most romantic honeymoon. He also said, he'd rather have us go commercial and so arrangements were made for the airfare and an escorted tour of Botswana and Tanzania with a 'Williams couple' along for the ride.

Five days before the wedding, the Germans arrived consisting of Andrea's dad, aunt and two first cousins with their husbands and several of Andrea's friends and spouses. Dad had simply reserved the entire first-class section on a Lufthansa flight and told Angela to "fill-er-up".

Andrea's family and some of her friends had never been to the States and yet, all but Andrea's dad, spoke impeccable English. Andrea and Derrick hosted them in both Chicago and Milwaukee and took then out on our fishing boat on Lake Michigan. Andrea's dad's suit had been 'roughed' in and so they just needed to adjust the sleeves and pants length and they were all set.

The wedding day came and the weather was spectacular (whew!). The Capitol rotunda was simply spectacular with ferns and flowers everywhere and the set-up went off with military precision. Wilco Security, the Capitol Police and both State and Local Police departments were all involved because the guest list included the Governor, members of the State Supreme Court, Madison's Mayor, both US Senators and one Congressman.

Those passing through the Capitol were politely 'redirected' and the entire ceremony went off without a hitch. My only regret was that we'd elected not to have bridesmaids and groomsmen. I felt sorry for Annie as she would have been my maid of honor. To make her feel special, I had a corsage and special seating that I think appeased her sensitivity.

The processions were flawless with each of us entering down a red carpet from a different side to the oohs and aahs of the ladies in the audience at our different dresses. Two red velvet couches were aligned at the front of each family section. One was for the bride and sponsor and the other for the groom. Amelia had Uncle Rodney, Andrea had her dad and I had dad. Changing protocol, Jack asked if it was OK if his mom could sit beside him and we, of course, said "sure".

We all sat while Chief Justice Warren shared his thoughts on marriage and the joys and challenges it provided. As he completed, he sat as Uncle Rodney presented Amelia to 'V' while the Medicine Man went through the traditional Native American wedding ceremony with their special vows, pipe and all. It took some arm twisting by Uncle Rodney to have special dispensation from the Capitol Police as there's no smoking allowed in the Capitol building.

Next came Andrea's dad who was nervous, but made it through presenting her to Derrick. The minister from Bethel Lutheran Church presented the vows first in English and then in impeccable German as a sign of respect for Andrea's family, which put wide smiles on their faces and nods of gratitude as well.

Finally, it was dad's turn as he presented me to John David Harris and Reverend Thomas Moore from the Mount Horeb United Methodist Church. Dad kissed me on the cheek and whispered, "I love you," as he returned to the couch and then almost sat on mom. It all seemed like a blur, as the entire six months of planning went whoosh in a little over an hour.

As the ceremony ended, Chief Justice Warren returned to the podium and announced that the three couples were now legally and officially wed in holy matrimony. He then smiled and noted that all three ceremonies needed to be consummated by the dinner and party at the Madison Club to which the guests could either walk or take the trolleys that were located out the M.L. King exit behind him.

We stayed for the obligatory photos during the ruckus and racket of five hundred chairs being folded, but no one would ever know, as our smiles were frozen in time to be cherished forever. I'd asked Annie to stay as Teddy was home and made certain they had their formal photos taken with Jack and I and then had them sit next to us at the reception.

Speaking of the reception, it was spectacular with dad going all out with even some of the Terrill 150 Private Stock somehow being served. Iced caviar, shrimp, lobster, scallops and crab centerpieces were set on each table and then the guests had their choice of Terrill Wagyu filets or chicken, of which I think I saw two people eating chicken. Instead of a huge wedding cake that normally tastes like wallpaper paste, whatever wallpaper paste tastes like, we chose white angel food wedding cake with a whipped cream frosting and strawberry filling. It was yummy!

To make certain everyone felt 'important', we reserved two empty chairs at each table and every five minutes there would be a 'dinging' of the glasses as all three sets of newlyweds moved from table to table until we'd visited with all the guests. When all was said and done, everyone got fed, entertained and enjoyed themselves. Even the hoity toities were smiling and having a good time, without all the political nonsense that usually happens when you get a bunch of ego maniacs together.

While others were staying next door, it made no sense for Jack and me as it was less than a block walk and so, I went into a private room where a maid helped me change into 'civilian clothes' and we simply, quietly, went 'home'.

A week later 'V' and Amelia had their reception in Black River Falls and I guess Uncle Rodney went all out. To ensure focus on them, we all agreed we wouldn't go to each other's reception. A week after that, Derrick and Andrea went to Germany and had a big shindig over there. I guess they got dad 'loose' and had him singing German drinking songs. We decided to wait on our reception and went on our honeymoon instead, simply to give mom and dad a break.

Africa was INCREDIBLE. My God, what a journey. My biggest thrill was visiting Rwanda where my ancestors came from and sightseeing through the African Great Lakes Region including Lake Victoria, which included Lake Tanganyika, which is the world's second-largest freshwater lake by volume and depth and then Lake Malawi, the world's eighth-largest fresh water lake. For me, it was awe inspiring to see where some of my ancestors had lived while actually seeing people who were built like me in terms of being tall and slender with gentle smiles and great big hearts who would have given us anything.

We came home with hundreds of photos and thousands of memories and one other big surprise. As things returned to normal, Jack said he was hungry for steak and agreed to cook out. As the T-bones were ready and the salad prepared, Jack opened the cupboard and was going to pour a couple of drinks. I looked at him and said, "uh, you can have one, but I don't think I'd better."

Jack looked at me with a frown and then caught on. "We're going to have a honeymoon baby!" We waited until the end of summer to let mom, dad and Jack's mom know and also let me get through the God-awful morning sickness. We drove to Mount Horeb and let Jack's mom know and then Pine Lake. Mom looked at me and then Jack and she knew. Mother's intuition I guess. Dad didn't have a clue.

We had dinner and then I said "We think we'd like to build a house down by Mineral Point if that's OK. Dad said sure, but you just fixed up the condo.

"I know but we're going to need another bedroom," I replied.

Dad looked at mom and then the light went on. "You mean you're going to have a baby?"

"Yup!"

"When?" "Valentine's Day."

"Oh, my God!" dad said, as a broad smile crossed his face. "I'm going to be a grandpa!"

Sure enough, things worked out and on Valentine's Day, John David Harris III was born at Meriter Hospital and our world changed forever.

During our wait, we'd purchased ten acres of farm land from my Uncle Tommie just outside Waldwick. While I've written a lot about Mineral Point, I think I need to tell you about the hamlet we jokingly call 'suburban Mineral Point'.

Waldwick doesn't have any businesses, not even a gas station - just a few houses, where everyone's a neighbor and friend and we're almost all related one way or another. Second, the Terrill farm literally started Waldwick. Before Jack, Charlie and I arrived, Waldwick consisted of about a dozen homes and, even with us building our house, the town is still so small it has the 'welcome' and 'thank you for visiting' signs on the same post. There are books written by my uncles and cousins about Waldwick and the farm and an area called 'The Forest' that some say is haunted. I, like so many of others, believe it's a very special place, filled with beauty and peace called tranquility and that's why I felt like we're just "coming home".

Our house was designed to be located at the edge of a valley and literally away from everything. Two hundred yards off County Line Road, we could see the Forest nestled below us and the very tip of the roof of the Derrick Williams Foundation core building the MadCity guys called the silo. If I look out the kitchen window at the right time, I can watch the helicopters land on the helipad, which always makes me smile.

Jack was busy with football and so I made the initial design decisions concerning our dream house that we'd then discuss after supper. I worked with the architects while Jack and I agreed on a contemporary version of the Prairie Style architecture, such that our house would reflect and pay homage to the surrounding environment.

If you're not into architectural history, the Prairie style was made popular by Frank Lloyd Wright and was based on the principle that houses should serve basic needs without being too flashy. As Wright intended, we agreed on an open floor plan and also having the house 'blend-in' regarding the exterior with long horizontal lines and a somewhat flat roof that melds into the topography.

To give the house a 'natural' look and feel, we incorporated local stone, wood, and brick both inside and out, to let the natural light and color show through. Depending on the time of day and the season, the interior takes on completely different personalities, sometimes warm and inviting while other times a little dreary, to reflect days and times in all of our lives.

The only place where we didn't follow the Prairie Style concept was on the back of the house that overlooks the valley. While the Prairie style incorporates a series of small windows in a row that are arranged to give the illusion of a glass wall, we loved the window walls in the condo and incorporated the same photovoltaic glass that literally make you feel like you're a part of nature.

I had the joy of being able to consult with Captain Luke about making the house completely energy efficient and also have a zero-carbon footprint and worked with Wilco Security to make certain the house and property was properly monitored both inside and out, without taking away our privacy. The net structural result ended up with insulated concrete walls with a bluff limestone façade that was cut from the Terrill Farm quarry, highlighted by dark stained cedar trim and Spancrete floors with the same hydronic system for the house, walk and driveway that Luke used on the Foundation runway. We added solar panels to the back roof so that they couldn't be seen, that reduced our fossil energy consumption as well.

The interior design was quite simple with a wide-open main floor plan consisting of a great room that incorporates a great deal wood to highlight the fieldstone fireplace, a half bath and coat closet all geared to face towards the huge windows and the valley below. The second floor has three "suites", where each bedroom has its own bathroom and oversized walk-in closet while the primary suite incorporates a larger bathroom with a soaking tub, over-sized steamer/shower and dual walk-in closets with mine being so large Jack felt it was bigger than his apartment in Oshkosh. Sorry! I guess Jack shouldn't have let me do the designing.

The entertainment level, that people used to call a basement, is a 'walk-out' with glass 'walls' to the back, a great room with fireplace, theater, Jack's office and a playroom under the garage that will someday be converted into a gym, when the kids get a little older. We added a three-car garage with a spancrete floor and stairs to both the loft above and the area below designed for storage of outdoor seasonal items that can be entered either from the playroom or outside. Finally, we designed an inground pool situated down the hill from the house that was cut into the grade so that it's below the site line and doesn't detract from our view of the forest.

The house was completed in May and we moved in Memorial Day weekend. Jack opened a bottle of Terrill Reserve Pinot Noir to celebrate and I looked at him and told him I'd better not. His eyes opened wide as he inquired, 'you mean?', as I nodded in the affirmative, with another member of the Harris family scheduled later that year.

At the appropriate time, we made another trek to Mount Horeb to share the good news with Grandma Harris and then

Pine Lake as we told mom and dad, "Save some of that spoiling for next year as you're going to be sharing it."

Mom looked at me and said "I hope it's not twins". Thank God it wasn't.

I thought taking care of one baby was tough until Ann Marie Terrill entered the world. "Oh my God!" I looked at Jack and said, "Enough is enough! We're done, one way or the other."

Jack got the clue, went to the clinic and came home singing the song from the 'Wizard of Oz' – "Chop, chop, chop, clip, clip, clip, fa, la, la, la, la. No more kids for Melia from me in the merry old land of aahs!"

We settled in with Jack teaching and coaching and me doing what I always wanted to do - be a wife and mother with the official title of housewife. For some my life wouldn't be enough. For me it was my dream come true, enjoying every minute of it, as we began blending in with no one either knowing or caring who I was, other than the coach's wife, which was just the way I always dreamed it would be.

Annie:

Time was flying by. The kids were now four and three and my world was all I'd dreamed it would be. Unfortunately, Annie wasn't quite having the same happy life as me. While she and Teddy were still married, it wasn't working out very well and her music career was going nowhere fast with my investment in her CD seeing very limited sales and then only when she was doing gigs where she could sell the CD's after performing. While Annie started with a band, all the guys had seen their dreams crumble and gone back to 'real' jobs with the woulda's coulda's, shoulda's of a musical career shrouded in frustration and sadness.

I knew Annie was struggling, but really didn't know how bad until I took the kids to Madison and found out she was unemployed as the parochial schools had consolidated their music programs and Teddy was only sending a portion of what she needed to live on. Annie's dream was becoming a nightmare!

We met at Culver's on Cottage Grove Road and Annie looked stressed out and bedraggled, but enjoyed seeing the kids as she was Charlie's godmother.

"How's everything?" I inquired. "It's OK," Annie lamented.

"What's going on?"

Annie laid it all out regarding her band, husband and job and the tears in her eyes said it all.

"Do you need money?" I asked.

Annie vehemently shook her head no. The last thing I knew she'd want was a hand out. We spent some time and then said goodbye, promising to see each other more often. As she left in her beat up and grubby car, I could only think of how the fifty-two miles and totally different lifestyles had made our world's so different.

As we were heading back through the city, I thought I'd stop and show the kids our condo and explain that it was where mommy and daddy first lived. No one had occupied the premises since we moved out and it was like time simply stood still. As I showed the kids the 'magic' windows that turned clear and dark, a thought came to mind. Wilco had three buildings in the neighborhood and had realized there was more money in renting than selling condos and had quietly begun buying back our former properties. This meant someone from corporate would need to take care the tenants and Wilco needed someone to live on the premises.

All the way home, I pondered whether we could let Annie live in our old apartment and serve as the property manager. She was organized and intelligent and could certainly handle what was thrown at her.

I hit speed dial and called dad who picked up on the first ring. After all the pleasantries of how Jack and the kids were, I got down to business. "Dad, I had lunch with Annie and then stopped at our old condo. You know, it's been vacant for nearly five years. What would you think of hiring Annie as our property manager and letting her live in the condo. We're not using it and yet, we don't want to sell it or rent it."

Dad responded that he'd need to talk to the property management division. I then went for it all. "How about this, Annie manage all three buildings and we pay her a small salary as well as the apartment?"

Dad knew I loved Annie like a sister and responded, "Let me see what I can do."

That night dad called and said he'd talked it over with property management and thought it could work. Annie would become the property manager responsible for leasing and general maintenance issues while serving as the liaison between Wilco and the tenants.

Wilco had developed a program called condo deconversion where they were buying back condos in our buildings that they could then rent. Annie would be responsible for working with the condo owners to determine if they wanted to sell and determine how close those considering the deconversion decision were to allowing the company to reach the required 75% needed for a full purchase.

The following morning, I called Annie, "Heh, I have an idea."

"What?"

"Well, I stopped at Jack's and my old condo to show it to the kids and realized it was just sitting empty. I then talked with my dad who said the company was looking for a property manager for the three buildings we own on Wilson Street. We're wondering, would you be interested in managing the properties? You'd receive a monthly salary, health insurance and use of our old condo. Your job would be rental showings, vacancies and scheduling both general maintenance and repairs."

"I've never done anything like that." Annie replied.

"I know, but the property management team will train you and then work with you to make sure you have all the tools and resources you need."

"When would I start?" "The first of the month."

"You mean I could move into the apartment then?"

"You can move in now, if you want to."

I heard crying on the other end. Annie hadn't shared that she was being evicted and was planning on moving back with her parents – something no 34-year-old woman ever wants to do.

"You're not doing this out of pity?" Annie inquired.

"Annie, you're intelligent, diligent and professional and get along with people. You can do this and keep singing."

There was a sigh of relief on the other end. It wasn't what Annie dreamed of, but it was going to remove a lot of pressure that had been building.

"OK and thank you. How can I ever repay you, Melia?"

"You repay me every day simply by being my friend."

I called dad and the offertory agreement was created and e- mailed to Annie. Dad sent me a text and I called Annie and instructed her to go to the Wilco offices on King Street where she could sign the document and get the keys for the apartment. I told her she had two parking stalls and the garage door openers were in the cupboard above the stove. Annie couldn't thank me enough.

The next day, Annie called and said she was all moved in and was so grateful. It was the least I could do for my best friend. I knew she was heartbroken by the fact that, like so many others with stars in their eyes, her music career never lived up to her dreams and expectations.

Snake Eyes:

Perhaps I was biased. Perhaps, I was a poor judge of character. Perhaps, just perhaps Annie wasn't the right person for the job, who knows? What should have been something she could handle, simply didn't turn out that way. Tenants were complaining. Rentals weren't being taken care of. All the little things Wilco was proud of, just weren't getting done. How do you tell your best friend that she's not doing her job?

Dad and I talked and he shared the company frustrations. He knew how close Annie and I had always been and, yet, something needed to be done. Annie's heart was still in her music and everything else came second.

My entire life, I'd loved music, which I think I got from my great Uncle Hank whose passion for music and love of life were stories still being told in Mineral Point. When I began medical school, music had stopped, along with life itself. Now with Jack, the kids and the anonymity, I felt safe, secure and happy and music hadn't even been on my mind, except when I was with or talking to Annie.

I read on line about a television show called "The Choice". It was a music competition that started regionally and then the regional finalists would travel to LA for the national competition. In order to audition, all you needed do was upload songs and, from there, the judges would select contestants in person in Chicago.

I knew Annie needed a break and I still had a copy of the demo songs Annie had recorded when we were in St. Martin. I decided to upload the audition songs in her name and left it at that, using her name and the condo address to complete the application.

A few days later, the phone rang and it was Annie. After a few pleasantries, Annie inquired, "Did you send the songs we recorded when we were in St. Martin into some TV show?"

I admitted, I did.

"I really appreciate your looking out for me, but they've auditioned the songs and called and selected you as a contestant."

"What?" I said incredulously. "Me?" I'd forgotten we'd even recorded the song.

"Oh Annie, I'm so sorry! That's not what was intended. I thought I'd be helping you by sending it in and wanted it to be a surprise and forgot that we'd recorded your song. What do you want me to do?"

"Go for it, girl!" Annie said. "What?"

"Go for it!" You've always had a better voice than me.

"But Annie, I've done everything I could to become anonymous and blend in. The last thing I want is publicity."

"Mella, you have the golden opportunity other people only dream about. You've got to go for it."

"I've got to talk this over with Jack. I can't just change everything – especially after all we've done to create my anonymity!"

We ended the conversation with me agreeing to call her back before making a commitment either way. I thought my chances were slim, narrow and none to win any singing contest and really didn't want to take any chances. Yet, I also knew that if I only sang Annie's songs perhaps it would help her get her foot in the door as a songwriter. I sincerely believed there was a huge opportunity for her, if and it was a big IF, people would only give her a chance.

Jack came home from school and I explained what was going on. I outlined my profound desire to sustain our lives just as they were but, also, my sincere feeling that I was compelled to help Annie in any possible way. Jack was reticent at first and then softened as he asked what it would take. Annie sent over the form from 'The Choice' and we read it carefully. It said that from the thousands of aspirants, twenty-five were chosen for the regionals to be held in Chicago, including Annie, that actually turned out to be me, singing Annie's song, 'Dream'.

I called Annie and detailed everything. I told her I didn't believe I'd make it very far. I definitely didn't want the publicity and would only compete if I could sing her songs exclusively so that she would get national exposure. What went from anger and pain on Annie's part, evolved to one of profound gratitude, as she realized I was willing to sacrifice my own privacy, security and lifestyle for her.

Annie notified the producers regarding who the vocalist was and they redacted the offer to include me and I became an official contestant on some TV show.

A few days before I was set to audition, one of the producers of 'The Choice' called to congratulate me and indicated that a contract had just been mailed Express mail that needed to be signed and brought with me, before I could compete. He also noted that I needed to change my performing name for my own privacy and protection. I'd never even thought of that and had no idea what to reply.

An hour later, the phone rang and it was LA, as we began calling it. They'd done a marketing study and felt my persona and vocal strength was such that they had a stage name picked out. While I wasn't Swedish, they felt my vocal style and qualities were such they wanted to have my stage name be something else and the most logical thing to use was another first name like Roberts or Johnson. Needless to say, I was perplexed. I'd never thought of a stage name and was totally happy with Harris.

I sat down at the kitchen table with Jack and explained what was going on and he was less than enthused, but finally saw the logic behind it. His only comment was that he thought my stage name could be Melia Wilson. We hoped, I could become a one name entertainer and simply be called Melia. I called LA back and agreed, but formally requested that all references to me simply be Melia, unless there was another competitor with the same name.

I called Tommie Larson at Wilco legal who was my friend and made him vow to secrecy, explaining what was going on, and that I had a contract shoved under my nose and before I could compete, I had to sign it. I sent the contract to him and he went over the details. It said I had to remain silent to all parties regarding the results until the broadcast and that 'The Choice' retained ownership of all video recordings, etc. I asked about Annie's songs and Tommie added a paragraph stating that any and all songs under her copyright remained Annie's property. This slid past the producers as they thought I would be doing songs they put in front of me. When it came to royalties, the split was 75% to the producers and 25% to me and I'd be paid a performance fee of $1,571 plus meals for two hour shows,
$1,303 for one hour and $910 for the half-hour results shows.

Tommie pointed out that just auditioning for the show could be a huge financial setback for some hopeful contestants because they would need to pay for their own travel and accommodations if the auditions weren't held in close proximity to where they lived. I wanted to keep this between Jack and me and away from mom and dad, so Jack offered to drive me to Chicago for the audition. I knew that if I made it to LA, Wilco Security would need to get involved and the whole thing could become a three-ring circus, but assumed that was so far off, we could leave the lions, tigers and bears for a later date.

The first three rounds were going to be taped in Chicago and Jack and I could easily make it in one day. I was told to bring my own back-up music and so Annie had to literally un-mix 'Dream' so that I had the melody. Annie put the unmixed melodies on both a CD and a flash drive in case one or the other didn't work. Even though I thought I wouldn't make the first cut, the last thing I wanted was to have technical difficulties.

Tommie read the fine print that said the show only paid for travel once you made it to the top twelve and would then only pay for your ticket to Hollywood and the hotel, where you shared a room with another contestant. At that point I knew Wilco Security and Ops would need to be involved as I wasn't going to stay in LA week after week, but we agreed it could wait to see what happened.

Once the finalists arrived in Hollywood, 'The Choice' provided $100 per day for meals and a fashion budget of $450 per show, while providing on-set hair and makeup in Hollywood. Whoopee! Needless to say, none of this mattered to me. I already had my own wardrobe and personalized makeup and was certain their hotel versus dad and Wilco security's choice would be totally different.

The day of the scheduled audition, we dropped the kids with Grandma Harris and drove to the Rosemont Center in Chicago near O'Hare airport. The audition was scheduled to be taped in the afternoon so we could do my audition, turn around and go home.

We got there early enough to allow my nerves to calm down and I had time to vocally warm up. To say it was a nickel-and- dime affair would have been an understatement. Besides paying for parking, if you wanted to wear makeup during the preliminaries, it was up to you to do your own or pay $100 for a 'professional' make-up artist. Money certainly wasn't an issue when you've got $10,000 per week being added to your bank account, but I still did my own at home.

We arrived and parked the car and saw other potential contestants with license plates from all over the Midwest. The performances were being taped in small anteroom to the real auditorium inside the Allstate Arena in front of just a technical crew. From the initial audition we were told twelve regional finalists would be chosen by the producers who would then create a televised show, where the determination of the winners would be based on the viewer's votes. I learned what was happening in Chicago was also taking place in New

York, Atlanta, Dallas, Denver and San Francisco and there were six regional competitions. This meant the time for the initial winners in Chicago would be every six weeks, so it really wasn't that big of a deal.

Our showed aired three weeks later and the producers made the first cut to twelve where good things were said about my performance as the drama was created. At the end of the show, the live votes were tallied and I'd made the cut. It was then mom and dad found out our little secret. Needless to say, dad was not pleased, as he was afraid someone would connect the dots and there could be huge security risks. My rationale was I had so many different names who would ever figure it out.

Six weeks later, it was time for the second Chicago round and, after my first performance, where I didn't feel I did a very good job, I vowed to make it better. Jack and I repeated the journey and were surprised when Charlie Jackson, the 'live' host was there and called me Melia, which I appreciated. I realized we were entering the next level of competition and 'The Choice' needed to tie it all together with Charlie serving as the thread, simply because he was a national DJ on a satellite network and host of a daytime TV talk show.

With me at six-foot-two and Charlie at five-foot-seven, it would have been like the cartoon characters Mutt and Jeff, with me towering over what could easily have been a jockey. Instead, the producers placed an eight-inch tall platform on the floor that Charlie traversed until he was standing next to me. Because they only shot us from the chest up, no one at home could realize that it made Charlie seem taller and me smaller, which was certainly all right by me.

We put on the CD and as the music came up, I gave it my best, singing one of Annie's more laconic ballads called 'I Miss You'. After I was done, Charlie came out with his patented exuberance and informed the 'audience' I was a mom with two kids from Madison, Wisconsin, which he made it sound was this little dinky enclave in the middle of nowhere.

As my set was done and the cameras went dark, they reset for the next competitor while Charlie came over and said "You've got an incredible voice. Hang in there, I believe you're going to end up in Hollywood."

I nodded my gratitude and headed for the exit, waiting until we got outside to ask Jack what he thought. Jack looked at me and smiled and said. "Are you kidding? You nailed it!" It would be a week until we knew what the audience thought and it was back to reality of two kids, clothes to wash, crayons to put away and working with Luke at the Foundation on the annual donations.

The Chicago broadcast saw several of our neighbors come over to cheer me on. It was the first time I had a fan club. Needless to say, they all brought up the fact that Charlie said we lived in Madison, but I was glad, as it made it even more difficult to track me down. As the performances rolled, everyone waited for my appearance where I sang 'Try To Say Goodbye'. I didn't know that I'd been slotted last. Once again, I thought I did OK, but thought being last was the worst possible place to be. Only later did I learn that was just the opposite. Placing first to hook the audience on the current show and last to motivate them to tune in next time reflected the producer's opinions that our performances were the best.

The votes came in and Charlie came on to announce the Chicago regional winners as they summarized all the contestants. "In no particular order, the top three finalists are...." It was all a blur, I'd been chosen to go to LA and considered a semifinalist. While the other contestants were excited, I was concerned. What about my anonymity? What about the kids? What about Jack and my parents?

Dad called and congratulated me and suggested using Amelia[X] to fly me out to LA and include security. I thanked him and told him "No," not yet, as I didn't want anyone to know anything about who we were. Secretly, my goal was to make it on my own, with no help or influence from the family. No one knew in Waldwick or even in Mineral Point that I was a

Terrill and Jack and I wanted to keep it that way.

Reality sunk in that I'd made the final three for the Midwest Regional and would be competing against 17 others and it was time for the business aspect to come into play. The first phase would be shielding myself from the talent agents. While it's virtually impossible to get one when you're just starting out as a singer, actor or writer because no one will even listen to you or even have the courtesy of returning your mail or calls, just the opposite comes into play when you've taken the time, energy and cost – yes there's a huge cost to competing in a talent show in terms of lost income from your real job, going home when you want to and time away from your family.

At first, I admit I was a bit thrilled by all the attention, but then it became a real hassle as the agents will do anything and everything to take a slice of life from you. I knew from then on, Wilco's 'Williams' couple would be there and that suited me just fine, as I put on another modified Apple watch and thought of my time on St. Martin.

After Chicago, I also knew there would be four days of rehearsal, plus the show in LA and the sequence would last for up to four weeks or until I lost. I contacted Wilco Ops and told then what was going on, reserving Amelia III that could land at the Waldwick airstrip so that I could commute home each week. The entire Wilco team was both excited and concerned, as they knew precisely how much we'd done to create my privacy.

Count Down to Obscurity:

The first LA round meant reducing the three competitors from each region to two for a total of twelve participants. This was done with each of us auditioning for the judges where I sang *"I Miss You"*. It was quick to see the producers were actually making the final cuts to ensure they not only had musical talent, but styles that paralleled the celebrity judges. This became obvious because the producers believed fans of the celebrity judges would tune in to see the judges. For this session, I was in LA for a total of three days with Wilco Ops sending Amelia III, that was sitting at the Burbank airport after my last rehearsal to take me home in a little over three hours.

The next round saw each region reduced from two to one and, once again, I was in LA for three days where I sang *'Round Trip to Nowhere'* and, after the final tally, was named winner of the Midwest Region. I simply shook my head in disbelief as I thought I'd done terrible. I guess Madison television played it up big as I got a lot of texts from friends and neighbors. I was finally a 'legitimate' contestant and all the broadcasts from then on would be live shows, starting with the six regional winners, plus two wild card contestants 'chosen' by the judges.

I knew it was going to be a grind with auditions and promotional activity and had Amelia III pick me up for one last extended stay at home. It was great to spend time with Jack and the kids and go to the Foundation and say hello to the gang, who all made me feel very welcomed.

I made time to visit the Forest and sat on the bench by Great Grandfather's obelisk and asked for guidance. As I sat there, the great buck appeared again and nodded his head. To this day, I believe it was a sign that what I was doing was for the good of everyone, including me. Sunday was fuse day and we had an early dinner as I reluctantly said goodbye to Jack and the kids and told them that if I had the chance I would call every night and to watch me pull on my left ear after my song as my secret message just for them, that meant, 'I love you.'

Jack drove me to the air strip where Amelia III was waiting and I thanked him for letting me see if I couldn't help make Annie's dreams come true. He told me not to worry. We could Zoom with the kids to take away some of the loneliness.

I decided to stay in what we called 'The Pitts Motor Lodge' to be part of the 'group' even though I was nearly fifteen years older than the other contestants. The next day we were picked up and driven to rehearsal while they only taped us entering the studio and not being unloaded from the worn out, beat up school bus.

I was glad I brought my laptop as there was a lot of down time while the band worked with the others. Finally, I rehearsed and, for the first time in my life, was miked and staged with blocking assignments. The producers felt my attire was a little conservative and recommended spending some of the $450 weekly costume allowance on something more 'contemporary,' as they put it. I told them I felt comfortable in what I was wearing and was concerned because we lived in a small, conservative town and my family might be thought less of, if I wore something more revealing. I didn't let on that the outfit was custom made in Dubai and cost over $5,000. They finally acquiesced.

My song choice was one of Annie's ballads called 'Flawless'. The band listened to the cut from Annie's CD, nodded their approval, before making made a few minor changes as we went through rehearsal. The three dummy judges, who stood in for the live talent during the auditions, made comments, which were all polite.

After I was done, I sat in the audience and listened to the remaining contestants and felt I did as good as they did, but still believed I could have done better. That Sunday, the show aired and the tension was great as two of us were going home and I'd already packed. To the roll of the drums, the names of those leaving were announced as the first girl from Dallas slowly walked off the stage with her dreams crushed. There were now seven remaining contestants, including me. It was a blur as the rocker girl from LA with tattoos and pierces just about everywhere had her name called and I saw tears trickle down her cheeks, only then realizing, I'd made it to the final six.

After the show, I called Jack and he said I looked scared. I replied I really wasn't, but suffered from loneliness more than anything else. Two of the other contestants were Eddie and Claudette. Claudette, was my assigned hotel roommate and had a voice that was simply incredible. I think she could have sung the phone book and made it sound great. Eddie was openly gay and a real sweetheart who wore his heart on his sleeve, while he had this innocent tenor style that would have made Sinatra envious. We bonded and I think the other three were jealous. Even with all that was going on, I still greatly missed my kids, husband, home and Wisconsin, but knew better than to say a word to anyone other than Jack, thereby keeping a broad smile on my face.

Everything at home was just as it had been and that was good. Initially, while other's elected to stay in LA between rehearsals and the show, I was commuting and so I was only gone a few days each week. I'd leave on Thursday morning, arrive in Burbank, take a taxi to the studio, go through preliminaries and have full rehearsals Friday and Saturday with the show late Sunday afternoon and then fly home, landing at the Waldwick airport, where I'd get in one of the Suburbans and drive home. Thank you, Captain Luke!

I knew the next week was going to be the toughest as we were going from six to four and the pressure would be incredible, simply because the show would be losing two regional winners and the four remaining contestants had to 'sell' themselves enough to keep the regional viewers watching. What I didn't know was an angel was about to enter my life that would take away the blues and fill my musical life with purpose and joy.

The Coach:

Fortunately, Eddie, Claudette and I all made it through what the show called 'the cauldron' that was intended to show how versatile we were. It was easy to see that the producers were building our profiles so that we had enough viewer awareness the regional element would be minimized thereby making this a national competition. To help us, we were all assigned a vocal coach. While the three celebrity judges would be videotaped 'coaching', the real work was done behind the scenes by some vocal professionals.

Miriam White had been contracted as my coach. Her reputation had preceded her as a no-nonsense taskmaster who chose the artists she wanted and not the other way around. Stories of her walking out on renowned divas and chastising even the most famous recording artists of our time were rampant. Needless to say, I was both honored and nervous as I learned that she hadn't chosen to coach anyone on 'The Choice' in five years. I also learned that her normal fees were astronomical, periodically totaling in the millions and, yet, there was a waiting list of artists and record companies wanting her services.

I arrived at the rehearsal studio about fifteen minutes early and, unlike previous times, it was totally dark. I called Francine who was my handler, whose job it was to make sure I was where I was supposed to be, when I was supposed to be. A bit flustered, Francine assured me that the doors would be unlocked and Miriam would be on time. Francine noted that Miriam had certain requirements and one of them was that it was just going to be the two of us and there wouldn't be anyone else – no cameras, no recordings, no producers!

About five minutes before our appointment, a janitor unlocked the door and turned on the lights. I walked into the empty room and noted that it was set with a piano and a small cooler filled with bottles of water and ice tea.

At precisely 10:00 AM, Miriam walked in the room and politely said "Hello." I thought she was in her late fifties and looked like a spinster. She was about 5'2" and couldn't have weighed one hundred pounds. Her black hair matched her black glasses and was done up in a bun, while her clothes were much less than what you would expect in California.

Before she began to speak Miriam went to the piano and typed the keys individually and finally played some chords. Initially, I had no idea what was transpiring, but soon realized that she was checking the sonic accuracy of the piano. Shaking her head, she noted to herself that the 'B' key was 'a little flat.' It was then I realized her true gift was that of hearing and I shortly began to understand that she'd forgotten more about music than either Annie or I knew and was lucky to have her as my coach, as she was about to take the gift I had and make it better.

Miriam looked at me and pointedly said. "Melia, good singers like you are born with an amazing 'instrument' that includes the right combination of lungs that have excellent vital capacity, matched to exceptional breathing control and a larynx that allows you to stretch and squeeze your vocal cords to achieve the desired vocal range, while the shape and size of your pharynx, nasal cavities and mouth then correlate the expelled air that allow you to sing the way you do. Quite honestly, you have one of the most natural and gracious voices I've ever heard. There probably aren't a hundred people in the world who can do what you do and less than a dozen in the music industry."

I was humbled and yet, after the whirlwind competition where everybody and their brother kept telling me how great I sounded, I tried not to be too jaded as Miriam continued. "Before we begin taking you from being a very good singer to a great singer, we need to overcome your reticence and self-induced belief that you shouldn't be here. You represent one of the most natural talents I've ever heard and all you really need do is believe in yourself. I don't think people realize that the psychological aspects play a major role in their ability to sing. Those who are sure of their singing skills have a much higher chance of success than those who doubt themselves and so before we begin, you need to start believing in yourself!"

I looked at the ground and promised myself I would try. I knew that the subconscious doubts were there even though I'd visited with Dr. Oldman and resolved a lot of the issues regarding my childhood and medical school as were the nerves. Yet, I also saw myself getting better and stronger and more capable of doing what I'd only hoped was possible a few months before – namely helping Annie.

Miriam stood and motioned to the two chairs that were set face to face on an inexpensive, printed oriental rug as she added. "I read your bio and saw that you've been singing all your life and that's great. People who have been exposed to music from a young age and grow up in an environment where singing is encouraged have a higher chance of being good at it."

I shyly smiled and thought of mom and dad and how they provided so much for me as Miriam continued. "I sense that you grew up where the competition probably wasn't that great and you feel you're not that good. However, you've run the gauntlet through the regional competitions and beat them all and now you're about to go on a national stage. This is not a charity event. This is a competition and viewers all over America have seen you and believe enough in your talent to vote for you."

Miriam leaned back in her chair and continued. "I've studied all this year's final contestants, along with those from the past five years and Melia, you have the greatest potential acoustically."

I must have had an expression on my face reflecting that it was just some more of the fluff I'd been hearing since the whole circumstance began and Miriam caught it as she added. "One very important element that makes some people sing beautifully and others flounder are problems with intonation or pitch and you're almost pitch perfect, which gives you a head start on all the others."

Miriam had me stand as we went to the piano and go through the musical Do-Re-Me scale, while urging me higher and higher until I slipped into what she called my "head voice" or falsetto that existed beyond my normal comfort zone, where she had me stop as she added, "Pure mid-range, a little light in your upper register, but nothing too bad. Great vocal control, but what we've only done so far is simply make you eligible to be a very good, but not a great singer."

"While you were progressing in standard notes, we're going to work on taking you up in halftones, where instead of an eighth of an octave, let's see if we can't go for one sixteenth or even a twenty-fourth. As we work on this, you'll get comfortable taking vocal baby steps instead giant leaps and it will give you greater depth and flexibility in your presentations. My analysis of your voice has your inherent vocal strength one octave above middle C with your performances so far, registering about two octaves above before going into your 'head voice' where you start to thin out. Below middle C, your pitch also begins to flatten and so we need to focus not only your breathing in the lower register, but choosing melodies that will keep you in your sweet spot."

I sat amazed. In a few minutes Miriam not only analyzed me, but recognized both my strengths and weaknesses as she continued. "Melia, what you sing results from the three components of vocal production which consist of sound, resonance and articulation. Your 'voice sound' is the basic sound produced by vocal fold vibration when you talk. The difference between the way you speak and the way you sing is when you add your resonance, which in your case, is simply incredible. What you have reminds me of an actor by the name of Jim Nabors who had a squeaky speaking voice, but rich baritone singing voice. Your resonance is that wonderful collaboration of just the right throat, oral cavity and nasal passage development so that your songs come out smooth and full of tone and never with a nasal intonation."

I smiled and was humbled as Miriam added. "We really don't need to work on the basics other than make certain you don't overcompensate and ruin what God has given you. Assuming we can tweak the highs and lows, which shouldn't be that big of deal, I really feel I can be of assistance in your articulation and that's what I would like to focus on."

I thought of the typical 'how now brown cow', 'toy boat' and 'Peter Piper Picked a Peck of Pickled Peppers" until Miriam explained. "Technical components of singing are the platforms upon which your artistic expression stands. Normally, I need to work on these with the contestants, but you already have an innate ability."

Miriam had me stand up and press on my abdomen as she outlined, "Abdominal support is responsible for the height of the sound or how loud you can sing. By being able to control variations in the height of the sound, you can add dynamics for expression. Most contestants just belt it out. You have that innate ability to increase or decrease the height for effect and that's what draws the listener in. What's really impressive is your level of control. Normally, a woman with two kids, has lost a lot of their abdominal support and therefore their ability to control the height. While you're in good shape, I need to have you begin doing 50 sit-ups five days each week except for the day of dress rehearsal and the actual performance."

Ever since St. Martin with mom, I'd been following her regimen of fifty sit ups and almost fifty push-ups per day, but didn't interrupt as Miriam continued, "this will help strengthen your abdominal muscles."

A small smile finally crossed Miriam's lips as she sensed she had a willing student and not someone who thought they already had all the answers, as she added, "there are so many factors which influence the sound of a voice including the singer's physical structure. You're a tall woman of proportional weight and yet you have the lower register of a woman twice your size, which provides the vocal depth I heard. Your Vibrato is also incredible and, based on both your abdominal and upper diaphragm. It's what allows for your pulsating change of pitch, where you're adding expression to your music unlike a lot of the other contestants."

The teacher in Miriam was beginning to shine through as she began to relax. She looked at me and added. "Vibrato is typically characterized in terms of two factors - the amount of pitch variation and the speed with which the pitch is varied. With you Melia, you not only have your natural vibrato, but the ability to change vibrato speeds for emphasis which again, is a reason your voice resonates with the audience and you sustain their interest even when singing a-cappella. In order for you to have even better control of this, we need to put you on a breathing regime consisting of deep breaths while doing deep knee bends. Again, five days a week, but be careful, don't hurt your knees."

Miriam was teaching me things I never would have considered and quickly realized how wonderful she really was, as she continued. "Now we can begin working on the technical aspect where I believe I can be of greatest assistance, and that's enunciation. Music consists of the melody and the lyrics, which I call structure – where the lyrical structure consists of the syllables which should be stackable - one on top of each other - and placed on the central line of the body of the lyric."

"I don't know if you were taught enunciation or not, but you have a natural gift of speech. In terms of consonants, your articulation is both finite and pleasant without being brittle, while your vowels are succinct and not elongated like those who grew up in the south. This is because the place and manner of articulation in your mouth are both sourced at the soft palate, which few singers are able to control and where the secret of going from being very good to great really lies and is what made Sinatra exceptional. When it comes to consonants, it all depends on the location of your tongue in terms of its height and *frontness* or *backness* of its position in your mouth and the degree of stricture or rigidity you are eliciting, which is then affected by the roundness of your lips."

I sat in awe as the rose was being opened before me as Miriam's passion and understanding of music played on the stage before my very eyes as she continued. "When we rehearse a song and the lyrics become automatic, I'll have you focus on your structure to create muscle memory of your tongue for each note so that when you add this to your variations in both the dynamics and vibrato, you'll literally pull the listener in and affect them emotionally, which is what makes the total difference between a good singer and a great singer."

"We don't want you to become vocally brittle and the words need to flow smoothly and each word and syllable needs to be understood. So many of the contestants have the ability to expel great sounds, but no one understands what they're singing. Remember, music is the combination of lyrics and melody and the songs that are remembered are those where there is instantaneous recognition of the first four bars of the melody and the lyrics it supports."

I nodded and smiled in affirmation, thinking of all the songs I loved and how each one had a unique hook. I realized, I'd been doing some of what Miriam outlined, just never knew I was doing it right.

Miriam continued. "Once you've achieved mastery of these four components, you'll have achieved technical control of the physical sound. The next step is to 'dress it up' so that the song is original, emotional, exciting, affecting and, above all else, totally yours. This is akin to a figure skater whose costume and movements reflect the music that is accompanying the performance. With regards to singing, the physical sound produced must correspond with the style of music and the musical instruments used in its production."

Miriam continued, "Recently, I saw a pop singer deliver what was clearly a R & B song with a classical sounding voice. It didn't sound very good because the sound of the voice was so alien to the style of music being played by the band. She actually had a strong voice and, thus, would have received high marks for technical merit if there had been official judges, but also would have received a failing grade for her artistic interpretation. In this instance, the total performance was not achieved."

The tutorial was over and the conversation began as Miriam added. "I do believe that style can be taught. In fact, many singers approach me to coach them specifically because they want to sing a particular style of music where they see the greatest opportunity for acceptance."

"One of my recently signed clients was a dance/R&B singer who had a recording session booked and asked me to come along for assistance. When I arrived at the studio, the session was already underway and I quickly realized that the song they were recording was not the one we had worked on. Moreover, the song was very demanding because it required a combination of three distinct styles: pop, dance and R&B and required that she change styles as frequently as every second line. The producers were high caliber and definitely knew what they wanted, but were having trouble transferring their instructions on how to do it to the singer."

"My client knew what they wanted, but didn't know how to achieve it. This is where I stepped in and was able to provide some assistance. By quickly instructing her on how she could attain the requested stylistic elements, the song was recorded in much less time than even the producers anticipated."

Miriam took a small sip of water and added. "They all don't work out that way, but I've been blessed that enough of them do, so that the record companies keep knocking on my door."

"From the very beginning of instruction, I've always taught my clients the obvious, such as how to stay in key and project their voice, but also work on how to work on the stylistic elements of the songs they are singing. This is often done by breaking the songs down to individual lines and practicing the ways each syllable should be sung, depending on the style of music."

Miriam looked at me and noted. "The producers have you slotted as a ballad singer, which doesn't fit today's music scene and means they're putting you up for slaughter. To make things even more complicated, you've indicated you want to only take your friend Annie's songs and sing them, is that correct?"

I nodded 'yes' as Miriam continued. "This means you're doing original songs, that have no reference standard. This gives us a lot more freedom than taking someone else's melody and making it our own, but there are also risks. 'The Choice' is not Karaoke! This means we've got to take what your friend has written and look for the 'peaks and valleys' and how to best express the emotion you're trying evoke. Over the next few rehearsals, my goal is to take your voice and mold it to the music instead of having the music molded to you. This is true creativity and where I sincerely believe we can succeed."

She took a deep breath and asked if I had any questions.

I replied, "Where do you see me fitting in?"

"Where do you see yourself?" "As a balladeer," I replied.

"In other words, a stylistic, classical singer!" I nodded in the affirmative.

Miriam smiled and shook her head in the affirmative as she uttered "Know thyself," and then added. "The reason I'm here is because I don't like the direction the music industry is heading and sincerely feel you can help change that. We need true vocalists who can communicate not only words and melodies, but emotions. Melia, I chose you because I sincerely think you can achieve that and believe you can be the next one-name star."

I looked at Miriam and knew it was time to lay it all out.

"Miriam, I'm here for only one reason and that's to help out my friend Annie whom I love like a sister. She's got incredible talent and simply needs the break. I hope 'The Choice' will provide that opportunity and I will do everything I can to win…everything! But, it's not for me, it's so that Annie's songs can be heard and she can win as well."

I think Miriam was taken aback and yet, I also believe she saw nobility in my goal as she responded. "In our business, that's a rare act of kindness – someone who actually is using their talent to help someone else for which I am not only profoundly impressed, but truly humbled.

Miriam paused for a moment and realized that, because we were in a studio, others would soon be 'listening'. Gone was the icy lecturer and before me sat a kind, wonderful woman who simply asked if I'd like to have dinner with her, as the bond between us was beginning to develop. Little did I realize, it was one of the most important bonds of my life beyond Jack and my family.

"As she stood, Miriam leaned in and whispered. 'Bring your songbook, I think we need to plan everything and see if we can't shake things up a bit." Little did I realize what she had planned. Little did I understand the consequences of her strategy. Never, will I forget, what we did and how it happened.

Dinner 4/2:

Arrangements were made for what I felt was a clandestine meeting. I offered to Uber it to the restaurant and Miriam suggested we have dinner at her house. I agreed and she said she would have a driver pick me up at six. I expected something nice and wore my best clothes. To say I was underdressed would be no hyperbole.

First, I was picked up in a classic sand-over-garnet 1961 Rolls Royce Phantom with a chauffeur who opened the door for me. On the back of the passenger seat was a small bottle of wine and a note from Miriam. Being a nondrinker since getting pregnant with Charlie, I said thank you to the driver who simply nodded. As we drove from the hotel, the area evolved from the urban glitz of Hollywood to the rolling tranquility of Beverly Hills and finally Beverly Ridge that consisted of eleven homes on large lots, secured by a 24-hour guard and individual private gates, as well.

I glanced out the window at the estates and knew that these were where the really rich people lived. It was amazing to think that our family could easily buy the entire neighborhood, but it just wasn't what mom and dad wanted, nor the way we were raised. Jack and I were trying to live a normal life, where we wanted nothing more than a nice house and the ability to simply 'blend in' even though my endowment consisted of $10,000 per week, which didn't put a dent in the total that now exceeded even more than before.

As the car slowed, I looked at the tall vine covered walls and the electric gate that was slowly opening. The house was what they called Spanish traditional and was probably 100 years old, yet still immaculate with wrought iron highlights and gardens everywhere.

As we reached the entryway, the front door opened and Miriam was standing regaled in a charcoal gray silk pants suit. Gone was plain Jane. In her place was someone who had money and wanted you to realize she was successful.

"Welcome!"

"Thank you. You have a beautiful home'" I said, admiring the foyer.

"Come in. Would you care for a drink?" "Sorry, I don't drink."

"Good girl, alcohol is irritating to the mucous membranes that line the throat and has the potential to dry out a singer's vice, potentially rendering them incapable of hitting the high notes and preventing them from making the most of their range."

As is California style, we entered a large family room and I saw several Emmys and Oscars on shelves adjacent to a natural stone fireplace that reminded me of ours on Pine Lake. In the corner stood an ebony, concert grand piano with a vase full of red roses on top.

Miriam excused herself as I pondered the awards with the name Edgar Weiss engraved and photos of her with literally every top singer in the world for the past forty years. I perused the collection and came upon one of Miriam as a child sitting behind a grand piano at Carnegie Hall that dad and I had toured and then another photo with what looked like her parents and finally Miriam, with what appeared to be her husband.

Miriam returned from the kitchen and noticed my review of her photos. "That was me at age twelve playing at Carnegie Hall. That one is with my mother and father. I think it was the proudest day of their lives."

Laconically, Miriam lifted the last photo and perused the image. "This was my husband Edgar. He was the spark of my life and the center of my universe and then he went away."

"He left you?" I asked almost incredulously.

"No, God took him from me five years ago. He and I loved each other so deeply. He and I were partners and lovers, friends and above all else, collaborators on this thing called life. They tell me time heals all wounds and, yet, I miss him as much today as the day he died."

A soft tear slid down Miriam's cheek that she discretely tried to brush it away as she caught herself. "Edgar and I met at Julliard where we went to school. Edgar Weiss and Miriam Goldberg, two poor Jewish kids from New York who commuted each day to class. We came to LA to work on film scores together and that's how it all began. Edgar did the lyrics and I did the melodies."

"Do you have any children?" I asked.

Miriam gently shook her head 'no' as she answered. "Not that we didn't try, but it just never happened."

I knew I'd hit a soft spot and quickly changed subjects. "Do you still write music scores?"

"There's not much demand today as when we first started and Edgar was the true creative genius, while I was simply the technician."

I looked at the Oscars and asked for permission to pick one up, quickly learning that Oscar was heavier than I imagined, in more ways than one.

"Edgar decided to have it engraved with our real name and not our professional name. You know the whole Jewish thing that used to be so bad."

I just shook my head in disdain, realizing that the stigma was still there, not only for someone who was one quarter African- American, but simply because of the way you believed in God, as I asked, "Do you still play?"

Miriam raised her hands and I saw a pianist's worst nightmare – arthritis, that had taken her fingers and warped them, riddling them with pain, taking away their ability to constantly caress the keys she loved.

"So, you were a concert pianist?"

Miriam proudly nodded in the affirmative. "Then you needed to find something else?"

Again, an affirmation as I inquired, "How did you get into coaching?"

"We'd listen to what was recorded and Edgar and I would simply groan at how bad most of it was. One day, we were having dinner with an international recording star here at the house and he saw Edgar's piano and started fiddling with the keys. He thought he'd impress us by belting out his signature song. We'd all had a bit too much to drink and my reservations were gone. I thanked him for the serenade, but inferred he could do better. Instead of getting angry, he was man enough to ask me how and so I tutored him."

Miriam motioned me to follow her and we went into what had been converted into a recording studio with 'just' a grand piano in it. As we entered, Miriam continued. "I told him to sing it the way I instructed and we recorded it, then I played his original version and my way and his mouth dropped open as I'd removed years of drinking and debauchery from his voice. While he was vane, he could still see there was a dramatic improvement in terms of the richness of his timbre and tone that added fifteen years to his career. The car you came here tonight, was his way of saying "thank you."

"He gave you a Rolls Royce?" I said incredulously. "I made him twenty or thirty million dollars."

I just shook my head in disbelief.

Miriam continued, "Word got out. Soon, every over-the-hill singer wanted my advice. As they got their second wind, the record companies started calling saying they had this artist or that who needed work and so, I went back to school, took some physiology and physical education classes, hired a yoga instructor and developed the program we discussed this morning. Sadly, along came auto tune and every Tom, Dick and Harry who couldn't carry a note in a suitcase became ingratiated with the artificial ability to sing."

"Edgar and I did all right for ourselves and so today, I only do what I want to, when I want to, with whom I want to. LA is a big/little town and reputations go a long way, as do relationships and the last thing I wanted was to be referred to in the past tense. Today, I pick and choose the artist I want to work with, from not only their musical potential, but their personal integrity. Before 'The Choice' contacted me, I vowed I'd never to do it again, as the stars in the eyes of so many have been nothing more than grits of sand that has done nothing but create a mountain of sadness.

I never thought I'd see another natural and then, this young woman from some little, dinky town in Wisconsin shows up and bam, I was smitten. Even through lousy microphones and poor speakers, I knew she was the one who could allow me to make my last mark on a town, an industry and a medium that made us rich, that I've come to despise."

The furrows in my brow must have been deeper than I thought as Miriam looked at me with a slight smile and whispered. "It won't be long until Edgar and I are together again."

"What?" I inquired incredulously. "My time is almost up."

"You're a young woman," I countered.

"Melia, this is Hollywood. I'm old enough to be your grandmother."

I knew it was impolite to ask her age and left it at that. It was only later that I found out she was seventy-nine.

Miriam quickly changed the subject and invited me out onto the patio. The shimmering water of a small waterfall cascaded down into the pool whose rhythm eclipsed the sounds of the city, wherever they were. The table was set for two and I was offered a seat facing the pool. Shortly thereafter, the gentleman who had been my driver appeared and served a tall glass of ice water and Miriam a glass of Chardonnay.

"I hope you don't mind if I have a glass of wine." Miriam stated.

"No, not at all. I used to drink, but when I got pregnant, I stopped. After that, my tastes changed and I don't like the taste of alcohol anymore, but I certainly don't think less of those who do." I didn't mention the family booze business, as I thought that would be too much.

Miriam added. "When I was growing up in New York, my

dad would drink wine after going to Temple. It was always Manischewitz and he said I could have some because it was kosher. Those were the days when we all followed the rules. Today, heavens, I only go to Temple for the main holidays and even then, I really don't seem to get much out of it."

"What did your dad do?"

"He and momma had a small grocery store in Queens. We lived upstairs. Daddy would work and then come upstairs for dinner and go back down and work until it was dark. He was a good man who loved music and bought an old upright piano that I learned to play. My parents gave up everything so that I could go to Julliard. After Edgar and I 'made it', we bought them a home in Miami and they retired down there. Dad called it 'Heaven's waiting room,' Miriam said with a snicker.

Dinner was served and it was wonderful. Miriam and I were bonding and it was like sitting with Grandma Terrill on her front porch. For the first time in LA, I felt comfortable.

"I heard your favorite dessert is strawberry short cake," Miriam noted.

I nodded in the affirmative, wondering where that tidbit of information came from.

Miriam went to the kitchen and returned with a home-made, frosted angel food cake that reminded me of our wedding cake.

"You didn't need to do that," I responded.

"I don't do things I need to anymore. I do things I **want** to."

The very first bite took me back beyond our wedding to my childhood when Uncle Hank would bake the cake and infuse the strawberries inside and put a dollop of hand-made whipped cream on top. Miriam had made it exactly the same way as I inquired "How did you know?"

Miriam looked at me with a wry smile on her face and said. "We do have telephones here in LA and there really aren't that many people named Harris in Mineral Point." I was both honored and concerned to think that Miriam would go out of their way to make my favorite dessert, wondering what else she'd learned, especially my real last name.

I think Miriam sensed my trepidation as she added. "Melia, my job is to coach you and that means to not only teach, but motivate you as well. I needed to learn more about you as a person. I have but one basic goal - to have you do your very best. For some people, it means a lot of pressure. For others, it means a lot of hand holding. For even others, including you, it's really only about taking that drive you have, along with your intellect, and having it focus on what lies ahead and have it overcome your insecurity. With two kids and a husband at home, your plate is full and I know my job is to keep you positive and focused on the next four weeks. If I can do that, you're going to win. If I fail, then you'll fail and you don't impress me as someone who likes to lose."

I gently nodded my head yes. Miriam had me pegged.

"I do have a couple of questions," Miriam inquired. "I hope you don't mind."

I looked at this wonderful little lady and felt at ease as she continued. "What we share is between us and no one else."

Again, I nodded yes.

"Did you graduate from medical school?" Again, I nodded yes.

"Were you planning on becoming a pediatric oncologist?"

Once again there was a nod admitting she'd done her homework.

"You simply walked away?"

I looked down at the ground and then into Miriam's eyes as I nodded again, while responding. "My grandmother was one of the world's most noted experts in pediatric oncology and I loved Grandma Marie. She was my hero and I wanted to be like her. Sadly, the pressure was too much and my life was a shambles. I was lonely, disheartened and afraid."

"Afraid of what?"

"That I might follow in the footsteps of my uncle."

"Alcohol?"

"Suicide!" I replied.

A shiver went through Miriam as I continued. "On my first night in Pediatrics, during my first year of residency, I had a three-year-old girl die in my arms and I simply lost it. I was totally burned out and realized I'd made a mistake."

"And so you just quit?"

"I talked it over with my parents and they knew I was unhappy, but didn't realize how bad it was. They told me to take some time off and go to our home in St. Martin and clear my mind. I resigned my position and spent over a month at House- On-The-Hill recharging my batteries and relearning to enjoy the small things in life."

"Mom came down with me for the first week and introduced me to several different forms of relaxation therapies that helped calm me down. Each morning, we would get up at sunrise and walk the beach. Mom had leukemia when she was in college, nearly died and had done what we were doing and it wasn't long before I began to smile again, something I hadn't done in years."

Miriam nodded, realizing that my life had a different side to it as I continued. "Miriam, what I'm about to tell you is totally secret and it must stay that way or I will walk away."

Miriam nodded in agreement as I continued. "After nearly five weeks on St. Martin, I felt relieved and headed home. My time with mom was wonderful, but it was Annie who saved my life as she taught me how to let go of the pain I'd endured and not only laugh but smile again."

"I was only home a few days and dad took me to Dubai and I saw a different side of the world. While there, he bought me a totally new wardrobe that helped me get over my sense of defeat. I needed to do something with my life and because our family started the research foundation, I decided to see if I fit in there. I went into town for lunch and ran into a guy who'd we met on a family cruise six years before and it was love at second sight."

Miriam agreed and so I continued. "My family has

substantial wealth. Jack and I agreed we wanted to live a 'normal' life and so, while we have the resources available, we're trying to make it as if we were a typical middle-class family with me home with the kids, doing what I really enjoy which is be a mom."

"The Derrick Williams Foundation?" Miriam inquired.

I shook my head yes as Miriam added. "Melia, I know who your family is and the gifts the Foundation has given to the world. I know about the Nobel Peace Prize and respect not only your privacy, but the fact that you want to just blend in and lead a normal life. One of the things that attracted me to you is your integrity and decency as someone who hasn't allowed power, prestige and money take away your purity and innocence."

I nodded and quietly said, "Thank you," as Miriam continued. "To me you're Melia Wilson and nothing more. You're a woman with a God-given gift, who's been offered the opportunity to share it with the world. My only question is, what happens if you win 'The Choice?'"

"I've thought about that and as I shared with you this morning, it's why all the songs are those written by Annie. My goal is to win, you can be assured of that, but to do so without any leverage from my family, and simply open up the music world to the incredible talent Annie has as a writer and let her reap the rewards she deserves."

"You're really not doing this for yourself?

I shook my head and responded. "Not at all. I'm doing this completely for her. Our family went to great lengths to allow me to get escape from the challenges they face and if it wasn't for Annie needing it, there's no way I'd be here right now."

"But what happens if you win?"

"It's something you and I will need to figure out WHEN I win," which put a broad smile on Miriam's face.

As we finished our last bites, Miriam inquired about the lyrics. I nodded in the affirmative as I opened my purse and handed them to her.

"Why don't we do this? Give me a day or two to go over what you've got and we can discuss it when I see you on Wednesday."

"Annie recorded all these songs," I offered.

"I know, I've been listening to them and have had a focus group evaluate each song."

"Focus group?"

"Sure, we know what the demographics of the voting audience are and we need to pick songs that score the highest with them. Your opinion and mine concerning song selection might be totally opposite of what the voters like and what also fits your program persona."

Once again, my naivete was in place as I simply shook my head in disbelief while the ride back to the hotel seemed shorter than the one to Miriam's house had been. Little did I realize that the road would become well-traveled over the next several weeks. Little did I realize the brilliance of my coach and her attention to detail and how it was no longer 'just' singing, but actually building songs word-by-word, note-by-note, emotion-by- emotion until the message conveyed was one of audience emotional participation and not observation.

Cans of Soup:

When you start with eighteen people vying for the same thing, it doesn't take too long until, like high school, you split into smaller groups, where three of us Eddie, Claudette and I, began hanging around together. As part of the first week, we were being 'introduced' to the industry where the record companies came in to put stars in our eyes.

All the big boys were invited and made virtually the same presentation that dealt with airplay, former success stories and coordinating concerts, where the real money was. The blah, blah, blah was the same except Mike Carvahlo from Summit records who looked at us and simply asked, "What is a brand?"

Eddie had been trying for eight years to 'break in'. Claudette for six and they knew and accepted what Mike said as he looked at the group and added, 'The Choice' is not only about music, but about building your personal brand. The truth is, branding doesn't happen overnight or even in a few months, and one false step with one wrong person and your entire brand structure can collapse instantly. Building a brand is definitely a process that requires a strategy. However, the ongoing effort will result in establishing long-term relationships with your fans, who are actually your customers. If done right, building and maintaining your brand can lead to steady increases in new fans and subsequent sales."

"We are a record company, but more importantly, we are specialists in brand building. What is brand building you ask? Brand building is generating awareness about you using strategies and campaigns with the goal of creating a unique and lasting image in the marketplace, where a positive image, plus standing out in a crowd, equals brand success." I thought about it and realized that was exactly opposite of what I wanted. Yet, I'd already fallen down the rabbit hole and knew I needed to continue – not for my sake, but Annie's.

Most of us shrugged, never thinking of ourselves as brands and yet that's what we were becoming. Mike stated. "Simply put, you will be defined by a customer's overall perception of you and what other people say when you're not in the room. In other words, your reputation!"

I sat back in my chair and realized Mike was right as he continued. "In today's market, a successful brand has to be consistent in communication and experience and do so across many applications including what you sing, what you wear - including or excluding body art - your personal logo, what form of content publishing takes place concerning your life, interests and objectives and your fan club and not only how your website is developed, but everything from site design down to even the font style we use, as we become your most trusted associates who then sustain your tailored image."

Mike continued, "At Summit Records, your branding will be broken down into three phases. First is brand strategy, then brand identity and, finally, brand marketing. Brand Strategy will map out that you're not only different, but trustworthy, memorable and likable by your target fan base, who will be selected by us to include demographics such as age, education and socio-economic levels, where we will convey your purpose, promises and how you will consistently entertain your followers." Mike looked at us and flatly stated, "That's the first step you need to take when creating a brand even though 'The Choice' has already begun to established that for you. While you're sitting here thinking you've got a lot of momentum, remember, you're only being watched by six million people. This means around 350 million Americans are NOT watching."

Eddie sort of had a weird look on his face and so Mike addressed him. "Eddie, you wouldn't build a home without a blueprint or plans, would you?"

Eddie nodded 'of course' as Mike continued. "It's the same with you. You can think of brand strategy as the blueprint for how you want the world to see you. Summit records will build and develop an effective and comprehensive brand strategy that includes brand discovery, competitive research, target audience and finally your brand message and story. While you might think this is inconsequential, it is a critical and foundational piece for building your successful career and is the one area most entertainers overlook simply because they jump right into performing.

Claudette had a perplexed look on her face and asked. "What is brand identity?"

Mike smiled, realizing that she was at least paying attention as he responded, "Brand Identity is the way we convey your persona to the public with visuals, messaging, and experience, while the brand strategy we create will influence how you present yourself and align it with your chosen musical lane for the greatest impact."

Mike continued, "As we develop you, your elements of brand identity will be applied across all channels consistently. It's the way you become immediately recognizable. Once this is developed we will begin the brand marketing phase which will highlight and bring increased awareness to you amongst those who didn't watch 'The Choice' by connecting your values and voice to the right audience through what we call strategic communication. Here, we will amplify your brand image through content marketing, which places key words in your stories so that people who use their search engine will find your name pop up as it directs them to your website and social media, which we will control by building up your Twitter and Facebook base as our writers keep your fans aware of all that you are doing. If need be, Summit Records will even invest in paid advertising or promotions on different media to launch your newest and greatest songs."

I believe all three of us were in shock. We thought it was all so easy and our dreams would simply come true, when in fact, we were becoming cans of soup, who simply provide a service – music to sooth the savage beast.

Because Eddie, Claudette and I paid the most attention and asked questions, Mike began focusing on us as he added. "Each of you has developed a persona that the producers feed into the panel of judges they use to differentiate each of you."

"Eddie, you've been positioned as kind, sweet and sincere. Claudette, you're the rebel. Melia, the producers have settled on 'the girl next door' that every mother hopes her son marries or daughter becomes. For all of you, a positioning statement has been created by the show to make sure you have a distinct and unique image the viewers can identify with, differentiate from the others and, for your sake, hopefully, support."

Mike leaned back against the wall and added. "As you can see, there is a powerful purpose behind the brand image they're creating that we can extend. The back-story they're sharing has one goal - to show that you wake up every day loving what you do to entertain the viewers and the world through your talent."

"The producers have established the foundation upon which Summit Records will ask four questions when defining your purpose: First, why do you exist? Second, what differentiates you from other singers? Third, what problem do you solve? Finally, why should people care?

I must have had one of those 'looks' as Mike added. "Melia, studies show that 50% of consumers worldwide say they buy products based on brand values and impact. So, we need to dig deep and find those nuggets of truth that can distinguish you from others. Our goal is to sell records or downloads. We know that people don't buy **what** you do, they buy **why** you do it, and that includes the melodies and lyrics of your songs, along with your relative position in the global marketplace. Our goal is **not** to do business with everybody that might want to listen to you, but do business with people who believe what you believe and what you

Surprise:

My next session with Miriam was scheduled for Wednesday. It was going to be song selection. As was the protocol, the meeting was scheduled for 10:00 AM and would just be the two of us. I learned that Miriam's contract with 'The Choice' indicated that she was not to be taped and we were to be alone. At precisely ten, we both arrived and, after the dinner a few nights before, were both more casual.

"Melia, I've been looking over the other five other contestants and I see a stylistic opening. You've got two pop singers that will cancel each other out, one country and one R&B's and then a rocker. What would you think of singing 'Amazing Grace'?

My mind wandered through my options and, quite honestly, I hadn't thought of it as part of my retinue for the show.

"You've got to realize the producers are slotting you as the girl next door and there's a huge deep-south religious following of the show. Because the song is so well known, it won't narrow your field but will give you an open slot, before we start going after the others in direct competition."

I breathed deeply. Needless to say, I'd sung the song dozens of times as I finally nodded in the affirmative.

"Great, now there's one other little thing," Miriam said with a sly smile on her face.

"I want you to practice with the band and then come to my house. Are you free for dinner?"

I just smiled and nodded in the affirmative asking, "Same time? Same place?"

The other contestants and I spent the rest of the day in photo shoots, picking out our performance wardrobe where there was nothing and I mean absolutely nothing I liked and me going through 'Amazing Grace' with the band for the first time. It was 72 hours to taping and I was getting nervous.

Charles was right on time and the drive went well for Los Angeles. I arrived at Miriam's house, to find the warm smile I'd seen before and a much more casual attitude than even that morning. Miriam looked at me and noted that we needed to begin the training regimen for the taping session. I had no idea what she meant.

"We need to pretend you have a cold to protect your voice." I nodded in the affirmative.

"First, I want you to make certain you drink lots of water."

"I can do that."

"It's got to be at room temperature and not cold." Yuk! But OK.

"I have these vitamins for you that contain zinc and vitamin C."

I looked at the bottle and saw they were over the counter vitamins from Walgreens and nodded again.

"I want you to begin taking omega 3 fish oil capsules that helps boost your immune system."

I reluctantly nodded again.

"Next, I want you to begin taking this elderberry syrup which is antiviral and will protect your vocal cords."

Once again, I reluctantly agreed.

"Finally, three times a day and right before you go on, I want you to drink a cup of honey/lemon tea."

My expression must have given away my trepidation as Miriam added. "Strictly speaking, there's no 'tea' in the tea. It's just honey, lemon juice and hot water, where the lemon juice will help cut through any congestion created by all your practice and the honey soothes the throat."

Miriam handed me a cup of the honey/lemon tea that I actually found it quite refreshing.

"It's important that you follow instructions and minimize the use of your voice until after your performance."

"What about your attire?" Miriam inquired at which point, I pulled the Dubai thumb drive out of my purse and offered it to her. With her quizzical look, I offered all the details about my trip with dad and how everything was designed to match my complexion and 'aspect ratio', as Waseem called it. Miriam simply shook her head realizing that I had a huge visual advantage on the others who were guessing about what to
wear.

We looked at all the different combinations and Miriam asked, "Are all these clothes here?"

"No! They're in Waldwick," I replied. "How will you get them here?"

"Tell me what to wear and I'll have it here tomorrow," I replied, knowing that this would be my only "urgent" shipment. I intended on going home as much as possible and, because we were laying out the song choices for the entire show, I could also plan ahead concerning my wardrobe as I realized it was all making sense.

Miriam assured me, "I'll make sure everything is available back stage."

I just smiled as it was great having someone with leverage on my side.

"Now, there's just one more thing…" Miriam stated. "What that?" I asked.

"I want you to sing a-cappella." "What?" I inquired incredulously.

"Just you and the microphone without the band or even any background lighting. Melia you've got the voice and now it's time to have you stand out."

I was in shock, just the mike and me? My God!

Miriam smiled and nodded as we headed for the concert grand. "Come on, let's rehearse. If you remember my dissertation on vibrato, this is where we'll knock the socks off the competition by having you sing a different music style and do so with completely different tonalities and resonant factors."

Miriam continued, "I think you should do 'Amazing Grace' in a classical mode because of your natural talent. Normally, I wouldn't slot you there because of the demographics of 'The Choice's' viewership. However, because you have the range to do classical, where the style is definitely a vertical application - not rounded like in R & B or Pop, I think we can pull it off and impress both the judges and your core viewers, while pulling in the Southern Region that was vacated when the guy from Dallas went home."

After the mandatory warm-ups on the concert grand, we went into the studio where I saw that Miriam had taken the entire song and cut it into specific bars. Instead of practicing the entire song, we were only going to practice segments until they were right.

After two hours, we were done. I hadn't sung the entire song once.

"Tomorrow night, we'll put the pieces together."

The rehearsal ended as I glanced at my watch. The kids would be getting ready for bed and I hadn't called home. Miriam caught my drift.

"Do you want to Zoom your family from here?"

I smiled appreciatively as we went into Miriam's study and she beckoned for me to sit at her computer. In an instant I had Jack and the kids on the screen and there were smiles all around.

"Jack, kids, there's a very special lady I'd like to introduce you to. Her name is Miriam."

"Like in the Bible?" Charlie inquired, which brought a huge smile to Miriam's face.

"Is she Moses sister?"

Miriam let out a loud guffaw. "Yes, I'm his older sister."

I turned the screen so that the kids and Jack could visually meet the woman I shared so much about. The kids giggled and were their normal shy selves and Jack just smiled as he said. "It's very nice to meet you Mrs. White."

"The feelings are mutual," Miriam replied.

The kids were in their pajamas as the two-hour time difference meant it was bedtime. I informed them that tomorrow was a school day and so they got the message. I also told them that Mommy was going to be very busy because it was the day before her big show.

"Mommy, don't forget to pull on your ear to show us you love us", Abby instructed.

We said goodnight as the silence of love rekindled the room.

"What a wonderful family, Melia." "Thank you."

"How old are they?"

"Well, Jack's my age" I said with a smirk. "And he's the biggest kid, while Charlie is four and Annie's three."

"What's the pulling on the ear that Annie mentioned?" "My way of saying I love them," I replied.

Miriam smiled a soft, reflective smile and offered, "Carol Burnett used to do that a long time ago. The producers told her to stop and she simply said no, as it was her way of telling her grandmother she loved her. Word got out and the producers received telephone calls and letters saying that if Carol stopped, they'd stop watching. Needless to say, she continued on every episode until her grandmother passed away. Do it Melia! From one whose only regret in life in not having kids. Do it for them, for you and Jack and then for me!"

Dress Rehearsal

It was 'terrible Saturday' as we began calling it. Hurry up and wait! Hurry up and wait! All of us had a slotted time with the band for dress rehearsal and then dead time. For me, it allowed me to work on my long overdue correspondence with family and friends and finish up my education certification. While others were out at night doing whatever it was they were doing, I was in my room on the internet and my computer doing research into 'Contemporary Teaching Techniques in an Electronic Era' and the 'quiet time' allowed me to organize my notes.

When my time came to rehearse with the band, I informed them, per Miriam's instruction, that I was coming down with a sore throat and asked that they simply play the song, while I mouthed the words. The ruse worked!

That night Miriam and I got together and put all the pieces together. What a difference! Most songs begin and build to a huge crescendo. Because it was so well known, Miriam wanted me to start strong and then begin to focus on key words by changing the height or intensity of the words and then add some vibrato to the chorus. Because the first two words identified the song, Miriam had me hold both words for a full beat longer than what the band would have had played and then build to the line 'I once was lost, but now am found' and then end softly, gently and even tenderly almost in a whisper with 'blind, but now I see'.

Amazing Grace, how sweet the sound
That saved a wretch like me
I once was lost, but now am found
 Was blind but now I seeWas Grace that taught my heart to fear

And Grace, my fears relieved
How precious did that Grace appear
The hour I first believed
Through many dangers, toils and snares
We have already come

"What about the band?" I inquired.

"It's all taken care of," Miriam assured me. "But how?"

"Remember me telling you it's a small town in a big city?"

I simply shook my head as Miriam outlined, "The band director is trying to produce a new CD and can't get any record company to listen to him. By the end of the competition, he'll have a deal, IF he does what we want done."

I was simply taken aback. Miriam had enough power to literally create or destroy careers and she was willing to do so for me.

It's Show Time:

We were going live for the first time and you could feel the nerves tingling everywhere. Charlie Jackson had his mark and the show began with the band playing 'The Choice' theme song, as the judges were introduced. Charlie introduced each of us in the order that we were singing and we all went to the waiting area on the side of the stage.

Eddie was slotted first and came out and knocked it out of the park. While most pop singers have thin tenor voice, Eddie was down in the range where Sinatra and Dean Martin had their greatest strength. Wearing a white suit with a light pink open collar shirt the make-up artists made him look like he'd just come from the beach. All three judges stood and applauded, noting that Eddie belonged in the same group as Sinatra, to which Eddie had tears in his eyes.

The rocker girl from Denver was next, but I was so nervous, I didn't hear a note she sang as I was backstage waiting to go on. At the commercial break, Francine came over and wished me well. I whispered thank you and took my last sip of honey/lemon tea before going to my mark.

As the show returned from the commercial break, Charlie in his eternal effervescence said, "And here's your Midwest Regional winner, Melia Wilson, singing 'Amazing Grace'. I was wearing a pair of camel tan slacks and black turtle neck that Miriam said looked 'holy'.

The lone spotlight blasted my face as the stage remained dark. I couldn't see, but I guess the stage hands didn't know what to do and there was pandemonium in the control room until Tom Darden the assistant director told them to zoom in on 'half body' and hold.

I began singing and all that Miriam taught me fell into place. The change in dynamics, enunciation and hitting the high notes just as she had instructed, worked before softening the end with 'but, now I see' as I softly pulled on my left ear.

As the lights came up, Charlie reappeared. While there was a profound difference between rehearsal and performance, he was professional enough to act as if the entire set had been planned.

"Melia, what can I say?" he lamented. "You've just taken one of my favorite songs and moved it from my mind to my heart. Thank you."

I looked at the judges and there hadn't been any emotion at all, just opened mouths. The videos they'd seen of the dress rehearsals were no good. The screens in front of them weren't pertinent. Finally, Lance looked at me and smiled before looking down and then up again. "Melia, how can I tell you what you just did? You took me to church. Right here, right now! You took me to church and I thank you and thank God for you tonight."

I simply stood there. No one knew what to do until the camera's went black as they went to commercial and then all hell broke loose.

As I made my way to the holding area, the floor director came over seething. "We **DON'T DO THAT**! Who told you to break with rehearsal? You made us look like fools!"

As the commercial break was one of the long ones, running nearly five minutes, things started calming down and then the judges' video screens came to light and all the uproar was replaced by open mouths of profound shock. The floor director literally ran over to Charlie Jackson and whispered something as Charlie took his spot as we came out of break.

"Well America, what can we say? It looks like we all just went to church as Charlie segued into the country singer from New York as the other four contestants slowly inched their way to create more distance between them and me.

The final act was Claudette and oh, my God, she was incredible. As the show came to a close, I stood and really didn't know what to do or where to go until the director came out of the booth and I thought I was going to really get it.

"Melia. I don't know whose idea it was for you to go a-cappella and right now, I really don't care. I'm totally pissed that you did it and yet profoundly grateful, as well. Your presence! Your performance was simply spellbinding. I've been doing this for twenty years and NEVER seen a performance like that."

"In the control room, there was total silence and you could have heard a pin drop. No one wanted to move! No one wanted to change the image! All we wanted to do was be immersed in what you were singing. If you get voted off after that performance, the show just isn't fair. All I ask is that, should you decide to make changes, come to me, and only me, so that we can work it out."

"Right now, there's a lot of anger and frustration, but if what I think is about to happen does, I'm certain that anger will quickly go away. My suggestion is you get out of here right now and don't stop to talk to anyone as you leave."

I made it to the stage door where my little Jewish lady stood with a huge smile on her face. "You did it! You weren't wonderful! You were so far beyond that, I really don't know what to say. Let's go party!"

The Aftermath:

I called Jack from the car and the kids were screaming how great mommy did while thanking me for pulling on my ear as it was their 'secret message'. Miriam knew that the hotel was the last place I should go as the producers and press would be after me all night and was also afraid they'd be hounding her, as well. "We'd better let things calm down. I've got four extra bedrooms and security. Why not stay at Edgar and my cottage tonight?"

I was emotionally spent and total exhausted and softly nodded in the affirmative as we set out. While I was expecting the home in Beverly Heights, we continued west and through a gated community entrance where the security came out and actually inspected the vehicle and who was in it, before nodding and smiling.

I had no idea where we were and politely inquired as Miriam responded. "Edgar and I didn't take many vacations and so we invested in a little cottage that overlooks the ocean. You're in an area called Paradise Cove where the owner's names are unlisted in corporations and we have all the peace and quiet you deserve."

Charles pulled the Rolls into the garage with the door closing behind us. While the house in Beverly Heights was beautiful, the house in Paradise Cove was simply unbelievable. As we walked in, I could see the sun setting on the edge of the Pacific. All the west walls were glass as we sat perched above those below. While I love House-On-The-Hill, this was simply incredible and I'd never even dreamed that houses like this existed. The floors were granite with oriental rugs and in the living room was a white concert grand piano. The walls were covered in photos of virtually every major recording star in the world with each saying the same thing, "Thank you, Miriam."

I looked closely at the photos as Miriam stated. "Someday Melia, I hope your photo is up there, as well." My thoughts turned to Annie with the hope that it would be her photo and not mine.

The adrenaline that kept me going dissipated and a huge yawn exploded from my mouth. Miriam showed me to what was to be my bedroom with one of those California king beds with silk sheets as the stars began to twinkle where the sun had finally set.

"Do you need anything to eat?" Miriam asked.

"Not really!" I replied. "Perhaps a glass of water – ice cold water – would be nice."

With that, Miriam flipped a switch on the wall and the black- out curtains closed and departed for my water and her wine.

"A toast to you!" Miriam said as she raised her glass.

I looked at my friend and said, "L'Chaim," which I'd Googled and saved for a very special time.

Miriam nodded and said thank you in many ways. "Now get some sleep!" she directed as she walked out and quietly closed the door.

I went in the bathroom and there was a new toothbrush, toothpaste and deodorant set out, along with a set of casual jeans and clothes for the following day. What a wonderful hostess!

When I awoke, I had one of those 'where am I'? moments before realizing what all had transpired. I used the bathroom, took a shower and went out into the living room.

"What time is it?" I inquired. "Almost eleven!"

"Oh, my God!" I responded as I hadn't slept that late since St.
Martin.

"Come, have some breakfast. I know whole wheat toast and orange juice, right?"

I nodded and smiled at the same time, as I peered at a neatly stacked pile of paper."

"What's this?" "Take a look!"

Someone had scanned the internet and copied all the articles about my performance. To my surprise and Miriam's glee the responses were 'over the top', as she liked to say.

"You did great last night!" Miriam concluded, as I finished the last page. "The challenge now is, how do we top it?"

"What do you think? I inquired.

"Well, the New York cowboy fell flat on his face and so I think he's going home. This means the Country music fans will be looking for a new favorite. Do you think we could twang up Annie's *'Last Call in Heaven'* enough to make it a cross-over?"

I nodded in the affirmative. After the success with 'Amazing Grace', Miriam could have told me to sing *Mary Had a Little Lamb* and I would have done it. We, made our way to the piano and Miriam played the melody.

"Can I have a day to work on the melody and then let's see what we can do?"

I nodded in the affirmative, as I looked at the bright blue Pacific and had an idea. "I know Annie doesn't have any commitments, what would you think if she came out and helped? She's an incredible talent and I believe the two of you will make a fantastic team."

"You mean, the three of us, don't you?" Miriam inquired, to which I simply nodded.

I called Annie and asked what she was doing. "Trying to unplug a toilet in 404."

"Pack some clothes and go out to Truax. Amelia III will be there in an hour. Forget about toilets and come help Miriam get ready for next week."

"Really? You mean **she** wants **me** to come to LA and help the incredible Miriam White?"

"Yes, you can work on the lyrics on 'Last Call in Heaven' while she works on the melody."

"Oh Melia, this is incredible. I've got to throw some clothes in a bag."

"We'll meet you at the Burbank airport. Amelia III will contact me when they're an hour out."

Annie arrived and Miriam and I picked her up in the Rolls and took her to Miriam's house. Annie was floored! Miriam White! A Rolls Royce! My God, what an honor, especially when Miriam offered to let Annie stay at her house and work with her.

Thursday meant rehearsal and all the promotional stuff that the show had tied into it. It didn't take long for me to realize that Hollywood was certainly 'different' – not quite as nice as I thought it would be, nor as exciting while the safety and security lecture the producers initially provided certainly made me wake up to the fact that, *Melia you're not in Waldwick anymore.*

Last Call In Heaven:

After the previous week's surprise, both Miriam and I knew we'd better play by the rules if I made the cut. Sure enough New York cowboy went home and the strategy of 'twanging' *'Last Call in Heaven'* seemed like it was about to work, even though Annie and I were the only people in California who knew the song was written for a bar called 'Heaven' in Appleton, Wisconsin.

Annie and Miriam worked their melodic magic and we sliced and diced the lyrics to put in just enough country, while keeping it true to the original. After the 'Amazing Grace' episode, I had no idea where I'd be placed, but Miriam assured me I'd go last simply because of all the ink I'd received from the week before. Sure enough, the casting list was posted and I was last.

Eddie did a Sammy Davis tune. Claudette rocked the house. The other girl and guy sounded good, but I was beginning to understand what Miriam had taught me and how it really made a difference.

We were no longer sitting next to the audience when others were performing and actually had our own dressing rooms, where no one else was allowed. I watched on the monitor and waited for the rap on the door, taking my last sip of my lemon/honey tea as I walked out the door. Annie wished me luck and I gave her a hug, vowing to myself. "This one's for Annie."

I came on stage during a commercial break and found my spot. I looked at the band director and nodded. He smiled and gave me a thumbs-up. It seems that after all the hullabaloo of the week before, he'd become one of my biggest fans. While the week before I'd been dressed conservatively. This week I was in jeans and light blue Armani blouse and white neck scarf. As the lights came up and I began singing the judges mouths dropped open. The girl from Wisconsin who'd gone viral with an a- cappella religious song, had gone country on them, in terms of melody, lyrics and attire.

As the song finished Charlie reappeared and simply shook his head as he said. "From church to the farm in one fell swoop. Only you Melia, could have made the journey."

The judges were polite and I felt I did OK, but it was nothing like the mayhem of the week before and I only hoped I'd get enough votes to keep going.

My hopes came true and, once again, Miriam was spot-on, as the overnight reviews indicated that I could easily choose a musical country road to travel on if I so desired.

Daddy:

On my day off, I Zoomed home and talked with Jack to make sure everything was OK and to tell him I missed him. The kids came on and told me how daddy had made special pancakes and taken them to the park. It was right then and there, I knew what my next song had to be.

While Miriam preferred a different song, I said I really wanted to do a song Annie had written for her dad as a Father's Day gift. Miriam asked for some time to think about it and called back two hours later and detailed her strategy.

"Look we've got the religious folks and now the country fans, I agree we can go for the heart with the song about Annie's dad. If we do it right, I think you've got a cover song that's going to sell millions."

I didn't really care about selling millions. Annie had written the song for her dad and all the sacrifices he and her mom made so that Annie and her sister could begin their lives 'ahead of the curve' as he called it regarding being in debt.

Miriam dissected the song and the three of us began what had become our standard procedure of taking the lyrics and forming different intonations as we built to the end. Miriam noted that this was one of the most 'innocent songs' she'd ever heard and there'd be a lot of tears flowing. To ensure it went the way we wanted in terms of tempo, Miriam offered to play piano during the show. AFTRA gave her permission and she agreed to not only donate her fee, but quadruple it, as a donation to the nursing home for elderly actors.

"There were now four of us competing – Eddie, Claudette, a girl named Stacy and me and we had bonded. Once again, I was placed last on the show. Once again Eddie and Claudette both were simply incredible. I felt sorry for Stacy, as her coach had no idea what to do and it showed.

I came out in a plain black pants suit with a white blouse and small necklace of gold 'pearls. Miriam was at the piano and I gave it my all. As the song ended, there were tears everywhere including me. Charlie came out and simply shook his head, he couldn't speak. The judges just stood and applauded as I turned and motioned to Miriam and Annie. No one moved! Not the judges! Not Charlie! Not Miriam! Not me!

Charlie caught his composure and shook his head and then said. "Melia, we have a surprise for you" as Jack and the kids walked out on stage. I was overwhelmed. I didn't know what to say. I was so happy to see them and yet felt bad for Eddie, Claudette and Stacey. I looked at my family and couldn't hold it anymore and simply broke down and cried as the video went to black.

"What are you doing here?" I asked between tears.

Charlie was first, "Were you surprised, Mommy?" "Oh, my goodness yes! What a wonderful surprise." "When did you get here?" I said between sniffles.

"A couple hours ago," Jack replied, as I grabbed his hand.

"Wilco?" to which Jack simply nodded.

"We came in a jet from Uncle Luke's airport and the pilot let me look out the front window," Annie proudly announced.

"Who? How?" I glanced over Jack's shoulder and saw the answer, the little lady who'd played the piano as I cried again – "Miriam."

We walked over to the piano as Miriam wiped tears from her eyes and I simply said, "Thank you. Thank you so much!"

"How long will you be here?" I asked Jack. "We've got three days, if you've got the time."

It was then that one of the producers came out and said "Melia, we've made all the arrangements for VIP passes to Knotts Berry Farm, Disneyland and Universal Studios, if you want to take the family there."

"Thank you"

"We've also made arrangements for limo service as well."

"I don't think this is fair for Eddie, Claudette and Stacey," I replied.

"We made arrangements for them, as well, and they'll be highlighted on next week's show before the voting begins to make things equal."

I felt better and looked at Miriam as she smiled and Miriam looked at me and the kids and then Jack and offered. "If you like, you two can use the house at the ocean."

My hand went to my mouth. "Really?"

"As long as Annie and I get one night with the kids at my place."

Looking at them Miriam asked, "Did you bring your swimming suits like I told you?"

This had all been planned. What a wonderful, wonderful surprise.

The next day all of us, including Annie and Miriam, went to Disneyland and all wore mouse ears and had a ball. That night we had dinner at Miriam's house and then Jack and I went to the house at the ocean. The following morning, we met the kids and Miriam at Universal Studios, where we had a private tour and the full VIP treatment.

It was time for my brood to leave. I rode in the limo to the airport and saw the kids and Jack get on Amelia III and it almost broke my heart to see them go. I guess I'd had a severe case of homesickness and didn't realize it.

The Soldier:

As the plane lifted off, it was back to reality and that meant picking two songs for the semifinals. I chose 'You and I' and 'Come Home', as Miriam wanted me to do an ethereal ballad and also Annie's favorite and we began practicing. In two days, we had them both pretty much locked down. As I was sitting in my hotel room, I received a text from Annie that simply said "CALL ME" all in caps. I knew that something was wrong – call it women's intuition.

I called and Annie picked up on the first ring. "What's up?" I inquired.

There was a long pause on the other end and then Annie quietly noted, "It's Teddy".

"What?"

"They say it was an accident." "What?"

"Teddy was on a helicopter mission and it went down. "Is he hurt?"

"Presumed dead!"

"Oh, my God, no! Not Teddy! Not my friend! Not your husband! Not the only other man I've ever loved besides Jack."

"I didn't know whether to call you or not."

"Oh, Annie, I'm so glad you did," as I started crying, thinking of Teddy and what a wonderful friend he'd always been. The guy who got me out of my shell. The guy who stood up for me when I didn't think I belonged. The guy I loved like a brother.

I sat for a moment and didn't know what to say or do. Finally, I broke the silence and thanked Annie for calling. I took a deep breath and thought about 'The Choice' and my songs and realized I needed to do something to honor my friend. I called Miriam and she could tell by the tone in my voice that Annie had shared with me what happened. Annie hadn't said much about her marriage and so, between sobs, I told Miriam about Teddy.

She said Annie was too upset to function and Miriam was on her way to the hotel.

Thirty minutes later, Miriam was in my room. In that time, I'd scribbled some lyrics on a piece of paper of a poem that my great, great, great grandfather had written in the 1860's that I never forgot. I knew, I needed to honor my friend and it was the only way I knew how.

Miriam shook her head and looked at me. "The producers aren't going to let you sing this. The show is about sex and love, not about death and war."

"I don't care, can't we do it like 'Amazing Grace'?"

Miriam's head tilted back. "You mean blindside them?"

I smiled which was enough for Miram to realize I agreed. The smile told Miriam I was serious as she offered. "Let me see what I can do."

Two hours later the phone rang and it was Miriam. "Charles will be downstairs in twenty minutes to pick you up."

I looked out the window, then at the clock and finally went downstairs. Charles pulled up and I opened the back door. Sitting next to me was Tommie Thompson, the lead guitarist for the show's band.

"I'm officially not here," Tommie began. "This conversation didn't exist", as it was against the rules for the contestants to fraternize with the show's employees. I simply nodded my head. We rode in total silence to Miriam's empty vacation house as they'd already dropped Annie off at the airport. She was heading to Washington DC for God knows what besides tears and
remorse.

All Miriam had told Tommie was to come. Tommie knew something was up when we pulled into the development, went in the garage and closed the door before we got out. Miriam was waiting in the living room. "Tommie, here's the melody," at which time Miriam played the basic notes on the piano that she'd created to go with my lyrics.

Miriam noted, "I'm thinking this should be plain and

simple with you on guitar and Melia singing. What do you think?"

Tommie read the lyrics and his mouth dropped open. "Who wrote this?" From my facial expression, Tommie knew it was me.

"Melia, this is profound!"

Miriam filled in Tommie on all that had transpired.

"Oh, my God!" was all Tommie could say in response to the news. "You know this won't fly with the producers."

"Unless we do another *Amazing Grace*" Miriam replied.

Tommie leaned back and took a deep breath. "This one's a career maker or breaker."

Miriam looked at Tommie and then stood and walked over to him. Looking down, she said. "You're lead guitar in a TV show band. Do this for me and I'll get you in front of every major rock band looking for a new lead guitar player. If you lose this gig, I'll pay you until you find another."

Tommie ran his hands through his long blond hair. He was at a juncture and knew it. If we succeeded, he'd be on a roll. If we failed, he might just as well go back to Nashville.

"Fuck it!" Tommie exclaimed.

Miriam played the melody as Tommie began strumming his guitar. In fifteen minutes he had the chords down and we were ready to add the lyrics.

"Let's go into the studio and lay it down so that Melia and I can practice."

We went into the beach house studio as Miriam and Tommie repeated what they'd created and recorded it. Miriam dubbed two copies onto thumb drives and gave one to each of us so that we could familiarize ourselves with the tempo and the chording.

As we finished, we went back into the living room and Miriam handed Tommie an envelope. Only later did I learn it contained $5,000 for his trouble.

We rode back to the hotel and I was about to be dropped off when Tommie looked at me and said, "this will either make you or break you" as I opened the door.

The next morning, we continued to rehearse 'Flawless' and 'Come Home' as if everything was going to be the same. As we were wrapping things up and I was heading back to my dressing room, Eddie Jackson, who everyone called Bubba, caught up with me.

Bubba was a large African American man who you loved when you were doing what needed to be done and someone you feared when you didn't get it right. He was the assistant director who ran the booth like the Marine Corps drill sergeant he once was, making certain the product that was put out was first class all the time. The 'Amazing Grace' episode had him furious from a technical standpoint, but elated from both an emotional and creative perspective.

"Let's talk." Bubba urged.

"About what?" I inquired.

"How about in your dressing room?" I knew this was serious.

"When you sing your second song, I'm wondering if we just do a straight-on head shot with a black background like you did with *Amazing Grace*."

I looked at Eddie and believed I understood. Miriam had gotten to him and wanted maximum visual effect.

"Perhaps, you could pull back just a little bit and add Tommie, as he's going to be my featured musician."

"Do you want him sitting alone?"

"That would be nice."

"Melia, I don't know how to say this, but I'm going to anyway. I've been with 'The Choice' since it began. I've seen great talent come and go. I've seen winners and losers, but I've never seen anyone as brave as you. This business isn't about being brave, it's about playing by the rules until you don't need the rules anymore."

I looked at Bubba and softly smiled as I replied. "You only

have to play by the rules if it's important that you win. When winning isn't everything, then simply let go because the rules mean nothing."

Bubba looked at me and smiled a broad infectious smile and nodded his head as he gave me a big bear hug and whispered, "I love you."

All the pieces were in place. The semis were set and everything was rolling. Lance Carter was dressed up and not wearing his traditional jeans. Amanda Logan had on a low-cut dress that left little to the imagination and Clint Walker even wore a suit and tie.

We made it through the first set with me doing OK on 'Flawless'. Eddie, Claudette and me in our dressing rooms while they had some "established" singers filling the air. We were given the *'five minutes'* signal and met in the hallway outside our rooms.

"Eddie, you deserve to win this. Your voice is simply like maple syrup on a pile of hotcakes." I said in a very poor imitation of Clint.

Eddie in total falsetto wiggled his fingers and looked at Claudette and said "Claudette, you're one of the best rockers to come along since Janis Joplin and I know, because I sang with her, even though it was over 50 years ago."

I just giggled at my friends and took their hands in mine. "No matter who wins, we're all winners. All we can hope is that our dreams come true. You have been two of the best friends I could have asked for and I'm hoping it's a tie for the two of you.

We all went back out on stage as Charlie went through our backstories one more time, showing videos of our home towns with the producers choosing Madison instead of Mineral Point to my chagrin. Leaving Eddie to sing first, Claudette and I went back to the holding pen.

Eddie sang his heart out and when he was done everyone gave him a standing ovation. As he made his way over to us, Claudette and I both stood and bowed as if he were royalty, which got a giggle and an 'Aw shucks' out of our dear friend.

Next came Claudette, who did a rendition of George Gershwin's Joplin version of *'Summertime'* that brought the house down. Once again, everyone came to their feet with Eddie and I bowing as Claudette returned to the pen.

It was my turn as I noticed Tommie taking his place on the stool with his guitar. The judges looked perplexed. Charlie looked lost. I looked straight ahead until I reached the mic stand and let the microphone rest. I took a deep breath and looked into the camera. Looking down at the floor and then back into the camera, I stared for a moment and then reported. "If you're watching at home, you always see who wrote the songs we sing in our credits. Some of you might have noticed that, other than *"Amazing Grace"*, my songs have all been written by a wonderful writer named Annie Franklin who has the gift of taking words and turning them into emotions. Annie was my college roommate and is my dearest friend."

"48 hours ago, Annie called to report that Lieutenant Theodore James Franklin – her husband – had been killed in a military accident. In tribute to Teddy and Annie, I would like to sing a special song dedicated not only to all those in the military, but police officers, firemen, first responders and medical personnel who make this country better, safer and hopefully happier than it would be without them. I would like to ask the audience to stand and hold hands with the person next to them and sing the chorus with me. "You'll know the words when we get to them,"

The stage went dark and Tommie began with the intro chords with the spotlight just on him. I began singing the lyrics I'd written and the spotlight switched to me.

Look in a Soldier's eyes and tell me what you see, But blood and hate and battle and
needless misery.

Breathe through a soldier's nose and tell me what you smell, The pungent odor of death, the
rancid fumes of hell.

Peace, peace, peace my God. Peace is what we pray,
Peace, peace, peace my God on earth today.

Eat with a soldier's mouth and tell me what you taste? The tartness of desolation, the
bitterness of waste.

Listen through a soldier's ears and tell me what you hear, The moans of wounded
comrades, the screams of a child's fear.

Peace, peace, peace my God. Peace is what we pray, Peace, peace, peace my God on earth
today.

Grasp with a soldier's hands and tell me what you clutch. The lives of innocent children
and the pieces that they clutch.

And live with a soldier's heart and tell me what you feel.

The awesome disbelief that anything so horrible could actually be real.

Peace, peace, peace my God. Peace is what we pray, Peace, peace, peace my God on earth
today.

With each verse, I took my hands and motioned to the audience to join with me in the chorus. With each verse, the response grew louder and louder until I finally looked at the audience and went a-Capella one last time. *"Peace, Peace, Peace My God, Peace is what we pray. Peace, Peace, Peace My God, on earth today!"* with a hologram of an American flag at half-staff blowing in the breeze and the name "Theodore James Franklin" below.

I did an about-face and simply walked off stage. Not back to the pen, but completely gone, literally removing myself from the show. The stage went dark and then total silence as the house lights came up.

As I watched the video later on, I saw Charlie totally unable to speak. I watched Lance wiping tears from his eyes, as he slowly recovered from the shock of what he'd seen and heard. I saw Amanda with a hankie, wiping away her tears, while Clint had his head down simply shaking and crying in disbelief.

401

After the pause, the audience began again, singing the chorus again as Lance finally stood and began to clap. The show was over and yet the network refused to shut it off. For two additional minutes all you saw were people applauding, people crying and people hugging each other, before the network went to black.

Once again, I slid out the back door into the waiting Rolls Royce. However, this time I went out the other side and into a black Suburban. I didn't want the accolades. I didn't need the congratulations. I feared the recriminations, until I realized that I had won, not 'The Choice', but the right to choose not to be manipulated, nor controlled as Miriam, my dear, dear friend grabbed my hand and simply said, "You did it!".

Instead of heading for Miriam's house, we went to Urasawa, the most exclusive restaurant in LA, where you didn't get in unless you knew someone. As we walked in the front door, you would have thought royalty was attending, as the owner came to welcome Miriam and congratulate me as he noted. "What you did tonight will never be forgotten by those of us who served our country and I thank you from the bottom of my heart," at which time he bowed and directed us to a private table on the patio.

As we proceeded, it was like the world was stopping and the applause began. People who'd seen the show stood and cheered. Those who hadn't, reached for their phones and began watching my performance, before tranquility once again returned.

"Is this what it's like to be famous?" I asked Miriam. "On a good day yes, and you deserve it."

The table was large and the perplexed look on my face mentioned without words, that I was wondering why we were seated with seven empty chairs facing me. A moment later the door opened and a huge smile crossed my face. Mom, dad, Derrick, Andrea, 'V', Amelia and Jack entered the room, to my immense surprise.

I just shook my head in gratitude.

"You were incredible," Dad announced. "Simply amazing," Mom added. "Fantastic," Derrick offered.

'V' just shook his head and smiled.

"I think, I could have done better." I finally replied.

"Are you kidding me? That was one of the most moving performances I've ever seen." Miriam offered.

"When did you get here?" I inquired to dad. "A couple of hours before the show?" "When do you have to go back?" "Right after dinner."

"Whose taking care of the kids?" Although I already knew the answer.

"Grandma Harris."

Just then my phone rang and it was a Facetime with the kids. "Mommy, you were great!" Annie announced.

"Mommy, you looked sad!" Charlie added.

"I was sad. One of mommies' best friends has gone to heaven."

"Will he be with Grandma and Grandpa?" "Yes, he will. I'm sure of that."

Both kids said in unison, "Mommy, we love you and are very proud of you. When are you coming home?"

"Next week. I promise."

We ate what had to be one of the finest meals of my life. As we were finishing Miriam proposed a toast. "To Melia, for making my life so wonderful and showing the world that there still can be love in music."

The long goodbye was a reluctant one as Meriam and I headed for her house simply because reports from the hotel were that it was engulfed in reporters looking for a story. I knew the balance of the Terrill family was in the black Suburban and headed to the Burbank airport and Amelia[X] and would soon be home.

The Million Dollar Fantasy:

To say that the producers were angry about *'The Soldier'* would have been an understatement. They felt they were losing control of the show and there was nothing they could do about it. Messing with Miriam Weiss could be career suicide and they knew it. My dressing room was visited and I was warned that either I followed directions or never work in Hollywood again. It was a hollow threat from all perspectives. First, the ratings for the show had gone through the roof. Second the social media chatter hit all-time highs. Finally, I really didn't care.

We were down to the finals. This one was different, in that we each were scheduled to sing one song and then the show would do video montages of our 'growth' with all sorts of "stars" lined up, who were desperately trying to restart their careers. At the same time, computers would do a live tally of the texted votes that were being audited to make certain there was nothing fishy going on, all followed by a second song from the three of us together.

Called the 'Twenty-one effect', the enhanced security referred to the 1950's show Twenty-One and a contestant named Charles van Doren who supposedly was provided answers that allowed him to compete against and be victorious over Herbert Stemple. Nothing was ever proven, but the show went off the air and since then extra caution had been taken to ensure equity in all competition.

As for the warnings and threats, I guess I no longer cared. I was tired, frustrated and profoundly disappointed in all that transpired, feeling as if I was nothing more than a piece of meat and wanted nothing more than to go home.

The final rehearsals had been longer than expected and I was exhausted, when the limo took us back to the hotel. It seemed strange to be riding in a limo. For weeks it had been the dilapidated bus that took us back to the hotel. Claudette, Billy and I looked at each other and just shook our heads.

We were the three people who were the finalists, who came from different backgrounds, with different dreams and aspirations and were supposed to be competitors, yet we'd become such great friends. We'd changed hotels to give the impression we'd been treated like royalty the entire time we were in LA. Little did people know those first few weeks were spent in a hotel that was, well let's say, not as glamorous as the producers wanted everyone to
think Hollywood is all about.

As we were riding, Eddie announced, "If I win the million dollars, I'm going to buy my mother a decent house and new car." Like so many others, Eddie hadn't read the fine print at the bottom of the screen announcing the million-dollar prize actually wasn't a million dollars, but an annuity paid out over twenty-five years at $40,000 per year. Take out 45% for social security and state and federal taxes and your left with around $1,800 per month. Then, if you read the smaller print, it said the million dollars was based on 2.9% interest so that you could also take the 'million dollars' in one lump sum of $375,000 which would net around $200,000. So much for the house and car.

We entered the lobby, got our keys and due to exhaustion, simply nodded at each other and wished each other best of luck. Claudette and Billy went to the left tower. I went to the right and slipped into my room only to see the light blinking on my phone. The call was from Mike Carvahlo that the three of us began calling one of the *level heads'* who had hung around during rehearsals, wasn't in love with himself and seemed like one of the few nice guys I'd met during the competition.

Mike asked me to meet him for breakfast in the hotel restaurant in the morning. My schedule was open simply because Miriam had been somewhat banned from seeing me until after lunch and no one thought I was going to win. I shrugged my shoulders knowing that the marketing people would soon have their claws in me and with the anticipated loss in the finals, the incessant demands would soon be over. I called Mike's cellphone and told him I'd be honored and would be downstairs at nine. Then I called home and talked to Jack and the kids who were all excited about getting to see Mommy on TV again and loved all the special attention they were getting in school, as the last person from Mineral Point on TV was Alan Ludden, who'd passed away generations ago.

Riding Into the Sunset:

I didn't know what Mike wanted to see me about and when I walked into the hotel restaurant I saw him sitting in the corner without the usual smile on his face. He'd been really honest with us about the business aspect and I respected him for that. Mike instructed me to come alone and I did.

"Melia, have a seat," Mike said in a low tone as he looked around the restaurant.

I did as Mike directed, not knowing what the meeting was about.

"First I want to congratulate you. You've done an incredible job!"

"Thank you," I replied, trying to be as humble as possible.

"You're probably wondering why you're here."

I nodded in the affirmative.

Mike looked down at the table and then at me and I could tell there was both thought and consternation in what he was about to say. "When are you going back to Wisconsin?"

"It depends on tonight. If I win, which I doubt will happen, I'll be here for a while. If I lose, I'll leave on Tuesday," I replied, mentally going over all that was being planned for the next several days.

"Are you flying commercial?" I shook my head 'no'.

My response didn't register and so Mike offered, "Let me see if I can get one of the company jets to take you to Madison. Right now, going through LAX and putting you on a commercial plane just wouldn't be fair. There's too many people who want to meet you."

"Thank you, but it isn't necessary. I've been commuting on one of our family planes."

Mike had a surprised look on his face as he looked down at his menu and then at me.

"Family planes?" with an emphasis on plural. I nodded "yes".

"How many planes does your family have?"

"I'm not sure. Around thirty, but our family only has two reserved for us. The family plane, and, right now, my personal plane."

"I don't get it, Melia."

"Mike, my original maiden name wasn't Wilson, it was Terrill and my grandfather was Douglas Williams. Our family is the primary stockholder in Wilco Corporation and my father founded the Derrick Williams Foundation for medical research."

"And won a Nobel Peace Prize," Mike added, as I nodded in the affirmative as he questioned, "Why are you here?"

"Because my best friend is an incredible writer who hasn't had a break and she needed one."

"You've done all of this for her?" Mike added incredulously. "Yes!"

Mike looked directly in my eyes and asked. "What happens if you win tonight?"

I just shook my head, as I sincerely felt there was no way I was going to win.

Mike looked at me with an incredulous frown and repeated, "You've done all of this for your friend?"

"Yes."

"Again, what happens if you win? If you do, you have to realize that from now on you're a captive of your own fame. You won't be able to go anywhere or do anything that won't be observed, scrutinized and publicized in both positive and negative ways and you'll be accosted by the selfie's who'll want their picture with you."

"That's not what you told us in your sales pitch. You said that most contestants just fade into the sunset."

The server approached the table, recognized me and told me she loved my performance. I thanked her. She indicated her brother was at Camp Pendleton and all the

Marines loved *'The Soldier'* song. I nodded my gratitude. She asked if I'd mind signing an autograph for him. I asked for his name and wrote 'Mark, thank you for your service' and ordered wheat toast and orange juice. Television really does add fifteen pounds, so I had to watch my diet.

The Tail Wagging the Dog:

Mike had to be in his early fifties, had a California tan and that bright, white smile that comes from spending a lot of time and money in the dentist's chair. Mike fiddled with his water glass and finally took a deep breath, looked at me and smiled. "You've really taken it to them, haven't you?"

I had no idea what he was talking about, but hoped this wasn't what breakfast was all about. I'd already been told that a dozen times.

Mike, looked at me and flatly stated, "I've been doing this my entire career and have really seen things change."

Slowly shaking his head, he added, "Nothing is more incredible than how music has adapted to technology, instead of technology adapting to the music."

I politely agreed even though I had no idea what Mike was talking about, as he continued in an almost sentimental way. "Have you ever listened to an old-fashioned long-playing, or LP record, through a great set of speakers and compared it to either a compact disc, MP3 player or something that's been downloaded?"

I shook my head 'no', indicating I hadn't.

"Back in the 1960's and 1970's music was king and the stereo system was your most important possession. There were actually stores that only sold audio equipment and you'd go to the specialists who would set you up with a system to play your records on. When you went to buy a turntable, the audio guy would discuss how consistent the speed of the turntable needed to be as any variation would cause distortion called 'wow, rumble and flutter'."

"A good salesperson would then talk you into an amplifier that took the sound and made it louder, where they would talk about distortion or the percentage of pure signal you would receive, where the higher the percentage, the better the amplifier. Then they'd talk you into an equalizer to allow you to customize the sound to your own environment."

I sat politely listening, having no idea where this conversation was going as Mike added, "Next came the speakers that were always discussed by measuring three things, dynamic range, frequency response and efficiency."

I knew about dynamics, where dynamic range was the reproductive capability to duplicate the sound from the softest to the loudest passage as Mike continued. "Recorded dynamics is simply the difference between the loudest and softest part of the passage a person can hear, with a range of about 120 decibels, where every ten decibels is a doubling of what is called SPL or sound pressure level. Frequency response is the tone, with human hearing ranging from 20 cycles per second which is the lowest bass response, called Hertz, to 20,000 cycles per second or 20 Kilohertz, which is the highest frequency a very few people can hear.

What most people never consider are called 'harmonics', where a harmonic is a sound wave that has a frequency that is a multiple of the first, or 'fundamental tone'. As an example, the frequency that is twice that of the fundamental tone is called the second harmonic, while the frequency three times that of the fundamental tone is its third harmonic and so on."

I agreed, not really knowing where this was going, but was still interested in learning about the structure of sound as it applied to music as Mike added. "The goal of the speaker is to have the broadest possible range for both the dynamics and the frequency response, where the closer they get to the full spectrum, the closer the speaker is to duplicating an accurate representation of what is playing. It's this combination that made me fall in love with music and why I got into the music business as great music, played through a great system can be spellbinding and emotional."

I nodded in the affirmative as Mike continued, "In 1982 Philips Corporation and Sony introduced the compact disc or CD. The record companies loved them! Why? Because by 1995, material costs were 30 cents for the jewel case and 10 to 15 cents for the CD and the typical retail price of a prerecorded CD was $16.98. In addition, shipping costs for a CD were only 10% of that of records, meaning greater profit for the record companies."

Mike then added, "This is where the first major creative change took place. LP records could hold a maximum of 22 minutes per side or 44 total minutes and artists knew they needed to add something between the two and three 'keeper' or 'A' side songs that might hit it big on the radio or even be introduced as singles on 45's, while the rest of the album was simply fill."

"CD's could hold up to 74 minutes of music and could be compressed to hold up to 80 minutes, which meant more fill or 'B' side material, as we called it. This meant artists needed to add more less than exciting music. The introduction of the CD also killed 45's. I mean, why buy a two song 45 when you could have an entire CD?"

"What about sound quality?" I asked as Mike saw my interest in LP's beginning to rise.

Mike replied. "CD's have a dynamic range of 90dB, while records are in the 55-70 dB range, which means that CD's can actually produce louder and softer passages. CD's have frequency response up to 22.5 kHz, or above human hearing, while records normally begin at 20 Hz but actually have no upper limit. From a technical standpoint, digital CD audio quality is clearly superior to vinyl. CDs have a better signal-to-noise ratio, i.e., there's less interference from hissing, turntable rumble, etc., better stereo channel separation and also have no variation in playback speed."

"So much better, right?" I asked.

Mike countered. "Not really! The argument against digital audio comes from the fact that, no matter how precise the sampling, breaking down music from analog into binary data can never match the smooth and continuous nature of analog vinyl because you lose the harmonics to the point the music sounds brittle. While vinyl is undeniably prone to physical interference and noise, it continues to retain a reputation for a warmer, more life-like sound and where true artists really flourish."

"What about today", I asked?

"Most people listen to music played on MP3 players and through headphones instead of speakers. This obviously affects the frequency response and dynamic range simply because of earphone size. When MP3 was introduced in 1997, it was primarily intended for use with computers and then along came Apple with the IPOD, that put hundreds of songs at your fingertips in a product the size of a pack of chewing gum.

"And what happened to sound quality?" I asked.

Mike replied, "The frequency response of MP3 was compressed to 16-to-48 kHz meaning a loss of bass response and the subsequent harmonics, taking away even more of the smooth sounds you can enjoy with the right equipment and LP's."

Mike looked at me and noted. "As you can see, the change in music technology has transcended into different types of music and therefore totally different types of artists. Today, it's not a talented vocalist like you singing ballads or really technical compositions who dominate, it's pop and Rap singers with limited vocal range, whose music is dominated by the beat instead of the melody and lyrics that is currently so prolific most listeners are totally unaware of what they're acoustically missing that has also then been corrected by auto tune. Sadly, you no longer need to have a voice to be a singer, all you need is some sort of niche that allows you to stand out in the crowd."

I nodded in the affirmative as Mike shook his head and said, "But that's not what really changed the music industry. The change came when people began to watch music instead of listening to it, thanks to video streaming and the creation of music videos and the real reason why your genre as a true singer has declined."

I thought I was beginning to see where this conversation was going. Mike was trying to soften the blow of me losing 'The Choice'.

Mike added. "When MTV launched in 1981, no one could have imagined how it would affect the entire music industry. Today singing is no longer enough, you have to put on a show with women wearing what hookers wore when I got into the business." That made me think of my 'retro' wardrobe in St. Martin, gulp!

Mike was on a roll as he added. "Add to this, the reduction in acoustic quality of the transport medium and what has happened is a splintering the record industry into so many different genres and lanes, that are all designed to sooth the savage beast and keep the music production lines going, regardless of the type or quality of product being created and why I think you're so exceptional."

"Well, thank you." I replied looking down at my half-eaten toast.

"First of all, when we talk about singing, we're talking about two separate, but very related elements – physical sound and emotional style. Physical sound is achieved by proper utilization of the technical aspects of singing and you've got them all, Melia, and do it without the electronic manipulation, which makes it all that much more impressive."

I was humbled to have someone who was recognized throughout the music industry as a true judge of great talent evaluate my capabilities as Mike continued. "Where you really stand out is in your emotional panache, which is essentially how you relate to the song and anticipate and complement the different styles of music."

"But they're Annie's songs, not mine," I countered as Mike continued. "They're Annie's words and Miriam's melodies, which are incredible, but it's your voice that has taken the talent of the two of them and given it emotion, which is why you're in the finals. Virtually everyone you've outlasted has been technically very good, but emotionally limited and this has been your draw." Mike continued, "A common view in the industry is that, while the technical aspects of singing can be learned through instruction, repetition and technology, style is only developed naturally over time and yet you walked on stage with a natural presence. While others seem nervous, you've never lost control and never once failed to communicate, not only to the brain, but to the listener's heart and that's truly special. Some people just naturally have it and you're one of them."

I nodded with a modest semblance of gratitude and asked, "Where do I fit in?"

Mike looked at the French toast he'd barely touched. "Melia, your creative range is spectacular and you're so good at everything, I don't know where I'd position you." I mean you might fit in Alternative and/or Contemporary Folk or even as a Contemporary Singer/Songwriter, Folk Rock or even Acoustic Traditional Folk Ballads or even as balladeer. You proved to the world there's room for someone who sings songs and has the vocal versatility to cover a full range of music which is something we haven't had in a long, long time."

Dirty Laundry:

Mike kept talking as I slid back in my chair and questioned whether this was simply a sales pitch or someone speaking from the heart. I decided to keep an open mind and listen, as Mike continued. "The reason for our meeting is that people are already trying to slot you and that's why I wanted to warn you about what's coming. I know the producers of 'The Choice' didn't believe the audience had interest in your type product and yet viewership numbers during your songs went through the roof."

I must have looked surprised at Mike's comment as he added. "You probably think the entire show is random and yet, trust me, it's not. Everything and I mean everything, is controlled and tested to make certain it maximizes audience size and focuses on the desired demographics. You sang religious, folk, light jazz, blues and even country ballads and shocked everyone.   The audience research teams at the network sat in their analytics rooms and watched focus groups of teenage age girls watching the show with their parents to see how they reacted, simply because they represent the sweet spot of marketing – not the kids, but the parents – affluent, college educated, mothers with a high level of discretionary income and you blew them away."

"I always thought I've been winning fair and square. I had no idea!"

"Melia you are winning and it is fair and square, but you also totally screwed up the formula and now no one knows what to do. You have to realize that the entertainment business is based on trends and you've taken what the 'experts' predicted and threw it out the window"

I shook my head and must have had a perplexed look on my face and countered, "I don't understand, Mike."

Mike continued. "Melia, everything is measured before, during and after the show, as the ratings company have their computers collecting data called BMV's or Billion

Minutes Viewed, which simply takes the data it receives from a sample of forty or fifty thousand viewers who demographically represent the American population as a whole."

How do they do that?" I asked.

Mike leaned in as if to share a secret and continued, 'The Choice' uses a national ratings product that adds information from ten million cable and satellite boxes that is measured minute-by-minute regarding how many people are watching and even if they're recording the show and skipping the commercials. This is why the cable companies made it so easy for people to record all the programming – not for convenience, but for data they sell to advertisers. The researchers can measure which shows you watch, when you watch them and even the commercials you watch and which ones you skip. From this, they not only tailor the commercial buys, but sell the data to telemarketers who skirt the law and call you with all sorts of proposals as they invade your home and drive most people nuts."

I just shook my head and thought of George Orwell's 1984 as Mike added. "Because they know the demographics on who rents the boxes and dishes, the cable companies and the networks and advertisers, not only know who's watching and where, but what their socio-economic level is and, their purchase considerations. By simply matching the rolling numbers to the time slot and the contestant and then adding in the search data of the same viewers histories harvested from Google, TikTok and Facebook, the producers can determine levels of interest and even match viewer demographics in terms of age, income and gender to create what is called a measurement footprint they match with advertisers."

Needless to say, I was shocked.

"Why do you think the judges kept looking down at the video screens built into their desks?" Mike inquired.

I just shrugged my shoulders.

"Because they were getting instantaneous readings on viewership, told how to respond to your performance and also instructed about what to ask and what to say!"

"And?" I inquired.

"Melia, they never thought you'd make it through the first round, but preshow viewer interfaces had your Q-rating going through the roof."

"My what? "Your Q rating."

I must have had a frown on my face as Mike realized I had no idea what he was talking about as he expanded, "A Q, or QTS rating is a measurement of the familiarity and appeal of any celebrity or the combination of how many have heard of you and what they think of you, which, in your case, is simply off the charts, in a positive way.

I really didn't know whether to be proud or ashamed as Mike added, "You were such a dichotomy to the typical struggling musician who calls themselves an artist, the producers decided to add SEO's to your profile, not because the judges particularly thought you were a better singer than the others, but because the market research had you score high in the demographics they covet."

"What's an SEO?" I asked.

Mike responded, "a SEO is a 'Search Engine Optimizer' which consists of words that are included in your bio so that people who included a word in their search engine were brought to your site to familiarize them with you."

Mike looked at me, leaned in and confided, "They were going to drop you in the first round by burying you in the middle of the pack and limiting your exposure. You can always tell who scored highest in the BMV's by who's placed first and last in the contestant performance sequences. First place is intended to hook the viewer to watch the show, just like the headlines in a newscast, and the last position is to get the viewer to not only watch the entire show, but tune in next time. In your case, you threw them a curve. The producers didn't think you fit the show's demographic foot print."

"I don't understand."

Mike continued. "Melia, you don't have a strong back story simply because no one's interested in someone who comes from a stable, loving, what everyone believes is middle class family, who did well in college, is a stay at home mom, who dresses conservatively. Then, you didn't sing songs from a popular genre or even fit into the more finite 'lanes' that match the show's target audience."

I leaned back, somewhat dismayed. The whole thing had been structured and controlled as Mike added. "In round two, they really didn't know what to do with you simply because you stood your ground when they tried to 'coach' you out of your sweet spot to see if the numbers would hold."

I just shook my head in amazement, now feeling as if I'd been used.

Mike continued. "There are around 20 different genres of music ranging from alternative and gospel, to folk and rock. Then, within the different genre, there are the 'lanes' the judges kept talking about of which, I've counted over 450 different 'sounds' that fall within the twenty genres."

"On the show, they focus on what carries the biggest market segment amongst the target audience and that's pop and country, of which there are around 40 different lanes for an artist to choose from, and you simply didn't fit. Didn't it seem strange who the judges are. Lance, the aging rock star for the moms, Clint the country singer and then Amanda who is pop all the way, for the preteen and teens, all selected to not only boost their brand awareness, but appeal to the casual viewer?"

"You mean the draw of the show includes the fans of the judges?"

Mike nodded and continued. "While other contestants had a back story of death or poverty and some sort of musical 'hook' that matched the musical style of the judges, you came out conservatively dressed, with different songs each week, that didn't play to the judge's QTS and what their fan base represents. Then, you did something no one had ever done before, which has always been the kiss of death – you sang Annie's unknown songs – not once – but almost every single episode."

Mike paused and then added. "This took away the residual the show normally gets from the record companies for using the playlist to promote an existing artist and therefore cut into the show's gross revenue stream. They tried to 'channel you' to the songs they wanted, but your brand image rose too fast and after week three, they realized forcing you out of your lane would cause viewer discord and that's the last thing they ever want."

I was flabbergasted. I had no idea as Mike continued. "If that wasn't enough, you did something no one else had ever been brave enough to do before and that's sing Amazing Grace a- Capella and dedicate it to all those currently in hospice, which was beyond anything the producers expected. The next morning, the Internet was simply glowing at your purity and innocence, while the production value of the show tanked. To simply stand in front of a camera with a black background and a single spotlight on you for over two minutes is normally video suicide, yet the BMV's not only held steady, but exploded and the repeats were incredible.

"Repeats? What are repeats?" I asked, again not knowing what Mike was referring to.

"Repeats are people who went back and watched your performance again. Normally it's less than 3%. Your numbers were close to six."

"Six?"

"Yes, Melia, nearly six percent of all viewers or 350,000 households re-watched your performance, which is unheard of and that doesn't include those who Googled you as well."

Mike looked at me and shook his head with a wry smile. "Finally, you screwed the producers by singing 'The Soldier' with just you and the guitar back-up. The band was pissed, the judges were pissed and the head director was furious, because all the called video shots went out the window and you sang for nearly three minutes, with simple backlighting and one camera focused on you."

Mike leaned back with a meticulous smile on his face. "Because the show was live, there was nothing the producers could do. Initially, they were furious simply because they thought the lyrics were too controversial, as the subject matter wasn't about sex and love, which they believe are the only things that sell.

When you were done, no one knew how to react. The judges were frozen and in shock and then everything seemed to fall into place as this nice, conservative mother from a little dinky farm town in Wisconsin, who was married and had two kids and was only there because someone, somewhere submitted her song, dedicated 'The Soldier' to a friend who died serving his country and simply lit up the boards."

"Melia, 'The Solider' has received the highest numbers and greatest traction of any song in the history of any talent show, where profound anger went to profound excitement as the producers began seeing the number of repeats on the ratings charts of people going back and replaying your performance over and over, followed by the post-show 'chatter' on social media that simply exploded. Have you any idea how many requests radio stations have received to hear 'The Solider'?"

I shook my head no.

"Over fifty thousand. Fifty thousand and it's number one on Apple and all the other channels. Post production normally sees a few hits to stations, but nothing like this."

Mike looked at me and shook his head and smiled as he added, "Melia, they've never had a song where the audience began singing the chorus before! *'Peace, peace, peace my God, peace is what we pray. Peace, peace, peace my God on earth today.'*"

I just shook my head, affirming I was in a zone as Mike added. "The silence was finally interrupted when Lance

Carter stood alone and broke the spell and began clapping and then the other judges joined in. To see tears in the eyes of every judge, who've seen it all and then Charlie Jackson, when he came back out on stage, was also something they'd never seen before and so they let the applause continue for an additional two full minutes, which is a lifetime in video that calls for a new shot every six seconds. Wave after wave after wave of applause Melia. Symbols of affection! Symbols of respect! And most of all, symbols of gratitude."

"You were probably in some sort of postpartum zone and didn't realize the very long pause before the applause. This was because people were simply ingesting what you had sung and then the switchboard was flooded with calls with some people complaining and thousands upon thousands cheering you on, with social media seeing over five million hits in the first two hours while the post-show buzz still continues today and it's been two weeks since you sang *'The Soldier'*. Never before has a national news program ran a story about 'The Choice' and yet, network news had you as their feel-good story at the end of their night cast after your performance."

Mike leaned back and smiled, if only for a moment, as he added. "The song was spectacular! However, the thing that really pissed the producers off is the fact that you sat outside their machine doing what you wanted with products you or Annie own.

They know that you signed a recording contract on future recordings, but the songs you sang are your property, and they're only going to get a tiny piece of the pie. In the end, you literally broke every rule in the book and took control of who they've channeled to win away from them.

"Who's that?"

"Claudette! She's the one they'll make millions on. As for you, while they were all smiles in front of the cameras, they're seething behind the scenes, simply because you don't fit into the music machine the way they've planned."

Mike leaned in and added, "You have to realize that all of you have already started to become brands. Because of the show, each of you has some level of household recognition and a level of brand awareness, not only because of the number of different people who've seen you, but the number of times they've seen you as well. It's called reach and frequency in advertising, with reach being the number of different people exposed to the brand and frequency being the number of times the message has been received."

"Some of the contestants will be picked up by record labels who'll use analytics to monitor their progress in key areas including month-over-month and year-over-year awareness factors, including aided and unaided recall. From this data, the record companies will make tweaks each performer's brand and marketing activity and do so by leveraging those components that provide the greatest opportunity to increase unaided recall with the lowest possible investment."

I was totally engrossed by what I was learning and asked, "What are analytics?"

"Analytics is a systematic computational analysis for the discovery, interpretation, and communication of meaningful patterns. From that data the record company can determine if it's getting a high enough return on investment. To do that, they'll take the trend analysis and look for patterns to conclude whether they should be spending money promoting an artist or not, putting them on tour and if so, with whom, or even ending their contract. As you can see, the old days are gone. Today, it's a combination of the simultaneous application of statistics and programming, along with operational research that combine to quantify an artist's performance."

I shuddered to think that we were all nothing more than a pieces of meat, paid to perform until we couldn't do it anymore. None of us earned a dime on the show and we provided the heart and soul. The winner gets the ancillary reward of a recorded song, the losers go home with nothing more than a pocketful of memories and a whole list of woulda's, coulda's and shoulda's.

Mike added. "This is why so many former winners of 'The Choice' walk off the stage and into the sunset, never to be heard from again. It's a brutal business where you can make a ton of money, but the pressure to win is almost beyond belief. Quite honestly, you're too nice and too sensitive to be in this business and before it gets away from you, I wanted to make sure you're aware of what's about to transpire."

I took a deep breath and sucked in the last gasp of glory before reality slapped me across the face and I realized, I'd opened a door I prayed I could close, hoping I could be one of those who simply disappears back to reality.

Mike took a sip of water and inquired, "What song are you singing tonight?

"I've got two new ones that Annie wrote and Miriam arranged." I replied.

"What about the band, are they set with it?"

I knew Mike was asking because he knew I'd surprised them before.

I looked at Mike and finally let it all out. "Mike, you're one of the good guys. You wear a wedding ring, talk about your wife and kids and have never offered me drugs or filled me with lies and that's why I'm here. The only other 'real' people are Tommie Thompson, the lead guitarist, Bubba Jackson, the assistant director, and of course Miriam, who has been like a sister to me. Just like you, they've never hit on me and have become people I trust. The producers want this big spectacle with fireworks and all that other hoopla, but that's just not me. I've rehearsed what they want and feel totally out of my range. Tommie and I have been working on what I want to do with him playing the piano and Bubba has agreed to let me do my thing again as he's fed up with how phony the show has become. This afternoon, I'll rehearse what they want and then during the live show we're going to do what I want."

"You're going to royally piss them off, again," Mike replied. "Mike, I don't care. I never intended on getting this far in the competition. All I ever wanted was exposure for the real talent and that's Annie. I never expected to win the regional matches. I never dreamed of being on national television and I certainly don't expect to win, especially after all that you just told me."

"What are you going to sing?"

"It's a surprise. You'll have to watch the show, but you've got to promise me you'll keep this as our secret."

Mike looked down at his barely eaten breakfast and then at me and softly smiled. "You're a brave young woman and while I don't totally agree with what you're doing, I give you credit for standing up and being true to yourself, knowing that you're risking everything, and I mean everything."

"Mike I never want to be famous and a captive of my own fame, where I have to hide from the hordes in order to lead a normal life. I have Jack and the kids and sincerely feel wanted, needed and loved at home. If fame would take all that away, I'd rather be one of the masses."

I looked at my half-eaten toast and then declared, "Money isn't really necessary as our family is quite – uh comfortable, to say the least. You see, to me, wealth isn't only about dollars, it's about love and laughter and being accepted for who I am and not what some merchandising group has created. I want to be Melia, the person, and not Melia, the can of soup, who is marketed and controlled, limited and sequestered, expected to enhance this or limit that, simply because someone, somewhere believes it will mean a greater return on investment."

The breakfast was over as both of us rose while Mike looked at me with soulful eyes and said, "Melia, thank you simply for being you. You've helped me regain my belief that there can be goodness in this business. I want to wish you good luck tonight and congratulate you. Whether you win or not, you'll always be a winner to me."

I looked at Mike and did something I don't think he expected, I gave him a hug and said, "Thank you and thanks for your friendship and understanding."

Try To Say Goodbye:

Annie wrote a new set of lyrics on the plane to Washington and sent them via text. We didn't have a melody or score and Miriam - wonderful, wonderful Miriam – offered her talents once again, as she and Annie had become the dynamic duo that rekindled life in both of them.

Before, we'd simply taken the lyrics and basic melodies Annie created and Miriam enhanced them. Little did I realize Miriam's creative capabilities, until I saw the musical majesty she created, that acoustically conveyed the message and emotions I was trying to share, without being too obvious.

The title of the song was *'Try to Say Goodbye'*. This was to be a full orchestra ensemble designed to match my vocal range with a strong emphasis on the strings, where Miriam blended violins and cellos to match my voice with her on the piano. The producers were extremely reticent when it came to the size and cost of the orchestra but Miriam, being Miriam, convinced all the musicians to play for the union minimum and it was approved. I asked if, to make things equal for all three of us, Eddie and Collette couldn't also use the orchestra. It would reduce set up time and give all three of us equal footing. I think they were grateful and it was agreed.

The original lyrics dealt with a person asking their lover to emotionally say goodbye so they both could move on. A few changes and the song became my hidden anthem asking 'The Choice,' and also the world, to please let go of me so that I could go back home and lead a normal life.

Jack and I talked and I called mom and dad and told them that the open door in front of me wasn't one I wanted to step through. Everyone was supportive and the only other people who knew were Annie and Miriam. I felt I'd given Annie the chance she deserved and hoped I could simply ride off into the sunset - back to Barbies and Legos, parent/teacher conferences and football games on Friday nights.

The Saturday stage rehearsals went well and even the technicians stopped to listen and the combination of the musical score and lyrics had the 'classic' feel.

Eddie's coach had chosen Louis Armstrong's 'What A Wonderful World' which Eddie rehearsed with immaculate results. Collette sang Stevie Nicks' version of 'Landslide', which was outside her normal rock venue, but simply incredible. Her voice! Her intonation! Her emotions were such that all of us had tears in our eyes.

After we were done, Collette, Eddie and I went for our final briefing, where the producers outlined what would transpire. This was to be open voting via texting, that would remain hidden until the last thirty minutes of the two-hour show, where the only thing that would be visually provided were the percentages without anyone knowing who was in first place. We would sing our songs and then there would be fill-in performances by some 'stars' and finally the three of us would sing as a trio, where the producers had chosen Leonard Cohen's 'Alleluia' as our final number.

After the final commercial break, we were scheduled to express our gratitude to the show and judges for the opportunity to compete. I felt it was really tacky that the producers had scripted what they wanted us to say, justifying it by saying we needed to stay on script to ensure the right timing.

At one-hour-fifty the contestant in third place would be announced and they would depart stage right. Then it would be the two finalists with close-ups, as the band played some music intended to increase the tension. Charlie would open the envelope and name the winner at which time, contestant number two was instructed to exit stage right and glitter would fall on the winner, who would be given an opportunity to sing one last song. We'd all seen the show before, but even so, the producers ran a tape of the previous year and how it worked.

Sunday morning, I called home and talked to Jack and

the kids and then called mom and dad. They all wished me luck. All the BMV's indicated I would be chosen, but one never knew. At two, Francine called and indicated the limo was downstairs. Collette and Eddie were already there and we headed for the studio.

As had been my protocol during the competition, I kept my talking to a minimum and made sure I did all the protective things to save my voice. No matter what, this was going to be the last time I'd ever sing in public.

We all went through one more walk-through and one more pep talk and went to our respective dressing rooms. As I was getting ready, there was a knock on the door and it was the trio of judges who came in to simply wish me good luck, which had become a tradition on the show as Lance began. "Melia, words really can't express my gratitude for your ability and your bravery. Our industry has become so incestuous and almost a cliché and you've been the breath of fresh air we all really needed. Hang in there and good luck tonight."

I simply nodded and whispered thank you

Amanda looked at me and simply shook her head before saying. "I stand in the presence of greatness and only wish that I had the talent and moxie you've shown these past few weeks. Good luck tonight."

Chet smiled and added his own thoughts. "Melia, I hope someday you'll consider having my band as one of your back-up groups. I know your talent and determination will soon have you as one of, if not the top vocalist, in the music industry."

I shyly nodded and whispered, "Thank you for your kind thoughts."

A few minutes later there came a second knock and it was Miriam and Annie. Wilco had arranged for Amelia[x] to bring Annie back from Arlington National Cemetery for the finals. Both came in and gave me a big hug.

"Are you all set for tonight?" Miriam inquired. I looked down at the floor and then at my wonderful friend and nodded yes.

Miriam looked at the floor and then at me in a very pensive way with tears in her eyes. "Melia, you've been one of the kindest, greatest, friends I've ever had. If Edgar and I would have had a daughter, my dream would have been that she'd have been like you."

I stood and we hugged. I pulled back and looked at this dear, sweet lady and said, "Tonight isn't the end. It just the beginning of another chapter. I want you to come and visit us as soon as possible. I want you to be our kid's honorary grandmother, if you would be so kind."

I looked at my dear friend Annie and said, "This one's for you!"

Tears turned to torrents as Miriam sobbed on my shoulder and Annie wiped away her flowing gratitude that was only interrupted by another knock on the door announcing "thirty- minutes" and time for the orchestra to be on stage to begin warming up. Miriam, Annie and I clasped our hands together and I said, "you're the best friends a person could ever have."

All alone and with the door closed, I took some deep breaths and thought of all that had transpired. As my emotions returned to normal, I went through the scenario one last time and bowed my head in prayer asking only for the strength to do what I wanted to do.

At five minutes to curtain, there was another knock and I headed for the pit to join Eddie and Collette, both of whom were almost pale from fright. I motioned for them to stand and we formed a small circle as I whispered. "You are my friends. You are the people who have given me value and I'll never forget it. You're both winners and tonight there are no losers. If either of you win, it's because you deserve it. If neither of you win, this isn't the end of your career, only the beginning. Things might be a little 'different' if I win, but please bear with me, steps are being taken to ensure that the real winners are truly recognized and that's you. Now I want both of you to go out there and do your very best and simply win." We all hugged one last time and sat down just as the floor director counted down to showtime.

Charlie appeared from the side curtain to the roar of the audience and went through his typical spiel about how great the competition had been, while promoting the next season's auditions. He then announced how the program would run with the three of us performing where people could vote up to ten times via text. I'd learned from Mike, the multiple texting provided the producers with the names and addresses and, after cross checking, the demographics of who was voting.

Charlie introduced the orchestra and made it seem as if it was the show's idea. That's Hollywood!

As Charlie was speaking, Eddie was called to the stage, resplendent in a black tuxedo with white shirt and black bowtie. Eddie sang his heart out and gave his best performance of the competition.

Claudette and I high-fived each other as she was beckoned and took her place during a commercial break. While positioned as a rocker, market research indicated she'd been a little too 'hard' as they called it, and her coach decided to 'soften her up' by putting her in a conservative floor length dress. With a voice that simply could do anything, Claudette filled her song with beauty, majesty and sensitivity that simply shocked the audience. This hard rocker had shown a tenderness no one, except Eddie and me, knew she had.

As the audience applauded and the show went to another commercial break, I took my spot. My nerves were long gone, but I'm certain that, after the previous week, the producers and network were on pins and needles. 'Try to Say Goodbye' went just as planned with the violins and cellos carrying the tone and the double entendre meanings sliding totally over both the judges' and the audience's heads, with only the producers realizing that I was actually saying goodbye and they could do absolutely nothing to stop me.

During what was called the fill, the three of us went back

to our dressing rooms to change for our song together. As we were told 'three-minutes' we made our way to our spot and, after another commercial break, came back and nailed 'Alleluia' where we all gave every ounce of energy we had, to the tremendous roar of the audience and not only a standing ovation but one of those arms-raised bows of total respect from the judges.

Charlie came out and simply shook his head as he reported. "I've been honored to be on 'The Choice' for the past ten years and, quite honestly, I can't remember three artists with as much talent as these three. You've made this year the reference standard, not only for 'The Choice,' but for all music competitions and I simply want to say thank you."

It was time for our 'heartfelt' thanks to 'The Choice' and judges. Eddie went first and provided what was written for him as he thanked the judges, coach and the show for the opportunity. Claudette came next and, to my surprise, followed the script, as well.

I was last and could almost feel the tension in the air. I paused for a moment and then began. "First, I would like to thank my best friends for their assistance. My dear friend Annie Franklin, who took words and turned them into emotions and Miriam White, who taught me how to properly share those emotions with you. The beauty of music lies in what it does to one's soul and these are the people who deserve your applause, not me. Next, I would like to thank the producers and judges. Creativity begins and ends with the risks of stepping outside the box and their generosity in allowing me to perform will never be forgotten. Next, I would like to thank my fellow finalists. Their love of music, their passion to perform and their overall emotional generosity has established the value of votes we all receive. Finally, I would like to thank you, the loyal voters who've stuck with all three of us and watched us grow, which includes my family and friends. On every performance, you might have seen me pull twice on my left ear, which was a message to my husband

and kids that I love and miss them."

With that, I pulled twice on my left ear and said, "Tonight, this 'double-tug,' as my kids call it, goes out to all of you, with the same message of gratitude…thank you, thank you very much."

The camera light went dark and we went to another commercial as Charlie approached me with a smile on his face. "Melia, I really don't know if you're our winner, but you're certainly a winner in every other way and I want to thank for simply being who you are, one of the finest, bravest, kindest, contestants we've ever had on the show."

The stage announcer counted back from ten and we were live with the three of us standing, holding hands, as it was time for the final tally.

"In third place with 27% of the vote is……Eddie Jackson."

As Eddie bowed and threw the audience a kiss, I turned to him and pretended to kiss him on the right cheek as I whispered. "Go stage right, and stand behind the curtains. This might not be over yet."

After a pause as Eddie left the stage, the drum roll began to create suspense as Charlie returned with a new envelope. Opening it and looking down Charlie announced, "In second place with 33% of the vote is……Claudette Robins and the winner of 'The Choice' is Melia Wilson!" Gold confetti was released and the orchestra was supposed to begin playing my winning song, for which three minutes had been allotted.

I hugged Claudette and repeated the instructions I'd given Eddie as Claudette looked at me in disbelief as I whispered, "Hurry, but don't go far. You'll be back out here in a couple of minutes."

Instead of what had been rehearsed, Miriam presented an orchestral montage of the melodies of Annie's songs I'd sung as I took the microphone and walked center stage with a somewhat laconic look on my face. Looking down at the floor and then at the camera, I smiled and began. "When I was asked to join 'The Choice', I wasn't quite certain it was for me and yet, the challenge put before me was such that I knew I had to try. During the past few months I've come to learn the joy of music, the beauty of friendship and the passion of being involved with some of the most talented people I've ever met. After a great deal of thought, I looked at my life and decided that the joy of being a wife and mother means more to me than a singing career. For this reason, I'm resigning immediately from 'The Choice' and requesting my award be shared by the two people who not only have as much talent as I do, but the passion to pursue their dreams. Will Eddie and Collette please join me here on stage? Charlie, will you join us as well?"

Eddie and Collette reappeared, simply shaking their heads, along with a shocked Charlie as I announced, "I hereby introduce the real winners of this year's 'The Choice' competition!" as I held both their hands up high and whispered, "I love you".

Without looking back, I simply walked off stage and into the waiting Rolls Royce with the little Jewish lady and my best friend sitting in back and huge smiles on their faces.

The audience was in shock, as were the judges. I learned later that the smile on Bubba's face lit up the control room. At first, the producers were almost vitriolic, until the media ran story after story after story of the woman who won it all and gave it up to simply be with her family. The PR people had a field day talking about how the show allows anyone and everyone the opportunity to compete regardless of their dreams, which injected new life into the show's message and extended its run on television.

Instead of heading for the hills as I began calling Miriam's residence, we headed for the Burbank airport. Amelia III was waiting and I hugged Annie and Miriam one last time and invited Miriam to come and stay with us and spend time with her adopted grandchildren. As I was about to leave, Miriam handed me a wrapped box and said, "Open it when you're on the plane and out of here."

I said thank you and kissed both her and Annie on the cheek. As I made the last step before entering Amelia, I turned and threw Grandma Miriam and Annie one last kiss of gratitude and a wave goodbye for all they'd done.

The door closed and we were cleared for take-off. I took a deep breath and slowly opened the gift. Inside was a total shock – it was one of Edgar's Grammy Awards with a small note that said, "You deserve this! Love, Miriam."

And Now You Know The Rest of the Story:

They say fame can be fleeting and, in my case, thankfully it was. My one minute lasted a few weeks until the media went away and small-town reality set in. I'd gambled with my anonymity and therefore my happiness and fortunately won.

I returned to the life I love of simply being a wife and mother and did so until the kids were both in school, when I began teaching at the Mineral Point grade school. All that happened is now in the past and thankfully there are few, if any, comments about those times when I put it all on the line for my best friend, simply because that's what best friends do.

Mineral Point High School football began to thrive and Jack has been offered numerous coaching jobs elsewhere. We're happy where we're at and that's all that matters. It's not fame and fortune. It's not glory! It's about love and the realization that life is about the little things, the smiles and frowns, the ups and downs, that weave a tapestry of memories as times goes by.

Annie has remained in California where she and Miriam began writing music to the point that Annie Franklin became a creative force in the music industry. While not the singing star she set out to be, her creative verve and innate ability to take words and turn them into emotions allowed her to achieve the success she always desired, winning numerous Grammy's and even a shared Oscar engraved with the names Miriam Weiss and Annie Franklin.

At one of the post-Grammy Awards parties Annie was introduced to Mike Carvahlo's son Steve. They say it was love at first sight and they're married. "No kids, but trying", is all Annie reports in our weekly Zooms, while living in the house on the beach that Miriam bequeathed to Annie and Mike as a wedding present.

Miriam came to visit us and loved Waldwick and Mineral Point for its purity and innocence. Perhaps it was the solitude. Perhaps it was the tranquility. Perhaps, just perhaps it was the walk in the woods that brought tears to her eyes as she sipped from the cup of innocence and looked in the eyes of the big buck who simply nodded and made her finally feel whole again. This lovely little lady had become my dear, dear friend, who taught me so much and helped make my world go round with whom I would talk every week to share the ups and downs of our lives, replacing my Grandma Marie in so many, many ways.

Three years after 'The Choice', Miriam joined Edgar and I know they're creating the beautiful music that had been such an important part of their lives. It was one of the saddest days of my life and yet I knew she'd simply 'gone home' – home to Edgar and all that she missed.

Summit Records took Annie's lyrics and Miriam's magic and had Eddie and Collette collaborate on a platinum-selling album called "Let Go", thereby showing the world and record industry there are still people out there who love real music.

After touring globally, Eddie decided to 'settle down' and has become a major attraction in Las Vegas where he and his partner have a home filled with dogs and cats that Eddie calls his children, while performing five nights a week at The Mirage, where he keeps pulling them in.

Claudette has become the super star everyone knew she would for Summit records selling tens of millions of records and downloads to the point she no longer needs to play the game. Settled in a world filled with the glitz, glamor and excitement Claudette deserves, she realizes and accepts that she truly is a captive of her own fame.

'The Choice' continues on and with it, the hopes and dreams of so many talented people who want nothing more than the opportunity to share their passion with the world. While there's a structure, it's there for a purpose and in the end, it serves as one of the few ways those who have the ability, desire and dedication can try to make their dreams come true. The road is rocky and the incline steep, but you can never achieve your dreams if you don't try.

Mom finally retired as CEO from Wilco, but remains Chairperson of the Board. She and dad bought a somewhat rundown 18th century Chateaux outside Bordeaux, France with an adjoining vineyard they are redeveloping. Dad uses the house as his European 'Home Base' as he calls it, while Mom has been elected to the Board of Governors at the Musée des Beaux-Arts de Bordeaux that keeps her busy.

Annie and Charlie now have four first cousins and it's quite interesting when Derrick, 'V', Andrea, Amelia, all the kids and the Harris's get together at Pine Lake, Bordeaux, or Dad's new retreat called the 'Lighthouse' on the east side of Hope Hill overlooking Anse Marcel and Anguilla, where mom and dad can sit, watch the sunrise and sun set each day as they hold hands and thank God for allowing them to be in love more today than yesterday and not as much as tomorrow.

As for me…While I love to travel, I always yearn to be in Waldwick where I can look down in the valley and ponder who'll be next to trek the path of innocence to a destination called 'happiness'. As I sit in silence, I thank God I finally realized that all a person really needs to erase the pain is to sincerely feel the majesty of love, where love is really nothing more than what you're willing to give to others.

I've learned that every life is full of "peaks and valleys" and accept that, when we're "sitting on top of the mountain" we need to realize it may be fleeting and cherish the fact that the mountain even exists. At the same time, when we're "down in the valley" due to any combination of incidents, circumstances or people, we need to recognize that the majesty of life still surrounds us and our sadness can be fleeting if we allow ourselves to seek the profound joy of love.

If one were to believe all the TV commercials, the way to happiness would simply be bestowing on loved one's ooh-and-ahh gifts like puppies and pick-up trucks.

Happiness might seem to be about things or the ability to

go and do whatever you want, but it's not. I've been blessed with the ability to literally have whatever and go wherever I want, but I've come to realize that having, going and doing is **NOT** what creates happiness.

For some, happiness comes from reaching some pinnacle of fame or achievement that seems to be just out of reach. I saw that in Hollywood where I realized that one step up the ladder doesn't mean you've reached the top. It simply means you've got a different view and a greater distance to fall. The question then becomes, is happiness the result of striving for some goal or finally making it when it's really only one mountain peak and not the range called life?

Perhaps, happiness is found in having perfect circumstance

s. In other words, a life without anything bad ever happening. No doubt having some of those things might provide a measure of satisfaction, but very few people have that kind of luck. I've learned that life is actually pretty messy and really challenging for most of us and sometimes it's downright difficult.

If we look around, we can see that there are happy people who have acquired a lot and also happy people who have very little. We can also see happy people who have achieved a lot and others who are happy just getting by. Finally, there are happy people who have the joy of good health and even happy people who have a terminal illness. Happiness knows no bounds of age, income or achievement.

The opposite is also true . Some people who have everything health…wealth…fame and fortune are still miserable and that's really tragic, not only for them, but for the people who are victims of their sadness.

With two little ones who have dreams of being princesses and super heroes, I've asked them. "What can make you happy?" Together, we've developed the seven secrets of joy at the Harris house.

First, it's giving of oneself. It's been said that there's more happiness in giving than receiving. When we assist others, we think less about ourselves. Reaching out to help others doesn't necessarily require money. Some of the best things we can share are our time, attention and a listening ear, where one can see how giving to others brings happiness to oneself.

Second is appreciating what we have. No matter how little or how much we acquire, it's always best to appreciate what we have, which goes back to our attitude. We can all look at our life and see all that's wrong, or we can look again and see what's right. Even those who've been dealt what some call "a bad hand" can find things to be grateful for. When we appreciate the people in our lives, it not only helps make them happy, but adds to our happiness as well.

Third is believing in something better. When our kids were born, we started going to church and that led to learning that people who have a spiritual component in their life are often happier than those who don't, simply because they're able to recognize something greater than themselves that makes them feel less alone. Loneliness truly is one of life's greatest tragedies! *Fourth is having fun.* James Howell's 1659 Proverbs says that all work and no play makes Jack (not mine) a dull boy. Well, there's truth to that and that's why my Jack and I spend so much time with our kids doing simple things like sledding, skating, hiking, playing board games and creating memories from basic things like popcorn balls and snowmen.

Fifth is simply laughing. As I learned from Annie, laughter is strong medicine and happy people share it with those around them. It provides important natural defenses against illness, diffuses bad stress, enhances problem-solving skills and creates a new perspective. It elevates moods, counteracts depression, fosters better communication, improves cooperation and empathy between people and remains a significant lubricant of human relationships. I tell the kids all the time that a frown is just a smile turned upside down.

Sixth is compromise. Happy people don't insist on having their way all the time. They let go of the little things before they become big things and also know the power of admission and forgiveness. Happy people value other opinions while not passing judgement on those who don't look, live, think or do things the way they do and is the main reason why bullies and bigots are rarely happy.

Seventh is don't worry. Happy people don't worry about things they can't control. If you can't affect it, don't worry about it, which was the lesson I learned from my very best friend.

Those are our seven secrets of happiness at the Harris House. We're a long way from being perfect and yet, we know that happiness is a form of magic simply because it's already inside us and all we need do is **let go** of the trials and tribulations, angers and frustrations that consume us so that we're happy with ourselves and can share our inner joy with others and make them happy too.

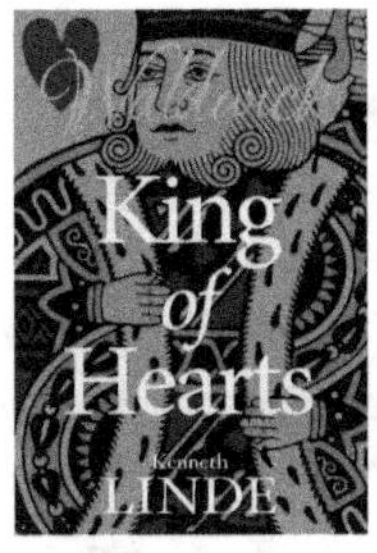

The King of Hearts has been reviewed as *"ambitious, extensively researched and deeply engrossing"*...a story that traces the actual Terrill family through 60 generations as it learns the consequence of wealth, power and prestige over 700 years only to have it all collapse around them. Using a blend of magic realism, lyrical prose and imagery *The King of Hearts* weaves a complex tapestry of a family's history from 65 BCE through sixty generations.

Beneath it all, the book is about friendship and the deep, mutual bond between people based on trust, support, and genuine connection that goes beyond just companionship—it's about understanding, loyalty, and being there for each other through life's ups and downs.

Little Spirit Based in contemporary Wisconsin, *Little Spirit* examines the concept of eminent domain and the taking of land and dignity, first from the Indian's perspective and then today, as seen through the eyes of George Terrill IV a descendant of the original George Terrill. Using flashbacks through a 94-year-old, blind, Ho-Chunk Indian elder, named Great Grandfather, George learns about the feelings and challenges of the Ho-Chunk nation and the taking of their land and also how contemporary America hasn't changed that much in terms of citizen rights.

Driftless revisits George and his wife fifteen years into their marriage. Reflecting on the challenges they face when their marriage becomes mundane while examining the profound question of which is worse... having nothing or everything. As the mystery of the Forest is revealed *Driftless* examines the consequence of technology and the power of special interest groups to control the status-quo for their financial gain, while addressing the issue of individual rights in time of personal need, where the one thing all people have in common is ... time!

The Hayflick Limit addresses the challenges of parenthood, while discussing a person's rights to live and die. When affected by an incurable malady the question becomes *"Would you choose five-to-seven years of normal mental acuity, at which time you would abruptly expire, or risk everything and allow for the slow, gradual decline with hope that a different, longer-lasting cure might come along?"* The *Hayflick Limit* addresses the role of government in establishing the validity of the Hippocratic Oath?

Let Go examines the consequence of bullying as Melia Terrill is affected by the verbal onslaught and her commitment to the only friend who has shown her the beauty of acceptance for who she is. The books examines the perks and perils of extreme wealth, the solitude of loneliness and frustration of achieving one's goals only to realize that all dreams can become nightmares when one risks everything for perhaps nothing as it delves into thoughts, emotions, joys, sorrow and consequences of being a captive of one's own past and fleeting fame.

Survivor...How Death Saved My Life looks at the consequence of an altered set of priorities and how it can take a near-death experience to "right the ship". Totally immobilized for six days, George Terrill examines his life and it's mistakes and vows, if he survives, to make things right. *Survivor* addresses the psychology of fear, the challenges of being told you have less than a 5% chance of living three hours and what you think about when you sincerely believe you're going to die.

Greed is a thought-provoking literary tale of ambition gone awry, exposing how the pursuit of wealth can fracture family relationships. This intense novel, explores the intricacies of human nature and the pursuit of meaning. It serves as a critique of modern society's obsession with wealth and status that challenges readers to reconsider what success truly means, making this book not just an exhilarating journey but a profound reflection on the human condition.

And/Or Using Newton's Third Law as a lens to explore relationships where every action sets off a chain reaction, *And/Or* journeys in ways no one can predict or control while asking difficult questions about resilience, identity, and redemption. As such, it ponders deep philosophical reflections and existential questions by drawing sharp connections between science and human nature, asking such profound questions as...Is it possible for a person to truly recover from betrayal? Can love survive after it's been broken? And when one loses everything, what's left? *And/Or* is a gripping, thought-provoking read that will linger long after the final page.